Des Dillon was born and brought up in the Lanarkshire town of Coatbridge. He has written poetry, fiction and drama, including *Me and Ma Gal, The Big Empty, Duck, Itchycooblue, Return of the Busby Babes* and most recently *The Big Q*. The stage version of *Six Black Candles* was awarded the TAPS Writer of the Year Award in 2000 and the Warehouse Theatre International Playwriting Festival Prize for 2001. He has worked as a teacher of English, a creative writing tutor and as a scriptwriter. Des Dillon lives in Galloway.

Also by Des Dillon

Me and Ma Gal
The Big Empty
Duck
Itchycooblue
Return of the Busby Babes
The Big Q

Six Black Candles

Des Dillon

First Published in 2002
by REVIEW

An imprint of Headline Book Publishing

10 9 8 7 6 5 4 3 2 1

ISBN 0 7472 6823 1

Typeset in Palatino by
Letterpart Limited, Reigate, Surrey

Printed and bound in Great Britain by
Clays Ltd, St Ives plc

Headline Book Publishing
A division of Hodder Headline
338 Euston Road
London NW1 3BH

www.reviewbooks.co.uk
www.hodderheadline.com

Dedicated to my sisters
Caroline, Linda, Angie, Wendy, Geddy and Donna –
cos they are fuckin magic!

For the general public
none of this is true
it's all made up:
Fiction.

Thanks for the assistance of the Scottish Arts Council.
Without the 2001 writers' bursary
this book might not have been written.

Three Dead Men

I've got six sisters. They're Witches. Real Witches. So far they claim to have killed quite a few people. Here's some examples. Brian McGowan that called Wendy a lezzy. Peter Bannan that called Donna *The Ghoul* one time too many. And John Cassidy, a plumber with the burgh that never plumbed my Maw's washing machine in right. They're all dead – Bannan, McGowan and Cassidy – and they died after my six sisters done the Six Black Candles on them. That's their top spell. The one they use when it's time to pull out all the stops. They know spells that come from Donegal way before the tattie famine. My Granny, Oul Mary, says they come from way before Christianity. Before St Patrick told the first snake to fuck off out of Ireland. Her Maw passed them on to her and she passed them on to our Maw, and our Maw passed them on to the Girls. They've had good teachers, my six sisters. The best.

When I say Girls what I really mean is women. They're all in their thirties except for Caroline who's just turned the big four oh.

That's as far as I can go telling their ages. You know how you don't give away a woman's age? Well, that rule applies even more when the women involved can cause horrible deaths at the flick of their black nail varnished fingers. Here they are from oldest to youngest:

Caroline
Linda
Angie
Geddy
Wendy
Donna

So what about Bannan, McGowan and Cassidy? Brian McGowan was screaming up Kirshaws Road on his motor bike. A Kawasaki. He'd been on the drink three days, and he was going faster than his rubberised reactions could cope with. His hand kept turning the throttle that little bit more without him knowing. Like a sleeping bird on a perch. When he rounded the bend at McKinnon's Knitwear (Kilts and Tartans a Speciality) he should've felt the centrifugal force pulling him towards the kerb. But he didn't. If he was sober he would have slowed down. Definitely. But this day he was full of Buckfast, and coming out of the bend he was hitting seventy.

Everybody knew there was a roundabout at the top of Kirshaws Road. Everybody except Brian McGowan, that is. He didn't even brake when he came to it. Hit the white bubble in the middle. And it's quite an incline, that thing. Brian McGowan flew into the air like a stunt drunk. The last thing he saw was the surprised face of the ASDA lorry driver as he was embedded in the windscreen. Witnesses said the back wheel of his bike was still turning. Like it never even knew it had left the road. McGowan's face was scattered with little stars of windscreen glass and the blood was running down like red comet tails. All points North as the comets blazed a trail to Brian McGowan's dead forehead.

Poetic Justice, said Wendy, *calling me a lezzy and ending up, excuse my language here, fucked by a big lorry driver.*

I remember the Girls cackling.

Number two was Peter Bannan. He died when a forklift truck fell forty feet onto his head. The odds against getting killed by a forklift truck are staggering. One falling onto your head? Astronomical. I've scoured papers and the internet and nowhere else have I come across a case where somebody's demise has been brung about by a forklift actually falling onto their head. Peter worked in the Klondike and one of the furnaces was getting overhauled. He was down there in the black dust sweeping the place out. He was a cloud of smoke with the head of the brush coming out the front every now and again. That created another front to the cloud and the whole thing moved forwards.

All up the inside and down the outside of the furnace this intricate scaffolding had been installed by the Callaghans. And they're the best scaffolders in Coatbridge. The forklift was going round the top with pallets of new firebricks. The top of the furnaces, being the hottest, are always the ones that crack and break and crumble. The forklift was laying them out for the specialist bricklayers to come in the morning. Willie Gann was driving the forklift and down below he could see Cloud Peter moving about the belly of the furnace. Two men going about their jobs. But they didn't know at the exact same time my six sisters were performing the Six Black Candles on Bannan. Sometimes the spell takes weeks. Sometimes it happens right away.

Bannan stopped for a fag. His cloud of black dust settled and fell to the floor as another cloud of grey fag smoke rose. Like he'd swapped one cloud for the other. Unbeknownst to Bannan, up above the tubes had started bending. Gann felt the structure lurch an inch or two into the furnace. He leapt out and jumped onto the steel beam on the walls of the Klondike, holding on like a lobster. There was a creak but there was that much work going on about him that the noises echoed into the furnace and were just a noise soup for Bannan. Then there was a snap but that was just a bone in the soup. It wasn't the noises that he should've been scared of. It was the silence of the forklift truck falling in holy stealth through the air. The only thing he noticed was its accelerating shadow. They say he was leaning against his brush with his fag in his mouth when it pancaked him. When my sisters heard the news they rejoiced.

That's him *a fucking ghoul now,* said Donna. *Baldy bastard.*

She laughed and done her starey-eyes thing. She sometimes, or quite a lot of times in fact, stares unfocused dead ahead and doesn't blink. It makes her look more mysterious.

Number three was Cassidy, the plumber with the burgh that never plumbed my Maw's washing machine in right. His fate was the worst by far of these three. He came to Maw's when it was only Maw that was in. Forty quid she paid him to plumb in the new Zanussi. But Cassidy was a skinflint. He thought he would save a few quid on materials. Rip Maw off. Instead of running a hot and a cold pipe to the machine he only connected it to the cold. He used a wee splicer thing to make his job easier so that the one pipe fed into the two holes in the back of the machine. He told Maw it was the latest thing in washing-machine technology.

Vorsprung durch Technik, Alice, he said.

And he laughed at his own patter. But he was a liar. Usually your machine fills with hot and cold to the right temperature and then sets off doing the washing. If you just fill it with cold it's got to heat the water to the right temperature first.

That meant Maw's machine took hours to do a wash. On a number six it took eight hours at full load. Eventually Maw phoned Cassidy back. She was nice enough but he gave her all sorts of abuse over the phone. There was a family meeting about it. The consensus was for everybody going over and kicking fuck out Cassidy. Not a hospital case, just a few digs to the head and plenty to the body. Maybe jump up and down a wee bit on his legs. Leave him in good enough condition to come back and fix the Zanussi. But we never got time to take it to a vote. Cos had Cassidy not been to the pub all day? To cap that he was in a right bad mood. And what had been going through his head but this argument he had had with Maw on the phone. He came staggering down the lane shouting, it sounded like Chinese, and papped a half brick through the scullery window. He couldn't have picked a worse time to do it. We were all there. Twelve counting Maw and Da and Oul Mary.

I wanted to kill him. To get that halfer that he chucked and break all his fingers with it. Crush them to dust. You're always more violent when your family's there. But he was covered with sisters when I got there and Oul Mary was trying to stove his head in with one of Gallagher's garden gnomes. Dopey, it was. They had five of the Seven Dwarves. As I stood looking for an opening for a boot or maybe a good dig, Cassidy, quite sharpish for a podgy guy, struggled free and shot down the lane screaming obscenities.

You might be ugly but you're fat, shouted Oul Mary.

Then, by a telepathic gift that none of the boys were blessed with, all the Girls, including Maw and Oul Mary said, *Six Black Candles* at the same time. Two weeks later they done the spell. Three weeks later Cassidy was dead.

He was in Jeannie Breen's house. Her Zanussi wasn't going right. He was fixing it to make a few bob for the drink.

What seems to be the problem? said Cassidy. He was looking in his bag for a stethoscope probably. Everybody always wanted to be a doctor and he was no exception. The thing was, he would soon be needing one. Or more accurately; an undertaker.

Sometimes the tub turns when the door's open, went Jeannie.

Of course Cassidy had a PhD in white goods. He sneered at Jeannie Breen and let a little blast of air out the side of his mouth through his teeth.

The tub!? You'd have a hell of a time if the tub turned, hen. It's not a tub it's a drum.

That was *her* put in her place. But Cassidy wasn't finished. He wanted to crush her. He never done the City and Guilds in Electrical and Electronic Craft studies for nothing, you know.

For your information, he said, *a drum can't turn when the door's open. There's an isolation switch on the door so that when you do this* (he opened and shut the door a couple of times) *the current that supplies the induction motor coils is cut off.*

Well, Jeannie Breen knew nothing about induction coils. She thought it might be something to do with pregnancy and contraception. She was about to speak but he told her he worked better with the women out the scullery. She seen the drum give a wee kick behind Cassidy. It turned a half turn even though the door was open. She was going to tell him but he'd said it was impossible so she went into the living room and read *Hello!*. Fantasized about celebrities. She was right into imagining a brief encounter with some prince from the Transylvanian mountains when she heard an unusual thumping noise coming from the scullery.

It was only when she heard the scream that she shuffled in at top fluffy slipper speed. There was the Zanussi on a full spin and Cassidy's big arse wobbling about to the reverberations of his smashed-in head as it rattled up and down and to and fro in the machine's big round mouth. *Oh,* the machine was saying. *Oh!* Jeannie ran over and switched it off. Cassidy's head came to a wobbling rest looking upwards and his neck was twisted like a wrung-out blanket. It's funny the things you think about in a crisis. Jeannie Breen was going to let it go to 'rinse' to clear away some of the blood.

He was dead anyway, she told the Girls, *but then I thought I'd switch it off and close the door. A rinse might have sprayed blood all over the walls.*

A practical woman, Jeannie Breen. Rumour has it when they took Cassidy to the mortuary he had his boxers stuffed in his pocket and a pair of Jeannie Breen's pink frillies on. Nice woman though she is, Jeannie Breen, you wouldn't want to wear her knickers. Not with the problems she's got with her waterworks.

That's one philandering burgh plumber out the road, Angie said.

And the rest of the Girls agreed. I felt a bit bad now about the doing we gave him. If only he hadn't lobbed that brick through the window he might still be alive. It's amazing the twists and turns that fate can deal. Just when you thought life was one thing it becomes something else entirely.

So that puts you in the picture about the Girls. I've not mentioned the lists of people they've exacted their retribution on in slighter ways, with less potent spells: limps, blindness and infertility all being par for the course. One man who took the last loaf in ASDA from under Angie's fingers doesn't know that it's his fault him and his wife can never have any wanes. He had three wanes to his first wife. There's trouble ahead for him.

Now, bearing in mind what I've told you already, try to imagine the meeting the Girls had when Bobby, Caroline's man, turned forty and done a runner with Stacie Gracie. Never before had they been offended at such a level. Even before they met we all knew somebody was going to end up dead.

To understand this story fully you need to know something about history. Not the history of Ireland and Scotland but the history of the Girls. The history of the family. The history of the immigrants in Coatbridge. Where it all comes from. My sisters didn't lick their talents off the grass. But this is no chronological history. It's the bits and bobs that I've picked up along the way. Stories. That's the main currency in my culture. Tale-telling. I can only do two things. One: tell you the personal history of the family through wee stories. Two: tell you the story of what happened one night last year.

Here's the thing that set it all off. The fuse. Bobby worked in ASDA on the fancy meat counter. Then this wee bird Stacie Gracie started there. She was alright in a pre-historic kind of way. A body that was perfect for sex but a face like a pterodactyl. She had one eye going for the messages and the other one coming back with the change. But there's no telling the ways of Love. Bobby fell for her like a bag of tatties off the top shelf. First time she sliced a quarter of chicken and held it delicately on her hand it was like she was weighing lace. Cupid done his thing. You always see Cupid in fields or meadows or city parks. You never think that he's sat there at the meat counters of this world too. Waiting for the sweetness and light of slices of corned beef on a pretty hand. Or the pastel pink of Spam being wrapped in cellophane.

Stacie Gracie and Bobby moved in together. A flat over in Greenend. That was the first Caroline knew about it. He went to work in the morning and never came back. Stacie Gracie phoned Caroline from the new flat and gloated. If she knew about Bannan, McGowan and Cassidy she wouldn't have went near Bobby at all. She's not daft, Caroline. Soon as she found out, she looked at the clock and it was only half past four. She flung her coat on and went straight up to Kennedy's to file for divorce and make sure she got the house. Her and Bobby bought their house in Old Monkland. A top flat in Kellock Avenue. They bought it just before the place started going downhill. Now all the other houses are boarded up or should be. Some of the verandas have been ripped off the walls so that flats have doors out into nowhere. Most of the people in the flats are drunks and junkies. The walking dead.

People who are dead but still walking and people who should be dead but we go on hoping. In a nutshell, she was a nutcase for buying a flat in the roughest street in Coatbridge.

The Girls asked if Caroline wanted the Six Black Candles done on Stacie Gracie. But she didn't. She preferred to deal with her own life problems without recourse to Witchcraft. She never was one for joining in much in the spells anyway. Never quite believed it. Donna, on the other hand, believed it fully. Caroline was always the most sensible of all the sisters. If one sister dissents then the Six Black Candles can't go ahead. They can shed a sister here and there for small spells but not the Six Black Candles. Weeks passed and Caroline was up at Kennedy's every other day making sure things were going smooth. The weeks turned into months.

Caroline thought she was coping; being busy can block out emotions for a while. In reality things were going from bad to worse. She found out that Bobby hadn't been paying the mortgage. He'd been spending all his dough on Stacie Gracie. Taking her everywhere. They went to the Meat Counter Servers' Convention in Blackpool and didn't go to any meetings or seminars. Spent a fortune the whole week on drink, drugs and partying. Bobby started planking the arrears letters so that as far as Caroline knew, things were ticking along nicely. The situation was now that she needed ten grand to keep the house. Five to pay the arrears and bills and another five to keep her going till she could get a job.

Bobby was in love and it's always best to wring people dry when all they need is the air they breathe and the one they love. Caroline was getting in there before the air turned sour and Bobby started to fight for his rights. He agreed to give her ten grand. But that was all he done; agreed. Every time she phoned him he told her he'd get it next week. If she didn't get it in the next month the bank was going to repossess the house. Caroline was in big trouble.

Caroline's History

What can we say about Caroline's history? She's the oldest. She's forty, good-looking with dark hair and greeny-blue eyes. But the past wee while has worn her down so her cheeks are hollowed a bit and her eyes are sunk into her head. From a distance, if you didn't know her she could be a junkie. As far as the Irish thing goes she's not too bothered about it at all. Considers herself Scottish, in fact. Even though she understands quite a bit of the Gaelic that she's picked up from Oul Mary and Maw chatting away when she was a baby.

One of the things she's been doing since Bobby fucked off is being undecided. This manifests itself by her walking to someplace like the telly unsure if she wants to turn it on or not and then walking away. She wears whatever she flings on now, when before she took good care of herself. One benefit is, all the worry has lost her at least a stone and she looks as neat as she did in her twenties in the body department. If she could puff her face out a bit she'd be a babe. A couple of weeks in Tenerife and a few cream rings would fix her.

As for her current psychology . . . well! You could say she moves from the collective action of the six sisters to the isolation of grief. She swings between those two fields. One day she's for the spell. Next day she's against it. Sometimes she believes it actually works; all this Witchcraft stuff. And on we go. Never quite rooting her emotions anywhere. Her one major flaw just now is letting other people make her decisions for her. She'd never have let that happen before Bobby done a bunk. She was the strongest out of us all. But now she's at the mercy of her sisters – the ebb and flow of their whim and ego.

What the sisters don't know is that deep down inside her she believes Bobby will come back. And then everything will return to normal. Give her her due; that's what usually happens. I've seen it a million times. About a year is the usual and the man, having had his middle-aged fling, comes back for the certain comforts of home. The familiarity of cheese on toast and farting freely. That is, of course, after the wife has exacted her revenge on the man.

Caroline did mention it once. To test the waters. She said that maybe if Bobby came home they could patch things up. Well! The Girls jumped on her. All except for Angie, that is.

Even if he does, Caroline, you'll hate him, so you will, hate his fuckin guts. That's what I was like, Geddy said.

The rest followed with similar advice.

Maw tells a good story about Caroline. About when she had her and it all went wrong.

Maw and my Da lived in Oul Mary's wee room. Maw was nineteen. It was the day Buddy Holly died in a plane crash. His plane flew into a snowstorm. Clear Lake Iowa, they said it was. Maw heard it on the radiogram and it sounded like a beautiful place to die. It was February the second. I know that cos our Caroline's birthday's the third. 'Peggy Sue' and 'True Love Ways' and 'That'll Be the Day' hadn't been off the radiogram all day. Half the day Maw had been watching the warm glow of the valves on the white distempered wall behind it; dreaming about having her own house. Her own radiogram glowing. Her and Pat, that's my Da's name, would be snuggled up on the couch with the wane sleeping in a wee cot. Not a drawer.

She was waiting on her pains coming but nothing was happening. Even by the time they were having their dinner nothing was happening. Oul Mary and her two sisters, Lizzie and Sarah, kept asking if she was alright.

Oul Mary had six sisters. There were seven of them, just like Oul Mary had seven daughters. And they say Oul Mary's Maw was one of seven sisters too but we can never be sure cos the family splintered when lots of Irish were fleeing to Scotland and America. After her dinner Maw always lay down on the wee room bed. So she went in and Pat went with her. He looked more worried than Maw. But she didn't feel right. She couldn't snooze the way she usually did. At first she thought she had indigestion and asked Pat about it.

Oh God I feel sick, Pat, I've got indigestion. Shouldn't have ate all that dinner so I shouldn't have.

Pat kept looking at the door and his eyes would squint back at her but his head wouldn't move. The Sacred Heart stared down on both of them. You could tell Pat wanted to go in the kitchen and get Oul Mary and Auntie Lizzie and Sarah. But he was stuck between two worlds. They stayed on the bed in silence for ages. Then she had another pain.

You better go in there and tell your mother, my Da said.

No, don't be daft. It can't be easy as that, having a wane.

Da kept on at Maw. They had to whisper cos they were living in somebody else's house. He eventually coaxed her and she went in and told Oul Mary.

That's you going into labour, hen, Oul Mary said. She said it like it was something simple. Something everyday. She never even put the teacup down when she spoke. A teacup she was reading for Lizzie and Sarah.

Don't you be phoning the ambulance now! Maw shouted.

Oul Mary said she'd not phone it unless Maw told her. All

the time her and Lizzie and Sarah were smirking at each other. They were smirking at the memory of their own firstborn. When they were Girls themselves way back in the early days of the Slap Up. When wanes died ten a penny. In fact, Lizzie and Sarah's first wanes *had* died – both in the first week. They told their men when they came in from the furnaces. The men consoled them for one night then it was back to the routine with a big emptiness that wasn't there before. Although having more wanes diminishes the darkness, it never quite goes away. They were hoping that Maw would be alright. Things were a lot better now but they could still go wrong. Maw went back into the wee room and lay beside Pat.

By about six o'clock Sarah and Lizzie and Oul Mary were coming in and out every couple of minutes. Alice and Pat got more cups of tea brung in that night than the rest of their life since.

How are you now, hen? they'd go with a wee smile on their faces.

Maw would bang the door shut, shouting at them, *Get out, they're not your pains, they're my pains.*

They shuffled off murmuring, *Right, right, okay, hen, that's fine, hen.*

Pat never knew where to look. Black affronted he was. He was stuck in the middle of a woman's world. He wanted to be in the pub with his mates. There was nothing he could do but sit on the corner of the bed like a big laddie. That's what he was; a big laddie. Aye. Right enough, that's exactly what he was. They had all stopped coming in the room but they had turned the radiogram right down and were talking low like a wake. Listening. Far as Maw was concerned, her and Pat were staying in that room for ever. They weren't coming out for anything.

But then she had this massive pain like a giant hand had just grabbed her round the waist and squeezed. Hard.

Get the ambulance! She screamed. *Oh Pat, tell them to get the ambulance!*

Oul Mary and Lizzie crashed into the room and rubbed her back and held her hands. They hunted Pat out. Sarah went running down to Mutchie's to use the phone. The men left their pints with beer mats on the top of them and came out into the street. The ambulance arrived at half six and off they went with the wee light going and the men smiling. The whole street was out. All the women. Everybody was waving goodbye. It was just Maw and the midwife in the back of the ambulance. When they left the gas lamps of Kirk Street Maw started to get really scared. Like they were all waving goodbye to her for ever. The men went back in the pub. They took Pat with them and removed the beer mats. Mutchie's had a habit of dust dropping from the rafters into the drinks. There was no ceiling. The men of the Slap Up got Pat drunk.

Bellshill Maternity was full up and Maw had to go all the way to Lanark. There was another Maternity there. Lanark might be quite close to Coatbridge now, but at that time it was as well being on the moon. Maw heard them saying to the driver that they'd have to go to Lanark. The midwife was looking over at the driver and his mate and glancing at her watch, biting her lip. She came back in and tried to speak in a voice that was calm. But her face was worried.

It's full here, hen. We'll just nip over to Lanark; they've got beds, she said.

Maw remembers swallowing and staring at her. She wished Oul Mary was there. Or Sarah. Or Pat. Lizzie even. The roads were windy, rolling her from side to side. It was the first time she'd been in a car even though it was an ambulance. She never knew anybody with a car. Three miles up the road she was sick as a pig. The midwife thought the wane was going to be born. She kept shouting to the drivers to hurry up. But they were going as fast as they could. The rain was battering off the roof and the noise of the window wipers going from side to side was making Maw dizzy. Now and then the whole darkness was lit up by lightning. The midwife got them to stop a couple of times cos she thought the wane was coming. Definitely coming. But it was a false alarm. All the time they were stopped at the side of the road there wasn't another soul went by. Nothing.

They got to Lanark and it was like a big drawbridge they passed over to get into the building.

Oh, this is a big prison, Maw said.

Ssh, shh, the midwife said.

As she stroked the back of Maw's hand, Maw looked about. It was like a castle. William Smellie Hospital. Going over the bridge, Maw thought there was a moat underneath full of strange fish sliding about like predators. Waiting for anything that might fall in. But there was no moat there. Just a big trough where there might have been one years ago. Long before the Irish came here to feed their starving wanes. It was dark and thunderous as they went through a tunnel then the sound spread out as they came into a courtyard.

It was half past seven. They done all these things to Maw going in. Weird stuff. Touching her in places that even Pat hadn't. But she never liked to say anything, them being nurses and doctors and all that. Once she was in her bed this nurse came up. She had a big clipboard with a pen. And she looked strange. Her face kept swelling up and pressing against Maw's. She felt like she was smothering, then the face would recede away to nothing like a ball booted up a park. Her voice sounded like an evil nurse off the radiogram.

Have your waters broken?

Yes, nurse.

When did they break?

That other nurse broke them for me when I came in.

She looked at Maw as if she was daft. *The other nurse broke your waters?*

Th . . . they poured all this water inside me when they brung me in.

No, no, no, no dear, that was an enema.

Right, Maw said.

She'd never heard of an enema. The opiate was starting to take effect. The nurse put Maw in a wee side room next to another woman, with a green screen to separate them. Maw could hear the woman moaning and groaning. On and on it went. She couldn't tell for how long but it seemed an eternity. What they said in Mass about eternity being immeasurable was starting to make sense. Only a few hours had passed but to her it was for ever. It was the gap between stars times a million. It was without beginning. Without end. Maw was freaking out. Paranoia. She thought people were trying to kill the woman on the other end of the screen. Maw pulled the blankets up to her chin. And oh God did she wish she was back in Oul Mary's wee room. Just her and Pat and Oul Mary and Lizzie and Sarah turning the radiogram down to listen. Eventually she conked out with all her family spinning in her head, their mouths opening and shutting. Praying. Saying Hail Marys. Protecting her. Keeping her safe.

When she woke up she was surprised. She could hear the woman in the other bed talking. She sounded happy. She kept shouting over to Maw.

I've got a baby boy! I've got a baby boy!

That's great, missus. That's wonderful so it is, a wee boy.

The fortune-teller told me it was going to be a wee boy and he's a lovely baby.

That's great, Maw said.

Yes, the fortune-teller told me. Aw, I wish you could see him.

Then a nurse came in and tucked her covers up. *There, there, go to sleep. You're tired.*

The woman was sleepy but she wasn't listing to the nurse. She was still talking to Maw.

You should see him, he's got blue eyes!

That was the last thing Maw heard before conking out again. She kept coming and going, in and out of a haze of crazy dreams. She tried to say a couple of Hail Marys but kept laughing. She never knew what was real and what wasn't. The nurses were coming in and checking on her.

How are you?

Maw just smiled cos she never knew if they were real nurses or dream nurses. Sometimes it was as if her body didn't exist; just her thoughts roaming about anywhere they wanted to be. And when she remembered her body it scared her. The size of it, and something else living inside it. When she tells the story that's the bit she comes to a stop at. The bit where language fails. Where the experience is outside the realm of explanation. You can only read the meaning on the look of her face.

How are you doing, dear?

It might or might not be a nurse leaning over the bed.

Fine. Okay, Maw said.

She widened her eyes trying to see if the nurse was real. Her face was like the moon and the wind was blowing big maple trees against the roof, crashing the branches off the slates. Branches were tap-tapping on the gigantic windows like they wanted in. Hailstones kept whooshing across the roof like railway pellets. Then a dead calm. Then *whoosh* it would go again. She can't remember falling asleep. She doesn't even know if she was ever really awake.

Then there was something not right between her legs. She felt the wet and put her hand down. Her bloody hand came out the top of the blankets like a horror film hand. She never told nobody. She just lay there like a wee mouse. Maw wished Pat was there. She didn't know what to do. Then came the voice of the woman in the other bed.

How are you now, hen?

I'm okay, missus.

Sadie, hen. Call me Sadie.

I'm okay, Sadie, Maw said.

She was glad to be talking to another human being. And even though there was blood on her hands she still wasn't sure if it was real. She'd seen a lot of strange things this night. The Sacred Heart had already flew past the window six times. But his eyes were the same blue as the wee woman's wane that Maw had never seen. But it was still the Sacred Heart that hangs on the wall in the wee room. The one that was looking down on her and Pat earlier. She lifted the blankets to check it wasn't a nightmare. The blood was still there and turned to jelly, some of it. If it was somebody else's blood it would have made her sick. She shouted through the screen.

Missus, did you take your period before your wane was born?

No – how?

Well, I'm all covered in blood! Maw says.

She held her fingers out the side of the screen. The woman started shouting right away.

Nurse! Nurse!

The nurse came running in and pulled Maw's bedclothes off. Her eyes went from the blood to Maw's eyes. The blood to Maw. Maw to the blood. Then it was *click bang clang* and the nurse was wheeling the bed away. Next thing, Maw was trundling along tiled corridors with lights you would never've noticed if you weren't on your back. They turned sharp left into an operating theatre.

In the theatre, time was sometimes long and sometimes short. Doctors and nurses came in with masks and gowns. They were pulling on rubber gloves and shouting out muffled orders through the masks. A nurse painted her stomach with cold yellow stuff. They started to measure her, down there.

She remembers them saying something about dialling. And thinking that was daft cos there's no phone that she can see.

Then somebody else came in and said the baby was too far down, they're going to use forceps. She never had a clue what that was. They gave her an injection and she didn't have a bit of pain or anything. They put her legs on wee stirrup things, and our Caroline was born. Maw watched her wriggling in the nurse's hands. She was focused on Caroline and she was a big, big wane. Ten pound twelve. Maw minds thinking, She's got an awful big head, and hoping she wasn't like Betty Maguire's wane that can't move anything but its eyelids. All the wanes in the street point and laugh at it. She said a Hail Mary to make sure everything was alright.

They showed Maw the wane.

Oh, she's lovely.

The nurses took Caroline away to clean her up. Maw shouted after them as they made their way along the tiled corridor.

That was nothing, nothing having a wane. I don't know what everybody complains about. That was absolutely nothing.

When Pat came up at one o'clock with Oul Mary and Sarah and Lizzie, she was sitting with her make-up on and her hair all done. She was never so happy to see anybody in her life.

You're sat up there like a film star, Oul Mary said. *Liz buckin Taylor.*

How are you, hen? Sarah said.

It was easy, Sarah! She was beaming as she looked at Pat. He wanted to know if it was sore.

Sore!!? It wasn't even as sore as going to the dentist!

Oh, Pat said, *that's great!*

I don't know what I was feart of, Pat! I could have hundreds of wanes.

The visitors at the other bed were laughing. So was Oul Mary and Lizzie and Sarah. But Maw and Pat only had eyes for each other and their new wane.

About six o'clock that night the epidural started to wear off. Maw was lying in bed. And she was crying. She was paralysed. For the next few hours she could only sit up in the bed through excruciating pain. When she got out the hospital she was walking like a cowboy and thinking she'd never have another wane.

Caroline's first taste of the supernatural was in the 1960s. In them days the men in the scheme had to steal; coal one night, spuds the next and back to coal the next. That was how they fed their wanes. Even a job didn't pay enough to feed them. Your time was took up with getting a fire up and getting chips to go with the bread and tubs of axle-grease (that's what my Da called margarine). There was about five or six of us then and more on the way. Maw had long since got over the wearing off of the epidural and the cowboy walk. Unfortunately Scotland's working classes hadn't got over their poverty. The houses in Kirkwood were damp and falling down discarded mine-shafts.

I can mind Maw singing in the living room back then as she looked out the window to see if the men were coming back from stealing the coal from the Brickworks. Now and then she'd press her cheek against the glass to see if my Da was coming up the street with Kim the dog and an Army kitbag full of coal. He went with Mr Harnes cos they had a lot of wanes too. I mind Maw's eyes sparkling in the black window panes like the only stars in the sky. Sparkling like stars. She'd be singing. She was always singing. And still does.

Oh Mary this London's a wonderful sight, where the people are working by day and by night . . .

Caroline used to sing it to her doll, trying to copy the words as they came out Maw's mouth. It was a Tiny Tears. If you were a girl and you wanted a doll, that was the one you wanted. The thing about Tiny Tears was that she cried real tears. I mind when the light was cut off and the candle's flame looked like it was burning in the doll's tears. Spooky! The white skin was like a dead baby's. It frightened me. I was scared of a lot of things, but thinking about dead babies scared me more than anything. I never let on. Angie said she seen it crawling over the floor on its own but when she told Maw she got slapped and got ten Hail Marys off of Father Divanny.

Maw stopped singing and her waving hand squeaked off the chilly glass. The deep woof-woofs of Kim came drifting up the darkness. I pulled myself up with the rest of the wanes so my eyes were over the window ledge. Maw was a slip of a lassie then. Madly in love with Pat and intent only on feeding the wanes and heating the house. It was a simple life and in some ways better than the life the next generation was to lead.

The front door creaked and the night sliced the rooms. We had no carpets in them days. My Da rushed through like a cold, black whirlwind and out the back door. There was the whine of metal then the low rumble of coal pouring into a bunker. Mrs Adams came in the front door cuddling a big parcel of butcher-meat tied up with string. The blood off the meat was seeping through the brown paper. Kim was right in there ripping at the edges. I was the only one that noticed.

Jack Frost's out and about the night. Youse wanes better get your bones up to the fire till your Maw makes your supper, Mrs Adams said.

She spoke different from us. She said Shoap and we said Shop. She said Doon and we said Down. She said Auld and we said Oul. She said Bowl and we said Bowel. She said Cauld and we said Cowel.

Another rumble. Mrs Adams's (whose man was dead) coal-bunker was getting coal too. That's why my Da took so long to come home this night; cos he had two bags of the coal. That's why she gave us the butcher-meat. She knew the butcher right well. She handed the parcel to Maw. Kim snapped up the bits of meat before they hit the floor. Gulp, gulp, gulp, all the way to the scullery.

My Da came back to the front door all red and shiny and breathing vapour out his nose like a bull. He smiled and rubbed his hands. Mrs Adams thanked him and pushed by Mr Harnes's arse as he bent over the railings smoking. In a big voice like a paper-seller Harnes was shouting on his sons.

Raw . . . nnaay! Jay . . . may!

Ronnie and Jamie appeared out the blackness. They swifted away a full kitbag each without words. Oul Mary turned up and spoke in a whisper that would grate cheese.

There's a delivery themorra night.

Oul Mary worked in the Brickworks during the day. That's how we found out when the deliveries were going to be. The hairs on my neck went mad. We all knew what that meant. The coal came from the Brickworks. You had to cross the viaduct and climb a steep embankment to get to it. Sometimes a train would come when everybody was halfway across and they'd have to lean out into the hundred-foot drop counter-balanced by the kitbag of coal.

Usually you had to be careful not to take too much coal and ruin a good thing. But on a delivery night you could take tons. On these nights the atmosphere in the street was like a carnival. All the Das and Maws went down and up all night humping coal till every bunker was full to the gunwales. Any woman that never had a man or a big son got her bunker filled and she'd watch for the polis or make tea for the wanes on her street. We all brightened up with the thought of a delivery. Next to Christmas it was the best thing.

There was a Watchie on the coal but he'd never said

nothing since the night he came out to my Da . . .

Right, what's going on here? he shouted. He was stamping down through the dross dust at my Da and Mr Harnes.

Woof, said big Kim.

The Watchie stopped twenty feet away, and shouted: *This is private property.*

Get yourself to fuck we're taking this to warm the wanes, my Da shouted.

The words don't sound much but it's the way he said them that told the Watchie he meant business. And he did mean business. People will go to any lengths to feed their wanes. To heat them. The Watchie took one short look, waved his arms down in an *ach!* movement, and went back to his hut. He never came out again; especially on a delivery night when you can't tell the coal from the people all black and moving. Over the years the women in the street took to sending him Christmas cards and bits of baking and maybe a knitted Aran jumper. Aran's off the coast of Galway. My Maw's cousin stays in Galway Bay. We've not seen her for years.

He's just a poor oul man from Bargeddie, no different to us.

That's what I heard Mrs Harnes say one day when Mr Harnes was talking about the Watchie.

Caroline was busy telling her doll that themorra was a delivery night and it would need to go to sleep early, when we were bundled off to bed. She bunged Tiny Tears into the Silver Cross pram after kissing her plastic nose. Four or five of us piled into one bed and all the coats were flung on. I got my two feet in a sleeve beside Linda, leaned down, folded the end, and conked out.

The next morning had white frosted ferns patterned on the window. Caroline reached up and rubbed a hole in it with her toe. I kept my legs in the sleeve. But everybody was warm and cosy cos it was delivery day and already the street was squeaking with people up and down collecting bogeys and prams and anything that went on wheels. The women could shove these while the men carried the kitbags. Up and down they would go from first dark to first light.

Night was a long time before it came. A silent gang assembled at the end of the street and a fog of breath hovered above them. There was a buzz suddenly rose when the last orange flakes of sun fell from the bare trees and a magnification of squeaking as off they went towards the Brickworks. A muffled cheer rose up from the women. All through the night them that never went came in and out the houses making tea and boiling spuds and giving out pokes of chips.

Are youse wanes alright?

We'd shout back no matter what we were up to: *Aye!*

We'd huddle on the stairs outside till we were freezing and then scoot back in for a roasting at the fire. It was better than Christmas. Our squeaky voices sang with pram wheels. The Das' and big sons' voices droned from moving black shapes lit by wet stars in a slippy sky. You could tell who was coming up the street by the drone. You never heard what they said but you could tell who it was. The wanes used to guess and they got giving everybody a good punch or a dead-leg if they were right and you were wrong. I never played it. I used to sit watching the black figures and the glinting chrome come and go at the end of the street. It went the way it always went that night. I woke up in bed and heard Da whispering to Maw about how it was a great night; this time the coal would last for months. I used to wonder what the coalman thought when he came round and nobody wanted any.

Waaaaaaaaaaaaah!

I woke up the next day to Caroline roaring her eyes out and the cupboards and bags tumbled out all over the floor. Maw came stamping into the room and grabbed her shoulders.

Wheesht, wheeesht, your Da's sleeping through the wall. He's been out at work all night, do you want to waken him?

That's when I found out Caroline wasn't as scared of my Da as the rest of us, cos she paused and screamed.

Waaaaaaaaaaaaah!

Maw covered her mouth with her hand. We giggled from the warmth of the bed. You couldn't see through the window for the ferns but you could see how white it was outside cos the room was lit up like summer. Maw took her hand away slow.

Now I can't help you if you don't tell me what it is.

My . . . my . . . my . . . Tiny Tears . . . she's away . . . she's ran away in the middle of the night. She's not nowhere and I can't find her. Waaaaaaaaaaaaah!

She wailed again like she could swallow the moon. My Da coughed in the next room and we all went rigid. Even Caroline lowered the wailing.

Don't be silly now, said Maw. I could hear laughing inside her voice. *Dolls can't just get up and dance a jig right out of the house anytime it comes up their humph,* she said.

I saw it crawling along the floor last week, Mammy, Angie said.

I could hear muffled slaps and murmured *awches* from under the blankets.

Just-you-keep-out-of-this, said Maw.

And she was hitting the blankets in perfect rhythm with her words. She hit everybody but me and they all started roaring and sticking their heads out of coats and blankets for attention. It was like a cartoon. Caroline screamed louder cos it was her thunder they were stealing; her time to cry. I burrowed into the world of coats and jackets where you might never be found. The door swung open and my Da coughed.

Silence.

What's going on here, Alice? he shouted.

He sounded angry. He sounded tired. Caroline sobbed hoping that he'd go out looking for Tiny Tears but I knew all he wanted was peace and quiet. I never needed my head above the blankets for that.

She's lost her Tiny Tears, said Maw. Her voice was so gentle that I nearly came out of the coats to see who was talking. It was like the dew falling on the grass.

She what? my Da asked.

She's lost her Tiny Tears doll. She put it in the pram, and now it's not there.

My Da thought for a minute. He remembered they had had the pram with them stealing the coal.

It wasn't in the pram last night . . . mind? We ditched the fuckin thing when the axle broke.

Maw stared into his face like she was watching a film and then nodded.

That's right . . . That's right, I would have seen it if it was there, she said.

Waah!! said Caroline.

The doll was gone for ever.

That's when the door went and it was Oul Mary. My Maw and Da gave her the whole story about the missing Tiny Tears while she puffed Woodbine after Woodbine.

Then, something strange happened. Her face straightened out. It was wrinkly as a plate of porridge most of the time and her eyes used to hide behind bags and layers of skin. There was always coal dust in her pores. For a second her face went flat and smooth and I could see a girl. The girl she used to be before life happened to her. She looked at Caroline with the same face.

Do you believe in magic, hen? she asked.

What . . . what kind of magic, Granny? sobbed Caroline.

It was the first I knew about White Witches and Black Witches and Banshees and all the horrible things that you never talked about. They eventually agreed that Caroline believed in White Witches cos they weren't so scary as the other things. Oul Mary got Caroline to do this wee dance on one leg, hopping about in a circle. She'd to stick a finger in her ear and keep her eyes shut and sing the song three times to the powers of the White Witch of Gweedore. It was a song about the Black Witch of Ballyshannon.

Nowhere I do declare
Her equal you could find.
She was humphy-backed and pock-marked
And one of her eyes was blind.
She'd feet for killing clocks with
And bunions on her toes.
She'd be a regular Dandy
If she had a shorter nose.

Caroline opened her eyes. The ice-blue eyes of Oul Mary shut them again. She sang on, spinning round the room on one leg. I was watching by now out of a coat sleeve that smelt of oul women and mothballs.

Nowhere I do declare
Her equal you could find.
She was humphy-backed and pock-marked
And one of her eyes was blind.
She'd feet for killing clocks with
And bunions on her toes.
She'd be a regular Dandy
If she had a shorter nose.

On she went without hardly waiting for any breath.

Nowhere I do declare
Her equal you could find.
She was humphy-backed and pock-marked
And one of her eyes was blind.
She'd feet for killing clocks with
And bunions on her toes.
She'd be a regular Dandy
If she had a shorter nose.

She came round, opened her eyes, steadied herself from the dizziness and saw that Oul Mary was gone. She screamed.

Whaaa!!

By this time we were rubbing holes in the frost following Oul Mary up the street. She went to the phone box.

It's okay, Caroline, said Maw. *Your Granny's away up the phone box to phone the White Witch and tell her about Tiny Tears.*

I remember being amazed at Witches with phones. I always thought of them with broomsticks but I never thought of one with a phone. Caroline wiped her snotters on her cuff and climbed onto the bed. She rubbed the steam of our breaths off one of the ice holes and caught Oul Mary going in the box and fiddling about with the dial. You could see she was stuffing money in and Caroline seemed happy from then till Oul Mary came to our door that night on her way home from the Brickworks. She usually talks to my Maw quiet in the scullery. That's why I was extra surprised when she asked to see Caroline. We all followed her into the scullery where she sat with both arms folded on her work-bag on the table. She had a crazy stare.

Well, wanes, she said, *there I was a-sauntering home from my work like I've done a million times . . . a million times. I'm looking forward to getting a bit food into my belly and a sit down and a good smoke at the fire. It's just like any other night mind and I comes up the lane at Mitchell Street there. It's black, as black as a night can be and a shiver runs down my oul spine of a sudden. I stops . . . you know the way when you just know there's something watching your every move?*

We all nodded and huddled in. Maw and Da were nodding wildly too. Oul Mary gave us a good staring each and went on.

I'm right there in the middle of the lane and I hears this voice. I stops dead and in the panic I don't know to run back or run away. I freeze . . . then I hears the voice again. It's right low and squeaky. Help me, help me, *it shouts. I looks round but can't see a living soul. I listens but there's nothing. Like there's nobody alive in the whole town.* Help me, help me! *it goes again. It sounds like a wane in trouble so I whispers, 'where are you? I can't see you.'* I'm in here. Is that you, Mrs Duffy? *Well . . . Jesus Mary and Joseph the fright it gave me, knowing my name and all. I thought I'd been sent for and was about to start praying the* De Profundis *when it goes,* I'm in here, in the pram! *In the darkness I never noticed the pram lying on its side so I strikes a match and leans down but there's nothing in it. Just a big empty space.*

Her eyes bulged at us to make sure we were listening. Oh, we were listening all right. We were as quiet as the insides of the coal-bunkers. She went on.

I was terrified by then and about to run when out of the empty pram the voice comes again. This time it's crying. Oh, Mrs Duffy please don't go away and leave me. I'm in the bottom of the pram, in the secret bit. It's Tiny Tears and I belong to Caroline Riley, twenty-four Drumpark Street. Please take me home. It's so cold in this pram and if I stay out another night Jack Frost will get me and I'll die! *Well! 'Help! Help!' I shouted and ripped open the secret bit at the bottom of the pram and there she was – crying real tears. And a wet nappy too.*

As she was talking, my Granny dragged the Tiny Tears doll out her bag.

Baby, baby, baby! screamed Caroline.

She grabbed it and ran away to the fire squeezing the life out of it. Maw and Da laughed with Oul Mary and the rest of us stared about the steamy room in puzzled amazement.

That was probably the first indication that there was more to our Granny than met the eye. More to our family history than your normal Irish genealogy. More than supporting Celtic and singing rebel songs.

When Caroline done a play in St James's Primary everybody went along to see her. It was called *The Upper Room*. Caroline came in and said she'd got a part in it. Maw was over the moon. Her daughter got a part in a play. An actress! All the wanes were astounded. I think the whole ten of us were born at the time but I can't rightly remember; things get so mixed up in your head by the time you come to write them all down. Especially here. But I do remember that we were all astounded.

What part is it? Maw goes.

I'm Mary, Caroline says.

Oh, Jesus Mary and Joseph she's playing Our Blessed Lady, Maw said.

Maw blessed herself. Caroline was well pleased and made a few faces at all us jealous wanes.

What do you do in it? Maw wanted to know.

I don't do nothing.

Don't be daft, you must do something. You're Mary, for God's sake – the Mother of Our Lord. Of course you do something.

When the time came we all went to see it and it was the creepiest thing you ever saw. Even Maw thought it was weird. Caroline was so white and ghostly-looking we all thought she was going to die. Whatever teacher put that performance on needed her head looked. The whole audience sat in dumbfounded silence all the way through. If it was art, it was art meant for middle-class snobs not for the immigrants and their offspring in Coatbridge. Call us oul-fashioned but we like out stories to mean something. Or at least be understandable. I've spent better days wandering about graveyards reading the names of the dead, God rest their souls.

Caroline's whole class was on the stage. Everybody was somebody holy although it was hard to tell which was which. Give the teacher her due, she came from the posh end of town and must have thought that this was the exact sort of theatre we needed to emancipate us. Free the working classes from their own stupidity.

Anyway, all these classmates were on the stage and they didn't have a clue what they were doing. Then all of a sudden there was this big *barrroom!* noise and thunder and lightning. The stage went dark. Then the back lit up. A curtain opened and there was Caroline aka Mary, Mother of God. Her face was in the clouds. The clouds were big pieces of card covered with cotton wool and held up from the darkness below on the end of sticks by Primary Five drafted in to help. The audience got a fright and took a sharp intake of breath. Caroline's face was deathly pale. She was wearing these off-white flowing robes and standing still like a holy statue. There was no music or anything. No lines and no movement on the stage. Just her staring out at the audience. It was her eyes you'd remember most if you were there. The front row got the shivers first and shuffled about in their seats. Then it moved back through the audience in waves. You could hear a pin drop and Caroline kept on staring. The whole hall was uneasy. People were getting nervous. Caroline raised an arm to one side, dragging the robes up. The audience were hooked on it. She raised her other arm till she was like the Angel of Death come to claim us all. The only thing missing was a scythe. There was a drum roll and she waved the robes about. Backwards and forwards then up and down too. Something terrible was about to happen. The drums stopped beating – and *ping!* The lights went out and the play was over.

When the teacher went up and brought the wanes out onto the stage for applause, all she got was a lightweight clap of disbelief and politeness. People were going about after it saying, *Oh my God it was lovely,* but you could see they were bothered. All the play had done was give them a reminder of their mortality. A mortality reminder was the last thing they wanted when they were going to see their kids perform and perhaps be a little entertained themselves. The teacher took the reaction as a compliment to her artistic prowess. Needless to say, she never lasted too long in that school.

As for me and the rest of the wanes, it was the singular most frightening thing I'd ever seen in my life.

When Caroline was sixteen she came in one day happy as a lark.

I'm going into Glasgow for an interview, she shouted.

At that time, even though Coatbridge was practically joined onto Glasgow and was a pretty poor and hard place itself, Glasgow was considered to be the big bad city. The place of roaming gangs and razor slashers. It was a place you never went near if you could help it. The facts were that Coatbridge was just as bad if not worse than Glasgow for poverty and squalor. But just as the grass is always greener on the other side so is it always dry and barren. Dangerous. The immigrant psyche is always a schizophrenic thing. So you can imagine, Maw was not pleased.

You're not going into Glasgow yourself, somebody might attack you. There's no way I'm letting you go into Glasgow yourself, she blurted out.

Maw got her fags out to play for time. But Caroline was always well prepared. She'd had this conversation in her head and knew what to say.

Mari Fergus is coming with me.

Maw looked at her. Going through her head like wee films gone wild were all the stories she'd heard about Glasgow. She was looking for a way to transfer this fear into Caroline's head. But if you could do that, you could bottle it and sell it to mothers worldwide. How to make your children scared at will; £200 a bottle. And when you get to thinking about the ramifications of that, you see why it should never be possible. The world would shrink. The sense of adventure would be reeled in, and in, until there was none left. The fears of the mothers would visit the daughters, and communities would shrink into parochialism and bigotry. It's as well Maw couldn't pass the wee films in her head to Caroline's head. Caroline jumped on Maw's stalling.

We'll get the bus at the Mill Brae and we'll come straight home, pleaded Caroline.

Oh, I don't know, hen.

Look, it's a great job and it's in an office.

Maw eventually let her go and Caroline went into the staff agency she'd seen the advert in. The job was gone but they asked if she would like to work at the agency. Caroline came out of Glasgow with a job. She was always lucky with jobs. Always lucky with money. And always lucky with love up until the Stacie Gracie incident.

She came home and told us all she'd got the job. Everybody was over the moon. It was the first person we knew with a job except for Da. And at that time the thought of one of us getting a job in an office was way beyond our expectations. The best you could hope for with an Irish Catholic name was the machines in the Mothercare factory or McKinnon's. But still Maw's face was tripping her.

Oh my God, Maw said, *I don't know if I want you going in and out of Glasgow.*

Caroline took the job anyway and she done really well in it. It was through that job she met Bobby. And if that was a good or a bad thing time can only tell.

It was years later when Bobby came in looking for work. He came from Ayr and he wanted to work in Glasgow. There was no work for him but Caroline took a fancy to his brown eyes and curly hair. And his funny accent. How he used to call eyes *een* and a car a *caur* and cows *kye*. She kept him up to date on the vacancies that were coming up. Eventually he asked her out. By this time Caroline had a car and a few bob put by. She was on her own can in the house and handed in twenty quid. For that she got her own room. The boys were shoved into one room and the rest of the Girls were shoved into the other.

Caroline started driving down to Ayr to see Bobby. Sometimes she'd stay overnight and Maw and Da said nothing about it. Oul Mary was down reading the tea-leaves for the neighbours this night. We'd just put our cups beside the sink and one of them was picked up by mistake by Oul Mary, thinking it was Mrs Gallagher's. She'd read all the cups and promised the usual things but this cup was different. Oul Mary took a physical jolt when she looked into it. There was murder in the cup.

There's blue murder in this cup, she said. She looked Mrs Gallagher straight in the eye. *Beware the open road and the rows of lights. I see rain and darkness. And the chase is on. There's a baby in here,* Oul Mary said, *a wee wane.*

Mrs Gallagher was shaking with nerves. She took the cup off Oul Mary and looked in it.

That's not my cup, she said, *I take milk.*

Oul Mary looked at the cup and it was black tea that had been in it. Whose cup was it then? All the women held their cups tight to their chests. No way were they letting such a bad reading be attributed to them. What Oul Mary did notice was the arc of lipstick on the lip of the cup. She took her money from the ladies of the scheme and bid them all goodnight. Mrs Gallagher refused to pay on account of the fright she got. When they were all gone it was late and all the wanes were in bed. Oul Mary crept into Caroline's room and bent in close to her lips. In the moonlight she could see that she had lipstick on. She didn't have to compare Caroline's lipstick to anyone else's. In them days women never wore lipstick unless they were going out anywhere special. And anywhere special usually meant weddings or wakes.

Knowing what she knew and knowing Caroline didn't believe in the Witchcraft stuff – she was much too pragmatic and practical for that – Oul Mary set about her business of weaving a protective spell round about Caroline. A spell that might well have saved her life.

Every Friday Caroline drove to Ayr to see Bobby. Things were going to be different when he got a job in Glasgow, but for now they were stuck with her driving down there every week in her wee Mini. To get there she drove down to Bothwell and over the bridge up to East Kilbride. Then she had to go through Eaglesham and across the Fenwick moor. That was a bleak place at the best of time. High windswept moorland. The habitat of grouse, pheasants and TV aerials. Not a tree for ten miles. Not a house or farm. On a grey day this place was as close to nothing as you would ever get this side of a Black Hole. Caroline never noticed it much. She was cocooned in the walls of her car with the radio on. Ronnie Lane's 'How Come'. If she knew how appropriate the lyrics were she would have laughed. But she never thought of these things at that age. She was young and she was in love. There was only her and the dark glass and the lights of the odd passing car. The pleasure of the radio nursing her all the way to her lover in the south. Beside the sea. Where his family used to fish till they took it all away.

So, this Friday night in late October, Caroline was driving over the Fenwick moor. The rain was coming down like broken steel rods, the rods splintering as their tips crashed into the tarmac. The Catseyes were like prisoners on a conveyor belt peering through bars, trying to escape; but there were always more bars. The rain was relentless. There was a warm glow in Caroline cos in the back seat was a box. And in the box was a nice pair of size nine black patent leather shoes she had bought for Bobby. It wasn't his birthday nor nothing but cos she was working and he wasn't she bought him something now and then to cheer him up. Such was young love.

She had been on the moor five minutes. Up and up the winding road went. It could be anywhere when you looked at it. The Scottish Highlands. South America. Ten minutes and she hadn't seen another car. None behind her and none passing from up ahead. The weather was so bad people had decided to stay at home. Watch the telly. But Caroline was in love. A little rain wasn't going to stop that.

Visibility dropped until she could only see twenty feet ahead. She pressed her face close to the windscreen. Drove on. And on. She dropped her speed down to thirty miles an hour. The rain was bullets on the roof now. She drove slower and slower. Then, up ahead, she saw something on the road. She strained to see what it was. The wipers were furiously going from side to side and she could only see the thing for half a second then it was gone in the wash of water on the windscreen. Slow, slow, slow. She got to ten feet away when she realised what it was.

It was a baby. A baby lying in the middle of the road. In the middle of the night. In the middle of the worst rainstorm for years. In the middle of the moor. She screeched to a halt. When she got out of the car it was like a scene from a film. Her car was lying askew on the road with the door flung open and moving to and fro in the wind. Threatening to bang and then swinging open again. Caroline paused halfway between the car and the baby. She was half drawn to the safety of the car; half drawn to the rescue of the baby. Finally she bent forwards and pushed through the gale that was howling all about her. The rain was biting into her eyes, but she had to get to the wane. She had to get to the baby.

It wasn't a wane when she got there. It was a doll done up to look like a wane. Not like a kid does a doll up but like an adult would do a doll up. Like an adult would do a doll up to look just like a wane. Exactly like a wane.

Caroline grabbed it by the plastic leg and took it back to the car. She never knew why she done that. It might have been the residue of love for Tiny Tears. But it was only a lump of plastic and she could have left it there or flung it in the ditch at the side but she took it into the car.

The water was running off both of them. She flung the doll on the floor at the passenger side as her arse hit the seat. Slammed the door and drove off. She was angry alright, cursing whoever done such a daft thing. On a night like this too. But her anger soon subsided. She had done a good turn really. It might've caused a crash. Two or three cars close together. Front one sees the wane. Slams on the brakes. A car's coming the other way. Bang. It could be a right mess. Aye, she might have averted an accident right enough. So she was feeling alright. The rain had died or at least wasn't horizontal any more cos she was on the down slope coming off the moor.

Headlights started flashing in her side and rearview mirror. She flicked the rearview mirror away; they never had the anti dazzle in them days. But the headlights were joined by the orange click of hazards. She wound her window down a bit and pulled the wing mirror back so the blinding would stop. Then the car behind's horn started going *beep, beep, beep.* Caroline pressed the accelerator. She got faster. The other car got faster. There was not another car on the road. Next thing, the car tried to overtake her.

Caroline instinctively pulled out and bumped it so that it was forced to fall back. Then – salvation. Up ahead were the lights and lines of Catseyes that marked the A77. She accelerated some more. Swerved onto the dual carriageway and put the accelerator to the floor. She had been in fourth gear all the time. She put some distance between her and the chasing car, but the other vehicle must have been more powerful. It was gaining on her. Catching up. There was no way she was going to risk stopping and trying to flag another driver down. Not on these roads. Not in this weather. Not in this darkness.

The car caught up and they were side by side tearing down the A77. The car was trying to push her into the side of the road. Not by nudging her but by getting its bonnet in front and swerving inwards so that she was forced to move closer to the kerb. Caroline braked hard. So did the other car. She got a look at the driver. He looked like a maniac. He was screaming and pointing for her to get onto the verge. He had his passenger window rolled down and his hair was wet with the storm, stuck to his cheeks and forehead. His eyes were bulging like they were trying to talk.

The road suddenly narrowed to one lane and he had to pull in behind her. That gave Caroline the chance to get away some distance. What she done was slam the brakes on so that the guy had to slam on his. He nudged her a bit and then braked, pulling back. As he moved up again she repeated the move. This time she braked before he shunted her. She's not daft, Caroline, and she repeated that manoeuvre another three times. Then she slowed down to forty. He slowed down. She pressed her accelerator right to the floor but at the same time touched the brake pedal with her left foot so that the brake lights came on. As he braked, her car was speeding away. She put at least five hundred yards between them. And she was just sighing some relief when there he was, right up her arse again. Caroline started to break down.

Help me, help me!

She was shouting and screaming to the other cars going in the opposite direction like little bubbles of hope floating up from a drowning man. One man, she remembers, was singing a song as his car whizzed past. But fuck it. No way was she going to let this maniac get hold of her. No way was she going to let him grind her down. She took the white line and made sure he couldn't pass. He went that way; she went that way. He went this way; she went this way.

All the way the chase went. Right to the Prestwick roundabout. Caroline bumped the edge of the roundabout as she screeched round the bend and onto the Ayr stretch of the A77. Cos she was full of fear she had the accelerator to the floor and had some traction going round the bend. Her pursuer didn't. He went straight into the roundabout and out the other end, spinning a bit on the road and facing the wrong way. Caroline laughed a long shrieking laugh. And out into the night she went. Just in case, she turned her lights off and flicked the full beam on so that she could see where she was going but anybody coming up behind wouldn't see her. Or at least would find it hard to make out what it actually was up ahead. She had seen the sign – *Ayr, 5 miles* – and felt better.

Bang! There was a jolt. The shunting made the doll roll about on the passenger floor, its eyes glinting and its face grinning up at her as the sodium lamps slid their ghostly yellow over its face. It looked like it was laughing. Christ, it *sounded* like it was laughing. The street lamps passed above like seconds on a terrible clock measuring out the last of Caroline's life.

She strained into the curve of the Ayr roundabout, and gunned the engine down into the town, crashing right over the roundabout and into the polis station wall. She got out the car, scrambling at first on her hands and feet before straightening up and running. The pursuing car came to a stop on the roundabout and the guy got out and chased her. She was nearly at the front door of the station when he grabbed her.

Leave me alone! she screamed.

He twisted her round and his eyes stared right into hers.

Don't kill me, don't kill me, mister, she was shouting.

But he put his finger on his lips and shooshed till she was quiet and only her hard breathing could be heard. He pinned her shoulders back to the wall. When he had her attention he spoke clearly and slowly. With the authority of a teacher.

I'm not going to kill you. I'm not going to hurt you. I'm not going to harm you in any way. In fact, he says, *I'm trying to help you.*

H . . . help?

Yes. Help.

How?

When you stopped to pick up that doll way up there on the moor, a man got in the back seat of your car.

What?

When you stopped to pick up the doll, a man got into the back seat of your car.

Caroline screamed and screamed. The polis eventually got off their arses and came out to see why there was a car smashed against their wall; one askew on the roundabout holding up the traffic and a crying girl crumpled beside a man. Once they had arrested as many people as they could, they unwound the story. When they went to search Caroline's car there was no doll but her back seat had been slashed to ribbons with the stuffing puffed out. They said a knife similar to the ones used in slaughterhouses for gutting was used. The black patent leather shoes Caroline had bought for Bobby were gone too.

They caught the slaughterhouse man three months later. He was standing on the roof of a car on the Fenwick moor with a woman's head in his hand. He was howling at the moon and the blood was dripping onto his nice size nine black patent leather shoes.

When Caroline had her wane we were all there. We were in the waiting room twiddling our thumbs when we heard her screaming. So we ran in and crowded round her bed wondering what was wrong. Caroline kept on screaming and screaming.

What is it? What is it? Maw shouted.

Caroline leaned up and her eyes were flicking about everywhere and her breathing was erratic. She nodded over at the Perspex cot where the wane was.

It's my wane, she said. *My wane's an alien.*

Maw went over and picked the wee thing up. You could see she was just about to say that there was nothing wrong with the wane. It must be the drugs still working on Caroline. But then she seen the pointed head. There was no getting away from it. This wane had a head like a rugby ball. Caroline could see Maw's reaction through the crowd of sisters.

See, see, it's an alien. Maybe I was abducted. Years ago even. It was on the telly about this woman in Kentucky.

Shhh, Maw said.

Maw was covering up the pointed head as best she could with the shawl. But the shawl kept slipping off so Maw tied on one of the wee white hats you always get for a new wane. Not blue or pink. Just straight white. She tied it but it was all wrong. It just wouldn't sit right. It was like the wrong snow cap on the wrong kind of mountain. But Maw was still trying to convince Caroline.

Look! Look, hen, he'll look normal with a wee hat on.

We were all amazed. The wane was like something out of a comic. *Astounding Tales*. We were half-expecting a map of his planet to be printed out on his back. Boy, was that one ugly wane. Meanwhile, while Caroline wasn't looking, Maw had the wane in a headlock under her arm and was trying to press its head down. It was screaming but that made Maw press all the harder. And all the time she was pretending she was shooshing the wane.

There there, she was going.

It looked like she was patting its back when she was applying two tons per square inch of pressure to its pink rocket of a skull.

Caroline couldn't feel her legs. The epidural was still working on her. Geddy came out with a cracker. I remember that.

What I can't understand, Geddy said, *about epidurals is: they jag you in the waist and it numbs you from the waist down. Why does it not numb you from the waist up?*

Binmen

To get into this world you've got to picture yourself walking up Wine Alley. Junkies and Buckie drinkers sitting in every nook and cranny. Staring. And if you don't live there or don't look at least as mental as them, you're in big trouble. Faces and bodies lean out of the dark close mouths. The odd red points of fags swing about like urban fireflies. It feels like night-time but it's a Sunday afternoon.

In the closes there's the smell of pish. A waft of human shite from the backs of the bin sheds. The crunch of glass under your feet. The murmur of another language: Nedeese. And the pressing of eyes. Waiting. Predators. You dare not falter or look too long or look too short. You pull in your signals cos they might be the ones that give you away. Even the two standard grades you got at school are beginning to show. That C in maths is burning under your skin. And your B in geography seeps out, you've had it. Best thing is to stop and tie your lace, or simply turn and walk down the lane a few feet, say, *Cunt*, like you've forgot something then turn again and proceed as you were. That always catches them off their guard. They think you don't even know they're there. And if you don't know they exist you've no fear. And if you've no fear they have nothing to get working with. That's their raw material, fear.

So you've dealt with the Neds and Nedesses. Look up now at the flats. Metal shutters on the windows of empty houses. Others with dim, 60-watt bulbs in them. If you were a dog you'd be able to hear the hum of a cheap light bulb merge with the thrum of the smelly oul fridge. The harmonics of poverty. In the main doorways crazy intercom systems have been ripped from the walls and their wires hang out like the guts of some do-gooders who decided a few new doors and fancy buzzers could sort out the deprivation down here.

As soon as Ziggy Cunningham's laddie got his fingers took off by one of them three hundredweight doors, that was the end of intercom. And it was the end of feeling safe when the doors were locked. It was the end of rolling your joints and shutting the curtains to watch the box or chill out to Floyd. When the laddie came home from the hospital, unable to count to ten on his fingers, he was plunged into a numerical world that ended at eight and a half until he developed his abstract mathematical thought process. Ziggy and a team of speed/Buckfast-fuelled Das spent a whole Thursday ripping every door in the scheme off and giving them to their wanes to play with. The older wanes stripped the aluminium off and took it up to the scrappy. They gave the wooden bits to the younger wanes and they made a bonfire. But a bonfire made out of doors doesn't amount to much so they added the contents of a few empty flats. You could see the fire as far away as Bargeddie.

Keep walking and you get to the middle of a square where you're surrounded by these flats. Some are burnt out and others have simply given up. But the ones with the lights on, the ups and acrosses of poverty, they're the ones we're interested in. The ones with the musical bulbs. There's a book could be written about what goes on behind every window. But the night we're only interested in one. Look dead ahead.

It's a close with the bottom flats, one left, one right, shuttered with metal. All over the scheme there are squares and rectangles of fool's gold: the orange street lights shining on the shutters so that they glow. One has a corner bent out so that a black triangle contrasts with the street light orange. The windows have a foot or two of black soot at the sides and much more at the top. They were torched by the kids after the burning of the security doors. Sometimes a pile of security doors and the contents of empty flats isn't enough. Kids eh!? I think all this destruction is a subconscious reaction to their predicament. An attempt to destroy the place they hate living in. Disaggregate it. Bring it to dust.

The flat on the bottom left has water running out the front door and out the close mouth. It's falling down the steps in thin sheets and blankets of water. In the right environment it could be beautiful. At night it can be quite soothing to lie back and listen to the falling water. But the usual shouts ring across it and an ice-cream van in the distance jangles out 'Greensleeves'. 'Greensleeves' used to mean cones and crisps and Rolos. But it means hash and smack and Ecstasy now. The dealers have found ways to course the arteries of the schemes. The whole scheme is a junkie. It's sick and sucking the better parts of town dry.

The first floor has lights only at the left. There's washing flapping on the veranda. Demanda veranda; a must for the outdoor woman.

The second floor has lights to the right. I don't even know the name of the people that live there. It used to be that you knew everybody on the scheme but now there's strangers lurking everywhere. Fear and paranoia.

The top floor has only one set of lights. Top left. That's where Caroline lives. Her and Bobby were happy there till Stacie Gracie came along. Yes, it's still possible to be happy in these places. You do that by living a decent respectable life.

And doing that, you automatically declare yourself out of the other cultures that exist. I have to laugh every time some politician or do-gooder talks about the working class. Who are the working class? I've never met them. There's no such a thing as the working class. That's a myth. What exists are the General Miscellaneous. Myriad sub-classes and cultures, and the only thing they've got in common is they live in the same areas. Areas that are similar to other areas across the country and across the world. And those that make up the words and phrases choose to call these culturemasses the working class. But enough of that. We have to get you into Caroline's flat.

Reach the top floor and it's a surprise. There's Van Gogh paintings on the close wall. Framed like a sudden art gallery. Lights. Stencils everywhere. A wee pine gate. Hanging plants and potted plants. It could be another place. But it's not. It's here. That's where Caroline lives.

Right, that's you got the typical Sunday in Kellock Avenue. Now to the story. Caroline's inside and she's tidying up. There's a living room with a veranda looking out over the scheme. Then the big Artex arch into the scullery. The Artex arch into the scullery was a prerequisite for any young couple in the 1980s. But the main thing in Caroline's house is the massive marble fireplace. The Artex arch has been relegated into second position. And now instead of it towering up like opulence it looks like a big white frown between the living room and the scullery. The fireplace smiles away and sends waves of warmth out across the room. Its flames are the height of comfort. The place where dreams can be born or nightmares burned to soot. It's obviously built for a much posher house. It takes up at least a third of the wall. The telly's blaring away so loud that it's just in the pause of the singing or preaching you can hear the lick of the flames and the chrinch of the moving coals. *Songs of Praise* is on, from St Theresa's in Possil.

Bind us together, Lord, bind us together, with cords that cannot be bro-o-ken.

Caroline comes into the room. She's looking better than she's looked for years. Since Bobby left she's been taking care of herself to boost her self-esteem. But she feels like shit inside. Her emotions rising and falling like an Irn Bru bottle lost in stormy seas. The channels between Burtonport and Arranmore maybe? She lifts a pair of boxer shorts from a pile of Bobby's clothes lying in the flamboyant hearth. Some cut up with neat clean slices. Others ripped and quite ragged. Some still intact. There's a few photos slashed or ripped or shredded.

Caroline holds the boxers between her thumb and forefinger. A fragment of photo falls from the mantelpiece which is just below eye-level. It's a photo of Bobby. His smile whirls down in cheesy circles and clicks onto the marble. Caroline stares at it rocking on its own arc and grinning up. She reminisces. Him and her in the Sharks Gub. Dancing. 'Love To Love You Baby'. Donna Summer. Oh, and the crack was good. It was certainly good. It'll never be that again.

She flings the boxers into the fire. They lie unchanged for a moment, then: *whoosh!* They combust and shrivel. Some of the wee bunny rabbits on them break free and run across the coals and white-hot flames. They're *whee-whee*-ing and screeching, trying to thrash to the safety of the cool marble. But they don't make it. They're fried. Their ears singe, turn brown, and curl up. Caroline swears she heard their tails go pop. She doesn't like where her feelings are taking her so she sings along with the telly.

Bind us together, Lord, bind us together, with cords that cannot be bro-o-ken.

But even that's no good cos she switches into the song Bobby used to sing when they were at Chapel. He'd sing it until the women about him would tut tut and move away.

Weld us together, Lord, weld us together with two big hot metal ro-o-ods. Weld us together, Lord, weld us together, Lord, weld us together we're Prods. We're Prods.

She picks up a few big kitchen knives lying here and there. It could be blood that's on them. Or it could be the red flames licking over the sheen of the blades. It's hard to tell. Caroline hates the noise they make. That slish-slash Edward Scissorhands noise. It's like nails down the blackboard. Her anger gets out. Loose. She grabs a pair of shorts and rips into them. It's a pair with strawberries all over them and she tears them to fuck with these knives. Three knives in her hand at once and jagging the points into the cloth and pressing till they start ripping. The flesh of the strawberries bursts. The blades go right through and she starts sawing into them. Imagining it's Bobby's flesh. Or better still, Stacie Gracie's. Her flat nineteen-year-oul stomach. Hairless except for those wispy hairs that look like feathers over her fuckin rave-dancing muscles. Rip rip rip. Down. The skin splitting. The trickles of blood racing the knives down the belly and winning so that the knives are following the blood like yacht blades in deep red streams. Cutting till the silvery strands of fat that look like fibreglass burst apart. Blood spurting out of veins. Then the guts tumble out like countless pounds of links spilling from a butcher's bag. She's still singing as her mind's cutting through skin and the elastic of Stacie Gracie's knickers.

Weld us together, Lord, weld us together with two big hot metal ro-o-ods. Weld us together, Lord, weld us together, Lord, weld us together we're Prods. We're Prods.

Caroline looks at the shorts. At the telly. At the fire.

Bind us together for fucksakes! she says. And she breaks. Flings the shorts in the fire and slumps over like yoga. The knives are sticking up into the living-room air. The telly blabbers on regardless.

And a favourite at weddings right round the country, that one.

Now here's the Possilpark Boys' choir with 'Pie Jesu', goes the telly.

Caroline rocks backwards and forwards soothing herself to the music. Comforting herself with the heat. She can see the glow of the fire through her closed eyelids. The intermittent red and yellow and orange is stroboscopic and hypnotic. She wishes she could stay there for ever in the just bearable pain of being curled up by the fire with the holy music lifting her. She doesn't know what the words mean but the telly is singing directly to her. For her and for her troubles. Who knows? Maybe there is a God. Maybe the priests were right. And so long as she concentrates on the song her pain stays away. The ice in the middle of her chest stays in the middle. There had been times when its frost crushed all the way out to the tips of her fingers and toes. Trapped her frozen in the chill of not wanting to live and being afraid to die. The flotation chamber of your own mind. She didn't want that. She needs distraction. And she gets it. A low rumble from outside and she lifts her head. She wipes her eyes, gets herself together, puts the knives on top of the telly and goes out onto the veranda. It's a bin lorry. Working on a Sunday. Caroline shouts down.

Are yees working on a Sunday?

You've got to take the overtime when you can get it, hen.

Are yees taking big stuff the day?

Big stuff the day, bins in the morning.

Wait a minute then, she says. She turns to go back in, then, as if she's scared they'll leave, she turns back. *Wait there*, she shouts.

We're waiting, hen.

Don't go away.

Caroline runs into the living room chanting his words like a mantra as she collects the stuff she wants to put in the bin lorry.

Big stuff the day, bins in the morning. Big stuff the day, bins in the morning. Big stuff the day, bins in the morning.

She opens the cupboard in the living room, takes a pause, a breath, as she looks at what's inside then flops a rolled-up carpet onto the floor with a heavy thud. There's something on it and it's sticky. She rubs her fingertips together and her eyes are remembering something they don't want to remember. Action gets rid of thoughts so she bends down to drag the carpet away. Another knife falls from the cupboard and tumbles through the air, sticking in the floor and thrumming from side to side like an accusation. She pulls it out, jams it under the front door to hold it open and drags the carpet so that it's half in the house half in the close. Who's going to come up there anyway? They usually stop at The Starry Night and think there's a right nutcase lives up here. Or if they know Caroline and the rest of my sisters they know that they're Witches so that's more the reason they stay well clear.

Back to the cupboard she goes, whips out a black bin bag and starts flinging all sorts of bits and sexy bobs into it. A pair of black knickers with red trim, cheap and tarty; just the way men like them. A suspender belt still attached to the stockings, a whiff of talcum powder from them, some make-up and a pair of white high heels. Out she goes to the close.

Holding the bin bag in her teeth like a crazy dog she drags the rolled-up carpet along the close and bumps it down the floors to the binmen. There's foam gathering on the bin bag. The *thump thump* as she pulls the carpet down the stairs is like a heartbeat. There's a long swish as she drags the carpet out the close and bumps down the waterfall stairs into the square. The close is empty. Just the cold wind coming in where the door used to be, up the stairs, and through Caroline's front door like heartache

The rumble and the crushing of the bin lorry makes it hard

to talk. But the three binmen are trying their hardest. If you're a man on your own your wheelie bin can lie unemptied till the winds strew it all over the streets. But a woman? Well! And a woman whose man's left her? Well, well! She's worth shouting over the machinery at. Well worth it. You'd risk a throat like sandpaper for her. They're round her right away grabbing the carpet.

Here, gimme that, hen. We'll get it.

Caroline chucks the bin bag into the crusher. She hears the ping of a stiletto heel shooting off like a bullet. Ricocheting the last of its sex round the inside of the bin lorry. The big steel teeth are coming back for more. When the wind dies down momentarily the faint sound of the telly wafts down the close. It's singing.

I'll walk beside you through the dark tonight.

Does that crush? Caroline asks the binman.

Down to a pulp, hen.

Even a carpet?

The wee fat one with the red splodge on his face knows the technical limits of the bin lorry.

Carpets, boxes, bottles, cats, dogs, mountain bikes. This fucker could crush a car, hen, he goes.

Not wanting to be left out, the mockit one, the only clean thing about him's his face and that's bogging, takes the carpet off her. Caroline holds one end but she's only holding the end shut so that the things won't fall out.

Here, gimme it, he says.

He chucks it in. They all smile as it drags the carpet foot by foot into the machine and crushes it. When it's fully in, lumps of carpet are bulging out through the high-tensile teeth. Once it's digested the binmen turn to Caroline looking for applause. A blow job each, even. But she's already gone. All they get is Caroline's arse all the way into the close.

Aye!

Aye, it's a good yin.

A rare wee arse that. Can't remember the last time I had both hands clamped on an arse like that.

St James's under-twelve's football team, says Blotchy.

The roar of the lorry is swallowed by two men laughing at one man standing with his teeth clenched and his lips pressed together.

Caroline hears the remark about her rare wee arse and it lifts her spirit a touch. Men looking at her arse. She feels good about that. She hadn't thought about that up to now. Other men. Sex. The freedom. The Liberation. And hasn't she got a nice wee arse anyway? For a woman just turned forty. Her arse is in tip top condition. Tip top.

Donna's History

My youngest sister Donna is thirty with long black Gothic hair and white skin. She'd frighten the Addams Family. Out of all the sisters she's the one that's closest to Oul Mary when it comes to the Witchcraft. You can trace the losing of the Gaelic from Oul Mary right down to Wendy who knows none of it at all. Maw knows it and can speak some of it. It loses its grip as you come down the sisters and stops at Wendy. But Donna has made it her business to learn Irish Gaelic. She goes to lessons in Govanhill. She jumps the buses and trains on the way home and if they ask her any questions she talks to them in streams of Gaelic and glares at them with Gothicness. They soon leave her alone. And she went out her road to find out all about the Craft. I'm not saying she knows more than Oul Mary but she's certainly read much more than her. Donna is the history of Witchcraft in Ireland. And Scotland too for that matter.

The difference between Donna and Oul Mary is that Oul Mary looks like a wee woman you might meet poring over the price of tea biscuits in ASDA (although there would be the slight suspicion that she was shoplifting). Donna, on the other hand, goes out of her way to walk and talk like a Witch. There's a core of doubt in Donna. She's found some meaning in the Craft and devoted her life to it hoping to find fulfilment. But the core of doubt is holding her back. Oul Mary simply believes. She doesn't need to search for the meaning of life. A cup of tea and a bun is more satisfying than reams of Kafka, Camus, Plato and priests.

What Donna wants is for the rest of the sisters to recognise her supernatural powers. But they mostly take the pish out her over her Witchiness itchiness bitchiness. Donna doesn't realise that it's only when *she* firmly believes that she will be able to convince others.

When they learn to accept people like me for what we are I'm going to London. To be famous.

They do, Donna, and London's full of people like you, believe me, said Wendy.

Donna frowned to the jeers and handclaps of her older sisters.

Donna's first brush with the supernatural, the incident that set her off in her quest to be special, happened many years ago on a wet spring day. I can't remember the exact year. That's why this is a history that might not be factual in some ways, but it is truth that underpins it cos there's nothing I can do but tell the truth. I can't tell a lie even if I wanted to. That's the way it is with me now. That's the rules here.

It was this time years ago, Donna had a touch of the flu and they were rushing back from Oul Mary's in the rain. Maw and all the sisters it was, some in the pram, some hanging off the pram and some walking. Donna looked up and the clouds were rolling over the roofs that fast it was like the houses were rushing through the sky. The pram was filled to the gunwales with coal we'd picked up off the ground over near the Vulcan. It was a bit where the seam of coal came right up to the surface. Everybody went there and got enough for their fires. The rain was going right through them and they were getting soaked so they went into St Augustine's and stood out the rain in the doorway. Three of them bumped the pram up. Silver Cross. The rain made the hood and cover shine like leather. The rain was splashing water drops onto the shining chrome and the black cover looked like an animal's skin. The pram looked alive. A monster on wheels.

They all pressed round Maw's legs. The wind blew her headscarf and the rain ran down her skin. Donna minds her skin was white. Definitely white. Maw was looking at the clouds and her top teeth were biting her bottom lip. It was like she could read something in them the Girls couldn't.

Won't be long, she goes. *Just a shower.*

And she was still looking up like she was scared. Like something was going to come right out that sky and bite off their heads. She walked the pram sideways up to the wood of the door. The wind crushed round the corner whistling and growling like the Devil. This cold came spinning up Donna's back and she dragged air in through her chattering teeth. She imagined she was in the North Pole on an expedition and the wanes were all huskies and the pram was a sledge and Maw was a polar bear. She was just wrapped up in that daydream and getting some kind of warmth from the expanses of imaginary white snow when Maw's hand came down softly on her head and flattened her hair forward. She felt Donna's temperature. Funny thing was, there was Donna freezing to death and Maw's hand still felt cold on her head.

You're still not well, hen, she goes. *It'll be your bed with plenty to drink the night. If God spares you.*

She said that all the time, about God sparing you and all that. Donna was thinking that God was right there, wondering if He was going to spare her or not. She stared into the flowers on Maw's dress; big red and yellow things. Linda's hair came whipping round in a gust of wind and hit her, stinging into her eyes. I was behind Linda sheltering from the storm. Donna turned and gripped Maw's dress, snottering and shivering into it. Maw looked down and pulled Donna into her.

I'm freezing, Mammy. I want to go ho . . . ome, Donna cried.

Right right, Maw was going. She was looking round and the rain was getting heavier and the wind was getting bigger and the clouds were mad. She looked at Donna. Donna was reflected in the watery blue of her eyes.

Away in there, hen, and pray that it'll stop raining.

Donna looked at her. *In there?* she said.

It was a big Gothic building with the spires pointing up at the rolling clouds, making you dizzy if you looked up. Then the door opened and banged like magic. But Maw was still asking Donna to go in with her eyes.

What'll I say?

Prayers that the rain'll stop.

There was no answering back in them days. Donna squeezed in behind the pram and she was halfway through the door when Maw spoke in a Chapel whisper.

And mind and sit near the heaters when you're saying your prayers. What have you to do?

Say my prayers.

What for?

For no raining?

And where have you to sit?

Down the front.

Down the front near what?

The altar?

No, a heater.

A heater?

Aye. Tell the priest your mother's out here if he sees you.

Donna closed the door and clicked the latch back on. The noise of the rain was muffled now. She slid into the warm quiet. Her feet echoed on the floor and she could hear the rain battering the roof and the stained-glass windows.

It was like a big bit of quiet was catched in by the big walls and high roof, she told the Girls later.

The candles burnt away at the other end like crushed stars and the sanctuary light was making itself into criss-cross lines cos her eyes were full of rain.

Right down the front she went, spinning round as she walked. Her mouth was wide, taking quiet breaths. Donna had never been in a Chapel on her own before. She felt better right away cos of the smell of some snuffing candles. Candles reminded her of family. Of weddings and Chapel. But not wakes or funerals cos she was too young for funerals. She got right to the altar and the stream was rising off her rainsodden clothes. If anyone saw her they would have thought she was a ghost appearing through mist at the candles.

She lit a candle and stuck her hands together and started to pray.

Hail Mary full of grace the Lord is with thee blessed art thou among women and blessed is the fruit of thy womb, Jesus. Holy Mary, mother of God, pray for us sinners now and at the hour of our death – amen.

On and on she prayed. She knew the prayers and how to kneel there with the back straight and the hands together and flat cos they'd shown her what to do at St James's but she'd not made her First Communion yet. After a few minutes she couldn't say the prayers right cos the heater next to her was making her dizzy. She closed her eyes to stop herself from falling onto the spinning marble.

When Donna came out the Chapel door the first thing to hit her was Maw's eyes. They looked like two holes bored through to the blue sky. Her mouth opened and the sunlight flashed on her teeth. Steam was rising from the ground and the rest of the Girls were already bumping the coal-filled pram down the stairs. But Maw's face changed when she seen Donna was eating a penny caramel and she had one held tight in each hand. At that time penny caramels were the size of shoe boxes. Maw asked what she was eating.

Mmmmmchchchchmmmmmmshlp, Donna said.

Maw prised open Donna's left hand and all the other sisters were staring through the sunlight at her chewing mouth. The green and white and red of the caramel wrapper was peeking out her fingers.

I want, I want, I want, is all you could hear as Donna chewed like mad till there was enough room in her mouth for the caramel and some words.

Our Lady gave me them, she told Maw.

What?

Our Lady . . . she gave me them.

Our Lady? What d'you mean, Our Lady?

Maw stuck her fists on her hips and shoved one leg out. Donna had seen that position before so she knew Maw meant business. She chewed furiously and made more room for more words. She swallowed a big chunk of sweet saliva before she spoke again.

Our Lady . . . she . . . she was up the altar. She gave me them.

All the eyes and ears had gathered round. Even the coal in the pram was listening. Maw looked up at the sky and then, letting out a long breath, goes, *And what did she look like, this Our Lady character?*

Donna only had the wee bit of caramel left that tastes like salt and the Girls were trying to open her fingers to get at the other ones.

She, she came down off the altar . . .

Jesus! Maw shook her head.

I was praying on the kneely bit . . . blue she was, all blue.

Jesus Christ . . .

It was Hail Marys and Our Fathers . . . and a candle. I lit a candle, and . . . and . . . I looked up, and this Lady . . .

Oh! Jesus, Mary and Joseph!

All the wanes were staring at Donna, then Maw and then Donna again.

What did she look like, hen? asked Maw. She reached out and felt the temperature of Donna's head again.

She was all dressed in blue and she floated down and she said, Why are you praying here, little girl? *And I said, 'I'm praying that it'll stop raining for my Mammy and my sisters out there.'*

Oh! Jesus, Mary and Joseph bless us and save us, she's dying. I knew I shouldn't've took her out in this weather.

Maw got her by the shoulders and crouched down so her eyes were right into Donna's. All us wanes came in close so we were like a secret circle.

Tell me, hen. Tell me what she looked like.

All blue. She appeared out of nowhere . . . she was all blue and she floated over. The candles were burning and they were blowing in the wind and there was no wind but they were still blowing . . . and I was saying the prayers like you said and she said, What are you praying for, little girl? *And I said, 'That it'll stop raining for me and my Mammy and my sisters,' and she said,* 'Go now and you'll find that the rain has stopped and the sun is shining, *and I bowed and said 'Thank you, Our Lady,' and genuflected and she smiled this big giant smile and . . . and . . . and . . . I got up and I started walking out, and the candles were flickering, and some were snuffing out, and . . . and . . . she shouted,* Hoy, you! *And I spun round and she floated over and stuffed three penny caramels in my hand and then she floated away and the candles flickered some more and she disappeared.*

Jesus preserve us I've got a saint on my hands here, goes Maw.

If ever there was a time for prayers it was now. Maw was blessing herself and giving it all this holy stuff and all the Girls had long amazed faces on and the coal in the pram was stunned and the sky was blue, definitely blue. The rain had definitely stopped and the sun was surely shining on us all.

We were a pool of light and amazement at Donna chewing away on the second holy caramel when

AAAAHHHHHHHHHHHJESUSMARYNJOSEPH!!!!

There was Maw screaming and waving her hands in front of her face cos the Chapel door was opening and a face was appearing.

Oh, hello Alice, said the face. The body stepped out. *Just out for a wee fag, hen.*

All the Girls were on their knees spouting Hail Marys like a fountain. Maw let out this loud laugh and its ribbon of echo was snipped off by the closing door. The cleaner reached into her blue overall pockets and got the smokes out. She gave one to Maw. They lit up and the smoke rose into the blue sky. The rest of us Girls were amazed at two things:

1. How Maw knew Our Lady so well.
2. That Our Lady smoked Senior Service same as Maw.

So that was how Donna got in touch with her supernatural side. And there's an argument that the impression that Gothic Chapel made on her manifested itself in her Addams Family lookalike quest. Who knows?

When Donna was fifteen my Maw took her up to put her on the pill. That might sound a strange thing to do when you're a Catholic, but so many of the sisters got pregnant before they were married Maw thought if she could save one, just one, from getting married too young she would do it. Wendy went with them for moral support. Her and Donna have always been quite close cos of the nearness in their ages. Donna is the youngest and Wendy is the youngest but one. It can surprise people when Wendy sides with Donna against the odds but it never surprises me.

It was a nice day so they walked through Langloan and along by the West End Park. The cherry blossoms were out on all the trees. From that vantage point Coatbridge looked nice, with the white and pink petals trembling in the breeze and the expanse of green grass behind them. In the distance the white figures of bowlers rolled their bowls along the green. And behind all that, the sandstone detached and semi-detached houses of Blairhill. They were the houses built for and by the owners of the iron- and steel-works and coalmines. The houses that used the Irish Slave trade. Still to this day Blairhill is held in reverence or resentment. Even though some of the immigrants have managed to get in there, it's still a castle. The further they got, the more scared Maw got of confronting the doctor to put a fifteen-year-oul lassie on the pill. The more scared she got, the more angry she got. The more angry she got, the more vocal she got.

See if it's that McMullen that's on. He's a right holy Joe so he is, at Mass every day. If it's him and he refuses I'm going to go for him.

They're not allowed to refuse if you're there, Wendy said.

But the closer they got to the doctor's the worse Maw was getting. By the time they reached the main street she was all for ripping McMullen's guts out as soon as she seen him.

By Christ if that big skinny drip even so much as looks at me the wrong way I'm going for him.

Wendy managed to calm her down and they met the usual hordes of people on their way up the main street. They kept their little secret well.

Hello, Alice, where are you off to?

I'm taking her up the doctor's.

Nothing serious, I hope?

Women's things.

Her periods are all wonky, Wendy would say.

Then they'd talk about the price of a loaf or who died this week. If anybody was pressing too much Maw would talk about reading their tea-leaves and that would get them. Off on a tangent they'd go, agreeing to a day, a time and a place. By the time they were near Jackson Street they were in such a hurry they just had to say, *Doctor's!* to anybody and shuffle off.

It just so happened that the doctor's surgery was having new chairs delivered that day. The boxes were being delivered as Maw, Donna and Wendy were closing in at some rate of knots along the main street. Joanna, the lassie that worked in the doctor's helped the men to bring the chairs in.

We've all been looking forward to getting these, she said. She was always batting her black eyelids below her blonde fringe.

When she had gave the youngest of the delivery men her phone number and they were gone, everybody ripped the cardboard boxes open. They were nice chairs. Foam backs, adjustable up and down with a hissing noise and they had double casters on each of the three legs. In the tin hut that apologised for being a doctors' surgery, they looked like extras from a Cadbury's Smash advert. The doctors and nurses and secretaries started trying to assemble them.

By this time the Mawdonnawendy armada was sailing past ASDA. They had the roof of the doctor's in sight. Down periscope and full ahead. Inside the tin monstrosity McMullen couldn't fathom his chair out. He was trying to assemble it as he talked to his patients coming and going. He prescribed Amoxil to the first three without listening. He had the casters on the legs but could he work out how to properly attach the back? No. In all the other rooms their chairs were assembled and they were kicking themselves off from filing cabinets and walls. The receptionists were zooming over to the wee sliding window, losing the smile, and talking to patients.

Yes?

I've got an appointment.

Name?

Pardon?

Name!!

James Johnston.

No.

Pardon?

No, you've no appointment. Next, please?

Joanna was swivelling and shoving her chair backwards and forwards. She was really too clever for the dumb blonde act. In fact if truth be told she'd a higher IQ than all the doctors in the tin palace. But she was a working-class lassie from Airdrie. She took up the dumb blonde thing and milked it for all it was worth. And she knew more than anybody that blondes have more fun.

Go and show Dr McMullen how to put his chair together, Moaning Minnie the receptionist said.

Joanna went in but McMullen didn't need any advice.

Joanna! Men have been building structures in the world since time immemorial. So if you'll leave me alone, thank you very much . . .

But Doctor, all you have to do is this and this . . .

As she explained and clicked the bits together and showed him what the bits he'd kicked under his desk were for, patients stared through the slightly open door. It's not often you see a doctor in a fix. It was a bit like looking in the priest's window and catching him watching *Coronation Street* while munching into a big outsider on jam and a mug of tea. Holes in his socks maybe. Even in the late 1970s doctors were gods in Coatbridge. A doctor could have cut your leg off as a cure for the flu and you would have thanked him as you hopped out the door.

Right y'are, Doctor. Thanks very much, Doctor.

McMullen was aware that his patients were watching but he couldn't close the door because the soft foam cushion was jamming it open. Every time he leaned forwards and swung the door it bounced quietly and came to a stop against Joanna's arse. His face turned red.

Listen, Joanna. I built my surgery in Zaire brick by brick, board by board, nail by nail. I'm sure I can assemble something as simple as a chair, thank you very much, he muttered as Joanna left his surgery.

That's when Maw burst in with a red face of her own and a purpose. Her fear was a nuclear pile now and she was ready to mushroom to the defence of Donna. The place smelled of bitter medicine and oul women's clothes.

Hi Wendy, Joanna said. *How's things?*

Great. How's the baby?

He's two now.

No? You look great.

Yoga, Joanna said.

She displayed her tidy little body. If she'd been born somewhere other that Airdrie or in a posh bit of Airdrie (there is one) she might have done a lot better with a body like that and her IQ. If she was in her early twenties nowadays she'd probably be running her own TV Production company. And even if she was stupid, which she's not, she had the body to shag her way, if not to the top, at least all the way to the middle.

Wendy told Joanna Maw had brung Donna to go on the pill cos every one of the sisters had got pregnant before marriage.

What age is she now?

Fifteen.

It's McMullen that's on.

My Maw says if he doesn't give her the pill she'll batter him.

Joanna wasn't too sure he would and they whispered on about how he was always moralising about relationships. But what use is morals when you're out there with a baby and a teenage Ned as a father. No way. Wendy was certain that Maw would attack McMullen. Joanna laughed.

I'm serious, Wendy said.

Joanna stopped laughing in time to see Donna and Maw being invited into McMullen's surgery. Joanna sighed and Wendy bit into her lip. They both moved up near the door but not so close the patients would clock on there was something up.

In the surgery things seemed to be going better for McMullen. He had his chair assembled and there he was twisting it round and shoving it back and forwards. Smug. He had his hands at chest-level with his fingers interlocking. They must teach that at doctor school.

Oh! and here's lesson ten of doctor poses; the interlocking fingers. This classic pose gives off an air of relaxation and aloofness at the same time.

Maw came in with Donna and closed the door. Donna sat in the hard plastic patient seat and Maw felt awkward cos there was nowhere for her to sit. McMullen swivelled in his chair.

Hello Alice, what do you think of my new chair? he asked Maw.

But Maw was in no mood to talk furniture. She was loaded and ready to go off. McMullen was taken by surprise when she launched into an unstoppable tirade. A torrent. Under the avalanche of words Donna and McMullen were being shoved back. Maw towered above the two of them, her mouth going fifteen to the dozen and her voice getting louder and more high-pitched by the second.

I want to put her on the pill I know you think it's a bad thing that young lassies shouldn't be on the pill and it's against the Church but this isn't the Chapel, Doctor, and you're no priest I'll have you know and I'm not going to stand for it I'm not going to let you fob me off with stories about morals and ethicals and all that . . . I'm here to get the pill for her and I'm not leaving without the prescription. All my daughters have been pregnant out of wedlock that's never going to happen again.

Is that right? McMullen said. He turned to Donna and asked if that was what she wanted. Donna nodded. She kept her head down so that she was looking through her hair and could only see his boots and a few nuts and bolts left on the floor.

Well, d'you know what I would do if I was your mother? he said.

What? Donna said like a wee mouse.

I'd kick your fuckin arse.

Maw looked at McMullen. I mean, you're a bit shocked when a doctor talks like that. Swearing. And he said to Maw. *I'm telling you, Alice, I'd kick her fuckin arse right down the road.*

Maw was speechless. His swearing interrupted her impulse to attack him. As she straightened out her thoughts he turned to Donna again.

Are you sure that's what you want to do?

Yes, Donna said.

She was using only her breath to speak. If you were more than three feet away from her the only way you would have knew she was talking is that a couple of wisps of her hair moved forwards. They were lucky cos McMullen had got a new chair and it had tilted him into the right side of happy. He decided to give them the prescription without any more moralising. Who cares? After all, he's got a new chair that wheels about the floor. Relaxed and calm he put his foot on the desk and shoved himself backwards.

The back flew off the chair. The chair went up in the air. Maw and Donna screamed as he toppled. McMullen landed with a hell of a thump. His arse and his legs were stuck up between the wee sofa and the sink. He was jammed solid.

Help! Help me! he was shouting.

All Maw could say was, *Are you alright, Doctor? Are you alright, Doctor?*

They didn't know what way to pull him. They could see his head. There was that much weight his ear was touching his shoulder. He was trying to wriggle loose but couldn't.

Wendy and Joanna crashed into the room. Maw and Donna were trying to pull McMullen out. Wendy and Joanna thought they were beating McMullen up. They tried to pull Alice and Donna off. A right mix-up it was. Joanna and Wendy eventually pinned Maw and Donna to the wall. McMullen struggled to his feet and explained.

The chair broke. The back came off.

Joanna held up a missing bolt. *Told you that bolt goes in there. But would you listen? Oh no!*

Fuckin thing! McMullen said. He lifted the chair and crashed it across the room.

The whole surgery was silent. Maw couldn't stop laughing. Neither could Donna. Joanna and Wendy too. There was even a mirmer of sniggering out in the condemned corridor. Oh my, how the mighty had fallen. On their arse. Their shoulders were going as McMullen regained some of his senses and twisted knobs and buttons on the chair.

When he got it working again he was dead nice to Maw. He sat down and wrote out a prescription for a year's supply of the pill. Donna was to start taking them at her next period and book herself in for a smear test.

Donna eventually got her black belt in karate. Anything that was black she wanted it. When Geddy was in having Alicia, Donna was there. Geddy was screaming her head off with the pain. The nurse started shouting.

Give her gas, give her gas.

So Donna, karate-style, grabbed the gas mask and shoved it on Geddy's face.

Take big breaths, Geddy. Take big breaths, she was going.

Geddy remembers her breath going

Out

In
Out

Geddy breathed long and hard. The pain went away a bit. The gas was really good. It really works, she was thinking. Out the side of her wild animal eyes she watched the doctor looking over at the wall just above the bed where all the wires and switches and gas came out. The doctor nodded to a nurse and then nodded to the wall. Geddy couldn't see right cos Donna's face was right up against hers with her Witchy eyes trying to hypnotise her into calm.

Breathe, Geddy, she was going. *Breathe in and out.*

Geddy squinted her eyes round. They were the only things in her body she could move cos she was pushing the wane out at the time. She managed to focus her trembling mind on the aluminium panel and there was gas hissing out from the connector on the wall. The nurse was trying frantically to fix it back on but she was all fingers and thumbs. Donna, in her exaggerated karate moves, had pulled it out.

The nurse managed to put it back in. That's when Geddy knew what pain was; when it started going away.

Geddy's History

Geddy's thirty-four with dyed blonde hair that's sometimes brown when she's fed up. She's always in for the glamorous look but that's a bit bright at half eight in the morning down the shops for bread and fags. If there's anything about Geddy it's the fact that she's sexy. When all's said and done she's the sexiest of the Girls. Not the best-looking and definitely not the cleverest, but the sexiest. She's for ever fixing her short skirts. Pulling them further down her thighs with her fists and bending her knees like she's trying to become a smaller person.

Once she's done battle over the length of her skirt she gets to checking her boobs to see that they're sitting right. There are rules for the amount of cleavage you show. I don't know them. There's no need for boobs and thighs and tight arses here where I am. But Geddy seems to get the right amount showing, about three inches of deep black gouge I'd say. Geddy gets that cleavage right and then tugs her jumper down another inch. Into the lands of too much. It happens when she's counting the price of beans or wondering whether to get the dear tights or the cheap tights. Her hand comes automatic up and covers that inch so that the cleavage is back to a respectable three inches. It's like she's two people; a prude trapped in a sensuous body. A virgin in a slapper's uniform.

Everybody thinks Geddy's as thick as mince. But she's not. Granted, some of the things she comes away with are crazy to the point of absurdity. But when you think them out yourself and discover the patterns of thought she's took to get there, you start to think that maybe she's not daft. In fact, maybe she's a lot more clever than the whole lot of us. But when she speaks she uses long vowels that only teenage girls or really posh women use. When really posh women use long vowels, like when they say, *rea-aly!* it only has the effect of making them seem more posh. But when the likes of Geddy says them it only makes her seem more dense. More of a slum-dweller.

Is that ri-ight? I don't beli-eeeeve that.

Geddy says that when something really unbelievable comes up in the conversation. But she offsets all this daftness by having an intimate knowledge of the political goings-on in the world. Geddy talks about political leaders and intrigue as if she's talking about her next-door neighbours.

What d'you make of that Yasser Arafat? I mean, one minute he's saying there's peace in the Palestinian territories and the next thing he's shouting the odds at Israel. Somebody wants to give him a right shake by the way. And that Clinton didn't do much fuckin good either, did he? Hoormaster.

She's not had much luck with men mainly cos she's always looking for that man who will transform her life. Everybody's looking for a resurrection. The only problem is, they're always looking for somebody else to do the resurrecting for them. Geddy looks for her epiphanies in men. If the truth be told she's always happier when she's not got a man. I have to be more exact than that. She's always happy when there's the prospect of a man on the horizon. The infinite energy given to us by hope. The men, even if they're a butcher with free steaks or a barman with free drinks, are always a big disappointment. After the disappointment she goes into a depression. Then she gets energised by the hope that the next man might be the actual one. That shooting star in the summer night with a square jaw and a pocket full of money.

As far as the whole Witchcraft thing goes Geddy doesn't believe in it much, although she moves towards it through her own superstition.

When we stayed in Drumpark Street my Maw had an oul ashpan. It was the one out of the bottom of the fire that had rotted right through and she'd flung it out. It was lying out in the back garden all rusted and ragged. The Girls were all playing on the wee wall. The top of the wall was covered in a damp green moss cos it lay in the constant shadow of the house. I suppose Geddy must have been about five at the time. Geddy pushed Donna and Donna pushed her back. The rest of the Girls joined in and there was one side against another. Bad thoughts went into the air. I don't think they were aware of their powers at that time but Donna, Caroline and Linda centred their thoughts on Geddy. Staring at her.

Stop it, youse.

But they stared.

Stop staring at me. Mammy, they're staring at me.

Next thing, Geddy fell off the wall and landed arse first on this oul ashpan.

A jagged point sliced right into her. When she stood up she was starting to laugh. The Girls were starting to laugh too but the laugh caught like a gurgle in their throats when they seen the blood. Geddy seen their eyes seeing something bad and twisted round. The blood was running down the back of her leg. That bit of your thigh you've got to twist round to see. A puddle had already formed on the ash and stones. Her white plastic sandals had acquired red soles. It's the red soles she remembers when she thinks back to that moment and the ear-piercing scream. The red soles merged with the scream and the fear and the blood. To this day she won't wear red shoes, Geddy.

Maw was peeling tatties at the scullery window and singing 'The Mountains of Mourne' when she heard the clatter and the thump. The silence and the scream. Out she rushed with the knife still in her hand. With the knife glinting in the sunlight and the blood and the screaming, if anybody had came along they would have thought Maw had stuck a knife in Geddy's arse. Maw clamped her hand on her arse to stop the bleeding. But it was no use. The blood seeped out through her fingers. Strange as it may seem, all I could think about was Jesus and the blood running out His hands. Out His side. We had pictures of Him all over the house with blood coming out left right and centre. I can't think of blood without thinking of Jesus. It's hard to imagine that people so used to seeing blood and hearing about it every week at Mass could become so hysterical at the sight of real blood. By this time Geddy had started to shake. Half because of the loss of blood and half because of the shock on everybody's face. We were all stood around like useless spectators when Mrs Adams came out. Her eyes were going everywhere looking for the answer to the question, What's all that racket out here?

What is it, Alice? What's happened?

She's split her arse open on that oul ashpan there.

Oh, for fuck sakes, hen, are you alright? she asked Geddy.

Geddy let out a long high banshee wail.

Jamie, take a penny out my purse and away up there and phone the ambulance, Mrs Adams shouted.

Away her big son went like the hammers of hell up to the phone box. In them days the ambulances sat about all day waiting on calls, playing cards and eating fish suppers. You never got as many accidents. You phoned an ambulance and it was there in seconds. All this new technology and organisation's slowing things down. Mixing everybody up. In fact, Jamie Adams was only halfway back down when it passed him with the siren going. It was my Uncle Eddie that was driving. He was an ambulance-driver. Married to my Auntie Sadie, Maw's younger sister.

By the time they got to Geddy, Maw had a big towel over her arse but Eddie whipped off his socks and made a tight ball out of them. He positioned them right on the wound and told Maw to press really hard. All she had been doing with the towel was soaking the blood up. Acting like a siphon. Making things worse than they really were. Off they went in the ambulance with Geddy face down and Maw pressing the big smelly socks hard onto Geddy's arse. She got eleven stitches.

When Geddy was a teenager she used to look at Caroline's clothes and drool. Caroline had the full caboodle in her wardrobe. It was the time that dirndl dresses were all the rage. Skirts that came right down to your ankles. With frilly white bits round the bottom and sometimes the middle too. Like gypsies. Caroline had three of them cos she had her job in the staff agency at the time. But she wasn't daft, the bold Caroline. Anybody with sisters'll tell you this. Keep your clothes under lock and key. Even your knickers aren't safe. Not only did Caroline have a lock on her door but she also had locks on her bedside cabinets and, more to the point, a big fuck-off padlock on her wardrobe doors. She used to keep the key of her wardrobe in this wee heart beside her clock. All the Girls knew that's where the key was. That wasn't the problem. The problem was the proper door and mortise lock my Da had put on her room at Caroline's request. Nobody knew how to get in there. They'd sit for hours when she was away to Bobby's trying to pick the lock with Kirby grips or bent-over nails. But they never managed to trip even one of the tumblers. Caroline sussed that they were trying to open her door and she warned them. She made sure Maw and Da had a word with the Girls too.

Keep out of Caroline's room. She's a woman now, she's got a job, was the war cry round about that time.

Caroline started pulling a hair out and licking it and sticking it across the door somewhere so that if it ever opened she'd know. Even that didn't put the sisters off. They were at the lock with all sorts. They even took the screws out of the handle one night and couldn't put it back on. Linda pulled the metal thing that joins the handles together out and the handle on the inside fell with a clunk onto the floor. Caroline went spare when she came in. She was running up and down the top lobby with the handle in her hand shouting the odds so that my Maw and Da would hear and come up the stairs. I think she had a drink in her.

But there's one thing Caroline never thought of. The window. It must have been a pretty sight when Geddy and Donna came up the street this summer night carrying a ladder they'd stole off the building site that turned out to be the Kirkshaws club. They got Angie to go in and make Maw a cup of tea and a big outsider on jam. She loved that my Maw. Caroline was away out to the Shark's Gub with Bobby. The boys were up to no good somewhere.

D'you want tea and a big outsider on jam, Maw? Angie shouted.

Maw came to the scullery. That was the signal for Donna and Geddy to get the ladder into the back garden and up against Caroline's window. Once they had it there, even if you looked out the living-room window, you wouldn't have seen the ladder. But there was another thing that always raised the alarm that there was something wrong in our house. Silence. If the house was quiet there was definitely something going on. Imagine it, my six sisters in the house, and three boys. There was always fights and arguments and laughter and music. There was every kind of noise you can imagine but the one noise you never got was the incredible hiss of silence. Even in the dead of night there was somebody snoring or tossing and turning in their bed. And Geddy spoke in her sleep. Sometimes she sang. One night Linda and Angie recorded Geddy singing two verses of the Bay City Rollers' 'Shang-A-Lang'.

Angie's still got the recording and she gets it out at parties. It's not Geddy singing that's funny but the suppressed laughter of the Girls in the background. But 'Shang-A-Lang' was unusual. More often than not what Geddy sang in her sleep was 'Jolene' – the Dolly Parton song. But she substituted Geraldine for Jolene. Now if the Girls had recorded that . . . Well!

So, as I said, silence would have alerted Maw. Geddy stayed at the back with the ladder propped onto the sill and Donna went in the back door and clomped up the stairs. In the room she flung on Bachman-Turner Overdrive, 'You Ain't Seen Nothin' Yet', and stamped up and down the lobby like an elephant. On top of that she went into mock coughing fits and kidded on she was shouting at Geddy and Linda. Wendy was in the room but she was having nothing to do with it and was finishing her homework.

Meanwhile the intrepid Geddy was sliding into Caroline's room. The window sill was pressing into her belly as her arse disappeared into the room followed by her legs. She got her palms on the floor and walked out until her legs came down with too much of a thump on the floor. She crouched and listened.

Donna was doing big giant steps for a few seconds. Then Geddy got up and closed the window. Mrs Brennan across in the flats was standing on her veranda smoking and watching the whole thing with laidback interest. It was a warm evening and she had a cup of tea.

Geddy got the wardrobe key out of the big heart on the bedside cabinet. She'd never seen it before. It was a big oul-fashioned key and rusty. It smelled tangy and made marks on her hands. But that didn't matter. She was a couple of clicks away from the dirndl dresses and wouldn't she look great at St Monica's Tuesday-night disco with one of them on. The black one. Donna and Angie could fight over the red and yellow ones, but Geddy knew she would look the best in the black. The belle of the ball. Angie and Donna could be her two ugly pals. She held the padlock in her palm like a dead bird and slowly put the key in. Turned it in small arcs until it opened with a beautiful click and heavy swing. She laid it on the bed. When she turned back the door had swung open and all the treasure was hanging in neat rows. Caroline even had wee labels stuck where everything should go. And right below where it said *dirndl dresses* were the three objects of desire.

She took the dresses one at a time off their hangers and folded them on the bed. Then she produced an ASDA bag from up her jumper and slid them into that, held the door shut with her knee and put the padlock back on. Getting out the window and down the ladder was a bit tricky with the ASDA bag in her teeth but she done it alright. Mrs Brennan shook her head, laughed and went in for another cup of tea. Geddy planked the carrier bag in the bushes at the back of the garden and went running round the front and burst in the front door.

Is Donna in? Is Donna in?

She's up the stairs clopping about like a Clydesdale horse, Maw said.

But Donna heard Geddy coming in and that was the signal to stop clomping, turn the music off, and come down the stairs.

Angie, are you not finishing your piece on jam? Maw shouted.

But the three Girls were racing out the house to examine their booty. First though, Geddy thought they should take the ladder back to the building site.

Somebody might've seen us stealing it, said Donna.

Angie pointed out that they'd need the ladder to put the dresses back so they planked it in Rettie's garden. That was a jungle anyway. You could go missing in there and never be found. That night Donna, Geddy and Angie went out with their rubbish gear on and headed up the swingpark with the ASDA bag. In the tunnels they stripped off and put on the dirndl dresses. Geddy had put the black one to the bottom and pulled out the red and slung it to Angie. Gave the yellow to Donna and kept the black for herself. It must have been a pretty sight, three teenage lassies in their knickers and bras in a concrete tunnel changing into dirndl dresses one black and the other two fighting over the yellow and the red. Donna ended up with the yellow.

Even though they had on dirndl dresses and were quite pretty, none of them got a lumber. They probably looked too sophisticated for the boys that went to that disco. They were more into Doc Martens and Levis-Sta-prest and fighting. Or just being sick on the floor with drink and lying in it till the priest got their Da up to punch lumps out them.

They got back home and went through the same routine again to put the dresses back. Only this time they had to get the ladder out of Rettie's jungle and made tea and pieces of jam for Maw and Da. But they got them back and Caroline never suspected. She did wonder at the time how the clothes smelled of sweat or drink or smoke but she was so certain of her tight security that she suspected nothing. The Girls borrowed the dresses every Tuesday until Paddy Maclehatton stole the ladder and started a window-cleaning run.

Years ago, some of the sisters were in the back garden. They were all still at home living with Maw and Da. It was sunny and they were talking about who would be at the dancing that night. Dolly Parton had 'Jolene' out at the time.

Geddy was always a funny one. She spent a lot of her time in her room, curling her hair and looking at herself in the mirror. She was pretty when she was in her teens. There's no doubt about that and her being a bit of a gymnast gave her a body men would kill for. And they did. Well, not kill exactly but kick fuck out of, stick the head on, whack each other over the head with Buckie bottles.

The Girls heard this singing coming from the room and they shoosht. It was Geddy. And if Geddy broke men's hearts she broke women's hearts too cos all the men would be eyeing her up and chatting her up. Sometimes she would steal them from their girlfriends and sometimes she wouldn't. When they were all quiet they could make out what she was singing up in the room. She was singing the song but substituting her own name instead of Jolene.

Geraldine, Geraldine, Geraldine . . .

The Girls fell into each other like a wigwam, laughing. The sun was dappling on the grass and moving like sound to light with their laughter. By the time Geddy came out into the garden they were ready for her.

One two three, went Wendy and they all started singing, *Geraldine, Geraldine, Geraldine . . .*

Not only that but they done a wee dance about the garden. The Gallaghers were peeping over the fence, but they were too drunk to understand what was going on. Mrs Donnelly knew alright. She shouted her man out. Just as he arrived Geddy grabbed Wendy by the hair and started tearing lumps out of her. Linda joined in by giving Geddy a hefty boot up the arse with her platform shoes on. It got Geddy right on the bone and as she fell her face folded up like an accordion. I don't know if you've ever had a boot right on the arse bone. It's like a funny bone with nothing funny about it. There's nothing you can do about it. You've just got to rub. Not very ladylike. There's Geddy on the deck rubbing her bone and all the sisters above her like a crazy birdcage and they sing it all over again.

But this time there's some venom in it. They're attacking her with the words. The *e* in G*e*raldine is pronounced with so much energy it gained a significance the letter e was never to achieve again until E for Ecstasy and e for email.

Geddy was up the doctor's this time when she was about eighteen or nineteen. My Maw went with her. There's nothing Maw likes better than a good visit to the doctor's. You've heard of Munchausen by proxy – where a mother harms her child in order to get attention for herself; like secondhand hypochondria. Maw went to the doctor's with anybody that would let her go. I guess you could say she went to get sympathy by proxy. Geddy had passed out in the pub the night before and Maw didn't like the sound of that. All you need to know here to understand the confusion that follows is that the pub she was in was called The Monkland. And there's a hospital in Coatbridge called Monklands General Hospital. Commonly known as The Monklands.

So in went Geddy and Maw to the doctor's. This was years after the arrival of the swivel seats and Dr Rousseau had his off to a fine art. Pushing back with his foot and forwards with his hand, braking as desired with his other foot. He was as good as a ballet dancer. In fact, it had become so much part of his day that on a stage it would have been beautiful to watch. If it wasn't just a doctor in his surgery in a swivel chair you'd swear it was art. Geddy and Maw sat down and he zoomed over and braked at the desk. Maw smiled as she remembered Dr McMullen arse over elbow stuck between his desk and his filing cabinet shouting for help.

Morning, Alice. So what's the problem, Geraldine?

I fainted in The Monkland, Doctor.

You were painting in The Monklands?

No, I fainted.

She fainted, Doctor, Maw said.

But things were getting more confused by the second. Rousseau's face was screwed up like a posh question mark.

What were you doing in The Monklands?

I was just out with my boyfriend for a wee drink, Doctor, Geddy said.

Now Rousseau was really surprised. *In The Monklands? Is your boyfriend a medical man?*

No, he's not got a job the now. He's on the bru.

Geddy was getting confused and uneasy. She shifted her arse about in the seat. Looking at Maw. Looking at the doctor and thinking it was her innate daftness that was causing the confusion. Maw couldn't figure out what was going on either. But Geddy sussed it out just as Rousseau came back with his next question.

Was your boyfriend ill?

I don't mean The Monklands Hospital, Doctor. I was talking about The Monkland bar down at Mitchell Street. We were out for a drink and I fainted.

There was a second of silence and Geddy spoke again with that racing way of speaking she's got, the words overlapping each other.

I went to the toilet and I came out and the carpet started spinning and down I went like a sack of tatties, Doctor, thump. I've got a big bruise on my arm – look.

He got it as she showed him the bruise on her triceps. Big and purple. Yellow at the edges. Rousseau laughed. Quiet at first but building up with his shoulders going up and his head hanging down. Each time he laughed his head bounced up a bit. And each time it bounced up it bounced higher than it did the last time. Like his crescendo laughter was leading to something. A destination. Maw laughed too, keeping her volume just under that of the doctor's and rising with him. It was a mark of respect. How would it look if you laughed louder than the doctor? Especially in his own surgery. Geddy laughed last. But she who laughs last laughs loudest and she didn't half laugh, Geddy. Maw and Rousseau got a fright when she burst out. But they looked at each other and laughed again. This time more or less in harmony. They wound up the volume till from out in the condemned corridor it sounded like a full-blown shouting and crying match. Joanna, by now the head receptionist, rushed along the corridor and burst into the room expecting to find Geddy and Maw battering lumps out of Rousseau. But what she did find was the three of them in fits, doubled over and red in the face with laughing.

What is it, Doctor? Is everything alright?

The Monklands . . . That was all he could say before he was caught up again in his own laughter.

The Monklands, hen, Maw said.

Geddy nodded her head in agreement. Joanna looked at Geddy. Scrutinising her at high speed. Same with Maw. But she couldn't find an obvious reason why either of them needed to be rushed to The Monklands.

You want me to get an ambulance? Joanna said.

No, get me a pint of lager, said Rousseau.

And at that the three of them folded over helplessly on the floor. Joanna stood exasperated at the door.

The Girls were waiting on their dinner this night. Geddy was making it. She put it all out on the table and she had this triumphant grin on her face. Everybody wondered what it meant.

As they tucked into the ham, eggs, beans and chips, Geddy stood back with her arse against the cooker and her arms folded.

D'yees smell anything? she eventually asked.

The Girls were sitting with their eyes wide like ping-pong balls. Asking the question, *What should we be smelling?* Geddy answered that with a question-cum-clue.

D'yees smell anything different about the ham? she said.

The Girls looked at each other and started sniffing the ham. Some of them lifting the ham up to their noses. Others lifting the plate and hovering their nose over the aroma.

No, Angie said, *I don't smell nothing different about the ham.*

By this time everybody had stopped eating and was staring at Geddy, who, unusually, was staring at them as if they were thick. Like they were the dafties. She let out a long, youse-are-as-thick-as-fuck sigh and fished into the bin for something.

Aha! she said.

It was the ham packet. Danish. Geddy held the packet up under her chin, wiggling it about like a clue. Then she whipped it behind her back the way you hide sweets from a wane or munchies from a dog. She whipped it out again and wiggled it under her chin.

Come on, come on, yees can't be that daft!

That made everybody worse. If they didn't have a clue

what she was on about earlier, now it was getting dangerous. Intellectual frustration was beginning to take hold. Adrenaline washing round the veins. Geddy was now hiding the packet behind her back and whipping it round with a *taa naa* or a *doo doo doo* trumpet herald. In the fuzz of frustration she took on the air of a mad Chinese dancer in an opium den. Eventually it was Angie that broke.

What the fuck is it? You're doing my head in here!

Geddy held the packet up at her left-hand side and pointed to it with her right hand.

A ham packet! grunted Angie.

Can yees not smell curry? asked Geddy.

While the Girls sniffed the air for any trace of curry, Angie stared right into Geddy's eyes. Almost daring her to say another word. One more fuckin word. If some sense didn't come out of those lips soon . . . Geddy was on the edge of Angie's wrath and she knew it. She pointed right to the bit on the packet that would solve the conundrum for one and for all. By now all the dinners were cold.

Look, you bunch of dunderheads, Geddy told them. *Curried bacon. Danish Curried Bacon.*

There was a pause as the Girls took it all in. What it said on the packet was *Cured Bacon.* Not *Curried Bacon.* All the Girls laughed except Angie. She stared at Geddy for a while, waited till the laughter died down and said three words.

My dinner's cold.

When Geddy was engaged to big Shaun they went to Spain together. I don't know what age she was but probably about eighteen, nineteen or twenty. It's hard to keep track of time here where I am now. Clocks and calendars are useless. But I'm sure that's what age she must have been.

It was the first time Geddy had been in Spain. The first time in fact that she had been out of Scotland. And certainly the first time she'd been anywhere with a man. Even if big Shaun was only a boy really. Being six feet six might qualify you for a rugby team but height alone doesn't qualify you for manhood. Geddy tested him for manhood the first week they were there. If you had seen Shaun lying in the sun sleeping, it wasn't the heat that was doing it. He was exhausted. Every time Geddy rubbed her oily toe off him he'd pretend to be still sleeping. He managed to keep the sexual athletics to night-time only in the second week. An added bonus was that he came home with the best tan he'd ever had. He hardly even got a drink cos to express a want for a drink was to express enough energy to go to the bar. Enough energy to go to the bar meant you had enough energy to go to the room and try a few more positions from *The Joy of Sex* Geddy had bought at the airport. It was mostly all pictures. Another ploy Shaun used to stay out of the apartment was the beach. He didn't really like the beach with the sand sticking to the suntan lotion and guys looking at Geddy's tits. But she persuaded him to go. Every time Geddy found a spot he'd say it was no use, too many people, too much noise or too near the road. On they'd go. Shaun would keep her walking until she sat down complaining and swore she was going no further. He'd roll out the towels and lie still as a corpse for the day in the hope Geddy wouldn't find an empty toilet or hidden nook where they might further explore *The Joy of Sex*.

On the second Wednesday about one o'clock the sun was right above them. Through his eyelids it was a yellow pink and sometimes blazing white. Shaun hadn't opened his eyes for two hours in fear Geddy might see him. She was sitting up at his side, her shadow casting away from them. And he needn't have worried cos she was in deep thought. Contemplative. It had been a long time without sex. More than four hours cos they had done page 44 before they left the apartment in the morning. Sex was paramount in her mind. The boys and men going past weren't helping much, with their tight peachy arses and the pocket rockets they were barely in control of. Even the women were oozing sex. Geddy hadn't thought before that she could see the sex in a woman. But there they were. Curves and little luminous swimsuits, green or yellow or blue. Long black curly hair bouncing off their smooth brown backs. My, them Spanish girls don't need to do much more than get out their beds in the morning. If a handful of them moved to Coatbridge, men would follow them about like puppies. And that's what got Geddy caught up in her conundrum. Spanish girls in the Brig changed to Geddy in Spain and a thought came up. A problem. It mushroomed in her head and went round and round. She had to ask Shaun. She had to.

Shaun was genuinely sleeping the first time she nudged him. He was coming round when she shook him with the palm of her hand on his pelvis.

Shaun, Shaun, wake up, she was saying. *Wake up.*

He woke. Squinted at the sun and leaned round on his elbow.

What is it?

He was hoping it wasn't sex. It wasn't. Except in a roundabout way. Geddy stared out to the thin black line of horizon then turned and looked down to Shaun. The sun was backlighting her head so that she looked like an angel and for all the ferocious sexual appetite Shaun saw why he was going to marry her. Her hair was lit up like candy floss as she spoke.

Shaun, see if I got pregnant here, will the wane speak Spanish? she asked.

She was genuinely worried. That's why her face fell when Shaun, after a beat, burst out laughing. He looked about to make sure nobody was listening.

Geddygetyourseltofuckyadaftcunt, he said.

He was running his words together cos he was holding back the laughter and incredulity. Then he done an impersonation of Geddy.

Will the wane speak Spanish!

The sun went down behind Geddy's head. Shaun got up and for the first time he felt safe from sex. He ran laughing towards the sea. A puzzled Geddy, none the wiser, watched him run in up to his knees, take a leap in the air and plunge into the sea. The water cooled every nook and cranny of his body. Every square inch was engulfed in aquatic serenity. But inside him was expanding, trying to explode. He surfaced spluttering water and laughing.

Geddy lay back and tipped her sunglasses from the top of her head over her eyes. In the heat of the buffered darkness she thought and she thought. Shaun swam and swam cooling all the time. Slowing. Feeling more in control. He eventually lay on his back and floated with his eyes closed. All he could hear was the pressure of water and the sound of his own breath. But Geddy bolted up. Another thought was terrorising her and she had to ask Shaun. She shouted and shouted but he was lost in the rise and fall of his chest and the line of cold water creeping up his body and falling away again.

Shaun, Shaun!! Geddy shouted but everybody that wasn't called Shaun was turning round so she had to stop.

When Shaun came back up she asked him the new question.

Shaun, she said, *will it not be bilingual then if I get pregnant here, the wane?*

Shaun flopped back into the sand with a thud and a sigh.

After Geddy and Shaun got married, Geddy and Maw went to B&Q to get wallpaper. Maw effectively picked it and even wanted to go round and help Geddy to paste it up. But she was firm on that, Geddy. This was something she was going to do herself. Maw told her to remember to match it. Her and Shaun spent the Sunday stripping the paper off the living room. They'd bought a wee flat in King Street. When Shaun went to work the next day Geddy put the paper up and was careful to match it perfectly and brush any bubbles out with the papering brush. She done a great job considering this was her first attempt. If the light came in a certain direction you couldn't even see the joins. She shut the blinds and put the lobby light on. Sure enough she couldn't find the joins and she was the one that put it up.

It was that good she phoned Maw and asked her up for tea and Paris buns. When Maw arrived the tea was set out on the living-room table and the blinds were shut. The lobby light was on. Maw loved the wallpaper even though she couldn't really see it right.

It's like midnight in here, Geddy, open the blinds till I see it right.

No. I bet you can't find the joins.

You don't get joins in Paris buns.

In the wallpaper.

Sure enough Maw couldn't find the joins but she noticed something up at the top next to the ceiling.

What's that up there, hen?

Where?

Up at the ceiling. Open the blinds a minute, youre joins are great, by the way. The best joins I've seen for years.

Geddy opened the blinds. Maw gasped. Right round the top of the walls was: MADE IN ENGLAND MADE IN ENGLAND MADE IN ENGLAND MADE IN ENGLAND MADE IN ENGLAND

Geddy had took the matching a bit too serious. At the top of every roll was a *Made In England* and she had went back to B&Q and bought fifteen more rolls so that she could match the paper perfectly. The woman in B&Q asked her what size her living room was.

It's just one of them wee flats in King Street, Geddy said.
And you need twenty rolls?

On the floor was twenty rolls of paper at a fiver each. Every one had ten feet cut off them. The rest was intact. You could have papered the whole house with them. When Shaun came in and seen what had happened that's exactly what he done. After he re-papered the living room. Waste not want not.

Caroline bought Geddy a new twin tub washing machine when she married Shaun. It was a great wee machine and Geddy's clothes were always spotless. She said it was a great wee washer and it made her whites whiter than when they were new. Especially if she used Daz.

But time it is a precious thing. And time brings all things to an end. Even Foster and Allen couldn't have saved Geddy's precious Hotpoint twin tub. When it died, it bled a colour wash all over the scullery floor. It had to go. You wouldn't think you could become emotionally attached to a machine. It was early morning and Geddy was crying when her and Shaun flung the Hotpoint in the canal. It gurgled a few times then sank so there was just a corner poking up. Then down it went for ever. They bought a new Zanussi automatic. It was bought, plumbed in and filled with washing by the afternoon.

A few weeks passed and the Girls started to notice things about Geddy only sisters could notice. She seemed a bit duller. Not as in your face as she usually was. Then a few more weeks went past and the Girls noticed that it wasn't Geddy who was duller but her clothes. Her reds had lost their sex and her blacks were tinged with grey. But most of all her whites had lost the summer cloud look to them. They were like everybody else's whites now. No, that's wrong. They were worse than everybody else's whites. Somebody had to say something cos, on top of all that, Geddy was starting to smell. It was Linda who said something. It had to be Linda cos this was after her operation when she was transformed into a truth-telling machine.

Linda wasn't that heartless when she told her. She told her in the scullery of Caroline's flat. The Girls pretended not to be listening from the living room.

Geddy, said Linda, *everybody's been saying that your clothes aren't as bright since you got rid of your Hotpoint twin tub.*

Oh I know!

And to be honest, hen, you and Shaun are fuckin stinking!

After Geddy stopped crying the Girls decided to march up to Geddy's house and see what she was maybe doing wrong with her new Zanussi. They all had automatics so it should be no bother for them to spot anything not right. And while they were there they could do a spell on Shaun and maybe knock his sperm count up a bit. Geddy and him had been trying to have wanes for years by then and they'd had no success. The tea-leaves said Geddy was alright, but when Oul Mary read Shaun's cup smuggled out of the house she tutted.

There's a gun on the rim of the cup, she said, *but not a bullet in sight.*

So the Girls had seen this as a chance to attack Geddy's BO problem and put some bullets in Shaun's gun. Donna packed the spell book and the candles and stuff.

When they got there they gathered round the machine and asked Geddy to describe what she done when she washed the clothes.

I do everything it tells you to do. Put the washing in. Set the wee dial to the right number. Let it do it all. It spins them great and then hang them out the back or over the radiators if it's raining.

The Girls couldn't work it out so they asked her to do a washing so they could watch and pick up any wee mistakes she might be making. Geddy opened the door and stuffed in some knickers and bras of indiscernible colour and age. She shut the door.

Mm mm. That's right. Nothing wrong there, the Girls were saying.

Geddy turned the dial to the right programme and switched the machine on. The Girls gasped.

What about the soap powder? Linda asked.

Eh?

It goes in that wee drawer, said Angie.

What wee drawer?

Donna pulled the soap-powder drawer open.

Oh that. I opened that and there was water in it. I shut it before I flooded the place.

What about the soap powder? Linda asked again.

What about it?

How do you put it in?

It's automatic!

But how do you put the powder in if you don't open the drawer?

It's automatic. It doesn't need soap powder. It washes the clothes itself.

So that was the answer to Geddy's washing-machine problems. A wee box of Ariel Automatic out of ASDA and it was fixed.

And the spell? That worked too. Maybe getting rid of the BO helped them to get it together more often but a month and a half later Geddy announced to all and sundry that her whites were whiter than white, her reds had the sex back in them and she had a wee bun in the oven. The Girls had a party.

Soon Geddy was swol up like a whale and smiling. Life was about to be complete. Her, Shaun and a wee wane to bring up.

When the time came to go into Bellshill she was all excited. Shaun didn't want to go so Maw went. In the labour ward it was long and complicated. There had been some concern that

Geddy's wane hadn't been moving much the last month of her pregnancy. So Geddy pushed and groaned. She never took any drugs apart from some gas now and then. No epidural.

When the wane came out there was a quiet descended on the room. Maw took the dead wane from the doctor. They done all the right things, cut the cord and seen to Geddy.

Is it a boy? No, I bet it's a girl, Geddy was shouting. *Maw, what does it look like?*

Maw gave a universal look and nod and the doctors left the room for a few minutes. Maw sat on the edge of the bed shooshing the baby. She had it wrapped up in a white shawl. A shroud. Birth and death in the one garment. Geddy looked into Maw's eyes and Maw looked into Geddy's. They didn't need to say nothing. Geddy started crying. Not bawling. She cried first with tears then with low sobs. She didn't feel sorry for herself, it was the wee blue wane she felt for. All the struggling for nine months and then to die at the moment of glory. The moment of light.

It's a boy, Maw said.

Let me see him.

Maw leaned over so that the baby's face was next to Geddy's. Geddy kissed him on the forehead. Tears ran off her lips and onto the skin. Maw remembers the tears like blue Spanish water moving down the baby's cheeks. Like the baby was crying for Geddy. And maybe he did, cos from that time on Geddy had a long fight with depression. A long, long fight.

I was going to call him Daniel, Geddy said. *Danny.*

She took her new baby in her arms and rocked it to and fro. A nurse nearly came in but this oul doctor stopped her. They watched through the window. Back and forth Geddy went with the wane. Her lips on its wee forehead and her breath spreading over the body. Death wrapped in life. Geddy was moving further and further away from reality. Maw could see it. Geddy and her wane, although they weren't moving anywhere, were running through a fairy-tale forest being chased by Death with his big scythe. The branches were whipping off Geddy's face as she ran and her ankles twisted and the pain was excruciating. But that didn't matter. Pile the pain on, any amounts. She'd suffer torments to keep this baby next to her breast. Daniel. Danny. Maw had seen it before in the Slap Up where wanes died at birth as a matter of routine. Her Granny was the midwife. Oul Biddy. Maw was at a lot of births. And a lot of deaths. She'd seen women, girls really, disappear behind their own eyes on holding a stillborn wane. After that they were never the same. And if they never had any more wanes they became women who lived their life out as if the end was a relief. A letting go. There were some strong women who came through it. But that entailed a long hard battle with depression and anger. Very few ever made it.

Maw could see Geddy was running towards a spot where she might never come back. She had to do something. She done what she done best. She sang a song. Low and sweet.

'Oh Danny boy, the pipes, the pipes are calling
From glen to glen and down the mountainside . . .'

Geddy started to stir. The one lone voice in the echoing chambers of the labour room drew the nurses, the midwife and the doctor to the window. They stared without saying a word and watched the miracle of humanity. A mother soothing the pain of her child who is soothing the pain of her own child who only ever existed inside her. The most intimate death. Maw sang on, starting to stroke the wane's head.

'The summer's gone, and all the roses falling
'Tis you, 'tis you must go and I must bide . . .'

By now Geddy was stroking the baby's head. Absent-minded

but stroking it all the same. And that was good cos that meant she was coming back from the place. She was out of the forest and Death was still in there swiping his blade at trees and shadows. All Geddy needed to do now was find somebody to give her wane to. Somebody nice. Somebody good.

'But come ye back, when summer's in the meadow
Or when the valley's hushed and white with snow . . .'

Maw paused after she sang *hushed* and the pause was filled with peace. The peace drew Geddy a bit more into the room.

'Tis I'll be here in sunshine or in shadow
Oh Danny boy, oh Danny boy, I love you so . . .'

Them at the window cried. They'd seen it all. What couldn't you see in a hospital that drew from Coatbridge, Airdrie, Bellshill and Motherwell? But that didn't matter. Geddy was out of the forest and onto fields of snow. Moving towards the hushed valley. Her feet crunching in the silence. Maw knew what she was doing. She was using the song to get Geddy to see that, when all is said and done, we end up together. It was the land of Together that Maw was leading Geddy into. Where all the spirits gather. She had to see her wane on the path and smiling. But more importantly Geddy had to see that the being of light the wane was walking towards was Geddy. A dead Geddy. Maw had to get Geddy to see that life here was just a passing of time before we'll all merged again. Maw didn't know if that was true but I do. It's true. Maw sang on.

'But when ye come and all the flowers are dying
And I am dead, as dead I may well be
You'll come and find the place where I am lying
And kneel and say an Ave there for me . . .'

That's what done it. That sequence of images done it for Geddy. What she seen in the fields of light was a gravestone. She walked up to it expecting to see Danny Harkins on if (that was Shaun's second name). But what she saw made her smile. Made her happy. Made her see things as they are, not as we think they are. *Geraldine Riley* is what it said and she died when she was eighty-six, a hefty age by any standards. And who was arriving at the grave but Danny. A fine figure of a man he was. He read the stone and knelt and prayed for his mother.

'Hail Mary full of grace . . .'

When he was finished he got up and walked off towards the hushed valley where she could see herself waiting to be reunited with her son. And they were all there. All the sisters and Maw and Oul Mary and people she barely remembered as a child. And people she never knew, yet she did. I was there too watching from a great distance. I am watching from a great distance. Maw's singing brought a smiling Geddy back into the labour room where she joined in and the two of them sang the last verse to the blue baby wrapped in a white shawl.

> *'And I shall hear, though soft you tread above me,*
> *And all my grave will warmer, sweeter be*
> *For you will bend and tell me that you love me*
> *And I shall sleep in peace until you come to me.'*

By the time the song was finished Geddy was holding the wane to her chest and the tears flowed freely. There was a slight noise outside but then it stopped. The doctors and nurses had inadvertently clapped. There's no telling what human beings'll do under pressure. They were embarrassed but behind them all the Girls had gathered and they were smiling and crying at the same time. They thought it was a pretty nice thing for the nurses and doctors to be doing and they thanked them. The Girls were happy cos they knew Maw had led Geddy through the forest and into the light. And Geddy had seen the light that none of them had seen. Only a very special spell or a very powerful moment allows us to see that light as humans. Maw had saved Geddy's life.

When all the Girls came in and gathered round, the nurses took the wane away. They thanked Maw for her lovely singing and went.

Three days later there was a wee funeral. From then on in it was an uphill struggle for Geddy.

It was well-known that Geddy's recurrent bouts of depression could be cured if she had a wane to look after. To take her pain away. Years passed. As I said, I don't know how many. Big Shaun with the low sperm count left her. He met another bird and banged two wanes out of her in jig time. Geddy said it was just luck. Meanwhile she was assessing the gene pool in Coatbridge. And to tell you the truth, if you were looking for the jigsaw and the bits and pieces that go into making up a new master race, Coatbridge isn't the place for that. There's been a high level of interbreeding since the Irish came there in the tattie famine. Don't get me wrong, there's hardly any high foreheads or *Deliverance* types.

None of that. Physically, that is. But mentally there's some strange thinking process evolved. One minute you're laughing at your best pal's joke. The next you're pounding her brains out with an empty Buckfast bottle (a full one would rarely be risked). Coatbridge has got a mentality where it's all laughter or all fists and feet. What it needs as a town is one ten-foot-across Prozac pill. The outcome of this geocentric mood swing is that the boys never become men. So when

Geddy was out hunting men she was really out hunting boys in men's bodies.

There's a lot of good-looking manchilds in the Brig. And Geddy's no dog herself, so a good time was had by all. Frequently. But could she get pregnant? No. No matter how hard she tried, none of the men could hit the button. It was obvious by the time big Shaun christened his second wane to Anna McCartney that everybody had got it wrong about him. It was Geddy that had the problem. There was no eggs rolling off her trolleys. All the Girls chucked in a few quid each and Maw and Oul Mary took Geddy off to Lourdes. It's usually for cancer and cripples and the like, Lourdes, but this was an exceptional case. Maw didn't take Geddy there to tickle her ovaries in the spirit of the Lord. She took her there so that she could get pregnant and in turn move away from the suicidal blackness that was descending on her once, sometimes twice a week.

As soon as Geddy plunged her arse into the miracle waters, between a one-legged man and a blind Polish woman, Maw got on a mobile to Caroline. Right there the Girls started the Fertility dance which involves the usual hocus-pocus with the added Postmodern practices of drinking wine and smoking joints.

There was nothing happened at Lourdes and nothing in Coatbridge. Geddy came home feeling a lot better for her few days away and more content with life. The Girls were sure her ovaries were in prime condition. By this time she had a wee flat of her own near Kirk Street. On the very site, Maw says, where Mrs Clark's close blew up all them years ago in the Slap Up. The 1940s I think it was. On the Friday the Girls took Geddy out and picked her a nice lumber. He was an Italian visiting his relatives that owned the chippy down the Whifflet. Really handsome with dark hair, nice tanned skin and brown eyes. If all the guys in the Brig were like that, the whole town would fall pregnant. Twenty-five years on you'd not be able to move for chip shops and pizza parlours. They were certain he'd be the one. Donna had a feeling about it.

So home the tally guy was took to Kirk Street and, on the site of Mrs Clark's explosion, set a few bombs off in Geddy's bedroom. She was sick in the morning but she never felt pregnant. When Massimo went away after greasing his hair and getting his threads back out of the wardrobe where he'd hung them Geddy started to cry. It wasn't the tears of a woman who feels used after a one-night stand. Geddy was well in control in that department. It was the tears of a woman who thought her life might change with a wee sperm crashing into a nice warm egg. She was sure there was nothing happening there.

She phoned round all the sisters but none of them was going out on Saturday night. There was a good film on the telly. *Who Will Raise My Children*. About a woman with cancer and her man's an alky and she's got to find decent homes for all her wanes before she dies cos that lazy no-good son of a bitch of a husband's good for nothing except drinking Thunderbird wine and crying his eyes out on the porch in the morning. He hasn't even got the decency to play a guitar or a banjo like the southern black men do when they've got the blues. This is one piece of white trash who doesn't deserve the woman he's got. And it should be him that's rotting away with cancer, not her.

Spending a night in alone was not appealing to Geddy. Spending a night in watching a film like that was even worse. Spending a night in alone not watching a film like that would only remind her that a film like that was on. So she decided to go out. She had dipped the Italian Stallion for twenty quid the night before. They never notice. They're that busy flashing their money about to show off they couldn't begin to tell you how much they spent.

Out she went. But not to Memory Lane or one of the classier nightclubs. No. Geddy went to The Barnyard. It's called The Barnyard cos it's full of cows, and other assorted farm animals. But Geddy was desperate to get pregnant. The best-looking guy in there was ugly as fuck but he sidled up to her and asked if she wanted to dance. 'Eye of the Tiger' wasn't Geddy's favourite song but she got up anyway and boy, was he some dancer. If it was a competition for taking epileptic fits he would have won first prize. Pure electrical brainstorm. You have to know what he looked like first to get the full picture. He was at least six feet two. Long red hair all the way down to his arse but thinning at the front so that it looked like his forehead had grown. Or maybe he'd bought it out the forehead shop and got one three sizes too big. The man had the forehead of a much bigger person. The last time his hair was washed is when he left the window open in his G reg Nova at the Whifflet carwash. Women are usually a bit embarrassed when the ultra-violet lights show up their bra on the dance floor. But this guy? His freckles showed up like a paintball fight. He had a denim shirt on with the Golden Virginia sticking out the top pocket and a joint behind his ear that was getting wetter with sweat the more he danced. His jeans were tight. Pure ball crushers. And to give the guy his due he had a nice firm pair of balls on him and a cock snuggled up beside them in a half-moon shape. Like it was resting before the coming action. He was stinking too. Smelled like an oul hospital apron. And this contraption of a man was swinging his sweat-soaked hair round and stamping his feet and screaming every word of 'Eye of the Tiger' right in Geddy's face. He had teeth alright. They were into double figures. Just. But a stroke of luck meant that his best teeth were mainly at the front of his mouth and the gaps and rotten teeth were at the back.

Yet he was the best man there. And something else. Geddy

was attracted to him. Subnormal he might have been but there was some primitive force telling her that here was a man who could do what she needed. Here was a man with target-seeking equipment the American armed forces would die for. She knew she was taking him home before the last crashing chord of the Tiger.

Good job that was when she decided cos the next song was 'Bat Out of Hell'. And that lit his fuse. His previous gymnastics were those of a meditating Buddha compared to these. As soon as Meat Loaf screeched his first line, Redhead-forehead went into action like an exploding box of tactical nuclear weapons. If the polis were there, they would have lifted him for his own safety – if they could have held him down long enough.

Two months after that weekend Geddy announced to everybody that she was pregnant. Maw thanked all the Catholic gods and all the other gods. Her child had been saved. From that day on she was never depressed again. The Girls rejoiced. They had visions of a mini-Massimo charming the women from birth to death. The Italian suave would be a great added ingredient to the family. Things were looking up.

Towards the end of the pregnancy Geddy took to her bed to be absolutely sure everything would go alright. The Girls were out buying bibs and Babygros that would match brown eyes and tanned skin. They could see Geddy in the summer outside Woolies with the sunlight falling on her and the wane and everybody pushing a pound coin behind the pillow.

What a beautiful wee wane – look at his big brown eyes! Is his father Italian? they'd be saying.

So it came to the day of the labour and everybody went to Bellshill to support her. There had been no complications with the pregnancy at all. Everybody put that down to the strong genes they picked when they selected Massimo from the crowd of deadbeats in Memory Lane.

This time the pain was unbearable and Geddy took the epidural and the whole kit and caboodle of drugs and pain relief. The wane was healthy and she knew that by the bawl it made when it came out. It would have drowned out Meat Loaf at The Barnyard. Easy. Maw handed the baby to Geddy. It was a wee girl but it was hard to see its Mediterranean complexion through the mess of the placenta and all the other gunge. The nurses took it away to clean it and the Girls sat and talked the biggest load of shite with Geddy, her being on the drugs and all. The main thing Geddy talked about was how beautiful the curtains were. They were right dreary, in fact, but they all agreed they'd look good with a wee valance in Geddy's living room. Fine. Now and then worry would flicker across her face and she'd ask where the wane was.

Where's my wee baby? Is she alright?

They'd all reassure her and off she'd go about the lovely table. The best table she'd ever seen. I don't know what you think of brown Formica with the edges chipped but the Girls told Geddy how right she was. It was the best table ever. In some circles it might be considered trendy; like the bricks showing through your plaster they sometimes have in yuppie flats. In fact, in some circles this table might even be art. And that's what it was to Geddy. The morphine had transformed a brown Formica table into art.

When they brung the wane back in, the Girls were first to see it. The nurse handed it to Caroline who passed it round so that it was on its way down the age groups and finally it would go to Maw and then be passed to Geddy like an Easter egg. There was something wrong but none of the Girls had the courage to say it. It was Linda who eventually said what had to be said. She looked at the wane in horror.

I've got bad news for you, Geddy.

The wane was purring and gurgling like a blocked drain so Geddy knew it wasn't dead. Nothing serious was wrong or else the nurses would have said something.

Don't tell me, don't tell me, I knew there would be something wrong. Does her ears stick out?

No. Worse than that, said Donna.

What is it? What's wrong? Geddy asked

Donna handed the wane to Maw and Maw handed it to Geddy.

It's a redhead, Angie said.

A right ginger nut, said Linda.

Geddy took the wane and sure enough it was a fully paid-up member of the red race. Destined to do badly at school and always gets picked out in a crowd. Arrested ten times more frequently than normal people. But all that didn't matter cos to Geddy its hair was as red as the rising sun. The freckles all over its face were the Milky Way on a still summer's night.

Maw looked tired. Not just labour tired but long-distance tired. The kind of tiredness that comes with wisdom so that the wiser you get the harder it becomes for you to exercise your wisdom. She was at the thankful end of a long journey to save her daughter's life. A journey that began years ago with the first lines of 'Danny Boy'. Geddy called the wane Alicia after Maw. It was her thanks for the long journey she had led her through. Alicia, despite everything, turned out to be beautiful.

Geddy has had a hard life. She deserves all the luck she can get.

Donna and Geddy

As Caroline is swallowed up by the darkness of the close she hears the remark about her rare wee arse and it lifts her spirit a touch. Men looking at her arse. She feels good about that. She hadn't thought about that up to now. Other men. Sex. The freedom. The Liberation. And hasn't she got a nice wee arse anyway. For a woman just turned forty. As far as the arse goes she's in tip top condition. Tip top.

It's Caroline's smile that comes back into the living room. The door into the living room is the front door. The door into the close. Don't ask me why, that's just the way they built the houses. She closes over the door and snibs it. Straight over to the veranda she goes and watches the bin lorry growling out of the street. A tiger with its belly full.

As she's standing in wide-eyed contemplation at the space where the lorry turned the corner her nose twitches. Once. Twice. Then it's going like a little bunny. She looks down at her hands gripping the veranda so hard the metal's starting to bend. There's a brown-pink residue on her fingers. When she lets go of the veranda there's the thrum of vibration as it springs. She holds her fingers to her nose and sniffs.

Euch! That is fuckin stinking!

She dashes to the sink and runs the tap so hard the water's

splashing out again onto the floor. Click, out with the Fairy Liquid and squirts it over her hands. She rubs them together hard, fingers interlocked. For a moment she looks like she's praying as the green slime runs down her hands and onto her wrists.

Fuckin bastard, fuckin bastard.

She scrubs frantically under the tap, cupping her hands and gathering water. Washing. Gathering water. Washing. *Bang bang bang!* the door goes. She starts round. She's a different kind of rabbit this time. Caught in the sudden headlights of a Nedmobile. She moves towards the door still washing her hands absentminded in the air. All the time she's looking round the room at this and that. If it wasn't that we already knew about the carpet we'd think she was just a woman checking her house was tidy before answering the door. Aha! She spots the knives and makes a silent bee-line for them.

Who is it?

No answer. It could be anybody. And they told her to be careful about opening the door. Caroline gathers in the knives and switches the telly off with her toe. *Bang bang bang!* the door says again like it can see her. She runs in and dumps the knives with a clatter into the sink. On with the taps. Hot. Not so good. Cold, strong and loud. But *bang bang bang!!* the door says and now it can see round corners.

Be there in a minute, Caroline shouts, *I'm just mnah mnah . . .*

That was a trick Angie taught her. 'The debt man mumble' she called it. To stall for time to get some money out of the telly meter or make up some excuses. Caroline pads over and presses her ear to the door. Nothing. Not even breathing. She peeps through the keyhole. It's so quiet she can hear her own eyelash brushing off the metal. Still nothing. A slight draught as she strains to see something. Anything.

Yearghgg! Fuck!

A hand pulses through and tries to grab her neck. Caroline reels back onto her arse. Her breathing is quick and her palms are behind her on the floor. She could be mistaken for a yoga student if her face wasn't so white. There, in the letterbox, hanging into the living room and flicking its fingers in a rhythmic dance is a hand with black nail varnish on. As Caroline is just coming to terms with what it is, laughing booms from outside.

Caroline, it's us, Donna and Geddy. Let us in.

You pair of fuckers.

Caroline reaches up and opens the door. In come Donna and Geddy. Grinning and holding each other up. They can't talk for laughing. Donna's all in black, long black hair, white skin and big laughing blue eyes. Geddy's down to eleven stone with her diet. A red mini-skirt and big mamma breasts pushed up with a Wonder-bra.

Yees had my heart in my mouth there, Caroline says. She's getting up off the ground and glad to see them really.

Maybe that'll perk you up a bit, says Geddy.

Donna looks about then listens for noise. *Where's the wane?* she asks. She heads in through the Artex arch and sticks the kettle on.

He's round at Angie's playing that Playstation thing. Angie's watching him for me.

My Auntie Sadie's watching Alicia, Geddy says.

Geddy flumps onto the couch and wriggles her red mini down to just below her knickers. But she crosses her legs and knocks it back up again. She lights up a Club King-size. Inspects Caroline then asks her the question that obviously her and Donna had been talking about on the way up.

Are you still going to let Bobby see the wane?

He's his father!

I'd let the cunt nowhere near him.

You can't punish a wane for his father's sins.

Geddy takes a long drag of the fag, inspecting Caroline up and down till she's uneasy.

Can you not? says Geddy.

Well, what would you do, Geddy?

I'd let him roast in his own pish. The bastard that he is.

Donna decides it's time to intervene. Can't have things getting off on a sour note. There's too much to do. Too much at stake to let petty opinions and resentments get in the road.

Everybody for tea? she shouts.

Mm Mm.

Aye. It'll do the now, I suppose, says Geddy.

As Geddy eyes Donna, Caroline sees the chance to break away from her scrutiny. She asks Donna about the others.

Where's everybody else?

They're coming round after.

All of them?

Same as the last time, says Geddy.

Just like the plumber with the burgh that never plumbed Maw's washing machine in right, shouts Donna.

Caroline keeps steering the conversation away from where it had started. The wane. Dealing with Bobby is bad enough without Geddy trying to force her beliefs onto her. What Geddy would do is not necessarily what Caroline would do. She decides to keep the conversation light. Keep it trivial. As trivial as it can be under the circumstances.

Wendy coming and all?

Everybody's supposed to be coming, says Donna.

Hmph! They say more than their prayers that lot, says Geddy.

Caroline walks to the veranda and stares out. She can feel Donna reprimanding Geddy with looks and frowns and glances. There's an uneasy quiet. This feeling of uncertainty starts at Caroline's feet and fills her to the eyeballs. She speaks without turning away from the window.

I've still not made my mind up if I want to do it.

That's like a red rag to a bull to Donna. Donna forgets everything in the scullery and directs all her energy out to Caroline. Some of it misses and flies over Caroline's head. A second later Davy Johnston's curtains flutter in its dissipated force.

You can hardly say that now, Caroline. We've came too far to stop now!

Caroline turns and tackles Donna's stare. *But I don't know if I can go through with it.*

Donna enlists Geddy's help with a wee glance and a nod. A nodette. Geddy swings her tits at Caroline. The heavy artillery is pointing right at her.

You can't stop now. Come on, Caroline! says Geddy.

Caroline is biting her bottom lip. Geddy is trying to pull the right answer out of her with her eyes. Meanwhile Donna is looking to change the subject. Divert Caroline's attention away from fear and into action. She sees her chance in the big new fireplace.

Oh Caroline! I like your new fireplace.

That's lovely, Caroline, agrees Geddy.

Geddy speaks right on top of Donna catching her drift. They could have used *Road Closed – Diversion* signs and Caroline wouldn't have noticed what they were up to. Not in the state she's been in recently. She smiles and goes over to her pride and joy all polished and intricately carved. Italian marble.

I got the coal put back in so as I could . . . She nods at the pile of clothes lying each side of the hearth. Geddy's eyes light up. She didn't notice them before.

Is that . . .?

Caroline smiles a real smile for the first time. A burst of pride. *That's what yees told me to do, is it not? Burn them?*

She leads Donna and Geddy to the fireplace. They touch it, run their fingers along it. *Ohh* and *ah* at it. Soak it in with their eyes. Geddy smells it. A long suck of the nostrils. Caroline stands tall and the two piles of Bobby's clothes cower at her feet. Trembling in fear of the flames. Donna's first out of her reverie.

That's brilliant, Caroline! Brilliant!

Oh, so it is. You're not as daft as I thought you were, says Geddy.

Caroline's fair took with it all. She's the boss now, she thinks. Back in control. She selects a pair of black satin boxer shorts from the pile at her feet.

Fuck! You've shredded them too, goes Donna.

Caroline holds them up for her sisters' benefit. With the light coming through the Artex arch from the scullery window the boxers look like a drunken barcode. Black and white strips moving in the breeze of three Witches' breaths. And if you ran your supermarket eye over the barcode your mind would register the price of heartbreak. The pain of desertion. Donna and Geddy register the heartbreak welling up in Caroline's eyes again. Quick as a Witch, Donna grabs the shredded boxers and flings them into the fire.

Burn burn burn, she chants.

Geddy joins in, flicking her fingers at the sudden flames that jump up out their slumber like a surprise.

Burn burn burn, go Geddy and Donna.

Burn and shrivel, shrink and die, says Caroline.

They watch the satin burn. Shrink. The red-hot flames sieve through. For a moment the shredded boxers look like a ploughed field over hell. The ploughman cuts the crust of hell and the fires are leaping up. Then the white heat buzzes like fission and *whoom* the shorts are gone so that the boxers are only a shadow, a shape, or an outline of something that might or might not be there. The flames lick their coal-black lips and snuggle back to sleep again.

Donna sees Caroline is rocking backwards and forwards.

She's got her arms wrapped round herself. Comforting herself. Donna snakes her arm round Caroline. And it's just in time cos Caroline's starting to cry. She's crying a third cos of what happened. A third cos of what's going to happen and a third cos her sisters have started to gather. A coming together. When it comes to the crunch blood makes more tears than water.

Shoosht! goes Donna. *Shoosht.*

The kettle boils up, spouts off steam, clicks and settles into silence. Nobody moves. They stand close to Caroline to comfort her.

This is murder, says Caroline. She's got her eyes firmly focused on the white-hot ashes. She can't get why the sisters are here out of her head.

Don't you worry yourself, says Donna. *We'll sort it all out the night.*

But Caroline's focus still won't leave the flames. Can't leave the flames. Geddy looks in like there might be something interesting in there. But she can't see nothing.

Murder? says Geddy. *I could murder a cup of tea. Come on.*

Geddy pulls Caroline back from the fire so that her link with the flames snaps. Caroline's back straightens. She looks at Donna. Looks at Geddy. Decides to take control. It's the only way to get over it. Get through it. That's it. Take control. Control. Cos if these maniacs take control there's no telling what will happen. Sometimes Donna and Geddy, and the rest of her sisters, have a habit of taking over your life. They're only trying to help but they can do more damage than good.

I need to get biscuits if they're all coming, she says.

Och, goes Donna, *don't you bother your arse about biscuits.*

But Caroline's diverting her anger into her biscuit mission.

I'm not having nobody talking about me, so I'm not. I'll need to go for biscuits!

Okay. Okay, calm down, says Donna.

Donna puzzles at Geddy. Geddy doesn't know what's up so she pokes away at the fire. Looks through the pile of clothes with a hint of an interest in what Bobby the bastard's choice in underwear is. Then she remembers that they'll have to get vodka.

Vodka, Caroline. You'll need to get vodka.

Geddy rumbles in her bag. A bottomless pit of lipsticks, foundation and oul phone numbers. She's not really been out with many guys since she had the wane. She plumbs the depths and brings out her dust-covered purse. Looks like talcum but could be anything. But there's no money there.

Here.

Donna hands Caroline a couple of tenners, then holds a pair of boxers up at Caroline and asks the question, *Can I throw them in?* with her eyes. Caroline nods okay to Donna and in they go. They're blue and white stripes this time. A good combination with the flames.

Welcome to hell, adulterer, says Donna, to herself mostly.

How much vodka will I get? Asks Caroline.

Get two bottles anyway.

Donna asks for biscuits without moving her stare from the flames.

Can you get some Indulgence, Caroline?

What's that?

They new biscuits on the telly. Have yees not seen the advert?

Caroline and Geddy obviously haven't seen the advert. Donna can't believe it. They shrug at each other and throw another shrug each at Donna.

Aw, come on, yees must have!

But they haven't. They shake their heads this time. Donna's not taking no for an answer.

Yees must have!

They still haven't. All they do now is squeeze their bottom

lip into their top lip by way of a response. So Donna describes the premise of the advert.

Eat one and the man of your dreams climbs in the window and shags lumps out you.

That's the memory jolt Geddy needed. Shags lumps out you. Now she remembers. She's animated like a windmill with a wee skirt on, if that's possible. It is now.

Oh that's right. I remember now, Donna. He's a right honey. You should see him, Caroline. He's lovely.

Caroline's on her own now. Guilty of not having seen the advert. Alone for the sake of a biscuit.

I've never seen it.

She's losing it again. In these situations it doesn't take much to break your confidence. One slight bump and your fragile hold slips. Donna jumps in to save her.

She'll not notice men.

But Geddy is still on a roll. The image of this abseiling biscuit romantic in the SAS suit is fresh in her head and she's not for letting it go. No sir. She tries to force the image into Caroline's head.

Aye, but he's more than a man, this guy. Dressed in black, swings down from the roof on a big rope like the Iranian Embassy siege. Black wavy hair he's got . . .

Donna puts the blockers on it by standing between Geddy and a folding Caroline.

She's not at that stage yet.

By her eyes Geddy can see that Donna's shutting her up. Caroline, however, has took some of the bait.

What stage am I not at yet?

It's still Bobby that's in your head every man you look at, Donna tells her.

A snow of silence falls on the living room. Even the last of the day's sun coming through the big Artex arch does nothing to melt it or take the curse off the chill. Now is the North Pole.

Caroline shivers. Her legs are about to give way. Donna and Geddy were only supposed to keep her afloat till the rest of the Girls arrived. Donna shakes her head at Geddy.

What? Geddy mouths.

She's right, it's not her fault. When blame is traced to blame, you end up at Bobby. Then on to Stacie Gracie. Then to the job they had on that fancy meat counter. You're forced to stand too close in that wee glass space. As Stacie Gracie bent over for the peppered pork, Bobby had some pork of his own he'd like to give her. Reminds me of the rhyme Angie used to do. *Old Mother Hubbard, went to the cupboard, to get poor Rover a bone. When she bent over, Rover got over, and gave her a bone of his own*. Every time I think of Stacie Gracie bent over the meats and Bobby eyeing up her arse, I think of that wee rhyme and it makes me laugh. If you didn't laugh you'd cry. Caroline is thinking of it too. Her knees are getting weaker by the second. But fuck it! No way is she going to let a nineteen-year-oul slag let her knees give way. No way she's going to buckle. She's going to be strong. Caroline fights back. Caroline is going to march out for biscuits.

Och, fuck this. I'm away. Indulgence, vodka – anything else?

Supers.

Many? says Caroline.

A dozen. Angie's coming, goes Geddy.

Angie's coming? Is she? Caroline like Angie. She was hard as nails. Took no prisoners. But much better to have around than these two egomaniac loonies.

She says she was coming, says Donna. *That's right, Geddy?*

Aye, and fags. Get some Club King-size. Don't get them out the shop, go to Maggie Kerr's for them. She's doing them at two quid a box.

That's the thing these days. People have took to selling fags and drink from their door. Half price of the shops. The real thing. So when you go out for fags or drink you don't go to the shops. There's a different door for each product. The Buckfast door. The vodka door. The fags. There's even one door now that specialises in Fairy Liquid. You can buy that half price in Europe and bring it back by the lorry load. That's the people's answer to Rip-off Britain. The new Co-operative Society. That's how Caroline's got so much. Half price. Caroline gets her stuff together and starts walking away, chanting.

Indulgence, supers, vodka and fags. Indulgence, supers, vodka and fags.

She's halfway out the door when Donna shouts that she needs tape.

Oh Caroline, masking tape!

Caroline's forehead's puzzled.

For the Six Black Candles! Says Donna.

The spell, goes Geddy.

Caroline nods with her mouth slightly open as she gets what they mean.

Oh, right!

She clicks the snib open before she goes so she can walk back in. Donna and Geddy hear her reciting her list all the way down the stairs and out the close.

Masking tape, vodka, supers, Indulgence and fags. Masking tape, vodka, supers, Indulgence and fags. Masking tape, vodka, supers, Indulgence and fags. Masking tape, vodka, supers, Indulgence and fags.

Stacie Gracie's Head

Soon as Caroline's gone Donna gets up and goes into the scullery.

More tea?

Geddy nods and sparks up a fag. Donna gets the kettle on again, gets out two cups as Geddy talks through from the comfort of the couch and the flames licking her legs. Even with the big Artex arch she's got to practically shout, especially with the kettle trying its hardest to boil the water. Donna was at the dancing last night and Geddy wants to know who was there and more important, who did she lumber.

Out last night, Donna?

Garfield's.

Good?

Aye. Some hangover but.

The kettle boils up and Donna's face is obscured by steam.

Good night then, eh!!

Great. In fact . . . Donna fills a glass with cold water and downs it in three gulps. The watery eyes of a hangover bulging over the top of the glass. *Ahh! That's better. Vodka and Irn Bru, kills you so it does.*

Geddy's got something on her mind. She's looking round

the room, trying to find a way of saying it. Smoke smoke smoking away. Peering at Donna. Thinking. Peering at Donna. At last, resting her eyes on the absolute apex of the Artex arch she gets it out.

D'you get a lumber?

Donna doesn't answer. She's too busy remembering last night. It has mirror-balled in her mind; fragmented so that only bits of it are still there. A head swinging this way. A smile. A nice arse. A woman's too. Guys, guys everywhere. Mmm. Oh fuck! The taxi. Another wee bit. The tarmac. Boots and screams. Blood and snapped nails.

Donna, I says d'you get a lumber?

Donna inspects her broken nails. *No.*

Geddy switches to phase two. Colombo would have been proud of her.

Anybody get a lumber?

Donna doesn't answer. She can't really remember because of the fragmentation. It usually takes her a whole day to piece back the night before. And even then there's big bits missing. Drink's not what it used to be. Now she wakes up in the morning like she's got treacle in her veins instead of blood. And the night has disappeared into feelings of remorse. Feelings of guilt.

Did they?

Wendy. She got a lumber, Donna says.

Mm mm. Mm mm. Aw aye, goes Geddy.

And she's sat there with her lips pursed thinking about Wendy getting a lumber. Wendy and her blonde hair rising up like a stunned animal. Her posh voice and teachery mouth. Fuckin Wendy; she might have know she'd get a lumber.

That Wendy's up the main street all the time.

Geddy stubs her fag out like revenge. Her fag ends lie in the ashtray like bodies. A massacre. She lights another one. The flame from the lighter moves over her face like another skin. A secret skin of fire. Her eyes're wiped out by its light. She looks hollow of life and filled with something else. Something not quite right. The vacuum of resentment that swallows everything else and never changes. Geddy is on the attack.

Aye, she's up the main street all the time and she never comes to visit me. I've seen her walking past a hundred times. You couldn't miss that hair. Even from space. The only two things you can see from space are the Great Wall of Hong Kong and our Wendy's sticky-up hair.

Donna ignores her by taking the milk out of the fridge and filling the cups. Her only answer is the clink of glass and spoons in cups. The language of silence. She's not taking Geddy's bait. Then, flash, she remembers something. There it is, a picture in her mind in bright colour of something that happened last night. It's a shock to her.

I punched this guy, she blurts out to Geddy.

Geddy chokes on her umpteenth fag. *You what?*

Donna walks over and leans against the Artex arch with one hand.

He was quite good-looking. Bang, I caught him right on the jaw. An uppercut. I think I felt it crack.

Who was it?

You don't know him. A doctor, he was.

No way! You whacked a doctor?

Learning to be a doctor.

Geddy's swinging her head from side to side. She can't believe three things. One, Donna battered a doctor. Two, Donna managed to lumber a doctor. Three, Donna had a doctor on tow and fucked it up.

He can prescribe something for his own sore head, says Geddy.

Shh! Don't mention heads.

Anybody listening would think Donna said that cos she's got a bad hangover. But it's not that. Not at all. Geddy laughs first. Her shoulders just. Then Donna. They giggle and stifle it. There's something conspiratorial about this. Something not right. And on top of that, or underneath, Geddy's still got her own agenda.

So yees were at Garfield's? Was John Ferry there?

Donna stops laughing. *Aye, he was in fact.*

Wendy talking to him?

Now she's dragged it back to Wendy. Donna parries it.

Dunno. Probably. I was out my box.

Geddy smokes some more looking for a way back into that disco. Donna looks about for something to say. There it is. The fireplace. Up against the wall. Lost. Longing for a much bigger house in a much more salubrious area. Slumming. A slumming lum.

It's something else, that, says Donna.

I'm not sure if I like it now, Geddy goes.

I think it's brilliant.

Not for this place, but. It's too . . . big.

She's going to do the whole place up.

Geddy looks at the wallpaper. The yellowing gloss on the skirting. The Artex on that stupid big arch. Bobby done that when he was drunk. And watching a Celtic game. It qualifies as the worst Artex in the world. If you fell against it you'd rip the face off yourself it's that sharp. Like a relief map of the Himalayas. It would be good for Caroline to do the place up. Not just cos it needs it, but it keeps your mind off your heart. And it stamps a new mark on the house. Your mark. The mark of a single woman. Not the mark of a couple and certainly not the mark of a man. Mark of a man. Now what the fuck was that? That's right. Old Spice. Now there's a nice after-shave. A right turn-on. Donna interrupts Geddy's mind-surf.

What d'you think?

Keeping your mind occupied is a good thing, I suppose.

Donna throws a pair of boxers on the fire. Geddy lights a new fag from the end of the one she's smoking.

You must admit it's perfect for burning things but.

Geddy starts remembering why they're there in the first place.

Talking about burning things, where's Stacie Gracie's head anyway?

Geddy gets up and starts looking about. She opens the living-room cupboard. No head in there, but there is a box of Trivial Pursuit.

There's Trivial Pursuit in here.

It's in the fridge, the head, says Donna.

Geddy makes her way through the arch, handing the game to Donna as she goes. Donna opens the box and starts laying the board out. Geddy opens the fridge three inches peering into the heavenly light of dairy products and rancid meat.

In here? Beside the milk and all that?

Geddy opens it squeak by squeak. The milk and Coke and Irn Bru. The two-for-one cheese. Canadian Mature Cheddar. The jars of pasta sauce you never use. The clear ice froze like disembodied tears on the back wall of the fridge. Crying for spilt milk maybe. Nothing else. Geddy moves a few things about. There's no head in there.

It's not here.

Donna hardly looks up. She can tell by the noises of the clinking bottles that Geddy's in the wrong bit.

No, it's the freezer it's in. The bit at the top.

Aw – she'll be pure white with frost.

Geddy shuts the fridge door with that *thimp!* that's peculiar to fridges. She opens the freezer and Stacie Gracie's eyes are looking right at her. Wide open and dusted with ice. The more she opens the door the more the ice refracts the light. There's a rainbow on her eyelashes. She's covered in glitter, Stacie Gracie. She looks like she's been frozen in time at a 1970s disco. Wizard: 'See My Baby Jive'. But she's not at a disco. She's in the fridge. Or to be more precise, the freezer. Geddy takes a breath and opens the door wide to the wall.

Hello there, Stacie Gracie!

Ask her how it feels to be out in the cold, shouts Donna.

Geddy reaches her two hands into the freezer. The fog from the ice is coming out and falling over the edge. It could be a horror film if it wasn't real.

Should we not thaw her out?

Donna jumps up when she sees what Geddy's doing. She shouts, *No! Geddy, leave her, leave her!*

Geddy stops in her tracks, her hands immersed in fog. Fag hanging out her mouth.

Don't do anything till Caroline comes back.

Geddy blows some smoke in on Stacie Gracie's head. It's a fog burrowing through another fog. And in the tiny clearing Geddy sees two lemon meringue pies; one at each side of Stacie Gracie's head. Like big yellow carnival-esque ears.

It'd be better if Caroline took it out anyway, Donna says.

Geddy knows Donna's right. She takes her hands back out. When they hit the warmth she shivers. Down her spine and back up again. Like a bad orgasm.

Brrr, how can Caroline sleep with that head in there?

Pour that tea when you're coming. It's sugared and milked.

Donna separates all the little pies in the Trivial Pursuit into their colours and sets the questions in place. Geddy dunts the freezer door shut, pours the tea, and brings it in. Soon as Donna takes a sip her hangover reacts and she turns whiter than she normally is. Geddy remembers the two big lemon meringue ears stuck onto the sides of Stacie Gracie's head.

Is that lemon meringue pie two for one out of ASDA?

Aye, they're doing great offers the now so they are.

They sip in silence. Thinking. Geddy's first to speak.

I'd need to get rid of that head but if I was Caroline. It's freaking me out already.

Donna shakes her head. And although she's a few years younger than Geddy, for a moment she looks like a mother.

Don't be fuckin stupid. How could we do the Six Black Candles with no head?

And she's got something there. That's the whole reason they're all turning up the night. To do the Six Black Candles. Donna shakes her head all the time, staring at Geddy.

Stupid cunt.

But does it not frighten you?

Not one bit.

They sit in silence for a minute. Geddy doesn't believe Donna's so cool about it all. That she's not scared. She doesn't want to say it but she does.

You take it out then.

Donna sighs, fed up with the whole thing. Goths are great at looking fed up.

I don't want her staring at me when I'm drinking my tea!

Geddy grins. She thinks she's got Donna here. She puts her teacup down to accentuate the challenge.

You're feart!

I'm not feart. Anyway, Caroline's the one that's got to take it out. It's nothing to do with who's feart and who's not!

She's got something there. Even if the both of them were feart, what does that matter? So long as they're there for Caroline. It's her night.

You're right. Leave it, goes Geddy. *Leave it.*

So Donna sips her tea and Geddy goes to the fireplace, flicking her ash into the fire. Donna reads the Trivial questions into herself. She can't make head nor tail of most of them and when she turns them over she finds the answers more puzzling than the questions. Especially green; Science and Nature.

That's good tea that, so it is, says Geddy.

Donna sips in confirmation. *ASDA's own make,* she says.

They savour the delights of ASDA's own make as, outside, the noise of wanes running about, the odd bottle breaking, shouting and 'Greensleeves' fills the darkening sky. The yellow street lights come on with a muffled buzz and go through their orange warm-up phase. Donna nods at the tea.

I think they're two for one the now and all. She's skint, Geddy. Brassic. *I don't cash my book till Monday,* she says.

Hit Wendy for twenty to shove you into next week.

They look at each other with a blank expression for a moment then laugh. Donna draws her cheeks in and does a pretty good impersonation of Wendy's imitation posh accent.

Oh, I'm afraid my salary's not due until the last Thursday of the month.

D'you get PMT with that? asks Geddy.

With what?

Getting paid once a month. A saa-laa-ray!

That's it; they fall about laughing. They see the same image of Wendy with her platinum credit card drawing cash out the machine across from ASDA. All crisp new twenties with that dry inky smell you get off them. Money looks artificial when it's new. Geddy thinks about how good it would be to even have twenty quid. That would get you two hundred fags off Maggie Kerr. They tail off with the laughing and fall into a happy quiet. Two orange smiles turning yellow as the sodium lamps get up to full blast. They smoke. Geddy sucks in the last of her tea. She pokes her nose in the cup and sniffs. A true Typhoo connoisseur.

That's Typhoo that, I'm telling you!

Donna sips and agrees with her eyes. She's been to ASDA days ago and bought the exact same tea and she knew it reminded her of something but now that she comes to think of it, that's what it is; Typhoo.

Ninety-nine pence for ASDA big giant cake of chocolate and it tastes like Cadbury's, Donna says.

Ninety-nine? I think I will ask Wendy for a tap right enough.

Aye, and lasagne, two for one. It's all good makes with ASDA label just, goes Donna.

So they sit and in their heads the peruse the aisles and freezers of ASDA. Drooling over what could be. Envying the heavy trolleys of them that's got money. Feeling sorry for the Giro trolleys that always seem to squeak and turn the wrong way. Like they attach themselves to the poor like misery magnets. There's always a wee woman in 1960s clothes pushing. Women of indeterminate age and kids with them so that they could be the mother or the granny. You just can't tell. There's no way of knowing.

Geddy and Donna are somewhere in the middle of the rich and the poor. Dignity has allowed them to select the best of trolleys, even though they might have to spread their purchases out to make it look like a respectable load. But they both think themselves lucky cos once or twice they've had to go into Shop Shite and in there's the walking dead. The alkies and junkies who live off the boxed remains of what the big companies wouldn't use. The salmon that John West rejected that makes John West Salmon the best makes tins of white-labelled salmon for Shop Shite and it's all bones and juice and gristle. Not fit for a dog. Thinking about the bones in the tins of Shop Shite salmon, Geddy remembers the head in the fridge.

What did she do with the rest?

Tea bags?

No, Stacie Gracie. What did Caroline do with the rest of her?

Donna had never thought of that. Her mind was focused on the task at hand. The Six Black Candles. She shrugs.

Dunno. Dumped it probably, she goes.

Right, says Geddy.

But Donna can see Geddy's still needing explanation as to where the remains of Caroline's cutting and slicing could be.

Couldn't have it in the house. Could you? Donna tells her, reading her mind.

But she's got the head, says Geddy.

That's different – we need that for the spell.

I know, I know. But . . .

There's no way Caroline could have kept anything that had even a tenuous connection with Stacie Gracie in the house. Once they've done the Six Black Candles they'll get rid of the head and all. Pronto. That way Caroline can make a fresh start. She'll be free to forget everything that's happened. Her world will be a sheet of blank paper again that she can write a new life onto. But Geddy is a blank sheet of paper herself with little hope of a pen or even a magic marker. Donna spells it out to Geddy.

She got shot of everything connected with Stacie Gracie. Anything that smelled like her. Looked like her. Tasted like her. Slung the lot.

But Geddy's not giving up. You see, Geddy's not too sure about the whole thing either. She's involved, alright. Up to her neck in it. But if she'd a choice she wouldn't be there. Geddy's got a morbid fascination with it all and that, along with a genuine wish to see her big sister alright, is what draws her to these things. Then Geddy remembers the carpet.

The carpet! What did she do with that?

Donna doesn't answer and Geddy goes over to the cupboard to see if it's in there.

It's not in there.

Fifty quid a week to shag somebody's man on the fireside rug! I wish I was a babysitter, says Donna.

Now she's talking Geddy's language. Getting a good ride on that rug with the flames licking off your body. That's movie-star stuff. And, truth be told, Geddy's always had a wee thing for Bobby.

Same here. He's no bad-looking, Bobby; for a bastard, says Geddy.

They stare into the flames and in their heads there's Bobby banging away at Stacie Gracie on the rug. Her wee arse, and it is a tight wee arse, flattening into the pile and rounding out again on Bobby's up strokes. Or out strokes. And Stacie Gracie maybe grabbing at the corners of the rug. And getting higher with every thrust. And moaning. And moaning more. Tugging at the corners. And coming. The carpet turning into a flying carpet and whizzing about the room. In and out the Artex arch, leaving her mark all over Caroline's house. A bitch in heat.

Donna imagines what it must have been like for Caroline to walk in and see them there. Wrapped round each other like a crazy eight-legged pink animal with one goal. The look on Caroline's face. The blood draining. Stacie Gracie almost smiling and her face in the last little contortions of orgasm. The short weak pulses that run through you after the ebbing away of the big one. Bobby's sheepish grin as he put his clothes back on and tells Caroline, *This is Stacie. We work together.*

Something Caroline knew – but all he could say. Donna gets a bad feeling. To be precise, she gets Caroline's bad feeling and she didn't think Caroline could have felt as bleak as she does. Instead of reading her mind, Donna is reading Caroline's heart.

I think Caroline'll do herself in if this doesn't work. Suicide.

Donna! Don't say that!

I'm just saying. Her mind's not right.

Let's shut up about it. Gives me the shivers, says Geddy.

So they shut up and look about the place again. Looking for something to talk about. Anything that isn't suicide and fear of losing a sister. Geddy especially knows what suicide is all about. She's been close to it so many times till the sisters, and Maw especially, saved her life. Their eyes can't rest anywhere. Everything reeks of Bobby and Stacie Gracie and that head in the freezer. An entity in a white tomb. Freezers will never be the same again. Geddy comes to rest on Donna's cleavage. There's nothing in that; women looking at other women's bodies. Even sisters. It's usually in admiration or just comparison. Geddy's tits are much better than Donna's anyway. Everybody can see that. But for her build, Geddy's thinking, Donna's got the perfect set. She's not had any wanes, Donna, so they're still looking more out to the horizon than down on the sand. But then Geddy sees something she doesn't like. No sir. Not one bit does she like it. It's a crucifix round Donna's neck, on the end of a wee gold chain. Upside down.

Upside-down crucifix. That stuff can bring you bad luck, you know!

Donna sneers and flicks the offending icon out of her black dress. The blood must be running to Jesus's head. And the weight that must be on His hands? All that inversion acting down on the nails. I know He was carting man's sins aboot but right now the weight on His hands must feel much more painful. Anyway, some of man's sins are pretty enjoyable when you come to think of it. That's what we talk about here all the time. What is sin? I mean, don't kill, that's okay. And don't give people grief for no reason. But sex? That's great, we all agree on that. That's a manmade sin. And His feet? They must be tugging so that there's no pain like it. Even for the Son of God. Or is it the Son of Man? Whatever it is, it's a hell of a treatment for the man that saved the world. Donna tries to pacify Geddy's superstition.

It only brings you bad luck if you don't know what you're doing, she tells her.

Geddy lights a fag by way of ignoring Donna. Donna gives the cross an enigmatic look, trying to look as mystical as she can. Anything for attention, that's Donna when it comes to things black magic. Anything that'll make her look mysterious. She wants to be a psychic. Supernatural. Candles burning in the bath and all that. Stinking incense and New Age this and that. Crystals in the corner of the toilet. Geddy changes the subject.

So, where is it then?

Where's what?

The carpet.

Probably took it out the back of the Wine Alley and burnt it. I don't know, do I!?

Geddy looks at the fire. It's big. Far too big for a detached house never mind a four-up flat in a close in Old Monkland. You could burn the whole house in it. Fold it into itself like a cartoon. Geddy points at the fire.

Even having the ashes in the house . . . know what I mean? says Donna. *Stacie Gracie's ashes.*

Donna and Geddy shiver.

You'd feel she was still here, goes Geddy.

They sit in silence again. The Trivial Pursuit is laid out on the table. Waiting for the players.

Game at Trivial?

Geddy nods yes and goes to the veranda to check if Caroline's coming back yet. Or if any of the others have turned up. Some Neds and Nedesses have set fire to a car in the swing park. It's called a swing park but there's no swings. Nothing apart from a few tussocks the size of hills and burnt-out cars that have been crashed halfway up them.

D'you see anybody yet?

Geddy comes back and sits down. *No cunt. I still don't think that cross is right, Donna.*

Donna is rolling the dice about in her cupped hands, rattling like mystery.

What colour d'you want? she says.

Geddy slams down the pink. Donna slams down the black. They pass a sniggering glance at each other. Donna leans forwards so that the crucifix drags off the Trivial board, across Art and Literature, coming to rest on Entertainment. That is it. Geddy's had enough.

You and your fuckin Witchcraft! It's a lot of shite so it is. That'll bring you bad luck, that. Mark my words.

Donna, hit by trance lightning, stares right at Geddy. Neither her face muscles nor her eyelids move. She is absolutely still.

Aw fuck not that again! says Geddy.

What?

What d'you do that with your eyes for?

I'm not doing nothing with my eyes. Donna makes her eyes wider and stares harder. Her face settles to stone.

Every time somebody mentions Witches you stare like that.

Donna looks about the room like she's looking for a lost cat. It's only her neck that moves; nothing on her face.

Witches? she says. *Witches?*

Aye.

Nobody mentioned Witches.

Aye, they did. Me. I mentioned Witches, Geddy says.

No, you never.

I did so.

What did you say? goes Donna.

I said about it being bad luck.

Aye, bad luck; this crucifix. That's what you said.

I know what I said. It was me that said it.

Aye, and you never said nothing about Witches but so you never.

Geddy copies Donna so that they're both staring each other out. The Trivial Pursuit had its hopes built up but now it's feeling sorry for itself, the questions lying unasked on the vast expanse of cardboard and coloured triangles. *Bang bang bang!*

the door goes. None of them moves.

It's open, Geddy shouts.

Come in, says Donna.

It could be anybody and them with a head in the freezer. You'd think they'd be a bit more careful.

Wendy's History

Wendy is tall and slim. Quite gorgeous really. She's got this posh accent that's put on but she's put it on for so many years now only the sisters can tell it's false. Even Wendy's not too sure what accent is hers and what one's been forced on her. After all, it wouldn't do to go into teaching talking like the very wanes that you teach. You're supposed to be better than them.

She's always well-dressed, wears designer gear and is very much the General Miscellaneous Girls done good. One thing about her is the way she really uses her mouth when she speaks. It's all about pronunciation with her. Pro-nunce-ee-ah-shun.

Out of all the Girls she was the quietest when she was growing up. The budgie incident shows what she was like and I'll tell you about that when we've got some other things about her out the road. But she's not really a snob. The Girls wind her up and force her into a position where she's got no other option but to act like one. Her main flaw is her Jehovahness. She started mixing with the Jehovahs when they targeted her as a single parent years ago. She was at that stage where she'd broke up with Jonesy and they were still having heated sex every now and then. Getting back together and then splitting up. The gaps between these meetings were getting bigger and bigger. It was obvious to everybody, including Wendy and Jonesy, that they were on their way out. That's when the Jehovahs got in the door. They did help her a bit cos she pulled her Monday Book socks up and got an education and became a teacher. This was with the spiritual backing of the Jehovahs. But she's got to keep her meetings with them a secret for three main reasons and a lot of other wee ones.

Maw and Oul Mary really frown on anything that isn't Roman Catholic. Being a Protestant's one thing but a Jehovah? It's well-known that they hate Catholics. Jonesy was a Proddy and they liked it when Wendy ditched him, hated it when they got back together.

The sisters ripped the pish out of Wendy about being a Jehovah so she never spoke about it to them. The current situation is that they're not too sure if she's still going to the Kingdom Hall or not.

The other big reason is that she's a primary schoolteacher in St Patrick's School and she's got to teach RE. There's nothing worse than a primary teacher in a Catholic school being a Jehovah. They'd be better off being in the Orange Lodge. Wendy has to go to Mass to keep the image up.

Given all that, she must be a pretty strong person holding all that together. And in the past few years she's started talking to The Mormons. I don't know if she's really on a search for peace and God and serenity but she meets them on a Wednesday, the Jehovahs on a Friday and Chapel on a Sunday. She meets her latest boyfriend on a Saturday and Jonesy, if he's in vogue, on a Tuesday. With all that going on you'd expect to meet some crazy mixed-up kid. But when you see her she's strength personified.

Linda says Wendy's the only married divorced single-parent lezzy Catholic Mormon Jehovah working-class posh person in

Scotland. Oh, and she's also a playwright, Wendy. She's writing a play about her sisters. She's a bit late cos I'm in there first with this story. But then she's not to know cos even though she's my sister and I love her very much as I love the rest of them, with all their faults and failings, she's never met me. In fact, the only one that's ever met me is Linda, and I doubt if she'll remember. But more of that conundrum later. To Wendy, cos there's nothing better than getting to know someone so that you can love them and not hate them. Never criticise a woman till you've walked five miles in her high heels. Then let loose with both barrels, in the knowledge that she's human and therefore the same as you. But don't let that stop you from having a laugh at her expense.

When Wendy was very young Maw had a budgie called Pepper. It was a nice wee blue and yellow thing that chirped away happily. The only time it was ever in the bad books is when it was put out in the lobby if *Coronation Street* was on. It seemed to be activated by Ken Barlow's voice and away it would go, shouting in budgie language. Nobody could ever figure out if it was whistling cos it liked the show or cos it hated it. I know now of course and it was because it sensed the draining of attention into the wee rectangle of light in the corner of the room. That meant there would be no attention coming to Pepper. Not that it wanted attention all the time, it was the knowledge that there would definitely be none for the next half hour that sent it off its wee yellow nut. But all the family knew is that when they put it in the lobby it shut up.

We had Pepper for years. It had a right good stretch of life in budgie terms. Then one morning Maw came down the stairs and it was dead. Most of the Girls took it in their stride and wanted to know when they were getting another one. But Da said no cos there was no telling what telly programmes it would sing at and he was fed up shoving it out in the lobby. On the morning of its death Wendy cried. And she was still crying the next week. That was an indication of the emotional turmoil that underlies Wendy's shell of many colours. If she could only tackle her emotions then she'd probably be okay. She's going about it the right way cos she's attacking her problems on a spiritual level. One thing I've learned to be true from those that I've met here is this: in your search for happiness, you should first keep yourself spiritually well. For if you're spiritually well you will be emotionally stable. If you are emotionally stable you won't make any rash mental decisions. And if you don't make any rash mental decisions you won't do yourself any physical harm. So the power comes from the top down. Spiritual; emotional, mental; physical.

Wendy was always in the right area to tackle her problems but maybe she's never hit on the right religion, the right spirituality. Anyway, back to the death of Pepper. Wendy was still tearful weeks after the event and the Girls used to tease her about it. One day Donna and Geddy cut a budgie out of bread, toasted it, and taped it to the perch. Maw and Da never flung the cage out for a year. I don't know if it was superstition or laziness. Geddy painted the budgie-shaped bread with food colouring and Donna went and told Wendy that the ghost of Pepper was back. It flew round the living room and landed in the cage. And it was saying, *Wendy, I want Wendy* over and over again. In the living room there was a couch that the front lifted up and you could store blankets and stuff in. When Wendy and Donna got in the living room Geddy had planked herself in the couch. And she was chirping like a budge and talking.

Wendy, Wendy, you killed me – it was your fault! I'm going to peck your eyes out. Cos you killed me.

Wendy took one look at the dead bit of bread and ran screaming out of the room.

Mammy, Mammy, Pepper's going to peck my eyes out!

When Wendy came back in with Maw, Donna had scoffed the evidence and was sitting on the couch alone. When Maw left the room the couch burst out laughing in a Geddy accent.

Maw took Wendy to the doctor's to see if there was maybe something wrong with her head. She was seeing the ghost of a dead budgie. She had a bit of a temperature and McMullen gave her something to cool her down. But ever since that day, until Wendy gained a bit of autonomy and strength by declaring herself a lezzy, all the Girls had to do to reduce Wendy to a sobbing wreck was sneak up behind her and whisper these words in her ear.

You killed the budgie. Pepper's dead because of you.

Just before her lezzy stage Wendy went through an introverted three years where she spent her time walking about the town with her back straight and her head tilted slightly up. She was the walking embodiment of disdain although that wasn't the image she was trying to project. What she was trying to do was go out in the open without actually having to deal with the open. She was using her body as a shell. A vehicle to take her into the terrible realms of agoraphobia.

Towards the end of that three years the painters were in the scheme painting the fences and shouting obscenities at passing girls. They shouted at Wendy this day.

Hey, Blondie, show us your beard!

Wendy gave them a mouthful of that feminist abuse fifteen-year-oul lassies pick up at school in English class. That just made the painters worse. Then a strange thing happened. Wendy started to walk past them more and more, ignoring the abuse. In her agoraphobia Hovercraft she could listen to the dirty talk, even be titillated by it, and pretend not to notice. By the time the painters were finished in the scheme Wendy was up to walking past them forty times a day at least. And never once did she openly react. Donna thinks that because Wendy trained herself not to react to men she mistook the situation for an aversion to men. It was right after the painters left that she went through her lezzy phase.

Wendy's girlfriend was a Gothic chick. In fact, you could call her a Gothic Horror chick. Gothic cos she was a right monster and horror cos she was a right horror. Her name was Clug. Fat as a beached whale, she used to dominate Wendy physically. Wendy was so weak she couldn't pull a cat off a glass table. They used to go about the town with big Clug dressed in black and the pavement bending under her feet. She was so fat she could have kept telephone books in the folds in her belly. Her skin was white apart from where the multifarious volcanic eruptions burst through. It made you sick to think of them having any kind of sex. And of course Wendy would kiss this Fat Sister of the Bride of Frankenstein in the main street right outside ASDA. You'd think the whole town would be disgusted. But they weren't. Or rather, they weren't disgusted at the homosexuality cos most people thought Clug was a boy. They were disgusted that Wendy, who was quite the pretty little thing, was kissing this Meat Loaf video extra reject.

Once Wendy had made her statement for the sisterhood she gave the lezzy business up for good. Clug tried to woo her back by crashing into pubs she was in and turning all the tables over. Battering lumps out the bouncers. One Friday she came into Memory Lane and stood next to Wendy as these young studs were chatting her up. She pulled a full bottle of Buckie out of her bag and smashed it over her own head. The wine was running down like blood. And if that wasn't enough she started jagging the smashed bottle into her head. You couldn't tell where the wine ended and the blood started. She got rushed to hospital. Poor Clug was soon up to twenty stone with the drugs the doctors put her on. She should've been put in care for her own safety. She was Planet Out-of-control. Orbiting Wendy. Running on the wrong kind of gravity. Everything was falling away from her so that the only meaning in her life now was recovering Wendy. Nobody knew what age Clug was – she could have been anything from nineteen to thirty-five stone. Clug the lezzy lost the plot. Her last-ditch attempt at gaining Wendy's love and affection was climbing up the verandas in Monkland Lane and balancing on the corner of the fourth one up. She told the whole world she was going to jump.

If Wendy doesn't come back to me I'm jumping. Wendy!!!

But Wendy was far away from being a lezzy now; she just wanted rid of Clug. Wendy had discovered the delights of men. Donna and the sisters knew how Wendy felt. Clug would be better off dead. It was a still summer's day with not a breath of wind. The Girls sent Geddy in to light the right number of candles and they chanted a quiet spell while the crowd egged Clug on to jump. A sudden gust of wind knocked her off-balance. The crowd moved back. Clug was just about to regain her balance when a big black crow landed on her head. Over she went with the slow topple of a space-hopper at first but then she plummeted and the ground shook with an almighty force. The crowd *oohed* and *ahhhed* and moved over to have a close look at death. There's nothing like death to bring a group of people together. When they got to her Clug was still breathing.

Somebody phone an ambulance.

Clug should've died, what with her weight and the force she scudded the ground. Momentum equals force times acceleration. The equation with Clug in it equals = a lot. But she was breathing. The only thing that saved her was her fat, the doctors said. But she's a vegetable now. A big one.

The man Wendy discovered was Jonesy. They got married and had a wane. Or she got pregnant and they got married and she had a wane. Jonesy was a taxi-driver. He was nipping about with this wee bird up the redbridge flats. One of Maw's pals seen him and went down and told Maw.

Alice, is your Wendy married to that guy they call Jonesy?

Aye.

Well, he's been winching a lassie up my close for about a year now.

That was enough. Maw didn't like Jonesy anyway. And to add to that, he was a Protestant. No matter what they said in Coatbridge, if you were a Protestant it was held against you to some degree. Maw went straight over to Wendy's and told her.

Sit down, I've got something to tell you, Wendy.

Is it about Jonesy? I know it's about him. What is it? Don't tell me.

Make me a couple of slices of scrambled egg on toast.

Wendy made the scrambled egg on toast and as they ate it Maw told her all about Jonesy with the young thing up the redbridge flats.

The bastard, Wendy said. *I knew there was something wrong.*

The first thing Jonesy saw that night when he came in was the Ken Hom wok over the head. Sweetness had turned to sour. The next thing he saw was stars. And that was the last he saw of Wendy for a while. But they eventually started getting together and splitting up like normal couples.

It was partly Maw's fault Wendy married Jonesy. When she fell pregnant she didn't really love him but Maw persuaded her to get married even though he was a Proddy. There was no doubt that Jonesy was a good-looking guy. And there was an oul maxim in our family about marrying a good-looking man. Maw reminded Wendy of that and it tipped the balance in favour of a big white wedding, albeit with a little bump in the belly of the bride.

Always marry somebody good-looking. At least when you're skint and hungry you'll have something nice to look at.

It's a wonder Wendy ever got anywhere in life. She was, psychologically, the weakest of all the Girls. But she ground a life out of what she was given and I suppose the route we all take to success is the only route we could have took. Wendy recovered and became a teacher.

Wendy was only a year in St. Pat's. She'd already proved she was a great teacher. The wanes loved her and so the teachers didn't. The teachers thought the wanes loved her cos she let them do anything they wanted in class. They couldn't be further from the truth. When Wendy's teaching, all the wee beady eyes soak up her every word, her every movement. The teachers, envious bunch that they are, thought it was only a matter of time till she got found out.

Wait till the exams, then she'll come crashing down.

But the exams came and went and Wendy's class done better than any class in Lanarkshire. So the teachers waited on parents' night.

Surely the parents will see through this young whippersnapper. Her big pretentious smile and hair sticking up like an electric shock.

But the parents loved her too. Wendy's colleagues were now all out to get her.

The school was putting on *Oliver* for Christmas. A big, well-publicised production. Wendy had been asked to video it and was doing a great job using two cameras. One on wide angle recording the sound with a microphone on the stage and the other hand-held so that she could cut close-ups and whip pans in once she got to the editing suite. The show was on for a week and she was halfway through the filming. She knew she had a good project on her hands.

On the way up the corridor the Headmistress, Miss Cotton, stopped her and brought up copyright law.

I'm afraid it turns out that we may be in breach of copyright law so we'll have to give the video a miss right now.

In the staffroom Miss Boyle was the first to speak. *What's the latest with* Oliver *then?*

Oh, nothing much. Wendy paused for dramatic effect. *Except that I've not to film it any more.*

That'll be the copyright laws, said Miss Green.

There was silence. But Wendy had took too much from these people. Things were building up inside her, coming to a head. *Munch, minch,* they were going, nibbling and chewing away.

It's nothing to do with copyright laws. It's personal.

Well, come on baby light my fire. Hi ho Paranoia, said Miss Green. Her eyes appeared laughing over the paper.

Let me tell you something, Miss Green, said Wendy. *I don't take shit from nobody and that's that. If this is your doing I might revert to type and kick your arse up and down the corridor.*

That's hardly the way to deal with it, said *Arts This Week.*

It might not be the way to deal with it in this namby-pamby culture here, Miss Green, but it's the ultimate way in mine. And another thing: used correctly it's the most respected asset you can have.

Miss Green shook her head and flicked her paper. *But isn't it a fact that you are now part of this culture, Wendy?*

She said Wendy's name with that finality a child uses when it makes a decisive point. The only things missing were hands on hips and wiggles. Wendy leaned across the table a bit. The rest of the teachers leaned back. They could see that this was going somewhere it shouldn't. They knew there was something about Wendy and her sisters. Not to be messed with. They had heard the rumours but didn't believe them.

Let me tell you something, Wendy growled. *I'm not part of this culture. I'm only visiting.*

Miss Green done a long sigh like Wendy didn't understand what she was on about. Like she was too deep for Wendy to get at. Too clever. Too downright academic. Wendy leaned in further to explain.

If you thought you could kick me about like a rag doll and get away with it you would. But there's one main factor stopping you. I would break your neck if you tried it.

World News grunted and went quiet. Miss Smith got up, poured a cup of tea and sat back down. Miss Green decided to try the box-Wendy-into-a-corner routine. She shoved her paper out and intertwined her fingers.

It's the job of our superiors to shit on you from great heights, Wendy. You are paid to accept that.

My superiors are paid to manage the school. I am paid to impart my knowledge to the children. And let me tell you this: if anyone attacks me I will always, without fail, attack straight back with enough power to overcome . . . it's my nature, it's a reaction and that's that. I never attack first.

Oh, is that right? Miss Green said. She pushed her paper well out of the way and you could tell she was about to play her trump card. *What about the Chicken Factory? The gaffers there? They must have shat on you there. Big hulking hooligans. What did you do there?*

Miss Green sat back, picked up the paper and flicked it. It looked like it was going to rip. She sure had Wendy there. Argument over. Except Wendy had a comeback for that too.

Well, she said, *if you want the truth, if it was a physical threat I'd crack them one on the jaw and then take it from there, win or lose. If it was verbal I just told him to shove his job and walked off.*

So you risked your financial security for your pride?

Wendy laughed and that surprised her.

No no, she said, adopting Miss Green's tone. *No no, you've got it wrong there, Miss Green. I kept my dignity intact by sticking to my principles.*

You've a lot to learn, said *The Crossword*.

It might be that I've been there, Miss Green, didn't like what I saw, bought the T-shirt, ate my piece and got the bus home, bored.

Listen! grunted *The Boxing Report*, *if you keep hammering your superiors into the ground they'll enlist the big guns and come looking for you and then you'll have to submit anyhow.*

Miss Green thought she had Wendy there.

What you're telling me is that if someone challenges me to a fight in a pub and I take them outside and knock lumps out them, then they go and get their big sister and I'm supposed to just stand there and take it?

Well, what else could you do if it was obvious you couldn't beat her?

What I've always done. Attack her right away and keep fighting till I'm unconscious. That's the way I do it, Miss Green, and if a few more people stuck to them principles, people like you would be fucked.

Then you'll be out of a job.

At least I won't be out of my mind.

I'm happy enough, said *Homemakers Weekly*.

How much is enough?

I'm telling you, with that attitude you'll not last long in teaching.

Oh, is that right? Sentence being passed – could you tell me, Your Honour, how long is Long?

I'll give you two years, Miss Green says, flicking the paper and curling her lip.

At the last night of *Oliver* all the local dignitaries were invited. Chain rattlers, priests, the whole bit. Miss Green introduced the show and said how proud she was of the wanes. Then she left the stage with a tear in her eye. She didn't notice the back row was filled with the six sisters and Maw and Granny. When the curtain opened the whole cast stormed out under the control of supernatural powers. They started singing the most obscene songs to the Lord Provost and his wife, then the Head of the school, then the teachers in general. It's a bit much to go into here but you'd never guess how many words rhyme with fanny, tits, cock and cunt. Half of the audience were mortified but the other half were in hysterics; they'd never seen anything so funny in their lives. Even when Green tried to storm the stage with the rest of the staff they were repelled by an unseen force. And the look on the singing wanes' faces told you they wanted to stop singing but couldn't. It was all over the local papers and the Education Department said they were *looking into it*.

Two weeks later Miss Green had to retire with a mild stroke. Wendy's teaching went from strength to strength. She bought a flat in the West End of Glasgow and went on to live a nice wee life, thank you very much.

Wendy

Bang bang bang! the door goes. None of them move.

It's open, Geddy shouts.

Come in, says Donna.

It could be anybody, and them with a head in the freezer. You'd think they'd be a bit more careful. Wendy bounces in full of the joys of life. Her blonde hair's shooting up like it's startled at the blueness of her eyes. They've all got blue eyes, my sisters, or greeny-blue. A mystical blue that's hard to explain. A blue that changes with their moods. Oul Mary calls it Donegal blue.

That's the colour of the sky in Donegal. Or the sea when it's angry. Or the sky in a storm. Or the calm blue straits off the strand, she'd go.

Donna and Geddy are still staring each other out. She strides to the centre of the room and puts her arms out for big hugs that will never come.

Hi there, sisters! she says.

But they don't answer. Wendy drops her arms. Ha! So that's what they're up to. Donna's up to her *I'm a strange human being, unique, one in a million.* Ego-tripper.

Right. Donna's doing her staring eyes thing again, Wendy says.

Geddy registers Wendy's support. Grins at Donna. But

Donna doesn't flinch. Not even an inch does she flinch.

See! See! says Geddy to Donna. *Even Wendy knows what you're up to.*

Mystic Minge, says Wendy.

That's pretty good for Wendy. She's not noted for good crack. Too rational; too matter-of-fact and proof-ridden. But she's here the night cos this is the only thing that breaks the rut of being Miss Prim of the primary school. The only thing that allows her to be herself. To be free. With Wendy staring and Geddy making faces, pulling her mouth sideways and waggling her tongue, Donna is put off. She breaks off and turns on Wendy.

Mystic Minge? I'm the seventh daughter of a seventh daughter, I'll have you know!

I've got news for you, Donna – there's only six of us!

Wendy's got her hands on her hips and her body bent forwards to hammer the point home, but Donna's not for letting go of her belief that she's special. That she's really got powers. And who's Wendy to tell Donna what she is and what she isn't? It's true. I'm the other sister.

Well, Maw might have had an abortion, says Donna.

Oh! God forgive you for saying that, Wendy says. She turns away in disgust. Even Geddy's not pleased.

Donna!! is all Geddy can say. But she lengthens the vowels for effect. Donna reverts back to starey eyes.

Anyway, my eyes are always like this, she says.

But by this time Wendy's ignoring her at the veranda window, cupping her hands on the dark pane of glass. Trying to see into the black and orange and red below.

There's some rough-looking little boys near the cars.

Geddy impersonates her. Exact same line; posh voice. *There's some rough-looking little boys near the cars.*

What other kind of boys d'you get down here? Donna says.

Wendy's biting her lip watching the dots of baseball caps

pass below. The street lights look like orange balls of Chinese lights disappearing into the night-time mist. Echoing through it are the laughs and giggles and in the distance it looks like a young boy and girl kissing.

And it is two kids kissing. Wendy can see them now as Donna and Geddy continue their argument in the background so that their voices are bees buzzing about in the summer. The boy and the girl unembrace and walk away backwards from each other. Throwing kisses and always being second last to say goodbye. Wanting to be last to turn and leave the glow of the lamps.

Wendy says a wee prayer to all her gods and wishes for that boy and that girl who are now a hundred yards apart and still facing each other, still walking backwards, things might be different. That they will succeed where all else have failed. That life will be good to them. The leaders of the future. Far away from home. From Donegal where they've never been. Maybe never heard of but they're Irish just the same. It was their Maws and Das and Grannies that put them there under the orange lights. On a fuckin hiding to nothing.

As the lovers fade into the dark, onto the stage walk a group of three then four stragglers grabbing a Buckie bottle off each other. Passing and swigging. Swigging and passing. They walk so close to Wendy's car they must be up to something. They brush against it like dogs. The car shines and their shadows pass over its panels like ghosts. Wendy could swear it trembled when they were gone. It had tensed up. Tightened its springs. Drew in its shock absorbers and waited for the crash of the laminated windscreen. Or the raw drag of a nail along the sides. Or the hefty dunt on the door panel to spring the lock open. But now it's hoping Wendy would just hurry up and take it back to where the cars are nose to tail and it can sit anonymous among the BMWs and the four-wheel drives that mothers use to get their kids through the West End jungle to school.

And from school the CRVs and Freelanders nose their way through thickets of narrow streets below flats with frightening price tags. Some of these flats harbour the most ruthless people of them all: TV producers. No wonder the women need their all-terrain vehicles. The terrain is in their brain. And all about them the harm is real. It's just not physical. Boy, are they glad when they get to the Café Bar Posh or wherever they go. When they nip at a bun and snigger with the girls. Each one measuring how much the other's buttocks are hanging over the edge of the seat. Fuck me; what a way to live. If I was Wendy's car I'd rather stay here. There's something honest about street violence and self-preservation. Your talent for violence is all that matters. And so long as you're not a complete coward you'll get by. Wendy's bumped back into the room by Geddy's palm thudding into her shoulder.

I said I heard you bought a new car. Is that it down there?

It's a Ford Focus.

Is that the one with all them fuckin weirdoes advertising it? Dressed in grey. They look like mental inmates. Bending about like ballet dancers with piles.

Those are arty people, Geraldine. Creatives, Wendy informs her.

Ohh! Donna! Creatives, they are!

Laugh if you like, you two, Wendy says. *It's so advanced you can't even hear the engine.*

Donna listens for engines with her hand to her ear.

Maybe there's no engine in it, goes Geddy, smirking at Donna.

But Wendy's not daft. She's not a teacher for nothing. And teachers have a whole bag of put-downs. They need them.

Just like you then, Geraldine, she says.

Geddy know it's an insult but she can't make the mental leap. Well, the mental hop. That's when Wendy first notices the marble fireplace.

Oh, now that is fan-tastic.

She goes over and runs her fingertips along it. You can hear the sound of her nails scratching along the marble. And her nails are black. Black nail varnish. The rest of her looks like a teacher but her hands, her hands look strange. Not teacher hands. Hands that would frighten the shite of the wanes. And they do. They call her Tree Claws at school. She doesn't know that, but that's her name. Tree Claws. They still love her as a teacher but every teacher has to have a nickname. And every nickname for a teacher has to be derogatory. Like Johnny Humph. Johnny Scratch. Miss Gorilla. Wendy just has to put her long fingers on a jotter and the kid in question shrivels with fear.

Please, miss, I want to go to the toilet.

Wendy bends down to inspect the hearth. The piles of shredded clothes. Some chopped-up photographs.

That's where she cut Stacie Gracie up, says Donna.

Wendy's fascination rises like Easter. She looks about the place for more story. More things that'll tell the tale of what happened, what is happening and what will be happening soon. She spots the new rug.

Is that a new carpet too?

Well, obviously. She had to sling the other one, goes Donna.

Wendy nods her head in understanding. Remembering Maw telling her all about it.

Oh I know, my mother was telling me.

Geddy's not too pleased with Wendy's relationship with Maw. She's been jealous since they were wee. Maws always love their youngest more than their oldest. It's natural. Maw's closer to Wendy and Donna than any of the others. Okay; Maws have always got something special for their first few wanes. She never talks to me at all now. She used to, when I was very young. But she done it less and less. And now she hardly talks to me at all. I'd be as well never having existed. But what am I talking about. This isn't my story. This is all about what they done to Stacie Gracie. What Geddy's jealous of is that she's in the middle. She gets none of that love a mother has for her early wanes and none that she saves for her younger wanes. Maws hang onto their last wanes cos they're hanging onto their youth. Maw still treats Donna and Wendy like pre-school wanes.

Youse two chinwagging again? What is it with you and Maw?

Chinwagging? Wendy asks. *Chinwagging? Huh. We hold conversations. We don't chinwag as you put it.*

Wendy makes it worse for Geddy by walking to the veranda as she talks. Lessening Geddy's importance with every step. Geddy's got to drill her eyes into Wendy's back.

Oh, sorry! I forgot to swallow my dictionary this morning! Geddy snorts out.

But Wendy ignores her. She doesn't even get a laugh out of Donna. Geddy and Donna are close. And they're against Wendy on a lot of things. But when it comes to Wendy's relationship with Maw, Donna and Wendy are one. The two youngest. Geddy accepts defeat by picking her nose and looking at it. Wendy talks into the sheer of the glass. Her words come out as fog and leave the trace of themselves in glittering mist on the pane.

Who's all coming? she asks.

Everybody, Donna says.

Geddy can hear their bond in her voice. She flicks the snotter into the fire and watches it sizzle like a whelk.

Are you paying it up, this Ford Focus? I bet it's on tick, Geddy asks Wendy.

Wendy doesn't take the bait. Geddy flicks her eyebrows up and down to Donna. Donna flicks hers in reply. They're back on good territory so she goads Wendy again.

Bring it up to my bit and let me see it.

I hate those flats, Wendy says. *Ring a buzzer they let you in. Ring a buzzer you let me in. Press a button wait on the lift. Press a button go to the floor. Press a bell and you answer. All that and you have to climb over drunks and drug addicts to get in.*

Wendy's on good form. Geddy retaliates.

We can't all afford a big fancy flat in Glasgow city centre.

West End, actually.

Aye, well, my Maw was saying you better not forget your oul arse! Geddy says.

Geddy looks at Donna and gets a smile. Wendy waits till she turns back and talks right into her eyes.

My mother? Was she, Geraldine?

Aye, don't forget who used to wipe the shite off your arse, she said.

Are you sure it was her?

Positive!

Donna's fed up. She lets out a long stop-this-arguing sigh. She doesn't know what side to be on. They're here for a purpose. This isn't a fuckin knitting bee after all, is it?

C'mon youse two; we're here for Caroline.

Oh, back out your trance, Morticia? Geddy says.

Even Wendy laughs at that one. Nice one, Geddy. Now nobody knows what side to be on. They're fragmenting when they're supposed to be coming together.

Youse two are only worried about yourselves.

Wendy hears what Donna's saying.

I know. You're right, let's calm down. It's Caroline's night, she says.

Geddy is reluctant. She's the most angry. But she gives a wee bit of ground.

Well, just watch you don't get too big for your boots, Windowlene!

She should know better. There's no getting the better of Wendy when she's on form. She fires a salvo at Geddy.

People don't get too big for their own boots, Geddy; they get too big for everybody else's boots.

Whoa! Does Donna like that? She whoops and claps. Geddy sucks her face in till it looks like she's just a pair of ears and screwed-up eyes. Her resentment's killing her. Crushing her. Donna has got to congratulate Wendy.

Well said, Wendy, says Donna. *Too big for everycunt else's boots. That's a good one. A cracker.*

She sticks her tongue out at Geddy and gives her a couple of seconds of the starey-eye thing. Geddy is off out of the room in a right folded-arm huff. The world at the other end of the Artex arch looks like Alaska now. If she could get there on the snowy plains of linoleum she could be alone. Safe.

I'm making another pot of tea, goes Geddy.

She stomps into the scullery. She can feel them holding their laughing behind her back but she's not for turning round. Alaska's a long way away. Every step is infinity when you're humiliated. When she's in there Wendy wonders where Caroline is anyway.

Away for Indulgence, answers Donna.

Away for vodka, Geddy shouts from Alaska.

How did she get on with that . . . that . . . hired thug? Wendy wants to know. She flicks through the Trivial Pursuit questions.

McGoogan? Says he'll get her the money the night.

So matter-of-fact does Donna say it that Wendy is horrified. One of her sisters paying a gangster to retrieve what money she's owed from her husband.

Do you not think she's being a bit desperate? Wendy wants to know.

Geddy pipes in from her ice floes. *If my man left with the babysitter and the bank book I'd be wanting half and all.*

And if she's not got the money for next week the bank's repossessing this house, adds Donna.

Geddy offers another gem of wisdom. *I always said a joint bank account. But would she listen? No. Would she fuck.*

He's a cunt, that Bobby, goes Donna.

There's no arguing with that. Wendy thinks Caroline's as well with the money than a dragged-out legal scenario.

Well, I suppose this . . . McGoogan person will scare it out of him.

And seven kinds of shite and all. Have you ever met McGoogan? goes Donna.

Wendy draws her an I'd-hardly-think-so look. What would Wendy, BA (Hons), PGCE be doing knowing someone like that? Geddy's keeping one eye on the teacups and one eye on the living room. The hurricane has stopped and it should soon be safe to make her way across the wasted plains of Alaska. Wendy is looking about for the paraphernalia of the Six Black Candles but she can't see a thing.

Is all the stuff here? she goes.

Mm mm, says Donna with a twinkle.

Everything?

Most of it, says Donna.

But Wendy's head's swinging about everywhere. She's looking for something but she can't imagine where it might be.

Where's Stacie Gracie's head?

Donna and Geddy answer in unison, nodding towards the scullery. *In the fridge.*

Freezer, says Geddy.

A nervous smile comes over Wendy's lips as she walks under the Artex arch into Geddy's Alaska. She opens the freezer door. Donna's up out her chair. Geddy's looking to Donna for what to do. Wendy looks like she's going to lift Stacie Gracie's head out.

Don't take it out! Donna shouts.

Wendy looks at Geddy.

We've to let Caroline take it out, Geddy informs Wendy.

She's taken with it, is Wendy. The head in the freezer. The

hair dusted with snow. The ice on the surface of the eyes. Her arms move involuntarily.

Don't touch it, Wendy. I'm warning you! Donna says as she moves to the Artex arch.

Wendy's arms drop back down but her head dips into the freezer so that she's breathing in the same fog Stacie Gracie would be breathing in if only she could breathe.

I only want to see what she looks like, says Wendy as if they're coming on a bit heavy to her. Donna's okay with that and Geddy resumes the tea-making.

D'you want ordinary tea, Wendy? There's no camomile, she goes.

Yes, please.

Donna is suddenly back in cahoots with Geddy. There's no telling what links are snapped and what ones are joined when three sisters get together. Just think what it'll be like when there's six of them. And Maw. And Oul Mary.

D'you want me to run out and get some sandal-eater's tea? Donna sniggers.

Fuckin tree-shagging tea? Goes Geddy, right in Wendy's ear.

But Wendy ignores them. She's trancing with Stacie Gracie. Getting some kind of contact through those iced-up eyes and rainbow glitter that the lights are flinging on her skin.

She looks terrified in there.

So would you be, says Geddy.

Wendy goes to lift the head out. Fuck. Donna's up like a shot and Geddy's looking for somewhere to put the cups down.

Don't touch her, I said, goes Donna.

She's in the scullery like she materialised there. Wendy drops her hands down again with a cross between a snort and a sigh, thrusting a pulse of carbon dioxide in at Stacie Gracie's face.

What d'you take in your tea now, Wendy? asks Geddy.

Wendy's still mesmerised. *Nothing. Just hot water. She's white as a ghost.*

Geddy pours three cups as Donna, satisfied Wendy's not going to take the head out, makes her way back to the couch.

Look at her, staring out the ice.

Geddy passes the fascinated Wendy with the cups. She nudges the freezer door shut with her shoulder as she passes, shutting Wendy off from the spectacle beside the peas, sweetcorn, and two-for-one lemon meringue pies. They all shuffle into the living room. Sit and sip their tea. Together but separated by more than joins them. In their own thoughts. And each of their views is the right one. Or, in Wendy's case, the correct one. The world is always from your own point of view. Still no Caroline. But they all know she'll have nipped into the pub for a couple of stiff drinks to get her on her way. Enough to get her back up to the flat and into the spell. Wendy blow blow blows on her tea to cool it. Geddy slurps and Donna sucks thin sheets of liquid in, cooled by the gap in her thin lips. Donna decides to break the silence.

Want a game of Trivial?

She never expected Wendy to burst out laughing.

With you two? Don't make me laugh, goes Wendy.

Through Wendy's laughter, Donna and Geddy exchange glances. Wendy might be clever but diplomacy's not her thing. Especially where her sisters are concerned.

We're not as daft as we look, retorts Donna.

Geddy follows with a gem of her own. *Aye, we're not as daft as we look.*

Wendy stares at them. She's a bit took aback that they don't realise how daft they are. Or more precisely, how much more clever she is than them. She feels a bit sorry for them. But to them it looks like she's took their reprimand on board.

Suppose it'll pass the time till the others arrive, she says.

Good, says Geddy.

Donna throws the dice. Or die as Wendy would probably call them. And probably will if one of them says dice. The dice roll along the board.

A three, go Geddy, says Donna.

Geddy picks up the dice and rolls them about on her palms.

Y'out last night? Geddy asks Wendy.

Garfield's, Wendy tells her.

Geddy lets the dice rip and roll along the board.

A two. Get a lumber? She asks.

But Wendy's mind is on other things. The wee Neds with baseball caps that walked past her car earlier with the Buckfast bottles. What if they're back by now? She gets up and walks to the veranda.

I hope my car's alright out there.

Wendy, it's you – throw, Geddy goes.

Wendy doesn't answer so Geddy pleads to Donna. Donna pipes in.

C'mon Wendy, sit down. Your car'll be alright.

Probably don't know what a Ford Focus is down here, Geddy says.

And they're away again. Rip the pish out of Wendy time. Donna goes first.

They'll think it's a UFO.

If they're going to wreck it they'll wreck it, says Geddy.

Geddy is smiling at Donna, secretly hoping they will wreck it. Teach that snobby bitch a lesson. Wendy comes back from the veranda and sits down. Donna hands her the dice.

C'mon, you need a six.

Wendy takes them. She even rolls them about her cupped hands with snobbery.

Who d'you lumber last night? Geddy wants to know.

Charlie Garrett, is Wendy's answer. Devoid of emotion or passion. She throws the dice and takes a sip of her tea. there's something about the tea she doesn't like. Something that opens her eyes in a glare, like two moons coming over the top of the cup. Two moons hovering over the Planet Geddy.

Geddy, this is tea!!

Eh . . . Hello! That's what you wanted.

Oh, look – a six. I said to put nothing in it, says Wendy. She's moving her piece. *Click click click* round the board as Geddy describes the contents of the cup.

There's fuck all in it.

I only drink hot water. This is toxic.

You said you wanted tea! Geddy rages.

Flinging the hot tea round her and ramming the cup into her face a few times is what Geddy wants to do. Wendy pretends she's interested in the game.

Who is asking the questions?

Me. What is it?

Green, goes Wendy.

But Geddy's not letting the tea incident go just like that.

You'll just have to drink it, she says.

I've just had my teeth polished.

Fuck, says Geddy.

She gets up, grabs the cup, veers off to the scullery and chucks it down the sink. Donna coughs like a game-show hostess, straightens her back and asks the question.

What is the coldest temperature possible in the universe? She's got to raise her voice over Geddy shouting through from the scullery.

So you lumbered Charlie Garrett last night then, Wendy?

Wendy answers Geddy and the wee card in quick and confident succession.

Aye. Minus two hundred and seventy-three degrees Kelvin.

Geddy pours hot water into Wendy's cup and Donna flips the card over. *Question; answer. Question; answer.* She can't make it out. The question means fuck all to her and the answer means even more fuck all.

What's that all about, Kevin? Donna asks Wendy.

It's Physics. Never mind. Wendy throws the die. *Brown,* she says.

Donna's looking at the brown question as Geddy comes back in with a cup of hot-water tea.

Sure it wasn't John Ferry you lumbered? Geddy asks Wendy.

Wendy has a look at Donna. Donna gives her a look back. You'd have to be Einstein to work out what those looks mean. Wendy gives Geddy an answer.

I think I can tell John Ferry from Charlie Garrett.

That shuts Geddy up and Donna gets on with the question. Art and Literature.

What Arthur Miller play is set in Salem?

The Crucible. It wasn't really a lumber though, Wendy tells Geddy.

But Geddy's excited now about something else. She knows the answer. Not so much that she knows this answer. She's excited because she knows *an* answer. Any answer. She knows the answer even though Wendy's just answered the question right. Or correctly, should I say. Geddy jumps in with her answer.

Stephen King. It's Stephen King! About Witches! A film. I seen it.

You're wrong twice. It wasn't Stephen King and Salem's Lot *was about vampires,* Wendy tells her.

Donna shrugs her shoulders and indicates to Wendy. Wendy throws again.

Could Charlie Garrett not get it up? Geddy goes. She's jibing at Wendy now. Donna and Geddy have a wee laugh at that. But Wendy stays cool. Keeps her chin up. Confidence.

We never got that far.

Did he not fancy you? Asks Donna. She's gulping her tea and trying not to laugh. Blinking at Geddy and Geddy moves in for a go.

Too posh for him?

Wendy waits till their mirth has died a bit and gives them it. She knows it's all about timing.

He fell out the taxi.

Donna splurges her tea all over the Trivial. *Fuck sake! What did you do?*

Aw, Donna! You've got that all over History and Geography, goes Wendy.

Donna, still laughing, tries to wipe it off with her sleeve. Geddy re-asks Donna's question.

What did you do?

I just walked it home.

No! Charlie Garrett! Is he alright? says Donna.

Wendy doesn't seem to quite understand that. *What?*

Is he alright? Is he in hospital or something?

Now she's really puzzled, Wendy. She looks at Donna like she's trying to read directions to Outer Bumblefuck on her face. Then it dawns on her what she means. She smiles and shakes her head. She forgot for a moment how thick her sisters could be.

It wasn't even moving when he fell out, Wendy says. *This is pointless, this game, anyway.* She gets back up and goes to the veranda. *I think I'll go and move my car.*

What d'you mean anyway, Wendy? asks Geddy.

Move it. Drive it. Get in and turn the key. Turn the wheel. Clutch. Gas. Mirror. Reverse.

No, about the car being the same as me. No engine.

Dhuu! Donna laughs.

Sometimes it takes Geddy a wee while before the penny drops. Geddy knows she's the point of ridicule again. But she can't figure out why. She reacts anyway by casting a spell on Wendy's car.

I hope your hocus pocus Focus falls apart with rust, she tells Wendy.

You're just jealous.

No, I'm not, says Geddy. She pulls her skirt down as if there's a predator about. Or maybe cos there's no predator about. Wendy ignores her and gets the nose up in the air. Geddy nudges Donna the nudge they've nudged a million times.

I really shouldn't be arguing here. With such a child, goes Wendy.

Oh! I wish I could video this and show it to your analyst, Geddy says.

Donna and Geddy like this a lot. But Wendy's got a trump card up her sleeve. The Atom Bomb for Geddy. The Jolene weapon. And what does Wendy do?

Geraldine, Geraldine, Geraldine . . .

Know something, Wendy? See if this works the night; see if it's real, I'm going to do a spell on you so I am.

Geddy swallows her anger. It goes down her throat like a Christmas tree on fire. The branches all folding upwards but the heat remaining the same. Wendy trails off and goes to the window sniggering. Glad to have won this battle but knowing that the war would always be there. You can't leave your background and expect every homecoming to be sweet as peas. Geddy wants to hit back but she doesn't know how. All she can do is reiterate what she said earlier with different words.

Maybe I've got special powers? So watch it.

And that's all she can come up with. None of them notices Donna doing her starey eyes again. Wendy glares at Geddy. Hey! She's winning. She doesn't need to take this shite. Why not hammer it home. Go for the jugular. Get right in there while the going's good. Between sisters and brothers and friends the whole world over, the language is artificially friendly. It's the subtext you have to watch out for. And Wendy knows all about subtext cos she fancies herself as a playwright and she's read *Teach Yourself How To Write a Great Play in a Day* by Shug Weedon. Wendy gets right to the subtext of the argument. The bones of contention that lie under the whole day. The whole relationship between the sisters.

Charlie Garrett fancies me and not you, says Wendy.

What?

Geddy says *what* for two reasons. One, how did you know that? And two, that's not fair, you're not supposed to use the subtext in this game. But Wendy is breaking the rules and she gives Geddy another tug.

That's what all this is about. Charlie Garrett fancies me and not you.

There's a pause as Geddy realises that Wendy is in fact much cleverer than she gives her credit for. She turns the heat right up to confrontation.

Hmph! Stay back from my man. That's all I'm saying. Stay back.

Wendy's made her mind up. She's going for it. Geddy had knocked lumps out of her when they were wee. She'd a terrible temper when she couldn't get her own way, Geddy. And if you were in the way – thump. And she could hit, being a gymnast.

Got a man now? says Wendy. She says it flat but with a scorpion hiding in it.

John Ferry, says Geddy. She is puffing out her chest. Not that it needs puffing.

John Ferry is your man? Now there's something new.

He fancies me something rotten. That right, Donna?

Donna shrugs and keeps staring. If she's not getting attention now she eventually will. All she has to do is stare. And stare. And stare.

She's doing her eyes, Wendy goes, *leave her out of it.*

They look at Donna staring. Geddy waves her hand in front of her face but there's not a blink. Not a flinch. Wendy can see

Geddy is getting riled up. Right angry. She's only trying to turn the attention to Donna to take the pressure off herself. Wendy feels good. It's great to be on the front foot for once, with your opponent shuffling back all the time, throwing wild punches. Geddy can't take the loaded silence any more.

See if I was at Garfield's last night, none of yees would have got a man, she shouts.

That's Geddy's right hook. Wendy looks at Donna in disbelief. But Donna is still staring. Wendy's got another Atom Bomb. One that all the sisters share. But none so far have been able to fling it at Geddy. It's never been used in mockery or in anger. Wendy's had enough of being snobberised just cos she tried to better herself. Got herself a life out of that godforsaken hell-hole of a scheme.

What are you talking about? Wendy goes. *Every time a good-looking girl stands beside you, you move away to the other end of the Disco.*

Even Donna reacts to the immediate silence. The fire recedes in the grate. Draws itself in away from the danger. Waiting. Donna's head's not changed position but her eyes have swivelled and she's holding her breath.

What d'you mean? Says Geddy.

The voltage in the room has been turned right up but it's darker than it was a couple of seconds ago. Wendy couldn't back out now even if she wanted to. And she does want to a bit. But she can't.

I've observed you.

A quick snort and a face twist from Geddy. She goes for Wendy's language. Her accent.

Observed. Fuckin ob-served! Away you, back to your West End; actors, poofs an posh birds.

Wendy wades right in. *You go and stand next to the Huckleberry Hounds. Or the Deputy Dawgs. You're noted for it, so you are.*

So and I do!

By this time Donna's turned her whole head and her mouth's wide open. She wants to laugh. She's trying not to but her shoulders are going up and down. Wendy piles it on.

It's going to come to the day when you won't be able to find hogs ugly enough to make you look good. Then what'll you do?

Donna bursts out laughing. Wendy laughs. Geddy can't take it. The truth's always harder when you don't believe it yourself. Then suddenly you do. So suddenly she did, and rather than kill Wendy with a big kitchen knife, Geddy stands up and gets her things together.

Right – that's it. I'm leaving. I thought this Witchcraft stuff was a lot of shite anyway from the start.

If this was during Geddy's depression periods before she had Alicia then Wendy wouldn't have pushed her so far. But she's fair game now and a night in the huff in her own house wouldn't do her any harm.

Geddy's got all her stuff and is about to leave when there's a noise from out in the close. *Bump – bump – bump – bump.* The speaking of muffled voices.

Shh! Sounds like Linda, Donna goes.

And Angie probably, says Geddy.

Angie's History

Angie's in her late thirties. She usually wears worn-out clothes cos she spends all her money on her wanes. But they don't appreciate it. No, that's wrong. Some of them do appreciate it very much. She had five wanes before she was twenty-one.

Her face is the most beautiful of the sisters'. But that's offset by her manly walk. She walks a lot with her arms folded and generally looks tough. That's probably because she is tough. One of the things she does when she talks is to say the same thing twice, only the second time she reverses the order of the words. For instance here's one.

Jumping in that water would be daft. It'd be daft to jump in so it would.

On the night in question Angie comes in not believing in Witchcraft much at all. Even though she's seen it working manys a time she's made herself believe that she doesn't believe. But even though beneath that hard exterior there's an even harder interior trying to get out, Angie has something in her that helps the afflicted. She's got the perfect psychological make-up to cut through bullshit, to see what's needed and to apply herself to that. If you're in any trouble, from CID to street-fights, Angie's the one you want at your back. And all this might be giving you a wrong impression of her. Okay, she might have been ground down by five wanes but she's got a great sense of humour and in some ways I suppose that's the very thing that's brought her through life.

The worst of her sons is Dessie. He's sixteen now but he aged her two years for every one of his. The rest of them picked up her humour and easygoing attitude. And her quick right hook. Angie thinks that once Dessie gets a nice girlfriend he'll settle down. One night she happened to say that to Linda. That was a mistake. They were all talking about ways to bring him under control. Every solution was offered, from taking him on holiday to Spain and treating him nice from Wendy to electric shock treatment from Linda.

When my Dessie finds a decent bird he'll settle down. It's a phase, Angie goes.

That's the oldest one in the book. He'll probably murder her, says Linda.

When Maw had Angie she had forceps. It was a difficult birth.

By the time Angie was fourteen she was a right Bay City Rollers fan. She used to go down Mitchell Street in a brown college jumper with yellow hoops round the sleeves and the neck. Big white skinners on and Doc Martens. Nobody knew how it happened but by the time she was thirteen Angie was out of control. She was dogging the school and stealing money. The truth was she liked a wee drink. That's all it was. She could drink the Buckie to a band playing. And even though she still likes a drink now she's not got a problem. Yet if anybody had seen her then they would have sent her straight to an AA meeting. And there's plenty of them in Coatbridge.

But Angie had discovered the drink. There's an oul Chinese proverb that goes: The man takes a drink, then the drink takes a drink, then the drink takes the man. That's the way she was. Addicted to it for a wee while. She used to take carry-outs of booze off guys. And I'm talking here about guys at eighteen and nineteen. They'd come out of The Monkland with their cargo and Angie would go up. Slap the one with the bag right on the face.

Gimme that!

That's all she'd say, rip the bag out of their hands and walk away. Swagger away really. Only one of them ever retaliated. Wee Dooley. Angie got him down by the hair and kicked him round the place. None of his mates even tried to help him. And none of them went anywhere near the carry-out Angie had ripped off them. When she was satisfied that he'd had enough of a kicking to make things easier in the future she made him lick her Docs. Then she took his fags off him and the fifty-seven pence he had down his sock. Off she went down the burn to drink the booty.

Much later, when she was smoking the last of wee Dooley's Regal King-size and trying her best to stop her drunken head from flopping down onto her chest, Dooley and his gang turned up fuelled by drink they took off even smaller guys. They kicked fuck out Angie and flung her in the burn. It was a cold night. Her head hit a rock and knocked her out.

Angie woke up in the burn. She was fourteen and she was cold. Ropes of her hair floated on and off her cheekbones. That's the first thing she remembers., That's when she regained consciousness. A combination of the drink and the rock she hit her head on was holding her the wrong side of paralysis. Everything was wet. And up in the sky a thousand November moons spun round on helicopter rotors. The dizziness worked from her eyes to her belly. She retched and a rainbow fountain rose up above her like gastronomic magic. Down it came. She closed her eyes for a second and opened them. Downstream a Technicolor raft of vomit flooded away through moonbeams and foam. That's when she realised she was in the burn. That Dooley and his gang had flung her in. Now and then as she took in breath the water was coming into her mouth with the air. It was frightening. She had to move. I was willing her to move. I could see everything she was going through. I could always see everything the sisters were going through. Think their every thought and feel their every emotion. But there was nothing much I could do about it except will for things to happen. Make things happen by thinking. It was, and still is, a case of you can look but you can't touch. I think I made her think the thoughts about her legs. Made her know that she had to move. From here on the other side things are much more confusing than with the living.

Angie tried to move her legs. There was no sensation. They weren't there. But she could see them moving in the water, the white linen pressing into her skin. She tried again. The legs. Nothing. Then she tried to move her arms cos the water was covering her more as her head slid down the stone and into the burn. The burn wasn't deep when you were standing up. Buy lying down, it could more than cover your head if it wanted to. She made an effort to move her arms again. But they were still. Still except that they were undulating in the flow and ebb of the water. Her fingers, all pointing upwards like she had an invisible tennis ball in each hand, were piercing the water's meniscus. Protruding from the burn into the cold slabs of night. She watched them rising and falling. They were stabbing sine waves in the air.

Then panic. Her ears sunk into the claustrophobic terror of water. They surfaced to a loud hiss and sunk to a muffled burble. They sunk and surfaced and surfaced and sunk into the chill of being young and drunk. Afraid of staying in the burn and afraid of going home to Maw and Da who would not be too pleased at all. Afraid too of not going home. The confusion of puberty mixed with the confusion of drink on top of the confusion of fear. She was truly paralytic. She had to get up. She commanded herself to get up. She was shouting inside her own head. Nobody could hear her but me.

Rise, white skinners.

But they were green with moss and still.

Rise, Doc Marten boots.

But they were filled with slime oozing into the bootlace holes.

Rise, Wrangler jacket.

But that was a shroud of dark blue lead now.

Rise, college jumper.

But that was soaked to her skin and going nowhere unless she was. But she couldn't. She was breathing in and breathing out tubes of breath. Above the breath the mad moons were still spinning. Oh, she felt sick sick sick. She let out her first words since she came to.

Oh Hail Mary full of grace . . . God remove me from this mess . . . now and at the hour . . .

That was it. It came to her. The place where she had to get the strength from. Death. *The hour of our death.* If she didn't move this would be the hour of her death. To die alone in the burn. The night sucking her soul out into the stars. Angie wanted to live. Fuck it! She was going to stand up no matter what it took. She grunted and rolled over so that her face was down into the burn. She arched her back like a cat and compressed her body so that her head rose until she could see the glossy hiss of the surface, and the noise of cars on the road above was like Christmas to her. Her fingers dug into the slimy bank and she dragged herself upright. A hanging willow branch bent down and waved in front of her like magic. She grabbed that and somehow got up onto the bank where she lay panting for a minute or two like an oul bust dog. At least she was out the burn. But her clothes were hardening up with the frost. She had to keep moving.

How she ever stood up she'll never know. I was beside her every inch of the way. How did she stagger home on liquid legs? All the way up the drunken paths and pavements people were pointing at her and saying her name.

Is that the wee lassie Riley?

They were stepping aside. The numb echoes of their voices were guilt. She'll never know how she made it home through alleys and blackouts. How did she ever stand up from her cold funeral water? She let any innocence she had drown in that burn that night and went home neither girl nor woman. One thing was for sure. She would never, ever, be pushed down again.

When she came to sometime the next day, stinking of sick and Buckfast and burn water, she told the rest of the Girls the story. Dooley and his gang had to get it. That was the first time they really all got together and deliberately done a spell to get back at somebody.

One night the next week there was gale-force winds and rain like you've never seen. There was flooding everywhere and most of the roads in Scotland were shut. The telly was saying not to go out unless it was an absolute emergency. Dooley and two of his gang stole a car. They went roaming about the place to see what they could steal. They came to a bridge across the burn. It was the very spot where they had chucked Angie in under a week before. The burn was up so high it was coming round the arched bridge and onto the road. Dooley reversed back a hundred yards and took a run at the bridge hoping to go into mid-air on the hump and land with a splash in the water on the road at the other side. When they got to the middle of the bridge, there wasn't one. Down they went into the tumbling abyss of water. They found the three of them downstream once the floods had subsided. Dooley was halfway out the window but his two pals' hands were locked round his ankles.

The time my Maw decided to put Donna on the pill, Angie got Donna to send the smear-test letter to her house so as my Da wouldn't find it. He would have went ape shit. I'll never forget the time Brian came over to tell him Linda was pregnant. She was only seventeen. But more of that later. Ninety-nine times out of a hundred the smear test comes back alright. But there's always that wee element of worry at the back of your mind that you might have cancer or something else.

Dessie might be a wee shite but sometimes he comes in handy for something. He had stole a typewriter out the butcher's. Don't ask me why the butcher had a typewriter. They say there's a book in everybody and maybe the butcher was going to write one in between wrapping up a pound of links for Mrs McGinty and eyeing up the next lamb for the laughter. Angie had a go at writing a book too but she got to two pages and gave up. Dessie had three hundred pages of the maddest stuff typed up with spelling mistakes and no punctuation but some of it made great reading. He could have been a genius if he only had a brain.

Anyway, he's another story. The typewriter had been gathering dust and promises for about a year when Donna's letter came through. Angie and Geddy were in and they steamed it open. It was the usual with the hospital logo at the top and a few lines giving her the all clear with her test. Angie got the letter photocopied in the school. But not before she covered the typing up with a plain sheet. So what they had was a clean white bill headed A4 from the hospital. They set about typing up another letter to Donna and sealing it back into the envelope. They arranged to meet the next day and got all the other sisters round to watch Donna's face fall.

The next morning Angie phoned Donna at my Maw's and told her there was a letter there for her. Donna arrived with a piece of toast in her mouth. When you're young these things are important. You half hope you've got cancer for the effect it would have on your street cred. Death is a fashion accessory. Till it confronts you.

Come in, everybody's down, said Angie.

She sat Donna at the other end of the table from the five sisters and they watched her light up a fag and talk out the side of her mouth while slicing the letter open with a knife. The sisters all chatted idly about the curtains and the price of mince but they kept a suppressed laugh and a beady squint on Donna as she unfolded the letter and read it.

It's from the hospital.

That'll be your smear test, said Geddy.

Came through this morning, said Angie.

Donna's face started to fall. Her eyes were darting all over the letter and the sisters had to turn away to hide their laughing. Caroline and Linda were over at the sink pretending to be getting a cup of water.

Pour me one, Caroline, snorted Linda.

Caroline disguised the gurgling in her throat as a sore throat. Donna's face was falling and her fag was stuck to her lip, hanging down on her chin. She looked at Angie, who was doing rather well at keeping a straight face.

Angie, is all Donna could gasp.

What is it? said Angie. She spoke with all the care and concern of a mother while the rest of the Girls sniggered and snottered and bent over double pretending to be fixing their tights. Donna spoke again.

I've got AIDS.

You've what?

I've to go in for more tests. I've got AIDS.

How can you have AIDS? You've hardly had sex.

I've done it about fifty times, said Donna.

Let me see it, Angie goes.

Angie took the letter while the sisters comforted Donna. They were so close that their snortles and sharp breaths sounded like tears. That made Donna all the more scared. Angie read the letter out loud to the mock dumbstruck family.

Dear Miss Donna Riley, We regret to have to inform you that your recent smear test shows you are HIV positive. We have to ask you to contact the clinic for further tests in order to ascertain whether or not you have full-blown AIDS. The current life expectancy for a young woman such as yourself with AIDS is about three months. Please contact the following number and ask for Mr Lyon: 0141 771 1185. When you speak to him tell him you want to come in for an AIDS test. All the best. Dr Toomuchsex.

Geddy was proud of herself. AIDS was just out at the time and cos she watched all the current-affair programmes she picked that disease. Angie had wanted to give her syphilis but that wasn't funny enough for Geddy. And anyway, they couldn't spell it between them.

They took Donna out for a drink and convinced her it must be some mistake but they never let on it was a practical joke. Just to be on the safe side they convinced her she should stay with Angie and the sisters that night and phone in the morning. Then she'd have all her sisters there for moral support. Donna felt a bit better until they told her she'd have to contact all the men she'd shagged and tell them they had AIDS too. That way they got to find out all the men she'd been with. A very enlightening night it was. Donna, even at that young age, was a big, big hit with the boys. They let her phone the clinic the next day and ask if she could put an AIDS appointment on.

This is the way the conversation went. Donna dialled up with the sisters gathered round her in moral support.

Hello, could I speak to Mr Lyon, please.

Pardon?

Could I speak to Mr Lyon, please. I've to phone for an AIDS test.

An AIDS test? Is this some sort of joke?

No. I was told to phone this number and ask for a Mr Lyon. I've got the letter, d'you want the reference number?

There's no Mr Lyon here.

Is that not the hospital?

No, this is Glasgow Zoo.

If you were outside Angie's house that morning you would have seen five sisters running out as fast as they could go, considering they were falling about laughing, and Donna catching up with them, dishing out blows with a frying pan, shouting about AIDS and smear tests. Quite surreal until you know the background behind it all.

Angie might have lost some of her sense of humour now but if there was one thing she was noted for it was that she was always up for a right good laugh.

Angie was out doing her driving lessons this day years ago. About that time Dessie was getting into a lot of bother with some local guys.

Angie was still at the stage where she was going out there and standing up for her boy. If Dessie got beat in a fight Angie would turn up and you had big trouble on your hands. By the time she was thirty she could take on any man in the Brig and give him a right good go.

She had to stop sharp turning the corner at Mitchell Street. The brakes screeched and this big guy turned, stooped and zoomed his head into the windscreen. The instructor cringed, his nails dug into the seats. Angie had seen the iron bar in his right hand but the instructor only noticed it when it clanged off the bonnet.

Oh my God – look! He's got a metal thing. He looked at Angie wondering why she wasn't panicking.

It's only Big Drongo, Angie said.

Angie was calm as Big Drongo leaned further into the dim light of the car. His face was framed by a great twist of metal.

Oh my God, what's that stuff all over his face? the instructor screamed.

Drongo's jaw was held together by metal scaffolding. He looked like Hannibal the Cannibal. The instructor breathed rapidly and ripped the seat, breaking his newly manicured nails. He was a suspected poof in Angie's eyes, the instructor. Panic set in. It costs a lot of money, a car with pedals on two sides.

Drive back! Drive back! He shouted.

He twisted away from the evil grin and smoky breath on the glass as Drongo raised the bar into the night, focusing on Angie's face. Two other morons high on jellies shuffled to the side window grinning. The drunk corner boys chanted.

Dron-go! Dron-go! Dron-go! Dron-go! Dron-go! Dron-go!

Drongo's scaffolding clicked against the glass. Angie could see the silver mesh and he could see her clearly for the first time. His sidekicks were bouncing the car to and fro to the chants of the corner boys. Drongo would have to do something now.

But he didn't.

He shouted something sharp and withdrew rapidly. His puzzled sidekicks scuttled away. Drongo gaped and nodded, holding a palm to the inside of the car and backed off.

What's he doing now? What's he doing now? the instructor wanted to know.

S'alright, s'alright. He's changed his mind, Angie said.

Angie drove on. She gave Drongo The Stare as she passed. The corner boys stopped singing and for a moment Mitchell Street seemed normal. They went under the railway bridge and stopped at the hotel car park to practise three-point turns. After a while they could hear sirens in the distance.

Looks like Drongo found a head for his iron bar, Angie says.

My God – do you think those police cars are for him!!?

Three police cars sped downhill blasting. An ambulance followed. The lights changed and Angie drove away slowly looking downhill all the while.

Do you really think that he's hit some poor soul with that metal thing? the instructor asked.

Probably.

He was crazy-looking. The instructor paused and then asked, all puzzled, why Drongo had walked away from the car.

Why do you think he never touched us, Angela?

Did you see the metal on his face?

Yes, all that stuff. What was that? An American footballer mask?

It's a broken jaw. His mouth's getting held together so it can heal up.

The instructor was more amazed at this culture by the second. In fact, it's Angie who's the instructor now.

He's got a broken jaw and he's out drinking?

It would only surprise me if Drongo was sober!

Do you think he's out looking for the people who did that to him?

I think he's out to get somebody for it, alright. But not the person that done it.

The instructor didn't understand. *What do you mean?*

Well, remember I told you my son Dessie got mugged a couple of weeks ago?

Yes?

And they took his Reggae Blaster and hundred quid leather jacket?

The instructor remembered. He nodded rapidly with his mouth shut tight.

Well it was Big Drongo and his crew that done it.

He couldn't make sense of what Angie was saying. She helped him.

I smashed his jaw. Got him up Wine Alley and kicked fuck out him, and I'll tell you something; I enjoyed every second of it. I got the stuff back first thing next morning.

The instructor never spoke all the way back to Angie's house. He dropped her off and headed for the safety of Blairhill. That was the last of Angie's driving lessons with him.

Even years after she was married and laden down with wanes Angie was always up for a laugh. Caroline had got hold of one of them rubber masks that looks dead real. The face looks like real skin and the hair like real hair. The only holes are for eyes and the mouth. The mask moves with your face and your eyes seem to become part of it. All the sisters had played jokes on each other with it. Every fright you could give anybody had been done. The best one was Linda lying in Geddy's bath with it on one night and Geddy coming in for a pee. She needed more than a pee after that. So the mask lay about for a year until one night they were all in Angie's drinking and playing Trivial.

Dessie had stole a load of building-site waterproofs, the ones that are more yellow than a bunch of bananas. There had been a crowd of Neds across from Angie's house drinking wine and making a right nuisance of themselves. Angie decided to teach them a lesson. She got into the yellow waterproofs and the mask and a big pair of yellow wellies that were lying about. She snuck out the back door and the rest of the Girls went out the front pretending to be walking home, slowly. When they got near to the Neds they stopped and argued about something. The Neds were shouting the usual abuse.

Gimme a swatch at your patch!

All that kind of stuff. But the Girls ignored them and they would have got worse except that one of the Neds spotted this figure in the distance. A funny man dressed in yellow. And he was coming right at them, still at a distance, but the Yellow Fellow had plotted a straight line and was moving towards the Neds like a Terminator. He was climbing fences, going straight through gardens and keeping a dead-ahead course towards the Neds. There was no doubt that they were his target. The sisters stood by to watch. The Neds started off lightly at first.

Hey you, get out of them gardens! Yellow bastard!

But on he came.

Hey cunt, are you deaf?

Seemingly he was cos on he came.

Hey, get to fuck or we'll give you a doing.

Yellow Fellow was within fifty yards of them. They fell quiet cos their presence didn't seem to be frightening him. The Neds talked amongst themselves for a wee bit.

Who the fuck is it?

I don't know.

He looks weird as fuck.

Like a mad fisherman.

Maybe he's just taking a short cut.

He was now over the last garden fence. The Neds were bristling with adrenaline but the Girls noticed that they were also trying to get behind each other. Some were drifting off to the side out of the line of fire. Some had their chests out. The leader, Polecat Malarkey, took two steps towards the oncoming Yellow Fellow, who by now was a mere fifteen yards away. Polecat stamped his authority on the situation.

Hey, Fatty, get to fuck before you get a blade in your ribs.

That would have frightened most people cos to tell the truth these Neds were a pretty scary prospect. They'd already stabbed a few folk just passing by. They held the whole scheme in their terror – but not The Yellow Fellow. Polecat made another two steps towards the oncoming monstrosity. His gang were just beginning to see the absurdity of the face forming in the lights. An oul wizened face coved in wrinkles. Unchanging except for a wee bit of movement around the eyes and mouth. Polecat stopped and his brain was trying to make sense of the situation. He reached in his pocket for his knife but it was a folding blade and he never had a chance to get it out cos The Yellow Fellow ran right at him, shouting:

BANANA MAN!!!!

Well, you should've seen it. The Neds scattered over walls and under hedges. Some ran screaming through people's houses. The Girls fell about. Some of the retreating Neds had even tried to save the Girls as they ran.

Come on to fuck, it's a mad maniac!

Chivalry, it seems, was not completely dead. Polecat was last seen heading west at high speed.

Help! Somebody help me! he was shouting. *Banana Man's after me!*

Angie aka The Yellow Fellow aka the Banana Man came to a stop at the Girls and lit a fag. By this time some of the Neds were crawling back on their bellies. What they could see was the grotesque man in yellow with the face of a ninety year oul and the body of a thirty year oul smoking and chatting with my sisters. After a while Angie aka The Yellow Fellow aka the Banana Man went away the way it came. Across the fences and through the gardens.

A little later again as the Neds started to appear round the Girls Angie appeared as Angie. The Neds asked who it was and what did he want. That was an opening for the Girls. They told them the truth of the matter.

He was a Russian hit man out to get them cos some guy they stabbed a week ago was the second cousin of the KGB. Polecat and his gang were never seen at that spot again.

A few years after that, Angie had the idea that if she had a caravan she could go on holiday every weekend away from the crumbling scheme. Angie needed to get out of the scheme at least once a week or she was going to go mad. Get Maw to watch the wanes.

But when she went to price caravans they were all too dear. Her man John had got a tow ball for their car in anticipation so rather than waste it Angie decided to build her own caravan. So her and John got sheets of knocked marine plywood and built a caravan in their back garden. It must be said that even though none of them were joiners they made a good enough job of it. Okay, it looked home-made and was pine but it was in the top division of rough-as-fuck home-made caravans. They made all the wee fancy bits too. Seats and tables. Bunk beds. Fixed them onto the metal frame of the trailer. John welded the trailer together in the garden with some equipment he got off his cousin. Sometimes the wanes would help but most of the time they wouldn't. It became an obsession for Angie. This wee box on wheels was her ticket to freedom. She'd long ago lost hope that one day she might make enough money to move to the countryside or another place where the people are sane. Somewhere, anywhere, away from this scheme. But that was not to be. The final dream of a wee cottage in Donegal faded when the house prices in the Republic went through the roof.

As winter passed, every day the caravan got bigger. Every

day the neighbours would ask Angie all about it.

It's looking good, Angie.

Isn't it, she'd say. Always returning their sly glances.

My, you're a bit of a craftsman, Angie. A true craftsman, they'd say.

It'll be good to get the thing out on the road, said Angie.

That was her standard reply every time she wanted to end the conversation and get back to work. You might think that it's a pretty ordinary thing to be chatting with the neighbours hanging over the fence watching you build a caravan. But there's something you need to know about the architecture of Angie's house.

Angie's house backed onto other houses. Her back garden backed onto another back garden. The houses were arranged in a big rectangle. There was no way in except up a skinny close. So when the neighbours were leaning over the fence saying how good Angie was at building the caravan, what they were really saying was something else. We're back to the subtext again that Wendy's so good at.

You daft cunt. I can't wait till you try to get that fucker out the close.

That was the thought running through everybody's minds. In fact, it was the talk of the scheme, Angie's caravan.

Before you start feeling sorry for Angie you need to know something else. Angie knew they were all laughing at her. That's the kind of place it was. She was onto them. She even led them along a fair bit.

I can't wait till I get this baby out on the open road, she'd go.

And they'd nudge each other and wink, the neighbours. Angie would even add bits on.

Aye. Me and the wanes out there on a Highland road. The wind in our hair. This place far behind.

They'd be trying not to fall about laughing by this time. But Angie would keep on going.

Maybe park up at a beach. Fry up the rolls on ham and move on in the morning. At a beach we'll park up.

She'd spill out her whole dream to them and they'd wait till she sank back to her work and draw faces and snigger. But they never seen Angie grinning as she tightened up the nuts.

So the summer eventually came and there was the finished article sat there taking up the whole back garden. Varnished pine, like an elephant's coffin. Angie couldn't even get a washing out. She was sharing with next door. They were letting her so they could talk about the caravan and have a laugh at her expense. The whole place thought she had finally lost her marbles.

Angie's caravan was now the talk of the town. She told them all she was going on holiday on the eighth of June. On the seventh all the neighbours were out in their gardens with carry-outs. Leaning over into Angie's and listening to her describing the journey she was going to take the next day. Right up to Skye she was going. A few days there and over to Inverness. Then up to Ullapool. Then Sutherland. That was where they were going. And the grander her scheme grew the more the neighbours got her to talk. They wanted her fall to be a long one. They wanted her to hit the ground hard. None of them mentioned the moving of the caravan. They didn't want to spoil the fun. They just wanted to be there when Angie tried it.

But she didn't move the caravan that day. They all got irked and hit the sack knowing that she would have to move it on the next day. The eighth.

When the neighbours got up the next morning there was the caravan on the front street. Shining. Bleaching in the sun. It was a blue day. A great day for your holidays. A great day for towing a caravan all over Scotland.

One by one the neighbours opened their eyes to the shining example of craftsmanship hooked up to John's oul Proton. Phones were ringing. People were coming out to see. Wanes were wondering what the commotion was.

By the time Angie and John appeared with the shorts on and Hawaiian shirts there was a good-sized crowd. They were looking in her front garden for evidence of a crane; tyre tracks or something. But they agreed that any crane that lifted this thing over would have woken up the whole street in the middle of the night. They couldn't figure it out.

Angie and John muttered a few good mornings and got in the car, *Vroom!* And they were off. The neighbours scratched their heads in a puffy exhaust cloud of bewilderment.

If they had waited up the night before they would have seen Angie and John quietly unbolt the roof. The four panels. The furniture. The trailer. They would have seen them in the dead of night carry the bits up the skinny close and reassemble them on the street. And when it was all done, if they listened carefully, they might have heard the two of them laughing quietly. They might have heard the same laugh as Angie and John wound their way up into the Highlands.

When Wendy was with Jonesy they sometimes used to batter lumps out each other. If the truth be told, Wendy usually won. But if there was even a mark on Wendy the sisters went looking for Jonesy. When they found him he'd invariably have scratchmarks down his face and a couple of big bruises where Wendy had whacked him. They'd leave it be. Eventually the sisters didn't go near when there were reports of Jonesy and Wendy fighting.

But that's not what it was like in the beginning. I sometimes think that all the sisters' marriages eventually failed because they were too interfering At the beginning. They watched a newlywed sister's life like a hawk and questioned the living daylights out of them if they seemed down or depressed. It can't be much fun married to a family of Witches.

So when Wendy married Jonesy the sisters kept a close watch on things. And if they watched, Angie scrutinised. Looking out for lumps, bumps, bites or bruises.

Angie gave Jonesy the benefit of the doubt the first couple of times Wendy looked bumped about. But this Saturday, when Wendy came over to Angie's with a black eye, Angie went off like a ten-bob rocket. She was boiling with anger but to see her walking to Wendy's you would have thought she was down for cookies, buns and rock cakes. Mints and coffee.

Hi, Angie, people said.

She answered back with a smile and a light nod of the head. When she arrived at Wendy's the door was open. The house was empty. Angie stood still and listened. It was one of them silences where you just know there's somebody there.

After a few minutes and a drink of water Angie went out the door. She shut it over and made some steps along the close. Then she snuck back, slipped in the house, and waited in the scullery.

Soon she heard movement up in the loft. It was a top flat they lived in at the time. Angie hid behind the fridge. Well, Angie partially hid behind the fridge. Next thing the lift hatch opened and down came Jonesy with a thump. He was muttering to himself coming along the lobby. All about how he was going to kill the bitch.

And sending that fat bastard Angie round. Fuckin total eclipse.

He came into the scullery and opened the fridge for beer. But Angie's voice came on with the fridge light.

Jonesy shat himself. He was pleading and begging and greeting. Blaming it all on Wendy. Snottering all over the place about how it was the drink and he wouldn't do it again. Angie let Jonesy drive himself further into despair. When he was a shrivelled wreck she told him exactly what would happen if he ever lifted his mitts again. Jonesy promised Angie the earth.

Angie walked along the lobby with Jonesy venerating her all the way. Thanking her for indulgences. Angie opened the door. Jonesy's heart was thumping to be rid of her.

She stepped out into the close, thought again, turned and cracked Jonesy an almighty hook on the chin. Knocked him clean out. Broke his jaw. Jonesy's jaw was wired up for weeks.

She waited till Jonesy came round. First thing he seen was Angie sitting on the stairs drinking the beer that was in the fridge. When she knew he could understand Angie told Jonesy the score.

I thought you might like to have an example punch to let you know what's coming if you ever lift your mitts to our Wendy again.

This is the measure of Angie.

Linda's History

Linda, like Angie, is in her late thirties. She's in a wheelchair through no fault of her own. To compensate for her lack of mobility she wears a sporty tracksuit and expensive trainers. She lost the use of her legs a long time ago although she can go to the toilet alright herself. But she wasn't always like that, Linda. Out of all the sisters, myself excepted, she's had the biggest change. She used to be the perfect Stepford wife and she's not now. But I'll tell you all about that later.

Another way she compensates for her lack of mobility is through her tricks with the wheelchair. She can do all sorts with it and takes part in races sometimes but doesn't like hanging about with *the cripples* as she calls them. When you press her for what she means she says it's the emotional cripples she hates. The ones who let their physical ailments get them down. Linda never lies. She might take the pish now and then. But she is sworn to tell the truth. And I'll come to why that is, later too. For instance, if Caroline was to ask her if she liked the new fireplace she'd get the truth.

No. It's a mess. A fireplace like that in a house like this is a monstrosity. What were you thinking?

But she's nearly always happy. She too has repressed her belief in Witchcraft. She does believe in it and has seen it work manys a time. Perhaps it would be right to say that she's a little bored with it. She thinks it doesn't live up to its promise and the sisters' early exploits in the name of Witches were beginners' luck and coincidence. But by the end of the night in question her faith has been restored and not a little fear and respect too.

She has a faith in the future and a belief in science. She believes that when science advances enough she will be cured and be able to walk again. Part of her cynicism about the Witchcraft is that the sisters have tried to restore her ability to walk with no success. She's been to Lourdes too. That was a laugh. It was a different time from the time Geddy went but Linda fell out the wheelchair and would have drowned if it wasn't for the fact her arms are so strong and she climbed up the Baptist's leg. One day she was boring the arse off the sisters with the latest advances in science and biology. Telling them it won't be long now till she's cured.

When they discover what's wrong with me I'm taking up jogging, canoeing and climbing. The whole bit, she said.

Aye! I'll have your wheelchair. My corns are killing me. I wouldn't mind getting shoved about all day, Maw said.

When Maw went into Bellshill to have Linda she had her easy. She couldn't believe that was her had a wane.

Oh my God that was lovely, Maw said.

Is this your first baby? The nurse asked.

No, this is my second, but she came out lovely – just like a fish.

The doctor came in. He was looking at her funny. Like he recognised her from somewhere.

How are you feeling now? You're looking remarkably well for a woman who's just given birth to twins.

Twins?

Yes – you remember. One was . . .

But Maw didn't remember. So he stopped talking mid-sentence. The reason Linda came out like a fish is that the first baby was stillborn. She remembered now. Holding the dead baby while the live one slid out. Then they took the dead baby and gave her the live one. Maw has held that secret all these years. That's why she was so good when it came to comforting Geddy at her bedside years later. I am Linda's twin.

She conked out when the memories came back to her. But when she woke up she had dealt with it. She came from another age, Maw. More connected with the late-Victorian Irish immigrants than with their nearly Scottish descendants. When the doctor came back in she was high on some more drugs they had just gave her.

How are you now? he said.

Yes, Doctor, I'm fine. I'd like to go home. You're a great doctor. I don't feel a pain nor nothing.

He looked at her and laughed.

You weren't saying that when I delivered your first child – Caroline, is it?

Maw looked at him.

Do you know many black men? he says.

Oh my God! What did I say, Doctor?

It was a stormy night, your first child, you were scared. I'm saying no more.

He walked away leaving her with an innocent wee wane in her arms. Linda. That was to be her name. Wee Linda.

The first time Linda came across anything supernatural was when she was about seven or eight. She always had this feeling that there was part of her missing. And at the same time another feeling that there was somebody with her. Her guardian angel. These feelings all stemmed from the twin she never knew she had.

As a consequence of her feeling the way she did; out of sorts and not really fitting in, always having that big empty feeling in the middle of her, she would hang about a lot on her own. During the day she'd go about in the graveyard looking at the names on the stones. She knew she was looking for something but never knew what it was. She never went near the graveyard at night but she hovered about near it hoping to catch a glimpse of whatever she was hoping to catch a glimpse of. That's when she started seeing McKraken. She started seeing him quite regularly and noticing these strange things about him. It's hard to say what it was but maybe Linda thought he was what she was looking for. She became, over a period of time, obsessed by McKraken.

McKraken was this oul man in Old Monkland who used to go down the graveyard every night with one flower; whatever one was in season.

He had one hand shaking behind his back all the time. Nobody knew what he done down there but rain, hail or mist he'd be walking into the dark. Linda followed him to the gates and watched him disappear round the tombs. She would peer into the dark through the metal railings on the gate as he disappeared round black edges of tombs. All she would hear was footsteps echoing and fragmenting on the teethy gravestones.

She asked Maw about the man with one hand shaking behind his back and a flower in the other.

McKraken? He had an electric shock after his wife died and he never speaks cos he was struck dumb the night he found her with her wrists slashed on the scullery floor. The blood was spattered on the salad.

Linda was horrified and to this day she doesn't know if that story is real or just one of Maw's made-up tales.

The story about McKraken was that when they found him, after his wife killed herself, he was sitting on the grass verge in the middle of the M8. He had this cornflakes box turned inside out and he was writing the same sentence over and over with a felt tip pen:

Poppies in a green field; flowers on the hillside. Poppies in a green field; flowers on the hillside.

He got put in Hartwood for a couple of years. The name Hartwood conjured up images of horror and pain for Linda. She used to think of wooden hearts burning and people screaming in agony. That was because Maw always used to shout something about hearts.

Yees've got my heart roasted so yees have. Roasted!

Linda mixed the two images up. It made perfect sense to her that once you had your heart roasted they would take you to Hartwood where it would burst into flames.

All that just made Linda's obsession with McKraken stronger. She watched him night after night but could never pluck up the courage to follow him into the graveyard.

One night she was hiding near his door. The whole sky was reflecting in her eyes. She'd been there for a while. And the empty feeling inside her was at its strongest ever. If there was ever a night when she was going to follow him, this was it.

McKraken's door let loose a barrage of clicks and falling chains like Fort Knox. Linda took a long breath and held it in. She lurked back into the hedges. Trapped water on the leaves came cascading down her chest. It was cold as hell. His bunch of keys thumped off the door. Linda still held her breath in case he seen steam blowing out the hedge.

He passed. His feet scliffed on the pavement. His hand was vibrating behind his back. And, as usual, he had a rose in his other hand. His coat was wrapped tight and his hat was low over his eyes. He walked at the same pace he always walked.

Linda slid into the orange glow of street lamps and pushed

through webs of drizzle. She followed behind, private-eye style. *Columbo* was on at the time and a crazy laughing inside her wanted to stop him and ask him questions.

Eh, Columbo here, just one more question before I go, Mr McKraken.

But she never. These surges were rushing through her body. It was only a short walk down Woodside Street to the graveyard gates. Before Linda knew it, McKraken was in there without even a look behind him. Linda skipped down and looked round the wall like a cartoon character. For some reason she couldn't help smiling but the smile felt like an insane grin and it frightened her. She bit her lip and searched herself for courage.

No problem. Okay, ghosts and goulies, here I come ready or not, in your graves, by one, by two, by three, she said. She was moving into the graveyard as she said it. Moving along quietly. Homing in on the scrape of footsteps heading through the tombs somewhere in the distance.

The orange lights shot in over the graveyard wall in sheets but none fell on the stones. It was truly black. She shivered and tiptoed on the grass avoiding stepping on the graves. That was real bad luck. Bad cess. She nearly caught up with McKraken.

She was only fifteen feet from him. But he couldn't see her. Linda felt like laughing but her heart was going like a frog's throat and her mouth was a badger's arse.

McKraken stopped at a white gravestone with a big angel sticking out the top. This time he was facing her but she had crouched down. It looked like he could see her but he couldn't. The moon rolled over the wall behind them and the whites of McKraken's eyes shone in the reflection from the angel. It was just him and this stone glowing in the graveyard. Everything else was black as a pit.

He bent down and planted the rose somewhere and

straightened up. There was a wind getting up and the twigs were clicking together like crabs' legs. Linda was thinking, Is that it? Is that all there is? Him bending down and sticking a flower on his dead wife's grave? Then McKraken started doing this Indian dance. Round and round he was going on the grave and murmuring low. It got louder and louder and he was saying over and over:

Hey for company. Ho for company. Happy would I be if a body brought a body spinning back to me. Poppies in a green field; flowers on the hillside. Hey for company. Ho for company. Happy would I be if a body brought a body spinning back to me. Poppies in a green field; flowers on the hillside.

Every time he done a revolution Linda could see his fingers shaking in moonlight. He was half bent over. Fear was consuming Linda. A white frost was forming over the whole place, from the epicentre of McKraken's dancing feet and he was getting louder and louder. Anybody out on the main road must have been able to hear him. Two wood pigeons flapped out the trees, breaking branches. When they flew over McKraken they turned to ice and plummeted, shattering like glass on the gravestones. Linda wanted to run but couldn't. McKraken heard and seen nothing. He was hypnotised by his own dance. He kept right on going round and round, crunching his feet on the frosting ground and singing out.

Hey for company. Ho for company. Happy would I be if a body brought a body spinning back to me. Poppies in a green field; flowers on the hillside. Hey for company. Ho for company. Happy would I be if a body brought a body spinning back to me. Poppies in a green field; flowers on the hillside.

Then WOOSH!!

This THING pulsed up out of the ground.

My God, my God, Linda was going.

But she was speaking through her teeth and paralysed. She tried to move but couldn't. There was no danger that he could see or hear her. He was enraptured by this *Thing*.

He was raving barking mad now and dancing faster. The Thing was all white like the frost and floating towards McKraken. He looked up and smiled. Linda was gravestone still with terror and they cuddled. McKraken and the Thing cuddled. Linda couldn't believe it. His hand was alright now! It was working its way up and down the Thing's back and all over its arse.

Next moment, they moved away. He was walking. She was floating. They walked down the path like it was a sacred Chapel and they were getting married, then disappeared in the fog.

Linda tried to run but she fell and cracked her skull off the edge of a gravestone. She got up and ran like fuck, slipping every couple of steps, was bumping off gravestones and whimpering and slipping and crawling and digging her fingers in the grass to pull herself forward.

The next morning she was bruised all over her arms and legs. She sat on the edge of the bed and thought about what had happened, trying to put it down to some crazy dream but she couldn't.

Linda had had her first connection with the other world.

The first time you fall in love is the strongest, everybody knows that. Linda fell in love when she was thirteen. And people often laugh at that kind of love. Donny Osmond was big at the time and he had 'Puppy Love' out. That was the perfect song for her and Nampa. That was his name. Nobody knew where he got it from.

And they called it Puppy Love. I guess they never knew . . .

That's what Linda would sing when people laughed at her obsession with Nampa McIntyre. They would go everywhere together holding hands. He took a right slagging off his mates but he was just as much in love with Linda as Linda was in love with him. He was slim with dark hair and dark eyes, really good-looking, and all the sisters used to try to steal him off Linda. But he only had eyes for her.

Nampa was a boxer. And a great boxer at that. He was two years older than Linda and when you're thirteen a guy at fifteen seems like a man. Light years away. He was the best boxer in Danny Duffy's Boxing Club at the time. They were talking about him representing Great Britain at the Olympics. He was one fight away from being ABA champion. His mates tolerated his buying flowers and chocolates and walking past the corner boys at Mitchell Street holding hands with Linda. But they had to give him a right shirriking when he started taking her to the Celtic games.

It was Celtic and some team like Forfar who were playing. This was the first game Nampa took Linda to. It was going to be the first of many and they were going to take their wanes when they got married. They would go in style cos by that time he would be World Champion and they would buy a house up in Blairhill beside the snobs. He took her to that game first cos it was a cert that Celtic would win. There was no need even to go to the game except for the day out. There wasn't going to be any drama except for how many goals Celtic might score against this diddy team. It was set up to be a walkover. And it was. Celtic won eight nothing. Linda loved it cos Nampa hugged and kissed her every time Celtic scored. It was the best day they had. And the last.

After the game Nampa took Linda down to the beach. They had the Shows there. They played the puggies and the penny waterfalls while the rest of the Coatbridge boys went on the waltzer. It was getting dark.

When you hear of bad stuff happening at Celtic games you always expect it to be a Rangers fan attacking a Celtic fan or the other way round. But this time it was a Celtic fan that came up to Nampa and tried to take money off him. The guy was in his twenties at least and Nampa was that wee and innocent-looking the guy didn't expect the *bam bam bam* on the face, nose and chin. Down he went like a bag of spuds. Out like a light. A crowd gathered as Linda and Nampa moved off to another arcade. He waved up to Glenny and Doc on the Big Wheel and they shouted some abuse down about him being glued to his bird. They'd seen the commotion below but they'd no reason to think it was any of their boys that were involved. Linda was oh so proud of her boyfriend, the way he took care of himself. Without a thought he had automatically done what was necessary to get out of the situation. No more. No less. A true gentleman. She was holding him tighter now than before.

Up above on the Big Wheel, Glenny and Doc were drinking Buckie and looking down. Standing up and being brave, all that sort of stuff. Rocking the carriage about. They thought nothing of the crowd that moved into the arcade where Linda and Nampa went. From the air it looked like a bunch of boisterous Celtic fans singing. They looked like they were walking fast but they were actually running if you seen them from the ground.

That was what Nampa seen as they poured into the Arcade. A waterfall of coins crashed down as they bumped past the penny push. And as the coins crashed to the metal Nampa seen the bloody face of the guy he gave the boxing lesson to.

Far above in the world of the moon and the stars Glenny and Doc trundled over the fairground below. They didn't hear Linda scream as a knife plunged into Nampa. Once only. Clean and sharp. He fell down as the feet scattered and his head was hanging out onto the ash. Linda stood with her hands exactly an inch in front of her face screaming and screaming. The breath was warming her face then her skin would chill as she breathed in. Then she would scream again.

She was an alarm going off at the shattering of her dreams. She wanted to but she couldn't go near Nampa. He wanted to shout for her. To at least see her but he couldn't move his head. He looked up above him at the inquisitive bodies gathering round. He looked beyond them to the blurring lights. Up, up, at a crazy angle through the bleepers and buzzers Nampa could see Glenny and Doc descend to the ground. They were punching on the safety bar trying to make the Big Wheel go faster and all the time they were looking down at him lying half in, half out the Golden Nugget arcade. A crowd of green and white jerseys were gathered round.

He's been stabbed, one of them said.

Linda was still screaming although she had lost a lot of the power in her voice by now.

The closer Glenny and Doc were getting to the ground the more Nampa was slipping away. Glenny got there first cos he jumped out the machine before it got to the ground. He shoved through the crowd and cradled Nampa's head. Doc ran over and got a hold of Linda. She was trembling in his arms. It was a weird situation with the buzzers and bleepers of the machines still going.

Come on, try your luck, said the wooden clown behind the glass.

The blood was gathering on the ash and it looked darker than what you would have thought blood should look like. Nampa was dying. Doc knew he was dying. In the distance they could hear the siren of the ambulance and the cops. Doc took Linda over beside him. Nampa looked up at Linda. He sang the first few words of 'Puppy Love' and laughed.

And they called it Puppy Love . . .

Nampa, you're a mad bastard, Glenny said.

Linda told him she loved him with her lips and Nampa died. His eyes were still open but his spirit had flown far above the world of the moon and the stars. Linda watched it go all the way up then fainted. She came to in the ambulance on the way to the hospital. Across from her, still and dead, was Nampa.

They buried him on the Tuesday. It was the first time anybody had seen Danny Duffy crying. His chance was lost too. The Olympics. Linda swallowed all the love she had and never really loved again.

Years later Linda met Brian. They went out for about a year and then Linda fell pregnant. It was a summer's day in July and I was watching everything from up on the roof. Nobody could see me. They had made a plan for how to tell Da. Oul Mary was there and Maw and the sisters were hiding in the rooms listening.

My Da and Oul Mary and Maw were in the back garden sitting at one of them wee tables with the parasol up and five chairs round about it. They were drinking – beer for my Da, vodka for Maw and Oul Mary. The sun was belting down. Even the flowers on the parasol were wilting. If you half shut your eyes it could have been France or somewhere nice like that. Not Coatbridge.

The only person that didn't know this was a plan was my Da. He just thought it was another summer's day with a wee can of beer and bees buzzing about in the climbing roses. My Maw went in and made up some nice salad sandwiches with plenty of cucumber on them. Fresh and crisp.

These are good, Alice, Da said. And he was munching through his second when out came Brian and Linda. It was good that there was two seats for them. The sisters took a big intake of breath cos they knew what was coming.

Can? Da asked Brian.

The can was already flying through the air when Brian nodded *aye* and caught it. He winked at my Da and crashed it open.

Nice weather we're having, Pat? Brian said.

Got to make the best of it while it's here.

Aye.

Aye.

So, how are yous two? Maw asked Brian and Linda.

Great, Linda said. *Great.*

Aye, great, said Brian.

Been fishing recently? Da asked.

But Brian hadn't been fishing for ages. He had a lot of work on. The sisters were by this time hiding under open windows listening for when Brian was going to tell my Da Linda was pregnant. She was only seventeen. Brian was in his twenties. My Da even spoke to him like a man.

They sat for as long as two minutes. Everybody nibbling on the special bad news sandwiches when Brian leaned forwards to speak.

Pat? He said.

The whole house held its breath. This was it. He was going to say it. He was going to tell him. Everybody shut their eyes.

Can I get a loan of your power saw?

No bother, my Da said. *It's in the cupboard.*

By the way, Linda's pregnant.

The first punch caught Brian on the forehead and his chair tilted back. Before the chair hit the ground again my Da was on top of him, punching. He'd knocked the table and the beer and the nice wee sandwiches all over the garden.

Once Maw and Oul Mary had pulled Pat off and Brian was wiping the blood from his face they agreed on a wedding. Soon. Half an hour later they were drinking beer and eating these other thank-God-that's-all-over sandwiches. To look at them you would have thought my Da and Brian were oul pals.

Linda was looking forward to getting married. What girl doesn't? But that night she went out into the garden at three in the morning. She lay on the grass and looked up into the stillness of the stars. She told Nampa she was getting married, that she loved him and always would.

Linda was the perfect wife. She had the house shone up like an MFI showroom. The breakfast lunch and dinner was always on the table at the right time. If you flicked your fag in an ashtray she would lift it, clean it, and put it back before you flicked your fag again. She was an automatic wife. They had kids and she had all their clothes ironed and shoes polished and laid out at six in the morning. She became an automatic wife in order to suppress the thwarted love she had for Nampa.

It went on like that for years and Linda became a byword in the town for good housekeeping. There's not much to say about that except that she led a pretty boring existence. Then something happened that was to change her life for ever.

She had an aneurysm.

At first it was this faint absence in her head. Like the way you feel when the flu or the cold's starting to come on. Then she started to imagine she was hearing a hissing noise. But she carried on with her housework and duties and never mentioned it. She never even thought about going to the doctor's. Then the hissing noise became a real hissing noise. She could even hear it in her ears. One night after Brian came in from the pub and she made him tea and cheese on toast with onion salt and just a sprinkling of pepper, she told him about it.

Brian was as good a husband as Linda was a wife. He done all the oul-fashioned things and handed all the money in so that the house could be a palace. Holidays in the sun. Cars.

The wanes were the first in our family to get all the things the posh wanes got. You might think he was a male chauvinist pig. But to Linda and most of the culture they lived in, he was a good man. Not to be judged by some other value system that simply doesn't apply there. It's a bit like trying to measure the size of the universe with an egg-timer.

Brian, there's this hissing noise in my ear.

In your ear?

It hisses every time my heart beats.

C'mere over.

Linda went over and he put his ear against hers. He might be a Joiner, Brian, who doesn't know much about medicine and biology, but he knew enough to panic there and then. And another lucky thing was Brian's Maw. She'd made sure that all her family got an education. Became doctors, most of them. She was one of the first people I can remember that broke the chains of poverty that the Irish brought with them when they came to the Brig. Best of luck to her for that even if she is a bit of an oul dragon.

So people helping themselves helped Linda. Brian was right on the phone to his brother, James, who was a doctor. He got his wife to drive him over cos he'd had a couple of drinks.

Brian, don't go to all that bother, Linda was saying.

But Brian sensed it. James came in and asked Linda a few questions before he done anything. Was she having headaches?

A bit. Now and then.

When did it start?

A month ago.

Did she feel it was getting worse?

Yes.

Only then did he look in her ear with one of them wee things that shines a light in and magnifies at the same time. Then he asked her to hold her breath and he put his ear against hers. After five seconds he packed his stuff.

Right, Southern General. Immediately.

Off they went to the Southern General. That's the main neurological hospital in Glasgow.

Maw and Da and Brian went. The rest of the sisters stayed on the end of the phone and got updates from Maw and then Da. It's hard now to remember how long they were in the hospital but it was three or four days without leaving. I was there too but nobody knew I was. Except maybe Linda. I was by the edge of her bed all the time. I was closer to her than anybody. And so was Nampa. We never spoke, me and Nampa. There's no need to speak here. Linda knew we were there and that comforted her a bit. The sisters used every ounce of will they had to save her life. They went to Mass every day with Oul Mary. And at night they done every spell in the book, every procedure that they thought might help Linda.

Linda had an aneurysm in a large enough vein in her head. The doctors said she must have hit her head on a sharp object when she was young. She couldn't remember the incident with McKraken. There was no question of operating. It was too deep into her brain. But they had a new procedure. What they could do was insert a tube in her thigh and work it so that the tube could be pushed all the way through her veins into her head. Once there at the place where thin artery walls had allowed a burst to take place they would blow up a wee balloon and seal off the leak.

The leak was getting worse and there was no time to waste. They decided to do it the next morning after they explained to Maw and Da what the procedure entailed. Linda was weakening by the minute. Maw, Da and Brian took turns at holding her hand by the bedside and going for cups of tea and a smoke and phoning the sisters to update them. Linda was crying. She had been alright but then the seriousness of the case hit her. She didn't want to die. She cried herself to sleep and Maw, Da and Brian, who had been at her bedside for a while, went out and managed to get a lot of their crying done while Linda slept. They never cried in front of her the whole time. They always talked about the future. What they were going to do when she got out and stuff like that.

They were out smoking and crying and not talking, cos this was beyond talk; there's nothing worse than a mother and father burying their own child. Linda woke up in the bed and found them not there. She was scared and for a minute thought that she might be dead already. But a passing nurse said hello and she realised she was alive. It's hard to explain the fear of death to people who haven't ever experienced it. It's nothing like fear itself. The fear you usually feel is the fear of life. When you feel fear, its ultimate function is to motivate you to take action to preserve your life. You have to go beyond that to experience true fear of death. The fear Linda was feeling was really profound regret. In fact profound isn't a profound enough word to explain it. The things she never done. And it was all spending time with her wanes and sisters and friends. The things she would never do. Those are only the thoughts that go with the feeling, but the thoughts can never project the power of the pain.

Linda was in spiritual agony. That's when she made her pact with God.

God, if You get me out of this, if You let me live, I'll never tell another lie again so long as I live. I'll never miss Mass and go to Confession every week.

Maw, Da and Brian came back in and they were happy that she was in better spirits. She even told them a few jokes. They laughed. Especially at the one where she said she didn't want a Mickey Mouse balloon in her head, she wanted a Daffy Duck. That night ended well.

But the next day didn't. The surgeons kept Linda awake

during the whole thing. It took six hours to manipulate this tube into position. When they inflated it, it never held. To make matters worse, the inflating of the balloon had opened the artery even more. They had to do something and they had to do it now.

Linda was all alone in a great white room. Sitting on a chair in the middle of it like an experimental monkey. They spoke to her through microphones asking her to move this way and that. Maw and Da and Brian looked in at her and she waved and managed a smile.

The doctors were going to have to cut the blood supply off to one side of her brain. That would definitely result in a stroke. There was a fifty-fifty chance that she could die. But if they didn't do something now she would die in the next two days. Linda agreed. Maw, Da and Brian said their goodbyes. They held her, all at the same time and hugged her. Then Maw and Da left Linda and Brian alone. As they did, the doctors gave her an injection. She didn't have to be awake for this one. Linda's strength ebbed away in their arms and Brian got an experience of what it might be like if she died. She looked beautiful lying there with her white gown on.

You'd be as well away for a cup of tea, the surgeon said. *This will take a few hours.*

Maw phoned home and Brian and Da got the teas. The sisters were crying but they regained their strength and some prayed and some done magic spells. Then they swapped round so that all the time there was praying and all the time there was spells.

It was four hours later when the surgeons told Maw and Da and Brian everything had went fine. She'd live and that was the main thing. It only remained to be seen how badly the lack of blood to the brain would affect her.

Linda could hardly move for the next few days. For one, the place was stowed out with flowers. And for another it was choked with sisters. And again she was trying out her body after half her brain had been shut down.

Across in the other room was Danny Connors. He had had the same operation but it went wrong. As Linda recovered, he deteriorated. But he had no sisters to come and lift his spirits. He had no family – none that wanted to take him in anyway. All he had was an oul mother who was too weak to go and visit him. The last Linda heard, he was took away to Hartwood. Linda vowed to visit him if she got out.

She did get out. The doctors were amazed that the only thing wrong with her was that one of her eyes didn't move. The rest of her worked great. The reason for that, the doctors said, was this: our veins and arteries come to an end and out of them are these other wee veins called capillaries. They meet at the top of your brain but don't have any function. In fact, the ones at the top are really joined but they're like flattened bicycle tubes. Sometimes, once in a million, these tubes can be forced open so that the blood from one side of the brain can feed the dying arteries at the other side. This was what had happened to Linda. Although the blood supply to the left-hand side of her brain was cut off, the blood was being supplied through millions of small capillaries from the right-hand side. It was well nigh a miracle, the doctor said. He'd only ever seen it in textbooks. The only thing was, she might end up in a wheelchair.

Physically Linda might not have changed much, except, as I said, for the eye. But in every other way she had changed. She hadn't forgotten her promise to God; she never missed Mass, and she never told any lies.

What do you think of my new hairdo? Geddy asked.

Linda looked up from the couch at the hair, then surveyed Geddy and gave her the answer she wasn't looking for.

You're too oul to have your hair as blonde as that. You look like a tart. That skirt is too short; makes you look fat.

Geddy stormed out of Linda's house as many were to do in the following months until they were able to put it down to Linda's illness.

The other way she changed is that she stopped being the Stepford wife. Once she was recovered enough for the sisters to stop chipping in to do the housework and get the kids ready for school and make Brian his dinner, Brian thought everything was back to normal. But it wasn't. He came in from work the first night Linda was on her own in the house and went into the scullery.

Where's my dinner, hen? he said.

Make your own fuckin dinner. I'm going out with Angie to the pub the night, was the reply.

It seemed Linda had took her vows to God seriously. Another vow she took seriously was to visit Big Danny in Hartwood.

Linda had a Magic Charismatic Leopard. He was five feet high. He was lime green, like teddy-boy socks with big black spots all over. He wore a pair of pink sunglasses and he was *coooool*. Her wanes gave her it when she got out of hospital.

Linda went out to her car one morning and sat him in the front seat, clunk click. Got some looks; big laughs. Wanes waved and jumped up pointing. Maws slapped and dragged them off, their faces twisting back to see the car.

Next thing she noticed was this leopard had powers. She went out to the car one morning and it was smiling in a million raindrops on the windscreen. Just when Linda was on a bit of a downer. She didn't want to, but this smile spread across her face like a Cheshire cat's.

That night she was going to Hartwood. Visiting Big Danny. She'd been going for over a year by this time. And her duty was repaying itself in a correspondent rise in her own self-esteem. Although her legs by that time were beginning to numb up a bit, she had reached such a good mental state that she now could handle any amounts of grief.

It was a weird place, Hartwood. First thing you noticed was the high fence on the railway bridge to stop the inmates jumping. Up till they erected the fence there was three dead bodies a year on the tracks below.

The last time she was there Danny had been on the drink. They didn't let him out. Angie usually went with Linda cos they were expecting her legs to numb up any time, the doctors said. Her and Angie plumped themselves down on Danny's bed. Danny was on a right downer so they drew him out of himself slow. He eventually grunted and rolled onto his elbow. His belly flopped onto the bed before he came to rest. He lit up a fag. Inhaled. Blew the smoke like a mad cherub slanty up into the yellow room.

Linda and Angie knew Danny was pished but they weren't letting on.

How've you been, big fellah? Linda said.

Aw, fuck me, man . . . it's slow in here. What a fuckin drag. These cunts get me down. Danny's hand swept the room like some Mafia boss. *Fuckin loonie tunes!* he shouted.

Then he cough-laughed himself flat onto the bed again. His belly was trying to find a centre of gravity. He looked pregnant with something big. The other loonies were hiding from the big man and a sadness painted itself into the walls. Danny fell asleep; Linda and Angie left.

This time was different. Angie sat in the back cos Green Leopard wasn't for moving. Angie cracked a smile and their three crazy grins followed the headlight beams into the east. They didn't talk much and soon they were up on the high moor road that leads to Hartwood. The bleak track above Glasgow is the last scene some people see before getting dubbed in Shotts Prison or Hartwood Asylum.

Victorians used to stick you in the loony bin for picking

your nose or scratching your arse. Your family would be black affronted that you were cookie-boo so they made sure nut-houses were in Nowheresville. You don't get anywhere more out the way than that moor. Spoo Key!

Angie and Linda were laughing. The rain was belting on the road like six-inch nails nailing the Tarmac to the moor and the Catseyes were staring rows of hari-kari cats' heads coming at them through the storm.

Shotts Prison, when they passed it, was drizzly through the orange lights like and American penitentiary.

Concrete's a good servant but a bad master, Linda said.

At least they cunts know when they're getting out, Linda. When the fuck's Big Danny getting out?

Linda felt one of her tirades coming on. She'd been prone to them since she left hospital after making her promises.

I'll tell you when! When the doctors and nurses stop playing fuckin God. I mean, you fling a cup off a wall – bang! five years added on. Not a fuckin judge or court in sight, just some specky bastard fresh out the doctor school. We'd be better off letting that mad Leopard say who's in and who's out.

Angie to this day would swear that the Leopard nodded.

They drew up at Hartwood Hospital. The Asylum. Victorian. Long dark empty windows and frightening sandstone. The Green Leopard blinked and smiled. He was going to like this.

Clunk clunk clunk, they all left the car. The gloom lifted. You have to buzz at the door. The attendant would let you in if you didn't look mental. So he thought two grown women holding up a lime-green, black-spotted, pink-sun-glassed Leopard in the icy Shotts night-time was normal.

Buzzzzzzz! And they were in.

The blast of heat hit them with the attendant's broad grin.

Hi aye, he said. And he was nodding like he had a Leopard the exact same five minutes ago.

There was the smell of pish in the air. In front was the now familiar sight of the long corridor disappearing to Ward One.

As they walked, patients crept up and were gone like ghosts into nooks and crannies discovered decades ago. Linda and Angie were looking through a membrane of reality into all the different perspectives of the inmates. Silence pressed on them from all angles, from watching pairs of eyes.

Leopard's magic started to work. Laughing twisted and echoed out from the shadows. Eyebrows lifted. Eye-whites showed. Faces creaked into smiles. Plenty missing teeth was the way to go here. Tombstone City in every mouth. Lopping tongues and squeaky gums. Linda, Angie and the Leopard gathered an army in the 200-yard walk to Ward One. The subtle commotion of sliding slippers permeated the membrane. Heads poked out of all manner of portals. Staff and patients were laughing. It was like the voltage went up in the lights and the whole building smiled. Leopard was a Messiah with his buzzing disciples shuffling and muttering in tongues and gums and slabbered lips. Linda and Angie were bearers.

This big laugh fired up like a passing jet. There was a wide-eyed pause and the dance continued. Big Danny bellowed at them and the Leopard. He was sober and tuned into their madness.

Ward One. They left their disciples pressing against the glass like a mad disassembled totem pole. They met the usual. Polite Fred Heathcliffe.

Hello Linda, hello Angie, how are you this week? Fred pushed his head politely forward, waiting for an answer. He seen the Leopard and smiled. *And who might this be then?* he said.

He's our new pal, Fred. D'you like him? We're looking for a name for him Fred. He needs a good name. He's a good boy, so he is, Linda said.

Fred ambled off, promising to tell Danny as soon as he gets

the right name for the Leopard.

Fred's Maltese. I'm sure when he was seven and swinging in some park in Malta, by no mad stretch of the imagination could you predict he'd end up in an asylum in cold North Lanarkshire.

Angie, I am Heathcliffe, he said one night, trying to explain. When he talked about Cathy it was real tears. But this night he was smiling. Magic Leopard seen to that.

Then, up came a patient called Jig a Jig, waddling.

Sweet, sweet!

We've none.

Cigarette, cigarette!

Danny chucked a fag. Jig a Jig pulled the bottom lip out at Leopard, lit the fag and shot off holding the fag at the burning end, mumbling. He was Pakistani. Ethnic Cleansed from Uganda by that mad bastard Amin in the 1960s. Scotland was where he came. Lost it before touch-down. Been here since. What nightmares hurl behind his two-word language of *sweet sweet* and *cigarette cigarette*?

Linda and Angie took Danny out that night through energy and laughter. Everybody waved. Danny made the lime-green, black-spotted, pink-sun-glassed Leopard wave back.

Lucky they had Green Leopard cos Hartwood stuck you on a downer. It was the building and the atmosphere.

Big Danny was calling the other loonies all these names. He had a different voice for each word like every word was said by a different person.

Idiots, eejits, dafties, lunatics, mentally disordered, insane, mad, lunatic, moonstruck, of unsound mind, not in one's right mind, non compos mentis, deprived of one's wits, deranged, demented, certifiable, mental, abnormal, psychologically abnormal, sick, mentally disturbed, mentally ill, of diseased or disordered or distempered mind, unbalanced, brain-damaged, raving mad, stark raving mad, mad as a hatter, mad as a March hare, off one's rocker, gaga, loony, declared insane, certified, away with the fuckin bongos!

They took him to his wee Maw's and had a bit of a crack. She suggested Pink Panther as a name.

I mean, c'mon! A fuckin lime-green Leopard called the Pink Panther. Are you mad or what? said Linda.

All the road back Angie and Linda fired likely names out. None fitted. The sky cleared and stars were out. The Catseyes looked more sane. They got back to Hartwood at eleven. The Leopard was grinning at the moon.

Night Linda, night Angie, Danny said. He leaned in the car, lifted up one of the Leopard's ears and whispered to it. *Night Hartwood,* he said.

Linda and Angie turned to each other and laughed the way you laugh when you've discovered the perfect name.

Night Danny, Angie shouted.

Next week, Fatty, said Linda.

Buzzzzz! The door opened. Danny waved. *Click!* The door shut. Linda and Angie zoomed off past dark windows interrupted here and there by pale moonlit faces. Some waved at the Leopard, others stared until the tail-lights disappeared.

Linda had a Magic Charismatic Leopard. He was five feet high. He was lime-green, like teddy-boy socks with big black spots all over. He wore a pair of pink sunglasses and he was *cooooool*. His name was Hartwood.

It wasn't long after that Linda lost the use of her legs, as the doctors said she would, and Angie started driving her about.

Linda and Angie

Geddy's got all her stuff and is about to leave when there's a noise from out in the close. *Bump – bump – bump – bump.* The speaking of muffled voices.

Shh! Sounds like Linda, Donna goes.

And Angie probably, says Geddy.

Bang – bang – bang! the door goes again like the polis. Wendy creeps over and looks through the letterbox.

It is them.

She opens the door. Angie comes in huffing and puffing, sitting in the wheelchair. She's a bit healthy-looking for a cripple.

They want to put fuckin rockets on these things, she goes.

Linda comes in crawling fast with just her hands. Like a crazy dwarf. Angie stands up out the wheelchair, stretches her legs, wiggles her arse and slumps down on the couch. Linda clambers up into the wheelchair climbing in with her arms tensile and her legs like rags. That was their standard joke. None of the Girls even notice it any more when Linda and Angie pull stunts like that. They do it all the time. In fact, if they had come in with Linda already in the wheelchair, then the Girls would have took notice.

What kept yees? says Donna.

I know – yees are late, Geddy goes.

We were up visiting Big Danny.

Linda's first to notice the new fireplace. *Check out that monstrosity,* she goes.

Nice fireplace, says Angie.

Where's Caroline? Linda wants to know.

Out getting biscuits, says Donna.

Out, goes Wendy.

For vodka, Geddy says.

That's three answers at the same time. Angie nods like she understands. But she doesn't. She couldn't make out what they were all saying. Linda wheels over to the monstrosity and picks up a pair of boxer shorts.

What's all this? she asks Donna.

Bobby's clothes.

What're they doing lying there? asks Angie. She's making her way over and leaning down holding on to Linda's chair to see the shredded clothes.

She's burning them, says Geddy all excited.

Oul Mary said we'd to . . . Donna says.

But Linda and Angie get it now. They cut Donna off mid-sentence.

The spell – right! Angie goes.

Nice! goes Linda. And she chucks a pair of boxers in the fire. *Whoosh!* Up they go in flames of many colours.

Fuck sakes, chuck another pair of knickers on the fire I'm freezing, says Angie.

Angie flings some more on. Wendy's getting all excited. She's jumping up and down clapping like the wee school lassies she teaches.

Talking about freezing, guess where Stacie Gracie's head is? Wendy says.

Don't get too excited, Gwendolyn, you might pish your pants, goes Angie.

Wendy and Angie exchange glares. Wendy recovers her enthusiasm but Angie still glares at her as she speaks.

But guess where anyway? Wendy says.

Linda and Angie shrug. Like they don't care. But they do. And Wendy knows that so she tells them.

It's in the fr— She's stopped mid-flight cos the door swings open and Caroline comes in, carrying some carrier bags.

Surprise! they all shout.

Caroline gets all emotional. Her eyes water up and they gather round hugging her. Linda's rubbing the flats of her hands to warm them up on an autumn night. She's developed all these ways of greeting people from a wheelchair since she lost the use of her legs. As they hug Caroline and kiss her they also search for what she's got in her bags. I suppose if any action symbolises what my sisters are all about it's that. The fact that they can genuinely care about another human being while simultaneously caring about themselves. Caroline manages to say something through the tears and the crowd of bodies.

Oh, thanks for coming.

Och, it was nothing! they're going.

But Caroline is still very emotional. *I don't know what I'd do without yees so I don't.*

They hug her tighter and that does it. She bursts out crying and they let her go. Let her pour it all out. She's standing with her head going up and down with every sob. Angie goes over and holds her. Holds onto her, in fact. No, that's not it. Angie goes over and lets Caroline hold onto her, that's it.

Don't you worry, everything's going to be alright, says Angie. She's patting Caroline on the back with a maternal rhythm as she speaks in a soft voice.

Get her a cup of tea, somebody, Linda says.

Aye, throw it over her face; hide these tears, goes Angie.

She's pulling Caroline in tighter and after a few seconds

gives her an Angie-special bear hug. Caroline laughs and recovers a bit as she struggles free. Then she remembers something not too good.

G-g-guess who I think I seen down at the shops?

They all shrug and look at each other like the answer might be printed on one of their foreheads. Caroline gives them the answer.

Bobby.

You're seeing things, says Linda.

It'll be your mind playing tricks on you. Happens all the time, offers Geddy.

Geddy goes on about how she was like that for a year when Shaun left her. Every guy she seen from a distance she thought was Shaun. They've half-convinced Caroline she was seeing things when Wendy remembers her phone call last night.

That's right, Bobby phoned me last night. Nearly forgot about that.

They could choke Wendy for that. They all look at Caroline to see if that's too much. If the edge she was on has slipped away and she's falling down into falling down.

What did he say? Caroline goes. Her eyes come up two or three watts as she moves towards Wendy. The glimmer of hope is sweeping away in the back of her pupils like a lighthouse beam far out at sea. On the shores of Donegal.

He just went on about McGoogan.

Did he mention me? Caroline says.

Wanted me to persuade you to call him off.

But Caroline doesn't give two fucks about McGoogan. She's got tunnel vision on what Bobby said to Wendy. What he sounded like. If there was anything in his voice that hinted he was prepared to come home and start all over again.

Did he say anything about me? Anything?

Just about McGoogan.

What was his voice like? Friendly? Was it friendly?

Sounded scared actually, goes Wendy.

Scared! That could be nervous. Was it nervous? Did he sound nervous?

Know the way you go when you've met a new man and you can hardly talk to him on the phone cos there's bats in your belly?

He wasn't nervous. He was scared.

But how can you tell? How do you know that for a fact?

I know scared when I hear it, Caroline.

The Girls can see what's happening. Wendy's unwittingly leading Caroline down the wrong garden path. Donna's in there first.

Stop talking about him, Wendy. You'll put her off.

But Wendy's stuck now. Caroline's not letting go of her.

Did you mention me? Caroline asks. She's got Wendy by the upper arms and is pulling her in.

Caroline! shouts Donna.

Did you mention me? Caroline repeats.

She's manic now. Wendy's saying nothing and Caroline's trying to shake an answer out of her. Wendy closes her eyes and lets her head flop up and down. Her hair brushes against Caroline's forehead every time Caroline shoves her back. And it brushes against it upwards every time Caroline pulls her in.

Caroline! Six Black Candles, Donna says.

In fact, she more barks it than says it, Donna. But there's no reaction. She goes over to her but she's still not listening. She's not listening at all. Wendy doesn't know what to do. Angie gives her a forward nod of the head and cut gesture. Wendy answers Caroline.

No. He didn't mention you. He was only concerned with McGoogan.

If she's not over the edge, she's got one foot hanging over, Caroline; into the abyss of abandonment. That's a sea that's deep and cold. Caroline attacks it from a different angle now.

What about the wane? He must have mentioned the wane?

Wendy shakes her head for no.

He must have! His own wane! He must have said something?

Wendy remains silent and Caroline starts crying again. These are bitter tears. Not the ones with the love of her sisters swimming in them like shoals of summer fish. The tears have fire and alcohol in them. And illicit sex. And a feeling that lives in the throat just at the base of the neck. Angie takes Caroline away from Wendy, hoping that will break the electromagnetic field of obsession. Caroline slumps into a chair trying to hold herself together.

Forget it, Caroline, says Angie.

See what you've done now, Wendy? goes Linda.

I can't go through with this, Caroline cries.

Donna reaches over and rubs her hand. It's a sight, Donna's long white fingers tipped with black nails. Like arrows pointing all the wrong ways. They look even more weird sliding over a pair of ordinary hands. Hands that have washed dishes for years for the same man. That roamed every inch of his body and thought there were no other hands roaming. That never had a blip in their marriage. That never wrung in anguish. Sometimes pain can be an inoculation for the big tragedies in your life. A couple of good heart-breaks early on in life can help you cope with a desertion. But Caroline never had any broken hearts. Everything went smooth for her in her life, and that's the problem. For folks like that, when it comes it's a flood. A tidal wave. A disaster.

You're past the worst bit, says Donna.

Caroline doesn't want to be past the worst bit. She's lost her bottle. They all pitch in about how they're all there for her. This is her night. They're doing it all for her. But the more they say, the deeper down she's sinking. Their words are lead weights and she's going down. And she's drowning. Eventually Angie steps in.

Leave her alone. You don't have to do it if you don't want to, Caroline.

Caroline talks to Angie. Only to Angie. The others aren't in the room.

Everything's whirling round and round in my head. I can't stop it. It's just wshhh wshh wshh! I can hardly handle just getting up in the morning as it is. Yees've got me into this and . . .

Donna puts her arm round Caroline but Caroline flings it off. Donna looks at Angie.

Let her make her own mind up, Angie says.

Stay out of it, Angie, goes Donna. But she remembers it's Angie and apologises with her face as soon as she does. Angie used to take carry-outs off guys down Mitchell Street, after all.

C'mon Caroline! Linda says.

Going to fuckin leave me alone?

Donna does an okay-okay! gesture. Caroline breaks down sobbing. Rolling into herself like a dog's tail. The sisters move in again and it's hugs all round. With the hugs and the silence Caroline decides she will go through with it after all. I mean, there's that head in the fridge and all the trouble the Girls have gone to. Not to mention Maw and Oul Mary who should be round any minute. Everybody's put a lot of work and effort into this on her behalf. She decides she's going to do it. Once the waterworks have subsided a bit, Caroline breaks free, stands up, takes a deep breath, and goes over to the fireplace.

Well, sisters! D'yees like my new fire?

Fabulous, Wendy says.

It's great, says Geddy.

It's a mess, says Linda.

Donna picks up a pair of the boxer shorts and dangles them

in front of the flames as she speaks. *Just right for setting your man's pants on fire,* she says.

It's like having the Vatican in your living room that fireplace so it is, says Linda.

Caroline takes the boxers off Donna, spins them round on her finger by the elastic a couple of times and flings them in.

It's amazing the satisfaction you get. Every time I remember them on . . . on that carpet, I fling another pair on, she says.

She must remember them again cos she picks up another pair. Black with wee airplanes on them, and flings them on. Time for a song, Angie decides.

One pair at a time, sweet Jesus, that's all my pants are to You . . .

Caroline's relaxed now. The dread's gone for the time being and she's back on the right path. She opens the ASDA bags and takes out the vodka, the supers, the biscuits, the masking tape. Donna grabs the tape and starts pulling long strips off it.

Right! Caroline?

Donna raises questioning eyebrows at Caroline. The question being, will we go ahead with the Six Black Candles? Caroline thinks for a minute. Looks round the room. Looks at all the sisters. The six of them there. Donna, Geddy, Wendy, Linda, Angie and herself. She looks at the boxers smouldering in the fireplace. These are her sisters. They've been there her whole life. These are her sisters. Through thick and thicker and thin. These are her sisters. What's a man compared to this? These are her sisters. Blood is crazier than water and water's always moving on, always spreading out. Always getting thinner. These are her sisters. Fuck it. Love bursts through all the wee arguments. And the big ones. All the infighting and bitching and outfighting. These are her sisters. Caroline shoves a Roman thumb up. The Gladiators roar with tickled pink delights and move into battle. Strategy. It's been handed down. From Oul Mary to Maw to daughters. Caroline asks what about Maw and Oul Mary.

When are they coming?

We'll get it all ready for them, Donna says.

Lock that door in case any unwanteds come in, goes Angie.

They're in action now. Caroline and Wendy drag the new rug into the middle of the floor. They position it just nicely and stroke their chins at it like women buying furniture. They adjust it slightly this way a little bit, that way a big bit, and are satisfied. But they're not women buying furniture. No siree. That's definitely not what these Girls are. Nothing farther from the truth. Angie gets the masking tape and draws long lines from it, sticking them up on the wall beside the ones Donna's already done. Donna is mumbling from a black book. It's ancient and it's beautiful, the book. Covered in black crow feathers that, from a distance, look like fish scales. That's quite appropriate cos in this game nothing is ever quite what it seems.

Linda helps Angie to start the process of taping the lines onto the carpet. It's all up a bit, down a bit and over here. Linda's using her wheelchair as a compass to arc out the tips and intersections of the Pentangle. It actually looks quite good on the surface of a stars and moons carpet; royal blue, gold stars and moons, white tape. They copy the diagram Donna produces from her book and draws on a bit of oul scrunched-up paper. In the absorbing precision of work the room falls quiet but for the odd crackle of the flames and the smooth rip of tape being took back up, moved or unwound off the roll.

Water

In the middle of the holy silence of preparation Wendy jumps up holding an Irn Bru bottle filled with murky water.

Taa naa! she shouts.

She frightens the shite out of the rest of them. When they eventually focus on the water there's wee bits of stuff floating and swirling about. The water is yellow. Some of the floaters are white as maggots, others are brown as worms. Others, there's no telling what they might be. There's a pause as the Girls recognise what's happening. What the water is all about. It's Donna that gets it first. The significance of the water.

Where d'you get it? she goes.

Out the stream.

Donna is as excited as a new rabbit on a green field of grass and clover.

Out what stream? Out what stream? No . . . don't tell me, don't tell me! she shouts.

Wendy gives her a you-know-what stream look.

No! Donna says.

Her mouth falls wide open and the others are half doing their jobs, half watching Donna and Wendy.

I di-id, says Wendy.

She resorts to the long vowels of her schoolkids and waits

for Donna's next barrage of questions. Inviting them.

Down the oul graveyard?

Wendy nods and Donna rushes over and kisses her a smacker on the lips. Linda wheels back to let her past.

Above the bodies? Donna asks.

Wendy does a smug no-not-above-the-bodies movement with her head.

Right at the bodies? Donna asks.

Wendy does another even smugger no-not-right-at-the-bodies head-shake. Then she stares at Donna daring her to see where she got the water. And Donna sees it. It comes alive in her head like a wee movie. She sees Wendy leaning into the stinking water and glug-glug-glugging the bottle till it's full. Letting the air bubble out till there's not a breath left inside. Yes, Donna sees it but she doesn't believe it.

No way? Donna breathes.

Mm-mm, says Wendy.

The bottom?

Right at the bottom, says Wendy.

She starts peering through the glass so that her face is bent out of shape behind it. The room to Wendy is grotesque with all these misshapen entities going about their macabre business. Donna just has to announce this. This is great news. The best water for the spell by far. Wendy has excelled herself here. Surpassed all expectations.

Everybody! Everybody! Donna shouts. She gets their attention. She takes the bottle off Wendy and holds it up like a trophy. Like a chicken with its neck wrung. She waits till they've all got their focus on it. *She got it below the bodies!*

A big cheer for Wendy. Geddy's mouth opens like a cheer but nothing comes out. Just a big silent O. She resents Wendy too much to cheer. And now here's another resentment to keep her going.

Aye! You're not even a pretty face, Wendy, says Angie.

That's a compliment from her, believe you me. For the first time in a long time Wendy is the beaming centre of attention. The first sister. Sistero numero uno. The hub of the wheel. They get back to their tasks in the fading light of Wendy's glory. Linda wheels up.

How's the teaching going?

It's good but it's stressful, Wendy goes.

But Angie butts in. Dessie's misadventures at school, like setting fire to it in the first year, have led Angie to hate teachers. All their holidays and easy job marking jotters with big red pens.

Should try working for a living, Angie says.

Listen to big Mamma Monday Book! says Wendy.

She only said that cos she was rising on the confidence of being number one sister. The accord that the water that washed through the corpses brung Wendy is gone. Angie is almost on the attack. Angie only knows one way to attack really and that's with her fists and her feet. And sometimes a wee nod of the head in the direction of your nose. She stands up and fires some abuse out at Wendy.

You try getting a job when you live down here!

I did live down here, Angela, Wendy goes.

Wendy and Angie square up but Linda wheels in between them. A quick change of subject.

Are you still teaching that wee Lynch? Linda says.

Wendy answers with one eye still on Angie. Just in case. You never know with Angie.

I'm up to here with him.

Can you not get him expelled?

Wish I could. I'm suicidal with the wee bastard.

I'll bring a big rope over and you can jump off the veranda with it tied round your neck, says Angie.

But it's not as bad as it sounds. It's got a tone that says, I'm willing to let this drop if you are. There's a sprinkle of humour over the words like icing sugar.

He groped her tits! Donna butts in with.

Aye, right! Did he, Wendy? says Angie. Suddenly welding herself to the defence of her sister who seconds ago was her enemy.

He did, says Wendy, *and all he got was suspended for three days.*

Linda asks Wendy to tell the Girls what Mrs Lynch said when Miss Cotton got her up the school. Wendy blows her body up as close as Mrs Lynch's size eighteen as she can and does a pretty good impersonation of her growling voice.

He feels my diddies all the time. It's just a wee bit a fun, hen.

All the Girls laugh and Angie describes how she'd choke the life out the wee cunt if he ever said boo to her.

People don't know how to bring wanes up these days, she says.

That gets a pot-and-black-kettle look but nobody's willing to tip the scales the wrong way again and mention a certain young man called Dessie.

Linda thinks it amounts to sex abuse, letting a wee boy grope his mother's tits. Even if it is just for a laugh. Geddy thinks the Social Work should look into the whole family. She's heard rumours about them for years. There's even talk that the youngest lassie's the oldest daughter's baby. By the Da.

I always said there was something not right about them, says Donna. *You just have to look at the size of their foreheads. Fuckin weirdoes.*

It's like incest that, feeling your own Maw's tits, goes Geddy.

Linda tells them how she met the very same wee bastard last week up the swing park. Linda was coming home from the betting shop, there was a good outsider in the three-thirty at Doncaster, and there he was. Dogging school. Straddling the path like an ineffectual John Wayne. Red hair and freckles on his face like a galaxy that doesn't know where to go.

When she passed he snuck up behind her and shouted in her ear. *Who shoves ya, baby!*

Then he tried to shove her down the stairs. But does the bold Linda not just apply the brake on one side and spin right round and catch the wee nyaff a cracker right on the jaw. Down he went like a shot dog.

He got up again and I span right round the other way and caught him an almighty crack on the other side of his face. Down he went again. His feckles were still floating in mid-air when he hit the deck.

They were all wondering in the back of their minds why this wee shite was using patter from thc 1970s. Surely people must have forgot about Kojak by now?

That's right, Kojak's *back on Sky, I'm following it,* says Caroline.

So that's what the shaved heads and lollipops are all about, says Wendy. She's realising how the wanes in her school have been using the same patter. Seemingly *Kojak*'s a cult among the young ones these days.

I know what I'd do if he felt my tits, says Geddy.

They all look at her. Cos they know what she'd do if he felt her tits too. And they look at her while someone makes their mind up to do the punch line. Angie does a Geddy impersonation. She opens her blouse down to the middle and hikes her skirt up till her knickers are showing.

What you doing on Saturday night, son? I like a man with red hair and freckles.

Aye, right yar! Ha fuckin ha. Hey wait till yees see this! Geddy says. She produces a big dod of turf from a shoe-box. It's the size of a dinner plate. She goes to put it on the rug.

Whoa! That's my new carpet! Caroline screams.

Geddy's standing like an eejit with the turf hanging over the side of her hand.

Get and ASDA bag somebody, Angie says.

Linda whizzes into he scullery and bangs a few cupboards.

Caroline tells her where the ASDA bag stash is.

In the cupboard under the sink.

She gets a bag, zooms back and gives it to Geddy. Angie goes back to her taping. Geddy sits the turf on the floor on top of the ASDA bag to the smiles of admiration from the Girls. It certainly is a good dod of turf.

That's a cracker, says Caroline.

All the turf-orientated compliments you can think of fly about as they settle into their work again. Angie sparks a wee chat with Linda.

How's Clare doing at school, Linda?

Aw, she's doing great. Loves it now. They do horse-riding and everything. And they take them away up the mountains. Abseiling in wee abseiling boats. They get elocution and all. Teach them how to talk right an everything.

How to speak correctly, Wendy instructs.

Aye right, Wendy. How to talk posh, Linda says in a posh accent.

I wish I had went private with my Dessie, goes Angie.

They can't help it. It's a knee-jerk reaction. Automatic at the absurdity of the idea. As soon as they've got some control of the situation they fall quiet. Stifle their laughter. But it's still there in the air and Angie can sense it.

What? goes Angie.

And *boom!* They all let their laughing out. Some louder than others. Linda's first to be able to speak.

Sorry, Angie, I just had a picture there of your Dessie playing polo!

Imagine giving him a big mallet, says Donna.

Or Dessie playing the piano, laughs Geddy.

She infects the others and they laugh too. It's not exactly fighting talk. The danger is that Angie goes over the top at being the object of ridicule. They really should be more careful but they can't help it. Inspired by her success as a stand-up comic Geddy goes for it and gives a crazy impersonation of Dessie playing the piano.

Doiing doiing doiing.

Who knows what key she's in. She's lifting her hands high in the air and dropping them onto the imaginary keyboard. A gorilla would have had more grace. Angie is not pleased. And sisters are just like any other animals. They've got pack-hunting instincts. When they see a wound they go for it. Wendy's in there.

Even if he was okay I don't think he's got the academic prowess.

Prowess! He's not a fuckin panther, Wendy. And he is clever, for your information, my Dessie, screams Angie.

By now she's right in Wendy's face. The sisters are loving the cabaret. Wendy considers Angie's comments with the gravity of a schoolteacher before she replies like she's talking in a debate on the nature of intelligence.

If you count intelligence as using the knowledge you have to your advantage, then I suppose he is clever. But they don't take just anyone in these schools, you know.

Like your Nikki? Says Angie. She says it like she's got something up her sleeve.

She's exceptional, my Nikki – right?

A fuckin donkey could pass its O-levels if you forced it to study morning noon and night.

Donna pitches in with a few hee haws and the rest of the Girls join in. A whole cacophony of donkeys. Wendy lets them die down and comes back at Angie.

Standard Grades actually.

What? says Angie.

They sit Standard Grades now, not that your Dessie will ever see one of those.

My Dessie's top of his class.

Murderers, rapists and junkies! That wouldn't be hard!

But as she says it Wendy knows she's crossed over the line.

She steps back one pace then another watching the volcanic lava rise in Angie. Linda wheels between them. There's something about a wheelchair as an instrument of peace. A metal contraption that can get more respect than Jesus. Linda appeals to Angie's sense of reality.

You must admit they're all crazies in that Secure Unit, Angie. A wet mop with its head shoved in a bucket would be cleverer than most of them.

Angie stares at Wendy for a while over the top of Linda. She cools herself down and speaks directly to Wendy.

Aye. He won't be in there for long but so he won't. Mark my words.

Linda pulls Angie gently down to the rug to resume the taping.

His panel's this week, Angie says. *They'll let him go. They'll see from the lies that the polis tell that he never done it, my Dessie.*

Linda thinks Dessie's better off in the jail where Angie knows where he is and nudges Wendy to come in on that too. Wendy does. She agrees. It's safer in there. There's more crackpots down Mitchell Street than in the jail anyway. Caroline thinks he's better away from the drink and drugging that goes on in these flats. It's like a jail here only there's no wardens. No polis even.

This is a fuckin hell-hole, Caroline says.

They reach full agreement on that one. That's when Wendy decides she'd better check her car again. Out she goes onto the veranda. Her car's alright. But the cold air calms her. She decides it's better to stay out there for the while with the orange sodium lamps and chiming ice-cream vans and baseball-capped Neds four floors below. They wouldn't see her if they looked up and she stepped back. She'd be a shadow among a million other shadows. She takes in some big Buddhist breaths. Raises her arms up as she inhales, dropping them as she exhales. And every time she gets calmer. It's strange to think that serenity can be had up there above the poisoned scheme and Linda and Angie finishing the pentangle inside through the dark surface of the glass. Very strange. Inside she's being discussed. She can't hear them. But even if she did it wouldn't matter. Arms up. Inhale. Hold for twelve. Exhale and drop arms. Do the lock that flies up. Hold for four. Repeat.

Check out that mad cow, says Geddy.

I'll take her posh head off one of these days so help me God I will, says Angie.

The very thing – do we need the head yet? says Linda.

She remembers why they're here and wheels towards the scullery. Donna puts her foot on a wheel.

Keep it in there the now, Donna says.

Should we not take it out?

Will I get it? says Caroline. She starts moving towards the fridge.

Leave it, Caroline, shouts Donna.

Caroline stops dead in her tracks.

Got to keep it nice and hard, goes Donna.

Don't want it getting all soggy and gooey, goes Geddy.

They'll be here in half an hour anyway, Donna says.

Caroline comes back into the living room. Wendy comes back in from the veranda. Calm and slow. She sits without uttering a word. Her body folds, her arse sticks out a bit and her palms come to rest flat on her upper thighs. She's the picture of tranquillity. There's nobody else there. The Tao of ignoring every cunt.

Where's the candles? Linda wants to know.

But nobody answers cos the door goes.

Bang – bang – bang!

Oul Mary's History

Oul Mary looks like your typical oul Irish hag. She was born in Donegal but came here to join members of her family that had came over in the tattie famine. She never lost her Irish accent. To see her you'd think she was really bitter and hard. But she's really quite soft and inside she's got a caring heart. Except for when it comes to Protestants. She doesn't like them one bit and had tried to pass that on to her children and their children. With limited success.

Along with Donna she's the one who forces the spell forwards. She's got great belief in it all and has more power herself than the rest of the Girls put together. She acknowledges Donna as the seventh daughter of a seventh daughter. She likes that Donna is trying to learn Irish Gaelic. Oul Mary can speak it fluently.

Her dress sense leaves a lot to be desired. In fact, when she comes up the closes people hide cos they think she's a gypsy selling clothes pegs. What she has is a right earthy wisdom. Some might say too earthy. She coughs up phlegm and swallows it as least once a minute and she picks her nose and eats it. Here's one of her gems of wisdom.

You can't hold your farts in and expect your breath to be rosy.

Out of all the women there she will be the one most unchanged by what happens. She's seen it all before. And worse. She believes when she returns back home to Donegal all will be well and she's made sure all the Girls know that she wants to be buried there.

Oh, when I go back home to live I'm going to sit by the fire all day drinking buckin vodka.

You've been saying that since I was a wane, Mother. Give it a bye. You'll never go back home, Maw would always say to her.

There's one other thing about Oul Mary. She doesn't swear. Instead of fuck, she says buck.

Oul Mary and Maw and some of the oldest Girls were brought up in the Slap Up. The Slap Up was the biggest populated area in Coatbridge. At the turn of the century it had a bigger population density than New York. The buildings were three high. Four houses on each landing. Twelve families in each close. Average size ten.

On Turner Street there was eighty-two families. There was hundreds of families in the Slap Up. Five thousand people in one square. One building. Craig's building was across from the Slap Up. Then you had Dundyvan Road, Bannan's Land, Woods Land. Then you had The Black Bull. Then there was a wee land called The Wee Black Bull. Landlords owned these lands and built, or *slapped up* buildings on them and filled them with Irish immigrants. There was a fortune to be had. But not for the immigrants. Beside The Wee Black Bull was the level-crossing then there was The Big Black Bull. Across from The Big Black Bull you had Hawthorn's Yard. All them lands became known as the Slap Up although technically it was only the Turner Street Square that qualified.

There was steelworks and ironworks and foundries and

mines. Everybody lived their lives to the factory buzzers. Every surface outside your house was covered in a thin film of black soot. The stench of chemicals, that would be banned the day, hung in the air. If the immigrants thought they were coming to a better life it was only relative to the 1846–7 famine. It was a better way to die, coughing your lungs up on a bar floor than digging up roots in the iron frost of a Donegal winter. From one hell to a slightly more bearable hell, helped on by the emotional anaesthetic of whiskey. Paradise, it seemed, would have to wait. At least until they built Celtic Football Club and named that Paradise instead. That was a Paradise you could get to much easier. It was only eight miles to the west. You could walk it. And many did. That's where the Irish were allowed to become Irish again, together. Instead of the scum that they were in the rest of Scotland. Dirty fuckin Fenian scum. Oul Mary came into the Slap Up when it had been up and running for seventy-odd years.

The trains ran right through the level-crossing on Dundyvan Road. They never stopped for pedestrians. Manys a drunk man was killed there. Right behind St Augustine's Chapel the train went. You'd hear it as you were in at Mass. Protestant drivers would blow their klaxons all the way past. The bell used to go sometimes as you approached the crossing. You'd stop with your pram and the train would run across. Although there was a lot of people gathered there you couldn't talk to them. The noise was too much and the ground shook.

When the cattle were coming for the slaughterhouse they'd walk down Dundyvan Road. Shitting all over the place. And so would you be if you were off for the slaughter. The cows used to sometimes escape all through the backs and into the closes. It wasn't unusual to wake up in the morning and see a sheep staring at you. It wasn't unusual either for a slaughtered sheep to be hanging above somebody's sink. If you'd a big family and one happened to wander into your close, and there was nobody looking, well! Sometimes you'd get up in the morning and the sheep would be everywhere. The wanes used to all run after them. Spend the morning chasing them. It must have been quite a surreal image, all them dirty wanes chasing sheep through the filthy tenements in an industrial landscape. If you made a film about it nobody would believe it. It was the cows the wanes felt the most empathy with. Their big eyes sad as the Sorrowful Mystery. Poor cows. They could smell death when they got off the trains behind the Chapel. And as the men whipped them all the way down Dundyvan Road they were thinking about escape. Some ran for the brief freedom of a close and into the high walled prison of the Slap Up.

There was always one escaped into Bannan's Land or Woods Land. It would run all round the place with everybody after it. The wanes used to all think it was great. They'd kid on it was a bull that was chasing them. Wave a red rag at it. Screaming through the backs with the clatter of the animal's hoofs out in front. The poor thing was terrified.

They drank their tea out of bowls, the Irishmen. Big bowls like soup bowls and saucers. No handles. The wanes always got cups but the men had a saucer and a bowl and they drank with both hands round it like they were trying to keep out the cold. A giant bowl of tea. That tradition was lost when the next generation was brought up on cups. Oul Mary was a cup person. The first step in the process of one culture trying to obliterate another. But it never completely succeeded because the Scottish were in the middle of resisting their own culture being obliterated by middle-English values. In some ways you might say the arrogance of the English helped save the Irish immigrants' culture in Scotland.

Oul Mary's Maw and Da never got on well. He was a very jealous-natured man. He worked in the slaughterhouse and had a killers' gun that he took home with him. All the killers done that, to clean them and oil them and make sure they worked right. That was the tools of their trade. His was a revolver that he used to shoot the cattle through the head.

She was away to a dance this night, Oul Mary's mother. She wasn't a bit of a woman or anything like that. She believed in the sacrament of marriage. The dance was up at St Mary's and it was mostly women who went there anyway. There was some young men but they were only there for the young unmarried girls.

She was on her way home just after leaving her pals at Dundyvan Road. Her man was hiding in the trees.

When she passed he fired a shot but missed her and it went into the tree. As she turned wondering what the splintered bark and the bang was, he fired another one. That shot clipped her on the leg and down she went moaning like a cow in the slaughterhouse. She never went dancing again. We've come a long way from them days to these of zero tolerance. Nobody said anything about it and the polis were never involved. Oul Mary was a baby at the time and was lying in bed snoring with her two sisters Lizzie and Sarah.

In the middle of the Slap Up, the O'Rourkes had a scrapyard. That was the start of the Irish going it alone. Getting their own confidence. An independence in the country that held their own country in a vicelike grip. There was a lot of politics about in them days. Who knows where it all went.

Oul Mary and her two sisters worked there from when they were fourteen. They were all well into their twenties by now though with families of their own. It was just a bit of spare ground with barbed wire round about it. Down at the oul Boltwork. There was no roof and they'd to work in the rain and snow and the frost. What they done was strip and burn the insulation off oul copper cables. It was a right dirty job and they were black with burnt cable and oil was engrained in the cracks in their skin. They worked like horses all day. The Irish bosses, it seemed, were as bad, if not worse, than the British ones. And as Oul Mary would say for the rest of her life: *There's none worse for ripping you off than your own kind.*

When O'Rourke came in he didn't say good morning nor nothing. He just grunted and told them to get on with their work. He wasn't paying them to sit about on their fat arses.

Ignorant bastard, Lizzie would mutter.

Mary (she wasn't oul then), Sarah and Lizzie used to unload the wagons dead fast to keep warm. And anyway, the day went in much faster.

Murren Nicol worked there too. She was getting married and they had a big chanty poe and they wheeled her all round the Slap Up on this chanty poe in a big wheelbarrow. All the girls from the scrapyard. She came from the highlands, Murren. Tomintoul. She was a Catholic too but oh so different from the Irish ones. She took the whole religion thing too serious. And she talked funny.

The day Murren was getting married all the women in the Slap Up wore big long evening dresses. Alice (Maw) was standing on the corner of Turner Street waiting for the nice ladies to pass.

Mary, Alice's Maw, put on a big lilac dress and a fur coat and came down the stairs. The wedding was in the Pie Shop a hundred yards along the street but Mary got into a taxi. She went past with the window rolled down and threw some coins out to the kids on the corner. A scramble. Alice and her pals were standing like rag-pickers and there was Mary throwing out pennies to them. That was when Alice got her first taste of nobody being worse than your own kind.

Eventually Alice and the rag-pickers got their own back. At the wedding a big fight broke out. It was like Lanagin's Ball. Murren got hit right on the head with a bean tin. Her head split open and she was rushed away to the hospital. The hospital was nine miles away in Glasgow. As the commotion went on, Alice and the rag-pickers snuck in and rifled the pockets of the wedding party. The men had hung their jackets neatly over the backs of the chairs before punching lumps out each other.

Poor Murren, and she wasn't the full shilling into the bargain. There she was in the Casualty with blood running out her head and these beans all down her white wedding dress.

She'd went into the Pie Shop with such glee and hope for the future, and she'd left it, her day ruined by an anarchic tin of beans. As she passed the wanes gaping up at her through the commotion she was sticking her hands out like she was trying to push them back. Like she was trying to push the world back and there in the white palms of her hands were these black lines running everywhere like tree branches on a winter street. The dirt in the Slap Up never left you. You ended up passing it on to your offspring and they passed it on to theirs. It was written all over their faces so that an Irishman dressed in a suit was either dead or the accused, and an Irish girl dressed in expensive clothes was a prostitute or a prostitute.

Murren moved in with her man to a single-end below Oul Mary. She had no luck at all, Murren. None at all. Oul Mary said it was on account of her taking nothing to do with the wee spells and potions and lotions the Irish had. The Craft was spurned by the Highlanders. They done straight Catholicism. Two years later Murren's man was dying. His lungs were packing in. Worked in the mines. Usually men got to their fifties before their lungs packed in but here he was in his late twenties and they were two brown paper bags.

He was in the box bed down the stairs this night and Murren came crashing in Oul Mary's door. Mary was stoking up the fire. It was getting dark and the flames were licking the ceiling. Oul Mary was caught up with them and dreaming but to this day she remembers what Murren said.

Mary, Mary, what like's the Deil? What like's the Deil?

What in the name of Christ are you on about, woman? said Mary. She always had trouble understanding Murren's Highland accent.

The Deil? What does he look like? asked Murren, all agitated.

Aw, Oul Nick?

Aye, Auld Nick!

Well . . . he comes in all different forms, Mary said.

She was about to go into one of her spiels about the Devil but Murren butted in and stopped her.

I've seen him! I've seen him! Murren babbled.

Mary blessed herself, so did Alice who was in the corner listening to every word.

What did you see, hen? Mary asked Murren.

I seen a big black shiny thing crawling in underneath the door.

Och, it's your imagination, Murren, said Mary. But you could tell by her face she never really thought it was imagination. When it came to the Devil Mary took the thing deadly serious.

Mary walked Murren back down the stairs to her single-end. There was a silence then a scream. Her man had died.

Murren had a wee boy soon after that and Mary used to look after him. Murren, after three years, fell in love again. She was going to marry this second man called Abraham.

Abraham's mother was right bitter. Wee Free Church. And even though Murren was a really nice woman that wouldn't harm a fly, the oul woman never liked her cos she was a Catholic. If the truth be told, the Highland Catholics were just like the Wee Free. They were anything but Free and took the world far too serious. Murren married Abraham anyway. He was a nice man with a big beard. Exactly what you'd expect an Abraham to look like.

Murren and Abraham's mother were fighting all the time. They shared a big two-roomed flat just outside the Slap Up. But Murren visited her Irish pals every day. Murren was not having a happy time of it. The oul woman was snapping at her every chance she got. She told Oul Mary and Mary, without telling Murren, done the Six Black Candles on Abraham's mother.

The oul crone took not well and she was dying. As she was taking her last, Murren went into the room. You see, Murren was never sure if it was the Devil she seen when her first man died. It could have been God or a guardian angel. But there's one thing she was certain of. She was certain that oul Maggie, that was Abraham's mother's name, was going to hell. If a bitter oul bastard like that wasn't going to hell then everybody, the whole world, murderers, hookers, polis and lawyers, were going to heaven. Murren figured that at the moment before she died Maggie would see the Devil. Murren would ask her what he was like, and if he was nothing like what she had seen sliding under the door of her first man's deathbed room she would be happy. She could assume that he would be in heaven resting in peace.

So, the death rattle was on the oul woman and Murren dashed in, pushing some of her family aside.

Maggie! Maggie! What like's the Deil? What like's the Deil?

They say the oul woman died with a look of terror on her face. They brought the coffin in from the close where it had been waiting. Murren, lacking the satanic description she needed to set her heart at rest, sat all night at the coffin. She wanted to know what the Devil looked like. She loved her first man. She wanted him to be in heaven. As soon as the Devil came in under that door to take Maggie's spirit away she would know.

She woke up in the middle of the night. There was a wee man sitting on top of Maggie's coffin with his arms folded. He stared at Murren but said nothing and never changed his serious expression.

Murren went running over to Oul Mary's. She burst in and dragged Mary out her bed.

Mary! Mary! Get up. Come over quick there's a wee man sitting on Maggie's coffin.

Mary went with her, asking Murren to describe the wee man over and over as they walked through the night. When they got to the death house there was nothing there.

Sure as God, Murren goes, *I heard a noise and I opened my eyes and this wee black man with green arms and legs was sitting on the coffin with his legs and arms crossed looking at me.*

The family were gathered and they were listening. This was serious. They knew all about Mary and knew that she had some kind of powers. Some kind of insight. Mary paused and sensed the room. She was dousing for evil. After a while, a serious thrill ran through her.

Go and get the priest, said Mary.

Murren ran out without flinching even though Maggie was a Protestant. The family were okay with it too. And the Wee Free hates Catholics more than Jehovah's Witnesses do.

Murren came back with oul Canon McDonald and he blessed the room and said it was Murren's imagination. *It was the deceased asking for our prayers. Don't think any more about it.*

But Murren believed Oul Mary, not the priest. From that day on she was a happy woman. She'd seen the Devil and he wasn't the thing that came in under the door all them years ago and took her man's soul away.

Aggie Cox had red hair. It was like flames lapping over each other when she walked. From a distance she was the best-known woman in the town. Her red hair was famous as far away as Airdrie. If you had red hair it was compared to Aggie Cox's.

She took no shit off nobody and had a renowned right hook. She knocked dozens of men out over the years. But still, I don't want you to get the wrong idea, she was a beautiful-looking woman. She married a Protestant and nobody had anything to say about that. Big Brian Macgregor was his name. A nice big fellah. She was pregnant but that's nothing, she would have married him anyway. They were in love. But she died soon after she had the wane, Aggie Cox. She fell off the Vulcan drunk. She bet Eddie Duffy that she could tightrope walk across it and fell. She fell into this wee brook beside the railway.

Brian was with the polis when they went and shone their big light into the brook. There was Aggie Cox's hair all floating on the surface and red as sunset. Her fingers and her face were pushing through the surface and her party frock was moving in and out with the current. In and out like bellows. There was all these wee flowers growing about the place. Like they were waiting on Aggie Cox to fall and die. Under all that there was rivulets of diluted blood making their way down the brook to the river; to the sea.

And ain't that where we all came from anyway!? said Brian.

Clouds of blood puffed out from the back of her head.

Like a painting, he said, *like a fuckin painting.*

And then he started crying and didn't stop till the funeral was over.

When Oul Mary got her cleaned and dressed up in her coffin, Brian said she looked beautiful dead. Oul Mary, amongst other things, washed the bodies. Aggie Cox told Oul Mary from the dead to watch over her young son and Oul Mary agreed to do that. It's the least she could do for the girl with the best hair in the town. The wane was only months old at this time. Months. His name was Joseph.

So Jeannie Cox, Aggie's Maw, took Joseph in. No Proddie was bringing her grandwane up. In them days there was nothing much a man could do if he wanted to keep a wane. It would have been considered strange. Mighty strange. And to be honest, Protestants weren't made entirely welcome in the Slap Up unless they had strong ties to a Catholic family. Brian had just lost his. They last they heard of Brian Macgregor was that he died of the drink somewhere in London. In actual fact, what happened to him was that he flung himself off the bridge at the Houses of Parliament on the anniversary of Aggie's death.

Jeannie Cox brought Joseph up well but there was always that wee bit missing. She could never shake off the fact that the wane was half-Protestant. There was always something not quite right, like tatties boiled without salt. Having said that, she done him alright. He had everything except love.

Joseph grew up and joined the British army. Jeannie put that down to the Proddie in him. Anyway. There was an accident and he got out the army with a wad of money. Thousands, they said in the Slap Up. He moved back in with Jeannie and by this time he never cared if she loved him or not. He was a quiet young man who never shouted nor fought. But when you spoke to him you felt, if he had to, he could kill a man.

Jeannie Cox was always trying to find his money. In the Slap Up nobody used a bank. Partly cos they had no money and partly because they were British institutions. Everything

British was tainted. The whole scheme waited on the day they could get back home to Ireland and then sadness would flee away. And hope, they believed, would sing its triumph.

Jeannie Cox was in his room every time Joseph was out at the pub, searching. He caught the TB. Jeannie kept him in the room. She wouldn't use any of his stuff. Scrubbed the door and the floor round about the room with caustic soda. Cleaned everything with Vim. Never spoke to him. It was more because she couldn't get into the room to search for his money than the fear of catching TB. A quarter of the population of the Slap Up had TB at any given moment. Joseph was like a prisoner, only he never had the fellowship of other inmates. The only person that visited him was Oul Mary. She said it was to say prayers but all she done was tell Joseph stories about his Maw, Aggie.

The finest hair you ever seen she had, son. She would have been the Queen of Donegal if her luck had been better.

I suppose the stories were prayers of a kind. Keeping Aggie's spirit alive. Keeping the promise she made to her after she died. Oul Mary never told Joseph about the promise.

Eventually he was took to hospital. That was what Jeannie was waiting for. She searched every inch of that room. Every inch. But she never found a thing. Not one single solitary penny did she find. She never visited Joseph, but Oul Mary did.

One night he'd been in hospital for months, Joseph. Back in the house Jeannie was poking away at the fire. She heard something and turned. There, crouched in the box bed was a flaming red-haired woman with white skin like all her blood had been drained. She bared her teeth and sprang, screaming, across the room shoving Jeannie up to her elbows in the fire. Five in the morning it was. Exact same time Joseph died.

Oul Mary was at his bedside. She knew he was going.

You're going to go now, son. Everything will be okay. You'll soon be with your mammy. Everything's going to be fine, she was saying.

She cradled his head in her arms and stroked his forehead. She wondered if she should say some prayers but she didn't want to embarrass him by saying Catholic ones, and not knowing the Protestant ones. Next thing, Aggie appeared in front of them and nodded to Oul Mary that it was okay to pray. He was at death's door just waiting for somebody to open it. Mary had to act quick. She blurted her words out.

Joseph, we'll have to pray now, d'you understand? It's time!

He let his head fall to one side. His breath was sour but that didn't matter. Bad breath, the smell of death, all that faded away to the beauty of dying with dignity. He whispered in Oul Mary's ear and she thought she was hearing things.

Take . . . the rosary from the wee pouch . . . in my pocket.

What, son? Could you say that again?

In my pocket . . . the rosary beads.

Mary dug in his jacket pocket and sure enough there they were. A beautiful pair of rosary beads. All red stones and well worn away. They had been prayed on, alright.

I didn't think you would have rosaries, Joseph.

They were my mother's.

Turned out he had said a decade of the rosary every morning and every night in memory of his mother. The accident in the army was when a private from Ayrshire had slagged him when he seen him praying on the beads.

Hey, Cox is a Fenian bastard.

Joseph said nothing.

Hey, Cox, put them away or I'll shove them up your arse.

Joseph woke up with his hands covered in blood. The Private lay twitching on the floor. He was in a coma for three weeks. The *accident* that Joseph Cox had was actually an *incident*. The rumours that he had money stemmed from that.

The whole of the Slap Up thought he was rich. He was, in spirit. For twice a day he prayed on the memories of his mother that Oul Mary had fed into him. Now he was going to meet her.

Mary started the rosary and took over in his bits when he was too weak to pray. His eyes said that he was a grateful and happy man. He died on the third decade of the Sorrowful Mystery.

Jeannie kept on looking for the money. In fact it became a madness with her. From the fire incident, or accident, Jeannie now had stumpy burnt fingers and melted arms. It was like rubber gloves had been burnt onto her arms. She spent the rest of her days and nights lifting the floorboards and digging under the building looking for the money. Thousands, they said it was in the Slap Up. Thousands. She digs and she digs. Her own unhappy grave.

One night in the Slap Up some woman was running about saying that a wane had went missing. It was one of the Donnelly wanes. It wasn't like it is the day, when you immediately think paedophile. It was hard in them days for paedophiles because strangers in a scheme like the Slap Up would have been spotted right away.

After a couple of hours had passed half the adults in the scheme were out looking for this wane. The rest were watching their own just in case the gypsies were stealing wanes. That's who used to get the blame for stealing wanes. The Maws would threaten the wanes with the gypsies coming and stealing them. Looking back now it's easy to see how such an easy myth can be attached to something much more sinister. Paedophiles have been with us for ever and I'm sure they generated the myth. Why would gypsies want to steal wanes when they were good enough at knocking them out themselves? The only group that could knock more wanes out of their women than the gypsies were the Catholics.

Things were getting tense and Mrs Clarke went in to tell her man she was going to be out searching all night.

It's not looking good, Jim, she said.

She went in to check all her five wanes were sleeping fine. They were. Only there was six of them, not five. The missing Donnelly boy was snuggled up in the middle of the five Clarkes. Seemingly when Jim Clarke had shouted at the wanes to get to bed, the wee boy was that feart he simply went to bed too. The search was called off and Big Jim Clarke took a power for it the rest of his life.

Can you not make enough wanes yourself, Jim, but you've got to steal them and all?

Oul Mary eventually got a job working in the slaughterhouse. Luckily her Granda had long since retired and hung up his gun. She was always scared that he would shoot her. She worked there till Alice was up and married. Four of the sisters had died at birth. The other two were Margaret and Sadie. Alice was the seventh daughter.

Sometimes Alice used to hang about the slaughterhouse looking at the lambs. She went up to help after school and fed them mouldy bread and any good grass she could tear up on the way over. She never really knew what went on inside the building. The lambs were slaughtered every day and a new batch was brought in. It never occurred to Alice that the lambs were different. To her it was the same lambs every day. She never thought it was a bit strange there was a field in the middle of the blackened landscape. That was to be the last day she ever spent leaning over the fence and baaing at the wee lambs. Oul Mary looked at her from the factory and decided she was getting big. It was time for her to learn a few facts about the world. Grow up a wee bit. The facts of life.

Alice, come up here and you can help me with my work.

Alice had that day etched into her head. She watched the men shoot the animals through the head and saw them slump to the ground. Heard the buzzing of the saws that cut the carcases in half, with water and blood and bits of meat flying everywhere. Oul Mary's job was to clean the guts and scoop the brains out of the skulls and put them in a big pot. It was horror everywhere Alice looked. Oul Mary looked at Alice and knew that the medicine was working. Gone were the woolly lambs of childhood and in their place was carnage. Alice watched the women and men hook the cows up by the legs and lower them into boiling water till the fur stripped off. Some of the cows were still alive as they lowered them in. Then they lifted the cows out, got a big knife and sliced their pink bellies till the guts poured out.

Gradually, as the butchering went on, she started to recognise the bits as butcher meat. That was where it came from. The tripe came out covered in shit. A special squad of women took that away and scrubbed the shit off it. They cleaned it and she remembers one oul hag chewing on bits of raw trip as she worked. Alice swore she would never eat tripe in her life. Oul Mary was watching her grow up in one big leap.

One day, one of the Clarkes came back from the Merchant Navy and popped into Oul Mary's house. Here's how the conversation went.

Have you seen my Maw, Mary?

She's at the doctor's. Come in here and wait on her, son.

I can't. I've left my bird outside the close.

Oh Jesus Christ, bring it in the cats'll eat it.

That was the introduction of the word Bird to the Slap Up.

Oul Mary

Caroline comes back into the living room. Wendy comes back in from the veranda. Calm and slow. She sits without uttering a word. Her body folds, her arse sticks out a bit and her palms come to rest flat on her upper thighs. She's the picture of tranquillity. There's nobody else there. The Tao of ignoring every cunt.

Where's the candles? Linda wants to know.

But nobody answers cos the door goes. *Bang – bang – bang!*

Angie and Linda roll up the carpet quick and bundle it in the cupboard. Wendy wanders about everywhere looking for a hiding place. She eventually shoves the bottle of graveyard water behind the chair. Caroline stands nervously near the door waiting for instructions. Geddy stuffs the turf in the ASDA bag, runs into the scullery, and hides it in the fridge. Donna pulls a smile across her whiter than white face. They all flop into chairs and onto cushions assuming natural positions. Wendy lays the Trivial Pursuit out and starts asking questions. I know it sounds like quite a lot has happened but it only took seconds before Geddy threw the dice across the board. Caroline is still trembling at the door as the dice trundles to a stop. Five Geddy gets and she click click clicks her pink slice of pie round the board. Wendy's asking the questions.

History. What were the pyramids once covered in?

Shite, says Angie.

That gets a laugh as Geddy puzzles this one out by searching on the ceiling for the answer. At the same time Caroline's got her eyeball at the keyhole.

Can't see a thing, goes Caroline.

Geddy searches out her answer in the Artex on the ceiling. Comb pattern. Painted with white eggshell.

Pyramids. Pyramids. Pyramids. What are they again? They big triangle things? Geddy says.

Come on, hurry up, Wendy goes.

That's all Wendy's giving by way of a clue. Caroline lifts the letterbox, taking a deep inward breath.

Read the question again, says Geddy.

There's nobody out there, Caroline whispers.

Angie signals to Caroline to shoosht in case there is. Donna grabs the question from Wendy and reads it out in plain English to Geddy.

What were the py-ra-mids once covered in?

Snow, she snaps.

And that's it. They all burst into fits of laughter. Falling about they are. If there's anybody at the door they don't care now. Geddy wants to know what the fuck they're all laughing at.

What the fuck are yees all laughing at?

But that just makes them laugh all the more. They're all repeating the word 'snow' like it's a laughing mantra.

Snow!

Fuckin snow!

The snow mantra is the doorway to happiness hormones. They don't even hear the door going again in all the din – not even Caroline who's laughing but not too sure what she's laughing at. And she's not too sure if she wants to be laughing either. Not with a broken heart the size of the one she's got. Wendy recovers her composure first and sweeping her hair away from her face repeatedly like that's the very thing that's stopping her laughing, she reads out the answer to Geddy.

Marble.

Well, how was I to know! I've never been to China, have I? Geddy tells her.

Well! That's it. They all fall about laughing again. As their laughing fades, the knocking at the door gets louder. They look at each other and choke back the last of their guffaws the way you choke back the last bit of melted chocolate.

Who is it? Caroline asks the other side of the door.

The Queen of buckin Sheba. Who d'you think!

The whole room relaxes and they flop into their real selves again.

It's Oul Mary, Caroline tells them. She opens the door and Oul Mary comes limping in with her knurled walking stick and her wee red plastic tranny stuck to her ear.

Oh my oul back's giving me gyp. I feel like a cracked bone in the jaws of a scrapyard dog. She's got a way with words, Oul Mary. A poet.

Was there anybody at my car, Granny? Wendy wants to know.

How the buck should I know? They all look the same to me, cars, Oul Mary says.

It's a Ford Focus, goes Wendy.

Like it's unique among cars. A square car in a round fashion hole. But Oul Mary's stopped listening to her. She's looking for a seat to plant her arse in. Donna's first up and giving her hers. Donna wants to be like Oul Mary more than anybody. She watches every movement Oul Mary makes. Every twist of the face and snort of the nose. Every squint of the eye and pick of the nose. Every flick or wipe of the snotters. Oul Mary rubs her arse into the wee seat.

You've a rare big arse on you, Donna. Sure you've heated this up better than Danny McGowan could have done.

That gets a wee laugh out the Girls. Danny McGowan was the fattest guy in the Brig easy. Donna doesn't bother cos she's not got a fat arse at all. Oul Mary fiddles with her wee red tranny. *Swiizzz* and *swooze* it's going as she gets it on the right station. And that station is short band. Police and emergency services. Death and ambulances a speciality. There's nothing she likes better than a good car crash, Oul Mary. Once she gets it right what exactly is happening on the tranny, she relays it to the Girls.

There's an assault down Mitchell Street, she says. Her eyes light up as she remembers something. When you're that oul, remembering something's an event that ranks with winning at the bingo. She turns to Caroline.

I thought I seen Bobby there with a bottle of Buckfast outside The Monkland Bar.

That does it for Caroline. Her obsession is back. She wants to know if Bobby looked drunk. There's only one thing worse than Bobby. And it's not two Bobbys; it's a drunk Bobby. All Oul Mary knows is that he looked rough, could be drunk; she couldn't tell and then there's another announcement about the assault.

No, sorry, it's not Mitchell Street. It's Southfield Crescent. Somebody stabbed. Serious. No, no wait . . . critical. Aye . . . definitely critical.

But Caroline won't leave it alone. *Did he notice you?*

I'm not even sure it was him but so I'm not.

Maybe he's decided to come back, Caroline says. She says it a third to Oul Mary, a third to herself and a third to the Girls.

Don't be so fuckin daft, Caroline, says Geddy. She's a woman who knows something about men. And Linda knows that if

Caroline gets tunnel vision about Bobby they'll never get the Six Black Candles done. Linda wheels over and grabs Caroline.

If he's coming back, he's coming back to do damage, Caroline Says.

How d'you know? You don't know that.

Oul Mary knows the way out. The way through this psychological impasse. The fireplace. If you're in trouble with a woman, always compliment her furniture. Gay men are the same.

Is that a new fireplace, hen? Oul Mary goes.

The Girls leap into action. Changing the subject degree by degree away from Bobby being at the shops. Caroline's obliged to answer the question from Oul Mary.

Aye. I got it . . .

It's a right mess, ain't it, Linda butts in.

A wee cup of tea, Granny? goes Angie.

Oul Mary rounds on her with a grin. *Tea? I don't want tea for buck's sakes. Vodka I drink.*

That's it. We're away. Side-stepping the Bobby issue like tango dancers. Caroline tried but she can't see a way back in. Angie wants to know where the other bottle of vodka is.

In the freezer chilling, says Donna.

Get me a vodka before I choke to death.

Angie opens the freezer door and fumbles about for the vodka. She takes it out but not before having a right good look at Stacie Gracie's head. A shiver runs right to her toes. It runs into the floor and right along the floorboards into the living room. It rises in the Girls. Angie wipes a tea mug and pours Oul Mary a big vodka. Happy out the side of her eye at the glug glug, Oul Mary switches to nice oul woman mode.

So how are you anyways, hen? she asks Caroline.

Well as can be expected, Granny.

Terrible so it is. Terrible.

I'm alright! Caroline goes. She's quite convincing and

anybody that didn't know her would think she was really holding it together.

What about the Sheriff Officers?

She still needs her ten grand to keep the house, Angie shouts in.

Donna joins in. *She's still not got it off Bobby yet.*

Has McGoogan not slashed the cash out that man of yours yet? Oul Mary says.

Caroline tries to talk but the words are jammed in that part of your chest where you feel grief. Just where the ribs meet. Oul Mary tries to cheer her up with a wee talk about how good McGoogan is at slashing the cash out of them that need the cash slashed out them.

St Patrick's pensioners used McGoogan to recover the day-trip money from McGlinchey Travel. Buckin rogue. Every penny we got back. And a free trip to Loch Lomond. Once McGlinchey got out the hospital.

Angie remembers something from the kitchen where she's been taking fly sips of the vodka; that's how she's taking so long to bring it in to Oul Mary.

Big John Doherty says he's sure he seen a guy like Bobby coming out the bank the day, Angie shouts in.

And that's it. The Girls nod. Oul Mary smiles and reassures Caroline that McGoogan'll get the money the night. Everything'll be alright in the morning. But the more they talk, the more worried Caroline gets. The more worried she gets, the more they try to tell her how McGoogan'll cut bits off Bobby's face. His ear maybe. His nose. And that's after drawing a few lines down his cheeks. Don't fuck with McGoogan. Ever! Caroline bursts into tears of half rage; half self-pity.

He'll be up here, Bobby. Full of drink. I know what he's like.

You don't even know if it was him my granny seen, goes Angie.

I think it might've been him. He'd that right rotten look about him, says Oul Mary.

Caroline's back on the Bobby trail. There's no way he's getting in that door. No way at all. Not after what happened the last time, and they all agree that there's no way he's getting in the door. Think what would happen if he burst in there and found himself amongst all them angry women? Then out of the blue, Wendy thinks Caroline's daft for buying a council flat like this in the first place. So at that Caroline starts bubbling. Linda puts Wendy in her place; they're there to help Caroline, not get on her case. And Geddy reminds Wendy that they can't all afford flats in the West End. That fracas gives Angie the cover she needs to slug some more vodka before she comes in with the mug half-full for Oul Mary. Oul Mary downs the mug of vodka in a oner and tips it upwards for another. Off Angie goes to fill the mug and her own gub.

Yees all been to Mass? Oul Mary asks and they all answer at the same time.

Aye, goes Geddy.

Mm mm, says Donna.

This morning, Linda tells her.

Half ten, is Caroline's answer.

St Patrick's, Angie says.

I was there at twelve, Wendy informs them. *There's a new priest.*

I was there, Wendy. I never seen you, says Geddy.

Geddy's on the attack again. But Wendy's more than the makings for her.

That's funny. I seen you down the front batting your eyelids at the priest.

Bang – and that's Geddy shut up for a wee while. But Oul Mary's getting suspicious. And she knows the surefire way to find out if one of them's lying.

Who took the offertory down then? She asks.

Biddy McGee and some guy, says Wendy.

Her fancy man, Geddy snorts.

Wendy can't believe Biddy McGee's going out with an ugly wee runt like that. And now Oul Mary knows both of them were there.

Right, you're right. You were there, Oul Mary says.

She admonishes them both. Linda gets an idea into her head. She'd thought Biddy McGee's man was in jail. And he is. Or was. Donna lets her know he was in Carstairs, the loony bin and he died in there. You could put the kettle on for what happens next. Every time somebody dies Oul Mary always says it. And this time it's no different.

Aye . . . there's people dying now that's never died before, she says.

So they moan and they groan and say, *Not that oul one again, Granny.*

She laughs and says, *Except for the Buddhists!*

She just found out last year at an ecumenical gathering that Buddhists get reincarnated. *They get re-carted, them Buddhists,* she says.

The Girls moan and they groan at the subsidiary jokes. Then Geddy decides to have a laugh at Oul Mary's expense. She nudges Angie to let her know she's about to go into action.

Anyway . . . I think you're jealous, Granny, Geddy says.

Me? About what would I be jealous, for buck's sakes?

Biddy McGee's got a man and you haven't, Angie goes.

Bright red Oul Mary goes and her lips purse to gather her voice so that it'll come out with some violence.

Buck's sake! He's the ugliest man this side of the luggie burn.

They laugh and make faces at her. She is not pleased. Not one bit is she pleased.

Look at her, everybody – look! She fancies Biddy McGee's new man! Wendy shouts.

As she shouts she gets up and dances round about the back

of Oul Mary's chair. Oul Mary stares at Wendy. At them all. She's acting like it's not bothering her. Like she hardly even knows what they're talking about. She gains some composure but her face is still tell-tale red and her voice is half an octave above self-conscious. She fixes her evil Donegal stare on Wendy.

His mother couldn't even love that fellah. Sure, he's got a face like a bulldog licking the pish off a jaggy nettle!

As I said, she's a bit of a poet, Oul Mary. And while they're all laughing she decides to launch an attack on Wendy. There's nothing like oul women when they get riled up. They've years of experience at frontal assaults. The best thing for an SAS division would be the body of a twenty-five-year-oul male and the mind of an eighty-year-oul woman. What a combination that would be! Rule the world.

Once the laughing has died to the occasional snort and sigh, Oul Mary comes away with it. *I hope you're not messing about with them Jehovahs still?*

No, Wendy says.

Liar! says Geddy.

Wendy's smile fell on the floor and she can't find it. Oul Mary throws another one.

Now who's red in the face? she says.

I gave it up, didn't I!? says Wendy.

She's looking about for support, but there's none forthcoming. None at all. In fact, Linda decides to join this little battle.

They were at her house last week, Granny, with their flowery frocks and jumble-sale suits.

Shut it, Superman, grunts Wendy.

Mistake. That weakness is a signal for the rest of them to attack. And attack they do – in that cutting way only sisters can. Sisters know more about manipulation than the CIA. Geddy sidles right next to Wendy. Touching shoulders. Oul

Mary is loving it. It's all entertainment to her. Life.

Come into the Kingdom, goes Geddy.

Get thee to Babylon, is Wendy's neat reply.

That leaves a puzzler on Geddy's lips. Her mouth is a squiggle on her face. Angie comes in a bit unsteady on her feet with Oul Mary's drink. Oul Mary sips it watching their performance. She has to ask. She doesn't want to, especially Wendy. But Geddy has to ask.

What you on about Babylon?

Figure it out, says Wendy.

She says it in her teacher accent. Geddy's not having it. But she doesn't understand it. She knows it's an insult but she can't tell what sort of insult. Is it an insult where you just laugh it off? Is it one where you have to come back with one just as strong? Is it one where you should escalate to see who is going to bottle out before the fisticuffs? Or is it one that is so bad that you have to go to fisticuffs as a reply? And Geddy hopes it's not the last cos she's missed her opportunity. There's no way you can go to fisticuffs after a remark has been unanswered for so long. Fisticuffs is an instant thing. A knee-jerk reaction. Or at least you've got to make it look like an instant reaction if you want justification. The time has passed.

No, you tell me!

That's all Geddy can come up with. But Wendy's still on her high hurt horse about the Jehovahs. Her true colours are shining through like a red light in a residential area. The sisters are loving it.

Don't criticise the Jehovahs till you've read the good book, Wendy says.

And that's all Geddy needs. It doesn't matter about her being the whore of Babylon. Not that she knows anyway. All that matters is the evidence coming out of Wendy's mouth.

See? See, Granny, she is still doing all that Jehovah stuff, Geddy shouts.

But Oul Mary's not listening now. She's tuned into the police reports again.

There's an accident down on the M8 . . . sounds serious.

Angie joins in on Geddy's side. Trying to get Oul Mary to tune into them. Angie goes for the long vowel thing.

I know, Wendy, what if any the parents found out? Angie says.

It's a free country.

Not in this house, says Geddy.

And not if you're working in a Catholic school. Jehovah! Jehovah! Geddy starts singing.

So they all start singing the Jehovah Jehovah song to Wendy. Wendy can't take it.

Jehovah! Jehovah!

Respect all religions, Wendy screams through them. Her head is on the end of her stretched-out neck. Her chin is out furthest of all.

Except them that claim to be the only true ones, goes Angie.

And them that want more than one per cent of your cash, adds Linda.

For a teacher and somebody that holds their own intelligence in high esteem Wendy's not doing too well. And there's nothing worse than a weak animal in the pack. They move in for the kill. Donna's first.

They always home in on single parents and nutcases, them Jehovahs, she says.

All Wendy can come out with are stock answers. Her brain's not working. Anger kills creativity.

Don't call them Jehovahs like that, she rages.

Jehovahs like what? Donna wants to know.

You know!

Geddy wants to know if this is what she means and starts chanting *Jehovah* all over again but this time augmenting it with a neat little dance not unlike the one Mud used to do to their hit single 'Tiger Feet'.

Anyway, I'm not a single parent, Wendy tells Linda.

Exactly, goes Linda. *You're a fuckin nutcase.*

When the Girls stop laughing at that one Wendy is still on the defensive. She doesn't realise that once she's disconnected from it all emotionally they'll leave her alone.

They were always alright with me, the Witnesses. Better than the Catholic Church anyway.

Oul Mary does not like that talk. Not in this house. Not on this night of all nights when they need all the luck they can get. Angie cheers Oul Mary on and hear-hears her. Cos she's got a point. They should all be sticking together this night of all nights. Caroline's night. Oul Mary dips into her extensive knowledge of theology to tell Wendy a few home truths about her precious Jehovahs. Like it being a well-known fact there's only about ten of them going to heaven.

One hundred and forty-four thousand actually, Wendy kindly informs her.

They'll be a bit lonely up there. Heaven's a big place, Oul Mary says.

Well! What if it's true? Wendy wants to know.

That gets a few laughs from the sisters. Angie lets Wendy know a lot of things might be true. That your man really loves you. That he doesn't lust after other women. That he doesn't run away with the nineteen-year-old babysitter. That UFOs are already here and under the sea with the aliens living amongst us; mainly as publishers, directors, film producers and TV agents. But come on! The Jehovahs the only folks in heaven?

It might be. It might be true. And if it is, where does that leave all you bigots?

Oul Mary comes in here with some more of her theology degree. Or it could be termed philosophy. Or spiritual-psychology (since the subjects of the thesis are actually dead).

And do you not think they've all claimed their places? All them Jehovahs? They'll not let some turncoat Catholic slide their arse onto a seat. You'd be better being a Protestant, hen. They're all going to heaven so they are.

Everybody laughs. Wendy, defeated, pours herself a drink. They cheer at her flinging in the towel. She wants to know if anybody else wants a drink so that she can judge how much arsenic she needs. Of course, being my sisters, they all want a drink. So Wendy's in looking out glasses and chipped mugs to go round. Geddy watches Wendy slug her vodka like it's water and wants to keep the attack going. Wants to grind Wendy down.

What about the Ford Focus? says Geddy.

I'm only having one, Wendy says.

Drinking and driving. A teacher and all? Geddy goes. *Tut tut.*

I'm having another one now so, na na na na naaa, Wendy says.

Wendy slugs her drink at Geddy and Oul Mary starts taking stuff out of her bag. A Catholic prayer book. A pair of crystal rosaries. Tells them there's an ambulance just away up the M8. It must be a bad accident. Linda tells Oul Mary how nice her rosaries are. Oul Mary holds them up and shows Linda how you can see rainbows through them if you look at the right angle. In the right direction.

How come they call them a pair? Angie wants to know.

Oul Mary throws her a stern eyebrow as she takes out a wee plastic Jesus. There's no way she's getting into a conversation about what, where, and why we call rosary beads what we do. No thank you. She'll just sit there and listen to the accidents. Watch the Girls puzzle out the unpuzzleable.

You're supposed to be intelligent, Wendy. How come they call them a pair of rosary beads? Angie asks.

Wendy picks up the beads and looks through them. *Tradition. Oh, you* can *see rainbows through them, Granny. That's great.*

Angie takes the beads off Wendy. And points out that there's millions of them. *How can you possibly call them a pair?*

Donna comes to the rescue and takes the beads off Angie.

They're nice beads, Granny, goes Donna. *Oh look, you can see rainbows through them right enough.*

Oul Mary's not too happy about them all handling the beads. *I hope that Wendy's washed her filthy Jehovah hands the day,* she says.

She takes out six brass candle holders and sits them in a circle. Linda takes the beads off Donna. She wants to know how they're called a pair and all. But Wendy grabs them back off Linda and lets them all know there's fifty-nine beads actually. To be exact. Angie tugs them back off Wendy and gives them back to Oul Mary.

Fifty-nine, is there? Well, that's hardly a pair then, is it? Angie goes.

I was right. Sounds like fatalities, says Oul Mary. She's got her tranny pressed against her ear with her shoulder as she arranges the objects in front of her. She looks round the sisters. Smiling. Loving the respect they give her.

C'mon, let's get on with it then. What are yees all waiting on? Oul Mary says.

I know! Get the carpet, Caroline, Donna orders.

Oul Mary pulls Six Black Candles one by one out of her bag and starts slotting them into the candle holders in a circle at her feet. Little brass sentries shining in the orange glow of the light coming in from the veranda. And she's chanting as she does it. It's Irish Gaelic she's chanting, but here's a rough translation:

I evoke the east and evoke the west. Blood and bone meet here. I call to what goes before me and what goes behind me. Bring to us the sun and the moon. Light of the beasts. The power of the stars . . .

What the fuck is she on about? says Geddy.

Caroline, being the oldest, knows bits and bobs of the

language cos she heard Maw speaking it to Oul Mary when she was young.

Something about blood, wood and bones. Or is it beasts? Donna buts in before Caroline.

Oul Mary bows to an unseen God. Or an unseen thing. Or an unseen being. Then she turns with her new Witchy head on to the Girls and asks them the all-important question.

Where's that we lassie Stacie Gracie's head?

In the freezer, says Donna.

Donna's eyes are lighting up like a cat. And she likes that, Oul Mary – the enthusiasm Donna's shown for the Craft since she was a wane. Ever since she thought she met Our Lady. Soon as she was born Oul Mary knew she had the gift. Oul Mary tugs Donna's cheeks.

Aye, Donna, hen, yees're learning.

We've had a great teacher, Granny, says Wendy.

All the Girls smile like primary-school children who kept quiet for the teacher while she nipped out for a fag. Oul Mary snaps out the orders and they all get into action.

Put the deep-fat fryer on and let it heat up.

Fuck, Granny, we forgot about that, Donna says.

She bolts into the kitchen, plugs it in, and turns it up to six. Caroline gets the carpet out the cupboard and rolls it back out. All the time Oul Mary's smiling. All the time she's smiling. They can take you out of Ireland. Starve you out. So that Donegal's just a memory of the things your mother told you about her mother. And a few visits. They can shove you in ghettoes and turn the name 'Catholic' into scum. They can build engineering works in your town and give the jobs to Protestants only. They can attack your schools and religion and whittle it down till it's only hanging by a thread. But there's some things they can't take away. Some things they don't even know about. And if they did? Would they believe it? Would they buck. Would they buck.

The tape has worked its way loose on the carpet. Linda and Angie get busy again lining it up. Getting it right. Linda uses her wheelchair as a compass. Holding one wheel steady and running the other round so that it scribes a perfect arc and shows an untaught knowledge of geometry. Of measuring out exact angles. Trigonometry. Angie marks the points with coins. Donna unrolls long strips of masking tape and hangs them on the fireplace for when they are needed. The scissors are lying amongst a pile of cut-up photographs. Black and white. Colour. Caroline and Bobby at the seaside. A visit to Dublin. Donegal. Wedding photos. All cut up. All shredded. So that their past is thin strips of reality punctuated by universes of space and emptiness. The vastness of pain. The infinity of loss. Donna flings the scissors over onto the carpet.

Meanwhile Geddy's wrestling a big dod of turf out of an ASDA bag. Oul Mary's lighting the candles. Geddy holds the dod up in the air and sticks her hip out the opposite direction.

How's that for a dod of turf, Granny!

Jesus, Mary and Joseph! I've not seen a dod like that since the Daniel O'Donnell concert in Dungloe, says Oul Mary.

She lights the fifth candle to the laughter of the Girls. She fancies herself a wee bit as a stand-up comic, does Oul Mary. But really she'd rather be a Witch. That's her true vocation.

That poof! Angie says.

I don't think he's a poof, Geddy says. Geddy doesn't want any man to be wasted.

You'd be able to tell right enough, says Angie.

There's not much Geddy doesn't know about men. Geddy's thinking of a quick retort. And if she came back a minute and a half later that would be quick. But she doesn't get the chance cos the door goes and they all freeze again.

Maw's History

By now you know quite a bit about Maw. But here's some things about her anyway. Maw's got a slight Irish accent but it's hard to detect. She picked it up off her Maw and now it's faded almost to nothing. She understands Gaelic but has all but forgotten how to speak it.

She's about sixty, I can't rightly remember the ages of people. Some would say she's fat, if they weren't standing too close to her. But for a woman her age she's not that overweight, I suppose. Her clothes are always smart, Marks and Sparks or something similar. She's always aspired to middle-class values. Admired doctors and teachers and people that talk with posh accents. She is a bit aloof when she walks, to the extent that Linda says Maw walks with a middle-class accent. I'd never thought of that before; that people's walks could have accents but I guess when it comes down to it they have.

As for the whole Stacie Gracie episode, it doesn't have any effect on Maw. The Craft is an ingrained in her as it is in Oul Mary. It's riding a bike to Maw. Her only problem really is that Da likes to take a drink. And he goes on and on when he's drunk. Talks pure shite. But she prays every morning that he'll stop drinking. She thinks that when he stops drinking he'll devote more time to his painting and sculpting. Then they can flit to somewhere warm and live an idyllic life. She made the mistake of having a conversation about it with Linda one day.

Aye, when your Da gets off the drink we'll sell the house and go to the Left Bank and he can paint.

What Left Bank is that, Mother? Linda asked.

The one in Paris where all the painters go.

He'll never get off the drink. The only Left Bank you'll see is the canal.

When Maw was born it was onto the floor in the front room in Turner Street. Once Oul Biddy came out of the room Danny went in to see his new wane. What he saw was Oul Mary and Alice, who had some size of head on her. Danny said later that he thought it was two women in the room and not a woman and a wane.

Where's the wane? he said.

On the carpet!

Jesus, Mary, he said, *that wane's got a bigger face on it than you!*

I know, Danny. The first thing she done was sit up looking for food.

Alice made her First Communion. There was her and Margaret Kearney. Marie Lyons leant them how to click their fingers when they were waiting on the priest any time they had to go to the Chapel for practice. She was from Dundyvan, Marie Lyons, and an only child. Maw and Margaret Kearney, Lizzie's daughter, were delighted when they got it right. But Marie Lyons hadn't taught them really to click their fingers. She'd taught them to click their nails off each other. Clicking the thumb nail off the forefinger nail.

When the Communion came everybody was more or less dressed the same. It was all standard dresses with white satin collars. Oul Mary put Alice's stuff on and a kirby here and there. One of the kirbys fell and her veil was away lopsided. But Oul Mary kissed it and kissed Alice on the cheek. She'd never done that before.

It was Alice and Margaret Kearney and Marie Lyons who were sat next to each other in the Chapel. They clicked their nails a few times and laughed. They thought that was magic. All through the Mass they sat doing that click click. People were looking all about trying to find out where the noise was coming from. But they sat upright like dolls. The teachers were furious, but too holy to shout and scream like they usually done in the school.

Then, in the middle of the prayers, Father Owens shouted out, *Right – who is making that confounded noise?*

Marie Lyons stood up and pointed at Alice. *Please, Father Owens, it was her, Alice Duffy.*

The whole place glared at Alice and the priest gave her a black glower then returned to the Mass. Alice hated Marie Lyons with a vengeance. Her head was down now and she was crying behind her veil. She kept staring into Marie Lyons's hand. Right where the fingers were clicking. Focusing all her hate into that point. Next thing the finger and the thumb started bleeding. Alice stared harder. They bled more. Blood was falling on Marie's dress. Wee dots like poppies poking through snow.

They all made their Communion and went back to the hall. They got tea, a scone, and a sausage roll. Then they got a cake of Lees Macaroon. All except Alice, that is. The teachers decided it would be fitting punishment for her clicking in the Chapel. Alice ran out crying and Oul Mary took her home. All she could think about was Marie Lyons falling down a hole.

Or getting stoated by a tram. Later Margaret Kearney came round and shared her macaroon bar with her. It cheered her up.

By the time Oul Mary traipsed her up the street to get her photo took Alice had put Marie Lyons right out of her mind.

One day about a week later Marie Lyons cut herself with a pair of scissors. She started bleeding. At first the teachers thought nothing of it. But the bleeding wouldn't stop. No matter what they tried to stem it with, it just kept on coming. She died. Bled to death on the staffroom floor. Alice was at the wake with her school pals. Marie Lyons lay in a wee coffin with a wee white veil. The same veil she had on at her communion.

In 1948 there was an eclipse of the sun. Everybody went out the backs of the Slap Up to say the rosary. Oul Mary took Alice to the Chapel. St Augustine's was packed and everybody was praying cos they thought it was the end of the world. Once the moon moved on from the sun and the sun shone out they proclaimed it a miracle and they all went back to their work.

The Slap Up had a massive party that night and their Scottish neighbours marvelled at the superstition these people had.

Alice and her pals used to play over at the slag hills. There was this wee iron fence there made out of steel. It had been about three feet high but over the years people had knocked it down. Alice and her pals used to lift a length of the fence and balance it on the wee sandstone wall. They'd play for hours like that. It was just like an iron see-saw. But that all had to stop when Margaret Kearney fell off and broke her leg.

On top of that, Raincoat Charlie was seen about the Slap Up again. The wanes had never seen him but he wore a big long raincoat. He met one of the O'Brian lassies over the Vulcan and opened his raincoat and showed her what was underneath.

Margaret Kearney had a big stookie on her leg. Alice was helping her up the stairs to her house. She lived in a tenement one up with maybe about twenty stairs up to it. It was the middle flat. Alice felt it was her duty to help, not cos she was her cousin but cos she was there when she fell and broke her leg.

They hobbled up the first flight of stairs and onto the landing. It was hard going cos her stookie was right up the whole leg and she couldn't bend it. They had a rest then struggled up the next set of steps. When they got to her door it was locked.

Oh, I don't know where my Maw could be, Margaret said.

There wasn't a soul in. That was unusual.

We'd better go round to my house, Alice said, *till your Maw comes in.*

Margaret looked at the daunting task of going down the stairs.

Put your arm round me and I'll help you down, Alice said.

They got down the first flight of stairs no bother and were on the landing having a rest when they heard a shuffle. They held their breath and listened.

Where is it? The front or the back? Margaret asked.

They listened again and heard the shuffle going through the back. Alice leaned over the banister and looked down. There, in the darkness at the bottom of the close, was a man in a raincoat. Panic stations!

It's Raincoat Charlie, Alice shouted.

She vaulted the nine stairs and ran. Margaret Kearney was greeting and stumbling down. Falling over and getting up.

Trying to get down the stairs and out the close before Raincoat Charlie got her.

Alice battered on the doors at the bottom of the close as she ran past them.

Help! Help! It's Raincoat Charlie! It's Raincoat Charlie!

Margaret arrived as the doors opened and the men came tearing out. They could hear two wanes screaming and they could see Margaret Kearney crawling along the close floor. She took to crawling cos it was easier. In came the man with the raincoat and the men set about him. It didn't take much for the Slap Up men to set about somebody. There was always a seething anger under their surface. It's easy to see where all that anger came from now but they were blind to it. Blind to the poverty and bad health. The short lifespan. The squalid living conditions and the loss of their Irish pride.

When they stopped kicking it was Jamie O'Rourke coming home from the back shift in Dundyvan.

Maw was just started school and this night she was lying in her bed. Sadie and Margaret had a room of their own. Maw was looking out the window. They had knocked down some of the Slap Up and built these new houses. Four in a block and you had a garden. Maw was lying watching the world go past outside, and the drunk men.

Next thing, this coffin went walking by. She shouted in to her Da.

Da, there's a coffin went by the window there.

Ach, don't be so bliddy stupid, he said. But he automatically stood up and looked out. Sure as fate there was a coffin going by. It had four legs.

Stay here, said Danny.

He ran out and chased the four-legged coffin down the

street. Turned out it was the fellah Regan and one of his pals. They had found an oul coffin and were taking it home for firewood. They had it over their heads like a canoe.

Danny, Alice's Da, was always one for the crack. One day when she was about seven the Orange Walk went past. Banging the big drum and throwing sticks up and the shrill flutes like train brakes. It was some racket. They always have, to this day, a big Orange Walk in Coatbridge. It makes plenty of sense when you consider that the majority of the population are Catholics. Alice asked Danny what it was when the last band passed under the railway bridge at the canal. He told her the Orange Walk was celebrating King Billy who invented oranges. All you had to do was stand at the side of the road with your apron up and they threw oranges into it. Alice couldn't wait till the Orange Walk came again.

When does it come again? When does it come again, Da?

Every July, hen, regular as clockwork, the last Saturday before the twelfth.

Free oranges was the sign that lit up in Alice's head and stayed lit till the next July. You've got to remember that oranges were a rarity then.

The next July the *boom! boom! boom!* of the big Orange drum woke her at seven in the morning. She was under the railway bridge at eight waiting on the walk. Round by The Fountain it came. And as they got closer the looks on the men's faces weren't the looks you'd expect from those who were going to give away free oranges. These men had hate on them. And another thing. Why was there nobody else with their aprons held up to collect the oranges?

There was some boys up on the railway bridge. Alice didn't know that they were there with the slops from all the houses in the Slap Up collected for the last month. There were dozens of pails of slops. The Walk was getting closer and the boys balanced the pails on the parapet of the bridge.

The funny man was dancing out in front, throwing the stick up and bending his body into impossible shapes to catch it. Behind him was the man beating the big drum and behind him rows of men in uniforms with flutes and drums under a banner of a man on a big white horse. That would be King Billy, inventor of oranges. Alice was scared and she didn't know why. The noise was too much and there wasn't an orange in sight.

Just then Ned Chambers came round the corner. He seen the Walk and stepped back. Then he seen Alice. He ran up and grabbed her.

What the fuck are you doing out here the day, Alice?

I'm waiting for them to throw oranges.

Ned looked up at the boys waiting to throw the slops and lifted Alice right up. He ran with her through the gas close and as he got to the other end he could hear the pails clashing off the ground and the barks and grunts of the Orangemen. A silence. Then a riot as the boys on the bridge were joined by a hundred men who started stoning the Walk.

The polis came in their black Marias. A hundred men were lifted that day.

Mary and Danny got one of the new houses near the Slap Up. A house with a garden. One day when Alice was about eight the Dummy came to the door with these plants.

Oh hi yi, Alice said.

The Dummy handed her a cardboard box with plants in it. *UG UG UG,* he was saying. And he was nodding at the garden.

Danny had just dug bits of the garden up at the weekend so Alice knew the plants were for that. He was quite handsome, the Dummy. Alice smiled at him saying, *Right, right,* all the time so he knew that she knew what he was on about.

The Dummy walked away backwards and stumbled staring at Alice as she stood at the door smiling like an idiot and nodding till it was just his head bobbing up and down behind the hedge. Alice stuck the plants on the scullery table and forgot about them till her Da came in from work.

Oh my Christ is this what's for my tea the night? he shouted.

Alice went in and he was trying to eat the plants with a knife and fork.

Remind me to tell your Maw never to let you make the dinner again, Alice from the palace, he said. He stuffed some leaves into his mouth.

No . . . No, Da! Alice shouted. *They're not the dinner. The Dummy brung them in. He says they're for your front garden.*

Well, that was it. Right away Danny was on his knees in praying position. He blessed himself and launched into a tirade.

My Christ, the Dummy can talk now. It's a miracle, my wee lassie seen a miracle! We should've called her Bernadette right enough. Hey, Mary! Alice from the palace heard the Dummy talking. It's a miracle! Get the rosary beads out.

All the time Alice was trying to tell him the Dummy couldn't talk. She didn't want him to go out in the street shouting that the Dummy could talk. But he was still shouting even though she was hanging off his arm trying to get him to stop.

It's a miracle. Get the candles out and fetch the priest round and fill him to the top lip with whiskey.

Every time Alice tried to butt in he talked over the top of her and kept right on going.

Oh don't talk to me, you're too holy. Away to the convent. Mary! Mary! Away up on that bus and bring Sister Mary Bridget down here to measure this halo round wee Alice's head.

He stared at the halo. Alice tried to grab it and he was going on and on.

Mary, she's trying to touch her halo – tell her. Don't put your hands near that halo, hen, it'll burn the fingers right off you.

Alice ran to the lobby mirror and there it was. Dim, but it was there, this halo. She felt like a cheater cos there was no miracle. The Dummy couldn't talk at all. She was about to burst out greeting with all the fuss when the door went. It swung open and there was the Dummy. He was grinning.

Ooh, he shouted.

Right, coming, Danny shouted back from the scullery.

Out he went. The two of them went into the garden and talked like demented windmills. After a while the Dummy went away and in came Danny.

Hey Mary, he shouted. *This one's not too hot at the oul miracles. The Dummy's lost his voice again.*

He looked at Alice and sure enough in the mirror the halo popped like a cartoon.

Alice and her pals were out in the street a few weeks later. Playing at skipping ropes and peever. Right outside the Dummy's window. They thought nothing of it when this big lorry came up the street. It stopped at the Dummy's and they had to move up a bit to play. These men started carrying the Dummy's stuff into the van.

Oh, look at all the lovely stuff the Dummy's got, Alice said.

Hardly anybody in the scheme had ever been in the Dummy's house. The wanes stood there mesmerised at the radiogram, the nice tables and chairs, the beautiful ornaments, brass and china. It was like a palace being emptied. The Dummy and his wife had no wanes. Alice could smell flowery furniture polish and the tang of the pine. It was like the furniture was wearing perfume. For two hours her and her pals watched the cooker, the couch, the piano, the four-poster bed and then the carpets and curtains come out the house. The only thing left was the wallpaper.

When they went home for their dinner that night the talk

was all about how the Dummy had the best furniture you ever seen. Nicer than in the Chapel even. But nobody listened. Danny and Mary were too busy talking about other things.

Nobody listened in any of the houses till the Dummy and his wife came home that weekend. They regularly went to Glasgow, Monday to Friday, to teach other Dummies how to talk with their hands. Alice always wished she could talk with her hands.

Alice was back out on the street after dinner with the other wanes by the time the commotion started. Every Maw in the scheme shouted on her wanes at the same time. The polis arrived in all sorts of cars and vans and plodding. The place was buzzing. Alice thought the Dummy was flitting but it was a robbery. Somebody had robbed his house while he and Mrs Dummy were in Glasgow.

Alice thought it was luck that she and her pals had been there. They described every bit of furniture and bedcovers down to the last nail and stitch, but could they tell them the registration number of the van? No. The colour of the van? No. What the men looked like? No. How many men? No. They were useless. The Dummy was stripped bare. Gutted. The scheme had a whip-round and the Dummy was supposed to have a right few bob anyhow so soon all this other beautiful-looking furniture made its way into his house along with a big crazy collie called Ug Ug. That's when Alice said to herself that she'd make sure when she saw anything suspicious in the future she'd remember the people best and not the stuff.

Years later, when Alice was thirteen, a woman nearly, there was a prowler about the scheme. He interfered with the lassies that worked in the chippy and the pictures when they were coming up the gas close. He used to peep in windows too. He'd been chased a couple of times but never caught.

This night Alice heard screaming from Isa's across the

street. There was Isa hanging out the window, shouting, *Rape, rape! Help, it's the Prowler!*

Isa was about twelve and if she was raped it must have been through the window cos a boyfriend couldn't get a hundred yards near the front door for her oul rosary-beaded Maw, never mind a mad-eyed rapist.

Alice ran into the street and right away she seen this big skinny guy bolting up into the backs. He had staring eyes and they looked white, like there was no colour in them. The backs of the houses went all the way up to the railway. Alice was trying to make out a description of this guy when somebody grabbed her. Her heart was in her mouth. She turned weak and shaking and it was the Dummy.

That way . . . he went that way, Alice said.

The Dummy ran up the backs after the Prowler. He caught the guy and Alice could hear punches and grunting and branches breaking. Then she seen this guy clambering the fence and stamping the Dummy on the face as he went. The Dummy was holding the guy's leg to stop him getting to the railway where nobody could find you. If you got onto the Coatbridge railways you could be somewhere else in minutes.

Then this team of men came pouring past Alice. She could smell the drink and that steelwork smell you don't get any more. The noise they made coming up the path disturbed the Dummy and the big skinny guy disappeared over the fence leaving the Dummy trying to point out what was happening. The men set about the Dummy. He squealed like a pig and the steel-toed boots went in and in. Alice was shouting that it wasn't him.

It wasn't him, it was this big skinny guy! Leave him, leave him! It wasn't him, it was this big skinny guy . . .

She could see the Dummy's dark eyes pleading in the mesh of darkness and grass and shining steel boots and grunts and men calling him all the fuckin perverts.

Alice fainted. When she came to, the Dummy was in hospital. The next week she was out on the street on her own and there was the Dummy and this other big lorry. All his new nice furniture was getting loaded on.

The Dummy and his wife came up their path trailing the mad collie. People were peeking out doors and curtains. The street was quiet as Christmas Eve. Alice was leaning on the railings. The Dummy's wife ran her eyes along the windows and spat on the street before she climbed in the lorry. The lorry drove a couple of feet and stopped. Alice was crying. The Dummy got out and walked up to Alice. He ran his fingers in her hair, bent over and kissed the top of her head. He smiled, turned and walked away. The van turning out the street was the last she ever seen of the Dummy.

Alice was out with Johnny Grogan this night. On the way home they stopped at this big railing and he tried to kiss her. She knocked him back and he touched her on the bust. Alice ran away from him and started walking when she got to the Slap Up. Anybody could see something was wrong by the look on her face. Mrs Gallagher stopped her.

What's wrong with you, Alice? she said.

This boy tried to touch me on the bust.

What boy?

Johnny Grogan.

Oh, that wee bastard. Mrs Gallagher marched Alice right down to her close. *Go right in there and tell your mother everything that happened,* she said.

Mrs Gallagher went away and Alice made her mind up never to tell Oul Mary. There was no way you could talk about things like that to your Maw.

Alice couldn't go to Confession for weeks either cos her Maw knew the priests so well and they knew Alice's voice.

Alice was friendly with them. Oul Mary cleaned the priests' house and she sometimes made them their tea.

A month later there was a Mission coming. Alice was waiting. It was like years, the waiting with that heavy burden of sin acting on her. She went in this week and it said Father O'Grady above the confessional. She'd never seen that name before. Must be one of the missionaries, she thought. In she went to let loose the weight of her sins. She done the usual.

Bless me, Father, for I have sinned, she said. *It's been three months since my last Confession.*

Three months, girl?

Yes, Father.

Go on, he said.

Alice paused and then forced it out. *Father, I've got a sin and I don't know how to tell it.*

Come, come child – just tell me.

She took a breath and spoke. *Please Father, I was out with a boy and he touched me on the bust.*

Was the bus crowded? he said.

Alice never knew what he meant but she carried on. *Please Father, it was dark.*

Come, come you must know if the bus was crowded or not.

Not the bus, Father, the bust.

You mean the breast, child?

Yes, Father. The breast.

You go home and talk these things over with your mother now. D'you hear me?

Right, Father.

Anything else?

No, Father.

Say three Hail Marys and an Our Father.

Yes, Father.

I absolve you from your sins in the name of the Father and of the Son and of the Holy Ghost.

Lord, I am so sorry I have sinned against Thee and I will not sin again. Amen, Father.

Amen, child.

Alice went away and knelt down to say her penance. She got up and there was Father Munn.

You're awful white, Alice, he said. *Where were you?*

I was in Confession, Father Munn.

Who were you in it with?

I was in with the Missionary Father.

The Missionary Father?

Father O'Grady, his name is, Father Munn.

Father Munn laughed low and polite. *He's the new curate, not a missionary. This is his first night in Confession. You run away over and put the kettle on. We'll be there in half an hour.*

Alice met Isa on the way over. She told her the whole story and they laughed their heads off.

Oh, I don't want to meet this new priest, Alice said.

Och, don't be daft, he'll likely not recognise you, said Isa.

So when she was in the priests' house making the tea she changed her accent to this really posh one. Oul Mary was there.

Anyone for some sugar? Alice was going. *Would you care for milk, Father?*

Oul Mary was throwing Alice these puzzled looks at her new posh accent. Father Munn was a bit surprised and all.

Where have you been, Alice? Maggie McCauley's? Oul Mary said.

Maggie McCauley was the local elocution teacher.

Alice and Pat were walking up the end of Kirk Street. They'd not long met and they were in love. Alice was eighteen. Pat was soon to become my Da. They reached the old redbrick bridge and up came Robbie Brown. Pat had never met him but Alice knew the whole family. He never looked daft, Robbie, and he only talked a wee bit funny so Pat thought he was just a normal guy.

Hi yi, Alice, said Robbie. *How's your Maw?*

Oh, she's just fine, Rob. And what about your wee sister – is she still in the hospital?

Robbie blushed, nodding away like a toy. His sister was in and out the hospital. Mad fits. They never knew that he was touching her up at the time. Anyway, Pat had just started going out with Alice and he was trying to impress – family, friends, the usual. He seen Robbie as a candidate and opened this poke of sweets and offered one to Robbie Brown. Did Robbie not go and take the whole packet out Pat's hand and stuff them into his own pocket without even eating one!? Pat's nostrils flared and his muscles tightened. He made a go for Robbie but Alice had already got hold of him cos she knew what they were both like.

Robbie plodded away and Alice told Pat the score about how Robbie was a mental case and all that. Pat unflared the oul nostrils and congratulated himself on his restraint.

Two months later Pat was at the dancing in St Augustine's Chapel hall. In them days the boys asked the girls to dance and if the girl refused you went and got Big Mick and he chucked her out. So mostly a girl would dance with any boy.

There was the girls lined up at one end of the hall and the boys lined up at the other. Pat looked round and to his left was Robbie Brown. Alice was the best-looking girl in the hall. She had a face like winning the pools. Long black curly hair, blue eyes and skin white as distemper. Four wide boys were coaxing Robbie to ask Alice up to dance. The music started the slow walk across. Boys to girls. Not too fast. Not too slow. Boys meandering in and out each other in the darkness, afraid to reach the other end first and afraid to reach it last. Nobody went near Alice Riley. You needed courage for that. Alice knew. It never bothered her that she was left without a partner the way it bothered Jackie Rettie's million freckles and red hair.

But Alice's face near hit the floor when she seen Robbie Brown making a bee-line for her. His face was a big grin in the darkness and people were looking out the side of their eyes to see where Robbie was going. Alice was creeping towards the girls' toilet but she was no match for the bold Robbie. He was right there like a homing pigeon.

Danth? he asked.

The whole hall was watching. A refusal and Alice would be kicked out.

Pardon? she said. She leaned over like she couldn't hear him.

D'you want to danth with me? asked Robbie.

I . . . I . . . I've got to go to the toilet.

I'll tell big Mick . . . MICK . . . MICK!

Big Mick was already moving out his doorway. He sensed something in the air. Jackie Rettie was sliding unseen up to Mick's ear and filling him in on how that bitch refused poor Robbie a dance cos she thought she was too good for him. Out came Mick's chest and he marched right up to Alice who was trying to sneak into the girls' toilet. But Robbie had got a hold of her dress and she couldn't get through the door.

You could see them arguing across the dance-floor. Everybody was dancing but nobody was listening to the music. Big Mick pointed to Robbie, who grinned, then to the dance-floor and then to the door. He was like a referee but everybody knew he'd told Alice to dance with Robbie Brown or get out.

The music stopped and everybody's eyes were molten rivets in the dark iron plate of silence. Alice jerked a nod at Robbie and he scuttled onto the floor. The whole place let out a sigh and the wide boys were knotting themselves.

As they danced Alice was looking at the ceiling and Robbie

was staring at her lips and breathing on the soft skin of her neck. He was talking and she was answering back but she was still looking at the ceiling. People were sniggering everywhere. Alice kept looking across to Pat but he was ignoring her cos he didn't want anybody to think he was jealous of Robbie Brown.

A white spoarts coat and pink ca-arnashun . . .

That was what Robbie was singing into her neck. Alice was screwing her face up to get away from his stinking breath. Then she noticed he'd stopped singing and was actually saying something over and over.

Pat was about to walk away when he seen Robbie waving something in the air in front of Alice's face. It was the bag of sweets. Pat's bag of sweets.

D'ye want one of Pat'th thweeth?

Alice was screwing up her face and Rob was slabbering down his chin. Big Mick was only halfway across the dance-floor when Pat had Rob on the floor and was laying the boot into his ribs heavy and hard.

One December Maw took Caroline, Linda, Angie and Geddy into What Every Woman Wants. It had just opened up and it was the place to be seen in. If you were a clampitt. She was in to buy them new coats and frocks for Christmas. The place was mobbed cos the stuff was half the price of the other shops in Glasgow. There was these lovely wee flowery dresses. Maw took a right fancy to them. They were going like hot cakes as other Maws shoved other Maws out the road to get them for their daughters. They could see, as Maw could, that their daughters, no matter how ugly they might be, would look stunning in these flowery dresses.

Get them they're lovely, Maw said.

No. They're too short, Caroline said. She held one up against

Angie and it did look a bit short so Maw moved it to the thinner Linda and it looked a bit longer.

There, see! They're great. Yees better get them before they're all snapped up.

Are you sure they're long enough? asked Angie.

Maw already had a film in her head where her daughters walk in a foursome down the street and the men can't take their eyes off them they're that beautiful. She went all out to persuade them to buy the dresses. Even took them off the hangers in all the right sizes.

They're lovely, Maw said, *they're modern. That's what they're all wearing to the discos these days.*

So Caroline, Linda, Angie and Geddy all bought one. The same cream colour with blue flowers on them. On the Friday night they went to the Community Centre disco. Bachman-Turner Overdrive was on. 'You Ain't Seen Nothin' Yet'. There they were dancing round each other waiting for the place to fill up with envious girls and lustful boys. But everybody seemed to come in at the last minute. They must have finished their carry-out up Wine Alley and walked down in unison. The first thing the four sisters noticed was that nearly all the girls were wearing the same flowery dresses. And about the same time as the boys noticed how short the dresses were, the four sisters noticed that all the other girls had their flowery dresses tucked into their jeans. That was because they weren't flowery dresses at all. They were flowery tops. Maw had watched too many James Bond movies. The ultra-mini-skirt was a long time in coming into fashion in Coatbridge. In fact they were raving to Techno by the time it did.

Another time years later Maw was in the same shop nosing about. Next thing she saw these big flash nighties. They were in the catalogue and were really dear. Maw decided she was going to buy them for her six daughters.

But when she went in they were really dear there too. She could only afford three. Geddy and Donna and Wendy were there that time, but Maw bought three nighties for the oldest daughters. They all came out with their faces tripping them, Maw especially. She had visions of all her six daughters pecking her goodnight on the cheek and one by one trailing up the stairs with their lovely long flowing nighties on. Three was going to look daft. They were about a hundred yards away from the shop when Maw turned to Geddy and Donna.

They were lovely. Absolutely lovely. I just wish I could have got six.

They went into the chippy under the Central Bridge and got a fish tea each. The Girls could tell that Maw was depressed about not getting the six nightdresses. As they munched Donna eyed the receipts and whispered to Geddy.

Maw, this receipt is wrong, they've charged you double. The nightdresses were only a fiver each, said Donna.

Were they not ten, hen? Maw asked.

Aye, on the labels, but there was a big Reduced To A Fiver sign beside them, said Geddy.

We'll go back up, Donna said. *Come on, Geddy.*

Let me see the receipt, Maw said.

But Donna and Geddy were off. They went into What Every Woman Wants and took What One Specific Woman Wanted; a dream of her six daughters dressed in the same nighties, wafting up the stairs like film stars. After checking the sizes, Donna stuffed the three nighties in the bag Geddy was holding open and they made their way out the shop. It was a long walk from the nightwear to the exit. They got stopped by the security but done the wee girly thing and showed him the receipt.

Sorry, hen, he said.

They came out and sprinted along the street through

shoppers with their hair and the carrier bag trailing behind them and big exhilarated grins on their faces. Wendy and Maw were away along at the Central Station eating popcorn when Donna and Geddy arrived.

That was great them being half price, said Maw.

One time Maw seen Danny, her dad, coming down the street with a halo over his head.

He won't be here at Christmas, she said.

He wasn't.

Maw

That poof! Angie says.

I don't think he's a poof, Geddy says. Geddy doesn't want any man to be wasted.

You'd be able to tell right enough, says Angie.

There's not much Geddy doesn't know about men. Geddy's thinking of a quick retort. And if she came back a minute and a half later that would be quick. But she doesn't get the chance cos the door goes and they all freeze again.

Oul Mary blows out the candles. And she's fair knackered at the end of that. Wendy opens the veranda and shooshes the smoke out. The wind is blowing in and swirling the smoke all round the place. Angie and Linda shove the carpet back in the cupboard again. Oul Mary licks the candles one by one and puts them in her bag. Don't want to set light to the pension book. It's a double dunt next week. Bank Holiday or something. Caroline hides the bottle of murky graveyard water behind the chair and Donna lays out the Trivial Pursuit again.

Caroline goes to the door and the Girls listen like statues. Oul Mary doesn't turn her head but she turns her eyes. Caroline presses her ear against it. She can't hear a thing. It's just the close door banging and opening on its hinges at the bottom. Banging and opening. She lifts the letterbox.

Who is it?

Kevin Barry, is the answer.

The Girls moan and relax.

It's Maw, says Caroline.

But they already knew that. Not even at the end of the sentence. But at the first word. Kevin. No, the first guttural sound. No, at the breath took in to announce the arrival of the first sound. There are some things in life that are so familiar they are you. And that's what everything of Maw's is. Them. The Girls. Her every move and motivation. Her every look and glance. Her every put-down – and there's a lot of them. Maw is the Girls and the Girls are Maw. Oul Mary is them all and they are all her. It's no wonder they're Catholics with all that transfiguration going on. Caroline opens the door and in comes Maw.

D'yees not hear me at that door? Yees deaf or drunk or what?

They all answer at the same time.

We're what, says Donna.

Drunk, goes Angie.

Both, Geddy says.

Deaf, Linda goes.

There's a beat of silence as Maw looks about the place. *Were yous talking about me?*

Aye! they all say.

Sniff, sniff Maw goes and sucks smokelets up her nostrils. *Got the candles lit already?*

Just taking them for a wee test drive, Oul Mary tells her.

Are you here, Mother?

No, I'm in buckin Donegal, cracks Oul Mary.

But Maw's not for being defeated just yet. The Girls watch in awe as these two giants of their lives go at each other.

Jesus what're you doing in Donegal, Mother?

Howking tatties; ten pound a hundredweight!

Laughter fills the room. Maw sits down and Oul Mary smacks her lips like a Roman Emperor. But Maw has to have some glory. If you can't defeat your superiors, attack your subordinates.

There's some wee boys at your car down there Wendy, she goes.

Wendy jumps up and runs to the veranda. Out she goes, banging against the railings and coming to a stop. Maw's making faces at her and all the Girls let their shoulders laugh for the time being. Out on the veranda it's just that light you only get in schemes. Metal shutters on the windows shimmering and empty streets. And the feeling that everybody is indoors planning something bad. Something violent. Something horrible. And if this house, Caroline's, is typical then maybe there are strange things going on behind all the doors. In the windows. If this is just another night in Old Monkland there's probably a story in every close. A movie in every street. Wendy decides it's time to go back in and face the laughter. In she comes. It's like looking at a pack of laughing-faced hyenas. They're shoving and dunting each other and pointing at Wendy. When they die down a bit Wendy turns to Maw.

Och, see you Mother.

Come on over, goes Maw.

Wendy goes over and automatically looks in Maw's hair for nits and Maw looks in her fair hair for nits. The habits that families carry on from childhood. It's become a normality. They don't do it in public places but they feel totally at ease in the privacy of Caroline's house. Angie decides it's worth a comment.

Look at them! I've seen monkeys more civilised, she says.

But it's nothing to do with the nits. Wendy's sat there searching Maw's scalp and Maw at Wendy's but just half doing the job. Rubbing her scalp absent-minded, just enough to keep Wendy working. What Angie is all about is this; Donna and Wendy were the young ones. They always got doing the nits. Angie was never asked to do the nits and now it's become a symbol of rejection. Geddy and Angie didn't belong to the biggies and they never belonged to the weeies. Relaxed now, Maw tries to spark up a conversation with Oul Mary again.

I was up at your bit there, Mother.

Was I in? says Oul Mary.

They all laugh again. Maw kicks her shoes off and flings two batteries to Oul Mary.

Here, I got these for your tranny.

Must be Christmas. Or you stole them. There wasn't a biscuit in the cupboard when she was young.

But by the end of Oul Mary's sentence Maw's not listening. She's turned her attention to Caroline. The reason they're all here.

Any more from Bobby?

McGoogan said he'll get the money off him the night, says Caroline. She's holding her tears at the back of her eyes. It's always emotional talking to your Maw even if she's quite cold. Even if she wasn't one for the hugs and the cuddles. Cos there's one thing for sure and that's this; your Maw's your Maw. And she says it all the time, Maw.

You can always tell your mother but you can never tell your Da.

And she added on that if everybody in this town knew who their Da was, there would be blue murder on the streets. But for now she's trying to settle Caroline down. Make her feel good. Give her some support.

I've got you a wee set of curtains for this house. Ten ninety-nine in the Barras.

Did you steal them and all? Oul Mary wants to know.

A grand Caroline paid McGoogan, Maw! Donna says.

Jesus! I would have done him in for fifty quid! Maw says.

She probably would have. Caroline walks off into the kitchen. That wee distance between her and them helps to contain her emotions. Donna joins Wendy on the chair and they're all looking in each other's hair for nits. Wendy's looking in Maw's. Maw's looking in Donna's and Donna's looking in Wendy's. It's like a Celtic knot. And there's quiet for the first time since they all started arriving. They're all caught up in their own thoughts and problems. Angie's first to speak.

How's my Da?

Fine. Maw answers through the ecstasy of being searched for bugs.

You sure? Angie wants to know.

He's great, Maw says. That's when she notices the fireplace for the first time. Her jaw falls open and her hair signals to Wendy's fingers to stop rummaging.

Jesus, Mary and Joseph! What's that monstrosity there? Maw goes.

Geddy tells Maw Caroline's been using it to burn Bobby's boxers. But Maw doesn't understand so Geddy goes over, picks a pair up and holds them at arm's length. Like she's in a telly advert. A model advertising divorce. Giving out advice on what to do. Shred the clothes and shove prawns in the curtain rail. That sort of stuff. But Maw still doesn't understand. In her day you never got divorced. Ever. You stayed with your man till he died. Cos in Coatbridge the men always die before the women. There's a joke in fact that Danny, Maw's Da, used to always tell.

Why do men always die before their wives?

Don't know.

Cos they want to.

Geddy flings a pair of Bobby's boxers in the fire. *Whoosh!* Up they go and the Girls laugh and applaud. They fall into a wee dwam as they watch the flames recede from blue to orange to red. Maw scans the size and ostentatiousness of the fireplace.

You could say Mass at that thing so you could, she goes.

Sacrifice goats, goes Angie.

Enough of that talk now, Oul Mary pipes in.

Who wants to pick my corns? Maw wants to know.

Donna and Wendy get down on the floor like two praying Bernadettes and pull Maw's shoes off. Get in about the corns. Digging their nails in. Maw sighs and relaxes. Sinking into the chair. That was another family pastime. Picking corns. Oul Mary used to get it done when all the Girls were up there. But she's past caring about her corns now. Her whole life is her wee tranny and helping the Girls out when they want to kill somebody or do them irreparable damage. It's much in the same way as if your Granda got a hatchet and came out to hander you and your Da against another family in the pub. But this of course is much more subtle.

Oul Mary might not be so much into getting her corns picked now, but Maw? She loves it. It's the best thing after looking for nits. The art of picking corns is, you don't dig your nails in and try to howk the whole thing out. That results in Maw shooting through the roof and a pool of blood on the carpet. And the corn, closely related to the wart, is a wee tube of gristle in your hand. So real you think it's alive and I've seen the Girls when they were apprentices get up and run screaming from the room. Getting out before Maw, or Oul Mary, regained their senses. Once you get the knack of it however, it's easy. You press the nail into the corn just enough to send some signals to the brain saying almost-pain. Any more and it'll be sore. And that's the pressure you keep on it. The expert corn-pickers are them that know that threshold like it's a football pitch. When you're young the threshold is a thin line that you can cross over ever so easily. So what you do is stay away from the line. Beneath it. And so Maw, or Oul Mary never get the satisfaction they want. But when you've reached the level of expertise that the likes of Donna and Wendy have you can get right into that line; it's a hundred miles wide and wander about while Maw, or Oul Mary, relax in corn-picking bliss. So that's much the situation when Linda pipes up.

Is he still off the drink, my Da?

Maw answers without even opening her eyes. *Thirteen weeks now.*

He must have had some, says Angie.

Not a drop. Can you do that one on my wee pinkie toe? It's killing me, hen, Maw says to Wendy.

Even though she's got her eyes shut she knows it's Wendy on that foot. She can tell her daughters by their touch. By their picking technique. Donna tends to dig the nail in a bit and pull and tug the corn. Moving round it steadily but slowly. Wendy on the other hand, or should I say other foot, tends to dig the nail in less. But she digs it into the surface and drags the nail over the corn with the same pressure. Changing direction with every stroke so that each sweep is a surprise to Maw. If the truth be told Maw likes Wendy at the corns best. But she prefers Donna at the nits. Aye, she can tell which daughter it is with her eyes closed. There's not a lot of mothers could say that.

That's the way they are. Reclining. Reposing. Resting. Caught up in Maw's bliss and the heat of the fire. The translucent haze of the flames. The hypnotic family togetherness. But the door goes and they're all suddenly alert as rabbits.

Bobby

They all stare at the door. It goes again. *Bang – bang – bang!* They stare at Caroline.

Who is it? Caroline goes. But there's no answer. She asks again. *Who is it?*

It's Bobby, is the answer.

The Girls look at each other, affronted at his brass neck. They've not even tugged the words of insults out of the treacle of hate when Caroline turns pleading.

It's Bobby. What'll I do?

You've got a cheek coming here, you cunt! Geddy screams.

Who's talking to you, Tina Turner? shouts Bobby.

Geddy draws him a look. A look so black that he probably seen it through the wood.

What d'you want? Caroline asks.

Oul Mary signals to the Girls to let them talk. And here's the conversation.

I want to talk to you, Bobby says.

Well talk then.

Through a door!?

I can hear you perfectly okay.

There's a creak as he lifts the letterbox. Two cartoon eyes swivel this way and that making sure none of them are standing with a kitchen knife or some other long sharp kitchen implement. He knows them so well.

Come on out here and we can talk.

I can hear you from here, I said.

Aye, and so can them fuckin Witches.

He should've knew better. That gets him a barrage of insults. But worse; it brings the sisters into his conversation with Caroline.

They're family. My fuckin family! Caroline screams at him.

That's right – family, says Geddy.

Bobby bangs on the door. This time he's angry. This time he's a man. This time it's an order.

Let me in, he shouts.

Not by the hair on my chinny chin chin, shouts back Angie.

That brings the house down. They fall about laughing, rubbing their bellies and sending the guffaw away up to the ceiling. Even Oul Mary's laughing. Her top teeth keep falling onto her bottom teeth and clicking and being replaced, and clicking. And being replaced.

Who's the fuckin poet? Bobby wants to know. *No, let me guess . . . Wendy?*

Angie actually, Wendy informs him.

Me, you fuckin hoormaster, Angie tells him.

I'm a playwright, says Wendy.

The Girls look at her. She did write a play once for Primary One to perform at the Christmas concert. So now she's a playwright. The voltage has went right up in the room. There's invisible lines of blue current running from the Girls to Caroline. She feels it. In her blood. In her belly. Her chest. Up and up it's coming. The anger she couldn't express. The words she couldn't say out of fear. Out of the low self-esteem bashed down like an empty bean tin when your man leaves you. Hooray and up she rises, and it's words that come out. Fearless.

How's Stacie fuckin Gracie?

Oh, the Girls like that. They rub their palms and smile. Hunch their shoulders waiting on the reply.

For your information I haven't seen Stacie Gracie for three days. She's away somewhere.

The Girls all give each other that knowing look that only Witches can give each other. Or sisters. They goad Caroline to keep it going. Bobby's behind the door confused. The reactions he got weren't the ones he expected. Caroline goes for him again.

Well, what are you wanting? Clean underwear?

I want you to call McGoogan off.

'I want you to call McGoogan off,' they all say. The sisters love impersonating his pathetic little voice.

Get him to fuck, Caroline, shouts Angie.

You're a dead man, Donna shouts.

But Bobby ignores them. He knows not to let them back into the conversation. He focuses and talks straight through the door to Caroline.

Are you going to let me in? he asks.

Not by the hair on my chinny chin chin. Angie sings it this time.

The Girls ignite and don't stop the rest of the time Bobby's at the door.

Say something else. Get him riled right up, Geddy says.

Caroline thinks with a half smile what to say. She looks like somebody that's been asked up to sing at a party but isn't too sure what song to sing.

I hope Stacie Gracie's not been charging you as much as she charged the rest of the boys in The Monkland Bar!

It wasn't as good as they expected but then Caroline was never noted for her patter. But they're sisters and this is a momentous night.

Geddy's up first and shouts right through the letterbox, *Fifty pence bent over the bar!*

A pound over the twin tub, is Angie's contribution.

Can we not act like adults? Bobby wants to know.

Oh, that's good from a man that's ran away with a nineteen-year-oul lassie, shouts Geddy.

There's a beat of silence as Bobby considers his answer. *I've got to get my fuckin hole somewhere.*

Ohhh! is what all the Girls and Maw and Oul Mary say.

Ask her, go on – ask Eskimo Annie the last time she shagged me! he says through the letterbox.

I'm not frigid. I'm . . . I'm . . . horny. Anyway, you couldn't satisfy a hamster! says Caroline.

The Girls cheer at that and Caroline walks away from the door. Okay, the hamster joke wasn't up to much but as I've said she wasn't one for the witty rejoinder, Caroline. As far as the Girls are concerned that was mighty from her. Fierce. Bobby thumps on the door and shouts the odds for a while but he soon gives up when there's no reaction from inside. They simply ignore him. Act like he's not there. Now Caroline's determined to do the Six Black Candles. Raring to go. She straightens her back and takes on a new attitude.

Right, she goes.

Right, says Donna.

Let's do it, goes Caroline.

What they don't notice as they talk is Bobby has stuffed his hand through the letterbox and he's got hold of the bit of string that's got the door key on the end of it. He's tugging it up. Albeit slowly cos he can only work with the tips of his fingers. It's a narrow letterbox. But he's tugging it up all the same.

This is great, says Linda.

Let's fry some head, Angie goes.

Wendy wants to know when Bobby said he last seen Stacie Gracie. And that stops Caroline in her enthusiasm. The mention of their two names in the one sentence crushes her and fills her with the ice of dread. The Girls glare at Wendy.

See what you've done now! Angie goes.

Behind her Bobby has the key inches from his hand and his fingers are still working deftly. Up and up, inch by inch all the time they key's going. Up and up. Caroline bursts out crying and Wendy gets glared at all the more.

What's that bitch got that I haven't? Caroline says.

In the background Geddy whispers to Donna, *Your husband, you daft cow.*

And nice tits and a tight arse, Donna says to Geddy.

Next thing, Caroline sees the key reaching Bobby's hand. All he has to do is pull it through the letterbox and open the door. Then he's in and there's no telling what'll happen then. Who's afraid of the big bad wolf time. That's probably what Bobby's thinking; what he'll do to them when he gets in there. He probably wonders what Caroline's screaming at as she runs at the door.

Ya baaaaaaaaaastard!!! she shouts.

Bobby's animal cunning tells him something is up. But his reaction is to make a fist. He makes a fist and pulls at the same time and he can't get free from the door. Sense overtakes his panic but it's too late by then. Not only has Caroline got a hold of his hand but the other sisters have seen what's going on. Oh ho! Trouble. Caroline yanks his arm through right up to the bicep. Bobby tries to pull it back but it's jammed at the elbow. Caroline sinks her teeth into his hand. She tastes blood and bites all the harder.

Argh!! What the fuck are you doing? Let me go! Bobby screams.

There's one thing worse than somebody biting your hand. Somebody biting your hand when you can't see it. Your brain thinks the worst. Bobby pulls and pulls but he's jammed solid at the elbow. He has to relax to be free. But his inside animal won't let him. Things are about to get worse.

The rest of the Girls join in biting, scrabbling with their long nails, kicking and punching. Piranhas in a feeding frenzy. Oul Mary has shuffled into the scullery and lifted one of them big black frying pans. Made out of iron. It's that heavy she's got to drag it towards them as they scream and bite and kick.

Let me go you bunch of weirdoes. I'm telling yees, Bobby shouts.

But he won't be shouting for long. Not with any coherence, that is. Oul Mary arrives at the door with the frying pan. She coughs and they all let go. She lifts the frying pan level with her waist and holds it out to the side like a baseball bat. Bobby's hand is surprised at being let go. His hand spreads its fingers in relief. Like a hand playing arpeggios on an invisible piano. That's when Oul Mary swings the frying pan with a hell of a force. Bobby gets half a sentence out.

Aye, just as well for—

CLANG!!! There's the sound of crunching bone as the fingers are splintered. Then the thud of the pan hitting the meat of the hand. Followed by the smack of the hand hitting off the door. There's a pause. Then

AAAARGHGHG!!!!

Bobby screams as all these different pains merge in his brain. The hand whips back through the letterbox. And that's without relaxing. It's the super-human strength you get with pain. Bobby screams all the way down the close. You can even hear him at the bottom changing his screaming pattern as he pulls the heavy security door open. Then his screaming comes in through the veranda as he runs down the street. Then nothing. The Girls cheer and relive the incident a few times.

Good enough for me and Bobby McGee . . .

Wendy starts singing and the rest of them join in. When they collapse into laughter they congratulate Oul Mary on her creativity. They would never have thought of that. A frying pan! No way. What a brain she's got. What a woman. They're so proud to have her as a Granny. Well chuffed.

Oh buck, I need a wee vodka after that, is Oul Mary's reply.

I'll get them, says Angie.

She tears into the scullery. The voltage in the room is so high there's lightning firing from sister to sister. From Oul Mary to Maw and on and on. If only they could see it they'd be amazed. Angie brings in the vodka and they all sip and reminisce over the very recent past. Puzzle as to which hospital department Bobby'll be in. Osteopathy or psychiatry. Then there's a bang outside. For a minute they think it's Bobby back but it's Neds and Nedesses going about down in the car park. Wendy's right out onto the veranda.

Hoi you, cunt! Wendy shouts.

That's the thing about Wendy. Her and her posh teacher voice. She loses it the minute she's angry. Except in the class that is, or she'd lose her job. But there's nothing the sisters like better than when Wendy reverts to type. It makes them feel at home. Like Wendy's not flew the coop after all. She's still a wee bird from the Brig. All the rest is just an act to fool the posh bastards she meets. One of the Neds shouts up.

Who the fuck are you?

Get to fuck away from that car or you'll find out who I am.

Suck my dick, is the reply. And he's got it out in case she wants to.

I'll bite it right off, Wendy shouts.

Maw hates it. She hates the reflected glory of Wendy's gold-plated life being dulled down by anything. It's all that keeps Maw one notch above the dirt and the scum that live round here.

Wen . . .dy! You're supposed to be a teacher, Maw says.

Wendy comes back in changing her crunched-up face and adjusting her poverty as she walks.

We've a right regular President Clinton out there, she tells them. Her voice is settled back into the poshness that befits someone of her standing.

I thought it was Bobby, says Caroline. Fear is wavering in her words again.

He probably flagged a taxi – with his good arm, says Wendy. Quite a good joke for her.

Bobby? That's the last we'll be seeing of him, says Linda.

Oh, d'you think so? goes Donna.

She's psychic again and knows something the rest of the sisters don't. She does her eyes for a few seconds just to back up her clairvoyance. Caroline's worried now that Bobby might come back. With them having took lumps out his arm and shattering every bone in his hand, he's not likely to be a happy chappy. Nobody wants to listen to that any more cos Maw's tearing into Wendy about the way she should talk, her being a teacher and all.

You shouldn't be talking like that, Maw chastises.

Speaking, Mother. It's 'you shouldn't be speaking like that'. Speaking, not talking.

Speaking or talking you shouldn't be doing it like that.

Ooh . . . naughty girl, Geddy goes. She's trying to stir things up a bit more.

So Wendy wants to know how exactly she should be speaking, being a teacher and all that.

Posh, Maw says. Her tone is laced with the finality of genius.

You are such a snob, says Wendy. That brings looks of pots and kettles from the sisters.

It won't be that when you get flung out St Patrick's for talking like a . . . a . . .

Like a what, Mother? Come on, Wendy growls. She's forcing an answer out of Maw.

Like the wanes you teach.

There. She said it. Wendy knew that's what she was going to say.

I knew you were going to say that, Mother!

Maw, that's the way we all speak, goes Angie.

That's the M8 clear now, Oul Mary says.

But Maw And Wendy are away. They won't put it down. Maw tells Wendy she shouldn't be speaking like that if she's a teacher. Teachers don't talk like that.

It's her that's the snob, Maw, Geddy says.

Hmph! Just what I expect from you, Geddy, Wendy goes.

You need to talk right if you're a teacher, that's all I'm saying, Maw says. *That's all I'm saying.*

Oul Mary coughs and starts getting the candles out again.

Would yees all shut buckin up. C'mon, she couldn't talk when she was born, Oul Mary goes.

So they all shut up and look at Oul Mary. They can feel she's just about to make one of her pronouncements. One of her wisdoms. And they're right. She does.

At least she can talk now. You don't hear the chickens arguing about how to cluck, do you? Come on, let's be getting on with this; the night's drawing in so it is.

It's a flurry as they take their positions again. Angie and Linda on the rug. Wendy with her bottle of dead body water. Donna with her stare. Geddy with her Daniel O'Donnell dod of turf.

Where's Stacie Gracie's head? Maw shouts through the frenzy.

In the electric fridge, says Oul Mary.

Maw smiles. A smile from daughter to mother. One Witch to another.

They're learning, says Oul Mary. *They're learning.*

She's lit the fifth candle and she's about to light the sixth when *tap – tap – tap!* the door goes. Angie tells them all to shoosht and they pad about trying to clear the place up. Angie leans over to the door. They all think it's Bobby back.

Who is it?

Eh, it's Father Boyle. Just paying a wee house call. From St Augustine's.

It's that new fuckin priest! Angie shout-whispers.

It's a madness and a half. Like a Charlie Chaplin movie as they accelerate into their clearing-up routine. There's no noise except feet brushing off the carpet and fingers leaving surfaces. Angie gets an idea. A smile spreads across her face. She whispers to Linda. Linda beams at Donna.

Donna! Donna! Get me out of this! Linda says.,

Donna and Angie drag Linda out the wheelchair and dump her onto the couch.

The Chapel's History

Father Boyle's new and doesn't know the Girls. He's heard of them alright and that's partly why he's there. To check them out. From a man's point of view for their beauty. And from a priest's point of view for their reputed Witchcraftiness. He has met Wendy briefly at St Patrick's, and thought she was a nice young lady with a gift for teaching.

What he's got going for him as a priest is that he is young and good-looking. And although he's a bit naive he already has that great priestly attribute of being quite patronising.

But that's enough of him cos in reality one priest's the same as the next. It's the Chapel's history I want to talk about here. Let's clear something up. The Chapel in question is St Augustine's. But Wendy works at St Patrick's Primary School. Father Boyle is from St Augustine's but takes in two or three schools since there's a shortage of priests right now. Which is a surprise cos there's no shortage of arrogant bastards.

Now that's *that* cleared up, let's look at the Chapel. One story from the Slap Up highlights all we need to know about the Chapel.

Paddy Cox walked with one arm out and limped like crazy.

The wanes used to take the piss out him.

Paddy Cox, nose like a fox, it's the way he walks, cos he's got the pox, they'd go.

He had red hair disappearing off his head. There was always scabs on his head standing out there against the red skin. The wanes used to give him pennies for throwing stones up in the air and headering them. The wee bastards. He was just an animated toy to them. The blood wasn't real. His screams mixed in with their laughter. Paddy Cox would stand there, his big blue eyes like Frankenstein when he can't understand why people are treating him like this.

Instead of saying W Paddy Cox always said B. And instead of J he said D. So a wall became a ball and a walk became a balk: a jockey became a dockey and jam became dam. He always had a bench to himself at Mass, did poor Paddy. He slept rough in the closes of the Slap Up. His mother, God bless her soul, had died. There was nobody to take him in. Nobody to put his clothes on and keep him clean. And you can't live on the wind so people used to take turns at feeding him. He was a sorry sight. No wonder he had a row all to himself at twelve o'clock Mass. He was stinking.

Anyway. There was this Sunday and these Missionary Fathers came to St Augustine's. Paddy Cox was in the row behind Danny, Alice's Da. Paddy always sat facing straight towards the Sacred Heart statue. Through the foggy haze of boredom Danny could hear one of the missionaries bumping his gums all about Jesus and saints and stuff. At the same time Paddy, who usually sat there stock still, staring into the compassionate eyes of the plaster statue, was shuffling the oul feet, grunting and getting restless. And he stank. The movement was sending waves of sour food and urine through the Chapel. On and on this missionary was going but nobody was listening cos they were all holding their breath cos of Paddy Cox.

We must give more to Jesus and that means hard cash. Prayers are alright. I'm not asking you to stop the praying nor nothing. Keep on praying. Pray all the more but these poor starving people, they need your money. Think how lucky you all are to have a roof over your heads and a job in the steelworks and mines. These people, they've got to eke their meagre living out the land . . . land that's baked hard or deep with mud. They roam around and sleep under trees. Dig into your pockets. Think of them when you're sat in your cosy little single-end there with the fire blazing away and the kettle on and all the children snug there in the bed. Imagine you didn't have that job to feed them children. No matter what we think there's always that bit more we can offer.

On and on went this missionary. You would have thought the people in the Slap Up had a good life, to hear him. Danny was nearly convinced till he thought of the six o'clock start and the twelve-hour shifts in the dry black dust of Dundyvan. New steel hot as hell. Christ, he was nearly convinced till he thought of his wanes that had survived all stuffed into the box bed, and him and Mary on a roll-out mattress on the floor. It was making him mad, so it was. Living in the Slap Up amongst the knives and the head-butts and the whoring and the drinking and the dying wanes and the dying men and the mourning women and the constant glow of gas lamps through the smog. Oh aye, he was fuckin glad alright.

Good to be alive Desus, Mary an Doseph look after us! Paddy Cox shouted out, interrupting the missionary.

Everybody looked round and laughed. There was the St Vincent De Paul pass-keepers ushering Paddy Cox out of the Chapel.

Div more to Desus. Div more, div all yous got. Be've got to div more to Desus, he was shouting.

Paddy screamed all the way out the doors. Danny could feel the cold blast of air and then the doors closed. The missionary was disgusted by the outburst but didn't let it get to him as he resumed his pleading for compassion and mercy.

When Danny left the Mass Paddy was sitting shivering in the snow. Some people drew him black looks but most ignored him and carried their Sunday serenity back into the high soot-covered walls of the Slap Up. When the priest shut the Chapel doors Paddy shuffled into the arches out of the reach of the sleet. The last Danny saw him, he was curled up and snorting warm air into the cold January sky.

Be must div more to Desus, he said.

Danny walked away. There was a storm brewing up. A big storm. Paddy Cox rocked to sleep murmuring to himself most nights so I suppose that's what he done that time too.

Danny went home and got his tea. The wanes were running riot so he went out into Turner Street just to see what was what. He was standing in the close out the swirling sleet, smoking, when he saw this red/pink figure running crazy out of the storm. There was a gang of wanes, none of them his, thank Christ, running after the figure. He was screaming and moaning and the shrill cries of the wanes cracked off all the buildings.

People come to their windows.

Danny remained immobile. It was Paddy Cox and he was stark raving naked. His cock was bouncing from thigh to thigh and it seemed strange that he had one, that he was a man, that he was a real fuckin man. Paddy Cox's balls . . . Danny was standing there but he couldn't believe it. Snowballs were hurling at Paddy ten a penny and they were exploding off his tight skin. He was screaming so loud and painfully Danny could see all his back teeth and he was thinking he was going to burst right through his skin any minute. Going to burst right through his fuckin skin. He looked to Danny for help as he passed. His eyes were all white screaming *HELP*. Danny couldn't do nothing. He lowered his head, ashamed. He couldn't even stop the wanes pelting him; they were too far gone in a frenzy.

The snow on the cobbles was slush and Paddy's feet were black. He slipped and got back up every few steps. His mother would be turning in her grave. They were kicking him and their Maws were whistling from the windows and throwing things. There was blood in the snow from his knees and his hands and there was blood on his body where the razor-cold snow had sliced the skin. He was writhing but still moving up Turner Street . . . up to the top of the hill where a gang of men, red-eyed from drinking, had gathered with their belts off and unrolled. The black leather and the buckles shone. Paddy Cox seen them and dropped to his knees. He looked up to the sky. The sleet was whinnying down and sticking in his face. The crowd of men surged forwards. Their eyes were picking out bare flesh to hit.

Our Fader hoo art in hivin . . .

Paddy started praying. The wanes were round him now, dancing in a circle and singing their song.

Paddy Cox, nose like a fox, it's the way he walks, cos he's got the pox . . .

They were scudding him with hard ice snowballs on the sound of Cox, Fox, Walks and Pox. The men were breaking through the dancers.

We'll show you, you pervert bastard prancing about like that with our wanes.

The men were rolling up their sleeves, spitting on the ground and moving in for the kill.

Oh my God he's dead, Danny thought, and realised he was moving at top rate into the dancers . . . through them

Paddy Cox was still Our Fathering away and Danny was on Big Joe Dillon. He lunged low on the way in. The steel on the soles of his boots slid along the cobbles. All the wanes looked round in time to see Danny spring up from a half-shut knife position and stick the head right into Dillon's face. The crunch rung up every close. Danny held onto Dillon cos they were going forward and they were going down. Danny let him go and ripped the belt out his hand. Blackout. A big polis had crunched Danny on the head and piled a few of them into the Black Maria.

Next morning they were all up in front of The Beak. It turned out that Paddy Cox had got into St Augustine's, took all his clothes off and folded them neatly on the altar. When he came out the wanes seen him and chased him up the street.

Do you have anything to say for yourself, Mr Cox? Goes the JP.

Paddy was standing there in a suit a mile too big for him. The polis and public were laughing. Danny and the rest of the custody cases were straining to hear what he had to say from the cells. Danny could see the side of his head over the dock. He looked up with pitiful eyes. His head was scabbed up where the wanes got him with ice.

I . . . I . . .

Speak up, Mr Cox, I can't hear you, droned the JP like he was the Pope of Rome.

I . . . I . . . dey said div more to Desus. Div more to Desus. My tlothes . . . I only hid my tlothes. Dave thim to Desus. Put thim on the altar . . . Desus'll div thim to thi poor black wanes, keep thim warm. Div more, thi said. Div more to Desus.

The court went silent. Through the bars on his cell Danny could see the sky darken.

Father Boyle

It's that new fuckin priest! Angie shout-whispers.

It's a madness and a half. Like a Charlie Chaplin movie as they accelerate into their clearing-up routine. There's no noise except feet brushing off the carpet and fingers leaving surfaces. Angie gets an idea. A smile spreads across her face. She whispers to Linda. Linda beams at Donna.

Donna! Donna! get me out of this! Linda says.

Donna and Angie drag Linda out the wheelchair and dump her on the couch. Donna jumps into the wheelchair.

Angie opens the door and in comes Father Boyle. They notice how young and good-looking he is. You'd think he was too young to be a priest till you walked outside and seen the age of the polis and the teachers.

The only one he's ever met is Wendy and that was fleetingly. In the school. But the main thing he won't notice is that Donna is in the wheelchair now and Linda is on the couch. And the conspirational air that's about the place? He won't notice that either. The only thing he'll be thinking is why it took them so long to open the door. Angie leads him into the centre of the room.

We were just looking for the hamster, Father, she tells him.

But that only serves to puzzle the man. Donna fills him in

as Geddy takes in every inch of his body.

The hamster, Father, it's lost.

That's how we took so long to answer the door, Geddy adds. She's looking direct into his eyes so that he can't mistake her lust. But he does. He's a priest. So Geddy shuffles her arse into the side of the couch, nearly breaking it.

Here, sit here, Father, she goes.

Geddy grins at the Girls and flicks her hair back as Boyle sits right next to her. His fabric rubbing her fabric as down he goes. A certain electricity. Wendy leans over and impersonates Geddy to Angie.

Oh, sit here, Father. Near my tits.

Angie puts her laugh into her shoulders as Boyle scans the room for a familiar face. His face is pink shiny priest plastic. Soon as his head's turned away Geddy opens the next button down on her blouse. Then the next, so that you can just see her bra. Maw frowns at her and does a load of close-your-blouse signals but Boyle catches them out the side of his eye and Maw, after a short hesitation, pretends to be scratching her elbow. Geddy ignores Maw and adjusts her tits. Maw signals to Caroline to offer Boyle a cup of tea. Caroline gets up and goes to the scullery.

Tea, Father?

Oh well, a wee drop then, he says. He looks round all the smiling faces. His eyes take a wee wander downwards as they pass over Geddy and he swings ninety quick degrees away. *So how are you all?*

Great, says Donna.

Magic, goes Angie.

Couldn't be better, Father, Wendy says.

In the pink, Father, Geddy goes.

Boyle makes the connection but thinks it's his own dirty mind. Geddy's bra's pink. He'd noticed that much. And the wee frills coming out the side. The wee frills. My God the . . .

He gets a grip of himself. He can't help but feel Geddy's arse pressing into his. His concentration keeps getting drawn to that meeting place. Geddy is forcing all her sexuality to that area. Caroline comes in with a plate of biscuits. Luckily Maw gets a look at the plate before she sits them down. Boyle's involved in small talk and holy chit chat with the Girls.

You can't give a priest an Indulgence. Have you seen the advert for these? Maw says. She gets up and ushers Caroline back into the scullery. *Have you no Wagon Wheels?* Maw says.

Boyle overhears the conversation from the kitchen. *Don't bother about biscuits for me,* he shouts.

You'll take tea anyway, Father? says Caroline.

Maw is panicking. She gives Wendy the nod and over she comes. Maw whispers to Wendy. *Run out and get some Mr Kipling. Here's two quid.*

Wendy tries to sneak out but Boyle sees her.

Just popping out, Father, Wendy goes.

Maw gives her the hurry-hurry signals as she closes the door peering through. Boyle notices Caroline is a bit down. Not as energetic as the rest of the sisters. There's nothing like a human being with a weakness to bring out the best in a priest. He decides to concentrate on her. Here's where he could make an impression.

And how are you, eh . . .

Caroline, Father, says Maw.

Caroline, is it? That's a beautiful name. How are you? Boyle says. He holds her hand in his. But he doesn't get the reaction he wants. Caroline bursts out crying. He's stunned is Boyle. Stunned.

Oh, she's all mixed up, Father, Maw tells him.

Boyle stands up and puts his arm round Caroline now. Geddy's face is tripping her.

There, there, he says.

Geddy's thinking, No! Here, here. But his sympathy makes

Caroline cry all the louder, He looks about for an explanation. Maw offers one.

Her man left her, Father.

No? he says.

He hugs Caroline tighter. Geddy's eyes get narrower the more he hugs her. Maw offers some more information.

For a young lassie.

Nineteen, belly button pierced, Oul Mary adds.

Belly button pierced, you say? goes Boyle. He says it in a detective's voice rather than a priest's. His forehead is all furrowed. All the Girls nod in that yes-she-definitely-had-her-belly-button-pierced-Father kind of way. That's with the eyebrows raised and the lips pursed while nodding the head. Caroline cries even harder now.

There, there, goes Boyle again.

Caroline gets up and goes to the toilet. They let her go like she's a passing wake and they're people that've stopped in the street out of respect. Once she's gone Boyle asks them a question.

Would it be anybody from this parish?

Stacie Gracie, Father, Maw says.

Ah! That wee girl. They warned me about her.

How's that, Father? Maw wants to know. And so do all the Girls. This is getting interesting. Very interesting.

Before I came to this Parish. The last priest, Father . . . Father . . .

Cooney, says Oul Mary.

That's right, Larry. Father Larry Cooney.

A noted slut in these parts, Father, that Stacie Gracie lassie, goes Oul Mary

Boyle's a bit took back by that to say the least. But that's not all he'll be took back by before this night's out.

Pardon my French, Father, apologises Oul Mary.

They call her the Chariot round here, Father, says Geddy.

Boyle's embarrassed. He looks about for something to do.

Something to fiddle with. They're no different to the rest of us, priests. When it comes to situations they need something to fiddle with. When do you ever see a priest on the altar without something to fiddle with? The books. The chalice. The communion. The Bible. The swingy thing they use at funerals that the smoke comes out of. Rosary beads. On and on ad infinitum. Boyle spots the flames and over he goes. It seems like a good way out.

Nice flames, he says. He notices the stuff lying on the hearth. He bends over and picks something up. Something to fiddle with. He feels stronger now that he's at the fireplace. Towering above everybody where he should be.

What's this?

Soon as he says the words he realises that what he has in his hand is a pair of boxer shorts. And not just any oul boxer shorts. No. Black boxers. And not just any oul black boxers. No. Silk boxers. And not just any oul black silk boxers. No. Black silk shredded boxers. He drops them and stands beside the fire like a right eejit. The Girls are sniggering and he knows it. And they know he knows. And he knows they know he knows. Oul Mary breaks the spell.

Sounds like a barney in Mutchie's pub.

That gives Boyle a chance to be puzzled. To be something other than the young priest standing like a wanker over a pile of shredded underwear of a man that left with a lassie that had her belly button pierced and was only nineteen. To think only minutes ago he tapped on the door with such confidence. Such authority. It would be a long way up to authority again for him. But he goes with the puzzled thing for the time being. Maw lets him in.

She listens to the police reports, Father.

Oh! he says, not wanting to give anything away.

It's her hobby, Angie goes.

There's a long silence and then, through the hiss and crack

of the polis reports comes the sound of Caroline crying in the toilet. Boyle is still uneasy. There's nobody offering a way out. And if things were bad, they are about to get worse. Oul Mary looks at the veranda and a big crow lands on it chewing at a lump of bread.

Wahrgrgrgr!!! Oul Mary screams.

Everybody jumps. Caroline comes running back in from the toilet. Boyle can't help it; he's halfway to the door with fright before he calms down enough to realise what he's doing. And it's just as he's calm that Geddy appears out of the sky and wraps her legs and arms round him. He's doing well not to collapse under her weight.

Save us, Father, Geddy's shouting. *Save us.*

Get off, is his answer.

Jesus bless us and save us, Oul Mary roars.

She's blessing herself. Everybody's looking round the room for what it was that sent Oul Mary into such a fear. Angie glances over at the freezer door just in case Stacie Gracie's head has rolled out onto the floor.

What is it? What is it? Caroline's asking in a panic. She thinks it's Bobby that's appeared back again.

Get off me! Boyle's still telling Geddy.

Oul Mary tells them what's up. *A big black crow landed, thump, nice as you like on that banana thing.*

Wendy corrects Oul Mary. *Veranda, Grandmother.*

They all calm down. It was a crow, a big black crow, they're saying to each other. They know Oul Mary's superstitious so there's not much more to say about it. Boyle is still trying to extricate himself completely from Geddy.

Geraldine! Get off that priest now, Maw shouts.

Geddy disentangles herself slowly from Boyle. Boyle looks indignant but he can't help admitting to himself that he liked it. It was good, this thing he's been missing. Well, not missing; you can't miss what you've never had. But there's something in his body craving for it. He tries to avert his attention but there's Geddy's skirt and it's rode all the way up her arse. Her blouse is all over the place like she's been chased through the woods by the monster. Any monster. But she's the screaming girl. And the moon is shining down. And the wolf is howling. Howling.

Sorry, Father, Geddy says. She's searching his face for the reactions that are automatic. She knows the face is the cinema of the soul. And there's a deep erotic thriller playing in the soul of this priest. Geddy's the director. By now everybody's got their breath and their senses back. If Boyle's breathing is a bit heavier than it was before it's not down to fear.

It's a bad omen that crow, so it is, says Oul Mary.

It's nothing, goes Linda.

A bad omen, Oul Mary says again.

Does that mean we can't . . . Caroline begins, but Linda moves over and shooshes her up before she says too much. Goes too far. Oul Mary's still got tunnel vision with this crow that landed on the veranda.

It might have been Oul Nick himself, she goes.

Boyle's right in there. *Don't tell me you're superstitious, Mrs Duffy? A good Catholic like you?* he says. His voice has regained its condescending authority.

I am.

You should put those things from you.

There's more to life than things you can see, Father.

They're not healthy, these things, he says.

Aye well! says Oul Mary. She sits back like she's finished with the matter. Like she doesn't want to discuss it any more. There's a pause. The Girls are looking at Boyle.

The Devil indeed! Ha! That's all Boyle can think of to say. But that's the wrong thing cos Oul Mary sees the gap and goes on the attack.

Well, that seems mighty strange to me, Father – a priest that doesn't believe in the Devil, she says. She wipes her hands and leans back chuffed.

Now I never said that, says Boyle. He is realising the theological implications of there being no Satan.

Mighty strange indeed, Oul Mary goes.

The Girls settle in. They love her most when she's up against powerful forces.

I never said I didn't believe in . . . him, goes Boyle. He's obviously buying time. Thinking up the next moves in the argument. What she'll say, what he'll say, and so on.

Mighty strange, repeats Oul Mary.

Now the Girls see she's not going to go down the labyrinthine routes of Biblical quotation and Catholic dogma. She's going to restate her position over and over, causing Boyle to raise his anger at every denial, and every denial will be him protesting too much till he loses the argument himself.

That's not what I said.

I've heard it all now, says Oul Mary, *that's all I can say. I've heard it all now.*

It's superstition I don't believe in, Boyle says.

Mm mm.

Big crows being the Devil and stuff like that. His voice is wavering and his face is puffing up. Angie joins in on the attack now.

I thought that's what Catholicism was, Father – superstition.

You're not listening at Mass, my dear, Boyle snaps at Angie.

But Angie's not Oul Mary's granddaughter for nothing. She comes back with an answer and she's got one or two stored up and all, if that goes wrong.

What? You mean all about big lumps of plastic being Our Lady and stuff like that? she says. *Our Lady being a lump of plastic?*

Boyle ignores her. He's staring defeat in the face. Maw steps in to save him. And save some face for herself and all. And her family, the heathens that they are.

Angela! Between Geddy jumping on Father and you talking like that, what's my family coming to?

It's okay, Mrs Riley. It's okay. They're young, says Boyle. He's grabbing the chance to extradite himself from the situation with both hands.

What must you think of my family, Father. We were so friendly with the last priest and all, Maw says.

Father Larry, says Geddy.

Quids in, Father. Quids in, says Oul Mary.

Geddy moves closer to Boyle and tells him Cooney might have been lovely but he's not a patch on Boyle. Not a patch. Boyle takes a big sideways step.

Och, this is just a silly misunderstanding about superstition, he says. He has a desperate lightness in his tone. But there he goes again, opening the door for Oul Mary.

Surely you're a wee bit superstitious yourself, Father? Oul Mary asks him.

Not in the least, he says.

He's trying to calculate all the possible places this can go to. What is that oul woman up to now? She tells him he should be superstitious. Very superstitious. Especially where he lives. Boyle snorts and wants to know why on earth would he want to be anything of the sort.

Cos of where you live, says Oul Mary.

Why? he asks.

Right on the very steps of your Chapel. He's been seen there, goes Oul Mary.

Who?

Shergar, Angie says. That gets a good laugh.

Him that should never be named, Oul Mary tells Boyle.

Of course there's no way that Boyle believes that him that should never be named was ever anywhere near the steps of St Augustine's Chapel. But Oul Mary's not letting it go.

I'm telling you! she says.

She has the confidence of a cat. She looks about and gets the affirmation of the others. Oh aye, and for sure, they're nodding as if they had been there. That they were the very people Oul Nick had appeared to with pitchfork and shovel and his big pointed tail swishing about behind him like a hand on a crazy mixed-up clock. Boyle's getting a bit fed up with all this.

Will I tell you about it, Father? Oul Mary asks him.

Oh dearie, dearie me, is that the time? I really must be going, says Boyle.

He knows he can't argue too much but he's got to claw some respect back. If he walks out now it's like repeating that he doesn't believe in the Devil. Oul Mary tries to persuade him.

It's good, Father, I promise you.

I've got a wake just over the road there.

He has got a wake. He's walking a thin line here. They might let him go with his respect intact cos he's got a wake to go to. And cos he's a new priest. But he's not sure. Not sure at all. Oul Mary sees where his thinking is going and offers him a compromise.

Tell you what, Father, if you're not interested you can up and go any time you like. How's that?

He wavers.

Get the Father another wee cup of tea, Maw says.

Angie runs in for the tea. Boyle knows he's trapped into a corner now. There's nothing he can do. He'll have to wait. Listen to their story.

Give me a minute, he goes. He whips out the mobile phone.

Two sugars in Father's wee cup of tea, Angie, Maw shouts.

Boyle's dialled a number and it's answered. *Hello, Hanna? I'm going to be another ten minutes – is that alright?*

Bzbzbzbz . . .

You start and I'll join in during the Third Decade – how's that?

Bzbzbzbz . . .

Great. See you then.

Boyle clicks the phone off and Angie shoves a cup of tea and a plate of biscuits in his face. Boyle takes a bite out of a biscuit. He's got to make up as much ground as he can. Bit by bit.

Mmm, these are nice. What are they?

Indulgences, Father, says Geddy.

What?

They're on the telly; eat one and the man of your dreams—

Donna! Maw cuts her off. Nearly.

Climbs in the window and kisses you on the end of your nose.

Maw sighs some relief out her nose. The door opens and in comes Wendy all red-faced and flustered.

They'd no Mr Kipling.

Shhsht! Linda tells her.

Wendy mouths, *what is it?* Linda tells her they're about to start the Devil on the Chapel steps story and Wendy brightens up. Great stuff, especially with a priest. For a second she feels sorry for Boyle. Trapped in here with eight women and them about to assail him with a story. And not just any story but the Devil on the Chapel steps story. Wendy turns off the big light so there's just the lamp and the sky dark outside and the flames in the big ostentatious fireplace licking every surface in the room. Oul Mary waits for the right moment and starts. Slow and easy she starts.

The Devil

In the 1930s all about St Augustine's was the Slap Up, Oul Mary says.

She's scanning everybody as she speaks. She's good, Oul Mary. Her very tone has captured Boyle's interest right away. She could be a hypnotist in another life. Of course, Oul Mary knows that. She's not the best storyteller in the Brig for nothing. Even the easy, throwaway style is calculated. That's the thing about General Miscellaneous stories; they're as worked out and considered as anything Shakespeare or English Literature has to offer. And what they have over them is their apparent simplicity. Their deliberate simplicity. So that to hear it or read it is to dismiss it as not being Literature, not being Art. And even that is deliberate. We want our art to be dismissed. To be accepted by another culture is the big betrayal. What I'm trying to say is every word of the story has been looked at like a brickie's brick. Tumbled round, the weight of it felt, its look judged against the other bricks, its value in the structure and its function as entertainment ascertained. All these things have been thought out by the same process a poet would use. The only thing different is the content and the language. Oul Mary continues.

The Slap Up was all these tenement buildings and narrow cobblestone streets.

Built for Irish immigrants that came to work in the ironworks, Angie says. *Irish immigrants they were built for.*

Thirteen to a room, goes Oul Mary.

One room, Father, men and women, all crushed together, says Geddy.

Crammed in there stinking, Maw goes.

The air was black as night and the daytime sun was always orange, Oul Mary says.

I can mind it, nods Maw, adding a bit of authenticity to the story. Boyle's pressed back against the couch again. Angie comes in with some facts.

At that time it had a higher population density than New York, the Slap Up.

New York, you say? goes Boyle.

And bang! They know they've got him. He's a fish on a hook and they can reel him in or let him out as they please. The head in the freezer can wait. This is going to be a momentous night. Almighty. This is another story they'll be telling down the time.

They never knocked it down till the sixties, Father, Maw says.

Imagine it, Father. The night was lit by the odd gas lamp here and there shining off the cobbles, Oul Mary says low and mysterious.

At that time all the pubs shut at nine, Maw goes.

I had two aunties – Mary and Lizzie, Father. They never married, says Oul Mary.

They read books, says Wendy.

They used to read the teacups and the palms and all that stuff, Donna says.

The Girls know what to do. When to join in or lean back and let Oul Mary run with it. When to move. When to sit still. When to lean in. When to lean back and leave Boyle feeling lonesome; the epicentre of a circle of Witches. Donna takes up the starey eyes again and Oul Mary gets on with the story.

They never drank . . . but they smoked like lums.

Chimleys, says Maw.

This night they ran out of fags, Oul Mary says.

They couldn't go a couple of hours without a drag, goes Angie. *A couple of hours they couldn't go.*

Out they went with their slippers on, says Linda.

Linda is talking from her position on the couch where to Boyle she looks like any other able-bodied sister. He's gave Donna a couple of glances in the wheelchair. But he's going for the treat-her-like-an-ordinary-human-being approach. Don't mention the wheelchair. Or ask what happened to her. That makes you seem mighty holy. Really sincere.

It was nine o'clock, but they were gasping, Oul Mary goes on.

The streets were dead, goes Maw.

It was dark, says Donna into his eyes.

And quiet, says Maw.

Oul Mary leans forwards so she's as close to Boyle as she can get without kissing him.

Jeannie Bogey owned the wee shop down Dundyvan and you could chap her back door for a midnight loaf or fags so you could. Aye. But this night Mary and Lizzie got there and Jeannie Bogey never answered.

Bang – bang – bang! Linda knocks the table right on cue. Wendy gets up and searches through her bag for a CD she bought on the way down.

Wait – wait a minute. We need music for this, she goes.

The Girls carry on with the story as Wendy sets up the CD. Although they've done this story hundreds of times before and they all play particular parts in it, there's always room for improvisation. Scope for improvement. It's a Paganini CD she puts on. Oul Mary carries on with the story.

Chap – chap – chap! They're going and nothing. Not a thing, Father. That was a bit strange cos Jeannie Bogey never left the

Slap Up except for weddings an wakes.

Wakes an weddings, Father, Angie repeats.

Oul Mary continues. *So there's Mary and Lizzie pulling their shawls criss-cross and pressing back home through the fog. Can you picture them, Father? Appearing in the light of ghostly gas lamps and then fading into the mist over and over along Buchanan Street. Can you picture it, Father?*

Whho! Hooo! screams Angie. She screams right into his ear and Boyle jumps out his skin.

Angie! Says Maw.

So Angie apologises. By now Boyle's eyes are shining. They're shining for a lot of reasons. One being the frightening way they're telling him the story. The other, the sheer power of all these females surrounding him. The sex.

Making it through the night without a fag was the only thing in their minds. They would have done anything for a draw, anything, Oul Mary says.

Anything, says Geddy. She moves closer, leaving no room for ambiguity. She holds his gaze till he looks away. If he ever had any power it was all but gone now.

Well! They go into the Chapel doorway, Oul Mary says.

St Augustine's? asks Boyle.

And they all nod like a weird machine.

To look for fag douts, says Maw. She gestures to Oul Mary to go on.

Next thing, this figure looms out the fog. They stop and let it move towards them. The noise of hard feet on the wet cobbles is echoing about the buildings.

Angie starts clomping about the floor really hamming it up. Oul Mary stops her with a glare. Donna takes up the story.

They couldn't see any buildings, it was that thick the fog. That right, Granny?

Oul Mary nods and carries on. *They could have been anywhere. But the footsteps kept on coming . . .*

For all they knew they could be at the top of some mountain wandering lost in mist, says Angie. *In mist, on a mountain.*

Angie passes it back to Oul Mary.

As they peered into the fog, clip clop, clip clop, the figure materialised. Top hat and tails, it was wearing.

Top hat and tails, Father, breathes Linda.

Immaculately dressed, Wendy tells him, and Oul Mary takes up the tale.

Like a prince. Mary and Lizzie are drawn by the intensity of his eyes. Tall. In the darkness.

About this size, Angie says. She stands on the couch. Maw takes the baton.

In them days, in the Slap Up, the only place you'd see a suit outside wakes an weddings would be the pawnshop.

'Good evening, ladies,' he whispers with no accent that you could make out, goes Oul Mary.

Maw stands up to add the next bit. *'G-Good evening, sir,' blurts out Lizzie. 'C-C-Can you sell us a cigarette, please?' And she curtsied automatic,* Maw goes. She gets up and curtsies like Lizzie in the story. The story, as always, was turning into a play.

The man smiled at them, Oul Mary says.

More a grin really, goes Linda.

Donna and Linda do big inane grins for Boyle. Oul Mary takes it up.

Mary blushed and looked away, peering into the fog. There's just the glow of a street lamp and somebody away in the distance singing 'Whiskey in the Jar'.

Wendy starts singing 'Whisky in the Jar' but tails off as they all stare at her. Improvisation's one thing but showing off's another. She shuts up and Oul Mary goes on.

The man replies, 'Sell you some cigarettes? Sell you them, ladies? I'll do better than that, I'll give you some cigarettes.'

Oul Mary stands up to do a wee bit of acting herself.

Caroline is losing herself in the drama. And that's good for her broken heart. Oul Mary acts it out.

The dark hand slid into his inside pocket and brung out a cigarette case. Solid gold, Father, the fag case. That's right, gold it was. Mesmerised they were. Can you imagine it, Father, eh – can you? She holds out an imaginary fag case right up to Boyle's face. *It shone and it sparked. Even in the dimness of the fog.*

Angie and Geddy stand up and become Mary and Lizzie. Oul Mary moves back and lets them be the centre of attention while she narrates.

Click – the lid flips open and the insides are padded like a coffin. He pushes it slowly through the darkness between them. Mary's eyes peer over the glittering edge. It's filled with row after row of cigarettes. He holds it out so they can help themselves. Lizzie curtsies again and slips two from the case. Delicate like.

Geddy curtsies and takes some imaginary cigarettes.

Then Mary grabs. One hand then the next stuffing them into the folds of her shawl.

It's like the box has no bottom, says Donna.

Fathomless, Father. Fathomless, Linda goes, her breath trailing off.

Angie does greedy Mary grabbing all these fags and stuffing them into the folds of her shawl. Oul Mary careers on with the story. It was a machine now and you couldn't stop it if you tried. Boyle couldn't get his arse out of the seat even if God Himself was there to help him.

Her hands are in and out and still there's rows of cigarettes lined up like little bodies. The man laughs and for a moment his eyes burn with fire.

Like there was flames inside his head, Father, says Maw.

Oul Mary does the sinister laugh. And the man sitting on the couch is nothing like the man who strode in and announced himself an hour ago. Oul Mary goes on, doing the Devil's voice now.

'Would you ladies care to smoke one with me now?' he goes in a voice as soft as a priest's. Sorry, Father, no offence.

None taken, carry on, says Boyle. He's enthralled. Caroline hands Oul Mary a lighter so that Geddy and Angie can act the next scene out. When they're ready Oul Mary carries on.

A red star pings in his eye. He cups a gold lighter in his hands and holds it out to Lizzie first. She puts a fag in her mouth. The three of them are lit up by the blaze from the flame. He's handsome.

The best-looking guy you ever seen, Father. Even better than him that's on the Indulgence advert, says Geddy.

Behind Geddy and Boyle, Donna is wheeling her way to the door. Oul Mary carries on.

And it looks like the skin on his face is a fine surface of fire. Lizzie leans into the flame puffing life into the fag. Mary fiddles with hers in her bony fingers. Lizzie sends a line of blue smoke burrowing up through the yellow fog.

Angie blows a line of smoke towards the ceiling. They crane their necks and watch it. In that long-necked silence where part of you always thinks you're going to get your throat cut Donna switches the lights off. Boyle jumps and they get a laugh at that. When they calm down Oul Mary gets deeper into the story.

The lighter clicks off and puts them into a further darkness. Then the man swings around and clicks again.

Donna switches the lights back on.

The blaze lights up his grin.

Boyle looks round uneasy. All the Girls have got big grins on them.

So, Mary notices his breath is stinking, Oul Mary goes.

Pure honking, Father, says Geddy.

Like sewage, Linda shudders.

Oul Mary brings it back. *She lowers her head into the crucible of light of his cupped hands. All polite like. Her eyes run down the black silk of his suit. Excuse my language here, Father. The groin . . .*

The thighs . . . The knees . . . The razor-sharp crease in his trousers take her to his feet.

She liked men, Father, Geddy says.

Angie runs screaming, *Jesus, Mary and Joseph* and all sorts into the scullery. Boyle's head is everywhere wondering if this is the story or reality. Caroline is loving it. For a wee while now she's forgot Bobby. Forgot her troubles. Forgot the head in the freezer. Her sisters' presence is working. She's taking the medicine and pain has flown away. Oul Mary carries on.

Lizzie looks at the man and either she's shrinking or he's growing, Oul Mary says.

Geddy shrinks to her knees leaning into Boyle's legs. Oul Mary goes on.

The lighter flickers on his face. Fear. She's immersed in it, Father. Sheer and utter fear. Then there's this noise on the ground. A clip clop from the cobbles and Lizzie looks down.

And freaks out, Maw says grinning hard.

Howling like a banshee, says Angie. *Like a banshee she's howling.*

Screaming at the two cloven hoofs sticking out the bottom of his trousers, Oul Mary says, hammering it home.

Boyle mouths the words, two cloven hoofs. Only it's *hooves* he mouths but that doesn't matter.

Two cloven hooves? He asks Oul Mary.

Oul Mary nods and goes in with the rest of the tale.

The man roars insane laughter. Lizzie tries to run but her feet are slipping on the cobbles. She sees two lumps appearing on his forehead.

Two lu . . . lumps? Boyle swallows.

Linda makes two horns on the top of her head to confirm it. Oul Mary takes it on.

They got home and boiled up pots and kettles of water and scrubbed and scrubbed.

Washed their mouths out with soap, says Maw.
Sprinkled holy water over each other, goes Angie.
And round about the room, adds Oul Mary.
Tied garlic over the door and window, Linda puts in.
Their clothes stank to high heaven with the stench of his breath says Oul Mary.
Like sulphur – that's what the Devil's breath smells like, Linda tells him.
So they burnt every stitch. And when they did, faces of demons and tortured souls writhed in the flames, goes Oul Mary.
The Girls dance and pull the faces of the demons and tortured souls. Maw comes in.
Cold sweat all over them, Father. Flames shining on their skin like mirrors.
It was hot but they were shivering, goes Donna. She resumes her starey eyes.
They sat naked, holding each other and shaking, Oul Mary says.
What . . . what happened to them? Boyle wants to know.
But Oul Mary's vague on that. London maybe. Aye, that's what Maw heard. London. That's what they say and the Girls agree that's the general thinking on it.
In a house of ill-repute, Father, Oul Mary says.
Good Lord, says Boyle to that.
They stare at his reaction. The wheels turning in his head. The disbelief being shoved aside by primitive fears and superstitions.
That is an horrific story, is what he says.
Gave you the creeps there, eh, Father? goes Donna.
Right on the Chapel steps, you say? he murmurs.
The Girls all nod in unison.
Cigarette ends, was it? he asks.
Aye, you can expect the Devil with the drink, but fag ends? Says Oul Mary.

Aye, they never expected the Devil for that, Donna says. *Not for that.*

Boyle gets himself together and shakes some of the story out of his head. If you looked you'd see the words and images coming out of his ears like water off a dog's head.

That can't be true, he says.

How d'you know it's not? Donna asks.

He says it's an urban myth but Geddy points out how can that be if they don't even know what that means – urban myth. There's not an answer to that.

A fairy-tale then, he suggests.

But Oul Mary thinks that's some fairy, that creature with big horns and red eyes and hoofs.

And minging breath! Donna reminds him.

I don't mean wee wings and three wishes. I mean lies. People hang onto these things for . . . for a great variety of reasons, Boyle says.

Oul Mary lets him know she's hardly going to tell stories like that about her own relatives now is she? Especially to a priest. The others support her. A man of the cloth . . . now would she be going and doing that? No way. A woman that's never missed Mass in all her days on the earth. No. Boyle has an idea. The same idea all priests have in sticky situations.

I know! Let's say a Decade of the Rosary, goes Boyle.

They all give him a what-for look. He gives them the priest answer. But actually he's just trying to regain some modicum of control.

To ask Our Blessed Lady to sanctify and purify the steps of the Chapel.

That should do the trick, Father. There's nothing him that should never be mentioned likes worse than the Holy Rosary, Oul Mary says.

Geddy turns to Wendy and wants to know where Jehovah is now. Like he might come in and save them from ten fuckin

Decades of holy misery. And in the background Boyle's going on about how comforting the Rosary is. For him it is. He's right there. But it's more boring than backgammon. The good news is he's only got time for one Decade. The Girls sigh and feign disappointment at that. But Angie says, *Aww*, too loud and Boyle gives her a dark look.

Watch what you're saying, Angie. He's on the Children's Panel this week if I'm not mistaken! Wendy tells her.

Oul Mary tells him it's the togetherness of it all that makes the Rosary such a holy thing.

The close proximity of other human beings. You're right there. One Decade then, Boyle says.

One it is then, Father, right enough, that should do the trick, Oul Mary says.

They all get into the kneeling position. Geddy kneels right beside Boyle. Boyle's got his beads hanging from his hands when Geddy pops the question.

You wouldn't mind blessing my back first, would you, Father? It's killing me.

She bends over and presents her arse to him so that there's no turning back. He reverses a step and he's got his blessing paraphernalia out before he realises what he's doing. Presenting a priest with such a lovely arse does that. He blesses it as quick as he can.

Grant this ars . . . back the grace to shoulder its cross in the name of the Father and of the Son and of the Holy Spirit . . .

As he carries on with his own particular wee spell Geddy's making faces at the Girls. Running her tongue round her lips; all that kind of stuff.

Amen, Boyle says.

Amen, they say.

He starts putting his blessing equipment by. Oul Mary sees an opportunity to get the house blessed.

Our Caroline's had a terrible time of it, Father, so she has. You couldn't bless her house, could you? she says.

If Boyle wasn't a priest you'd swear he gives it a fuck-this look. He tells them he's late enough for the wake already and they've still got the Rosary to do. Oul Mary promises that they'll say the Rosary for him that should never be mentioned on the Chapel steps when he's away at the wake. Five Decades they'll say. All he has to do is bless Caroline's house.

I've a busy night ahead of me, Boyle says.

But they look pleadingly at him. Begging girlies. Boyle gets the holy-water sprinkler out and starts flinging water about like a summer lawn.

Protect this house and those who live here in the name of the Father and of the Son and of the Holy Spirit, Amen.

A wee cup of tea, Father? Angie asks.

But he really has to go this time. He's way late.

I hear you're on the Children's Panel this week, Father, she says.

And he is. He is indeed. *My news gets around this town fast. Very fast.*

Angie tells him her Dessie's up the Panel this week. *It's my oldest laddie, Father.*

If there's anything I can do, Boyle tells her.

Angie thanks him. Boyle wants to know what he done, her oldest laddie. Of course the answer to that is nothing. All the Girls could have put the kettle on for that. They lift their eyes to the sky and Angie trundles out the case for the defence.

He was in this shebeen, Gallagher's house, they drink the wine in there, Father. Get it abroad and sell it like a pub. Anyway, they said my Dessie hit a guy with a hammer but I asked them all and they said he never. It's the polis! They've got it in for my Dessie so they have.

Oh, the hammer incident. I heard about that. It's a terrible thing so it is, Boyle says.

I know, Father, they're always blaming my Dessie. He's in the Secure Unit the now. They're all crazy in there. A bad influence.

A terrible thing for a mother to bear. Terrible, says Boyle.

He puts his hand on Angie's shoulder. She thinks she's getting a result from this dumbo of a priest. He thinks she must be heartbroken and Angie lays it on like lemon curd. She can't sleep at night. Hasn't slept for weeks. She opens one eye to see what he's going to offer her. And the Girls laugh cos he offers the usual. About how Mary must have felt during Christ's Passion. Holy stuff's no good. She's got to go for it now. She bursts out greeting. Geddy whispers to Donna that she's putting it on.

Dhuuu, says Donna to Geddy.

Angie shuffles away to the toilet crying. Boyle is affronted. But once she's there her tears disappear and she passes the time away having a fag, remembering to let out some artificial sobs now and then as she reads about the latest pop stars in a magazine. She doesn't know that in the living room they are talking about her in front of Boyle. Linda's tearing right in and telling Donna but really telling Doyle.

Sadie Brogan told me that when that fellah Brown was out for the count on the carpet her Dessie smashed him on the head with a hammer.

Linda! Maw shouts.

Three times.

Linda!

Here. Here. And here.

Linda, would you shut up! Maw goes

I'm just saying, goes Linda.

Maw's head sinks with the shame of it and Angie comes back from the toilet hoping her plan has worked. That he's ready to pull all the strings he can. The holy ones and the secular ones. The social ones and the legal ones. She's glad she came here the night. Boyle asks if she's alright. She says an aye that really means no. Boyle goes over to her. Yes! Here we go. Here's the help.

Jesus is a healer, he says. *A true God and also a great man.*

But what good is that? That's the same shite he was coming away with when Angie went to the bog. She'll have to humour him. At least a bit.

Good, Father. He was that. A true healer. Can you do anything for my wee Dessie?

I'm sure there's something, he says.

Angie grins at the Girls. But she ungrins at his next sentence.

Ask and ye shall receive. We can't doubt the words of Jesus.

Angie's face sinks. Boyle's working his way to the door now.

If Jesus was so great how did He not tell the disciples the world was round, not flat? Linda says.

That stops Boyle in his tracks. He wants to know what she said. Maw tells him it was nothing, just bumping her crazy gums about nothing in particular. But he heard it alright. He heard exactly what was said. Maw tries to deflect him by saying it was Donna she was asking the question to. And it looks like Boyle's accepting it. He gets to leave the house with his power levels back up a bit if he leaves now. But oh ho, Wendy of all people comes in now. She can't hold her Jehovah-ness back.

You know, I'd like an answer to that question too, Father. It's intriguing, says Wendy.

Linda is chuffed at having such an unexpected backer. Boyle's face boils up. He looks direct right at Wendy.

Well, I never expected it from you. A teacher in a Catholic school?

It's strictly philosophical, Father, strictly philosophical, says Wendy.

Boyle knows he can't get past strictly philosophical. He forgives Wendy with a pious smile. Geddy makes faces at Wendy behind her back. Faces like; you're dead when you get back to school. Boyle goes to leave again. But Linda pipes up.

But I want to know the answer, she says.

Boyle looks at his watch and sighs. *Well,* he says, *there's some things we don't get to know till the time's right. The world wasn't ready for that sort of . . . eh that sort of knowledge as yet at the time, you know. Contemporaries of Jesus knew what they had to know. No more.*

There's a pause as the dogma sinks in. Linda lets the pause fizzle itself out. At the maximum silence she says, *Well, it would have saved Christopher Columbus a lot of fuckin bother, Father.*

Linda! Shouts Maw.

Linda, says Oul Mary.

Boyle is buttoning up his tunic. He is raging. Mad. Geddy decides to have a go at it all now. Priest baiting is quite good fun.

Tell him about Jehovah, Wendy, Geddy goes. But Wendy ignores her. Geddy starts chanting, *Jehovah! Jehovah! Jehovah!*

Some of the others join in. Boyle is perplexed at the whole thing. What he can't see is Linda whispering to Donna. Conspiring.

Ask him, Linda says loud.

No, I can't ask him that, Donna says.

Donna's all coy and respectful again. Boyle looks down.

Ask me what, Girls?

The Miracle

Linda nods to Donna in the wheelchair. Donna in Linda's wheelchair.

She's feart to ask you, Father. You couldn't bless Linda's wheelchair, could you? It's not going so well. Squeaks a lot, Linda says.

Strange to be calling Donna by her own name but you never know if the priest already knows there's a girl up there in a wheelchair and her name's Linda. Oul Mary wants to know what they're playing at. There's far and there's too far. But this is too far by far. By fuck. She's mortified.

I suppose it's . . . Boyle says.

He wants away but Angie wheels the chair over to him so that there's Boyle and Donna in a space of their own. A space where he can stay and help or desert her. He gets the wee scarf thing out and kisses it. Unscrews the bottle of holy water.

Bow your head, Linda, Boyle says.

And Donna bows her head. Winking at the Girls as she does.

A little bit more.

She's shy, Father, says Linda.

I bless this chair and its wheels and all its moving parts . . .

It squeaks like an oul ASDA trolley, Father, Donna goes.

Boyle continues with the blessing.

...That it may swift Linda here to and fro with the greatest of ease. In the name of the Father and of the Son and of the Holy Spirit.

Her legs, Father, bless her legs, Linda shouts.

Boyle puts his hands on Donna's thighs. His hands are trembling, partly with fear and partly with womenitis. He makes the blessing up as he goes. It's actually quite a good one.

I bless these legs that Linda may walk and have the freedom of this earthly paradise to roam and be free. That the Lord take pity on these limbs and restore them to the beauty they once possessed. In the name of the Father and of the Son and of the Holy Spirit, Amen.

Amen. They all say.

That was lovely, Father, Maw goes. *Beautiful.*

Never heard it done better apart from Mary McGinty's funeral, says Oul Mary.

Boyle starts packing his stuff. The Girls try hard to suppress their laughter. Boyle's at the door when Donna shouts out.

I feel something. I feel something.

Try the brakes! Try the brakes! Angie shouts.

It's like a throbbing. I feel I could stand up, d'you know that! she goes. Donna struggles halfway to her feet.

Jesus Christ Almighty! Boyle gasps.

Father . . . Father! Donna pleads.

And she reaches out with her arms and walks, or stumbles, towards him like a beautiful Frankenstein. The Girls are just one big intake of breath, a pause, then a cacophony of amazement. Boyle's mouth is a black hole and if you look right down there in the thick of the darkness there is his sainthood like a little galaxy swirling about waiting for a place to create itself. This could be the one true call. He went into the priesthood cos of his mother. His family. Respect. But now here's the call that the other priests go on about. The one he's pretended he's already had. The voice of God Himself.

It's a miracle, says Linda.

Boyle looks at his all-powerful hands. The hands that seconds ago laid on the thighs, on the legs of this young girl. The very legs that are stumbling towards him. These hands. These hands.

Praise be to the Lord Jesus Christ! Boyle shouts.

Donna reaches him with her last wooden clog step and falls into his arms. He's so far gone he doesn't notice the press of her breasts against him. Donna makes some faces at Geddy.

My God, how long has she been in a wheelchair? He asks them

Years, Father, Angie tells him.

They all nod in confirmation.

I could get a Cardinalship out of this. This could be . . . this could be . . . Boyle can't bring himself to say it.

A miracle. It is a miracle, Father, she says.

Donna flops to the floor. Boyle tries to stand her up again but she's a rag doll; her arms waving like rubber in the air before slipping through his grip. Boyle is intense. The Girls all gather round her with the appropriate sympathy and help her back into her chair. Boyle clears them away and kneels by her side.

Try to stand up, he says.

Donna pushes up on the chair but she can't get any purchase. The Girls are standing round about like a holy painting.

Come on, Linda! Linda says to Donna.

She tries again. Gets an inch further but no more. The strain on her face is terrible. Boyle is rising up with her. The Girls are rising up with her. She's there. She's there. Her arse is two inches off the chair. She's going to do it. She's going to do it. Bump. Back down she goes.

It's no use, Father, Donna says.

But Boyle's not for giving up. He can see promotion in this. Then who knows? Who knows. There's never been a Scottish Pope. Right. He gets his blessing gear out again and lays it all on the floor nice as you like.

Not the water, Father, my hair!

Oh right. Fine. Right you are, Linda, he says.

So he does the blessing with his bare hands. That's where the power is anyway, is it not?

I bless this chair and its wheels and all its moving parts that it may swift Linda here to and fro . . . to and fro . . . what was next? What was next?

Greatest of ease, Father, Linda says.

With the greatest of ease, in the name of the Father and of the Son and of the Holy Spirit.

He stands back. The Girls are in awe of the impending Divine intervention. Boyle slowly raises his hands to the sky and tilts his head back. It looks like he's doing Tai Chi. He brings them down gradually so the palms are pointing to Donna's head. The Girls jump when he shouts. Donna nearly jumps out the chair.

Rise, woman!! I command you to be on your feet!

Donna struggles but can't get more than an inch from the seat. The Girls have to took to hiding their laughter now by turning away and sobbing like they're crying with joy. Boyle's seen religious fervour before so that serves to make him more insane. And the more insane he gets the more they sob with laughter. The more they sob the more insane he gets. It's a vicious circle. Only this is a hilarious circle.

What were my words? What were my exact words?

They stare at him blankly. Linda turning away and sobbing.

Come on, for God's sakes help me, he pleads.

That phrase tells you all you need to know about Boyle. He never said help Donna. He said help him. All the way to the Vatican he thinks he's going. The Girls know he'll be lucky if he gets halfway to the Whifflet Bridge.

You said something about wheels, Father, Angie says.

Watch what you're doing, Father – this might put Peter Thompson out of business, Linda says.

They've all got to turn away and sob this time. Even Donna. Boyle doesn't know Peter Thompson's the main supplier of wheelchairs and wheelchair accessories in Scotland. Boyle has a go at it again.

I bless these wheels and moving parts that it may swift Linda here to and fro with ease, in the name of the Father and of the Son and of the Holy Spirit.

The Girls stare with vacant expectation. Nothing happens. Boyle grabs them demanding to know what his exact words were. They all chip in.

Holy spirit bless my sprockets, goes Linda.

Leave her hair so shiny as she streams along the street, says Geddy.

Remove the margarine from these wheels and replace it with WD40, Angie says.

Oh Lord of the good place send these gammy legs to the bad place, Donna goes.

Boyle rises to his full height and fills his lungs with the Holy Spirit. *Get behind me, Satan! Now rise, child, and walk!* he screams.

In the silence left by his diminished words Donna speaks.

I can't, I'm crippled, Father, she says.

The Girls fold over at that.

Help me, help me, he says.

Boyle, Angie, Wendy and Geddy lift Donna upright. Donna's making faces and sticking her tongue out. Boyle holds Donna by the shoulders turned away from him. So that she and him are facing the Girls. Although Oul Mary wasn't too pleased at going so far with a priest she's right into it now.

In the name of the Lord Jesus Christ, when I remove these hands may Jesus and His holy mother Mary lay their spiritual hands on you and keep you upright and walking . . . walking! he shouts.

He lets Donna go giving her that extra wee holy push towards her sisters. CRASH!!! She thuds onto the floor and she's as still as a bit of wood. Unconscious. The Girls are down round about her. They crane their necks and look up at Boyle who's towering above them riddled with the bullets of disappointment.

Look what you've done! Linda says.

She raises a slightly crooked finger at him which is somehow much more effective than you'd think. Boyle is ashamed like a boy caught wanking by his Maw. And that actually happened to him. Who knows, maybe in some crazy academic psychoanalytic way it led to him becoming a priest. He was lying in bed that morning with the usual hard-on. He decides to get rid of it and starts chugging away. This is Belfast in the 1960s. he's just getting to the tickly bit when the Hoover comes into the room. There's nothing worse to put you off than a Hoover. Well there is actually – your own Maw. So there's his Maw on the end of this Hoover shooshing it about the room and bumping it off the bed and the skirting. Boyle's still got it in his hand, stroking it gently. Keeping it warm and alert. Once you lose a hard-on in these circumstances you can never get it back. The Maw's Hoovering away. And that jet-engine noise is going through him. He closes his eyes. That's his big mistake cos seconds later his Maw, noticing the bulge in the blankets where there shouldn't be any, whips the sheet off and there he is lying with his hand on his tadger. First thing is she's shocked by the size of it. Then she's enraged by the sin of it. Then she's affronted by it being her son, her own son. Then the thought comes to her. A thought she's never entertained. That he was wanking to her. His own Maw. Chugging away there as his own Maw's arse went left and right against the momentum of the sweeps of the Hoover.

You filthy little bastard!

She grabs him by the tadger. He's squealing as she flings him out of the room and down the stairs he goes. Before the two of them know it they're running down the street; Boyle with his hands cupping his shrinking tadger and his Maw running after him with the Hoover raised above her head. The neighbours never knew what to make of it. They'd never seen the likes of it. So Freudian analysis might lead you to think he became a priest cos of that. And who knows? They might be right. But for now that memory flushed through his head and brung the same feelings to this moment. In this house. With these eight women staring at him with the same eyes his mother had on her when she whipped that white sheet back.

I think it'd be best if I left, he says.

They stare at him.

Well, bye then, he says.

They stare more.

I'll drop in another time perhaps, ladies.

They continue to stare and he goes. Blessed are the meek, and the way Boyle clicked that door open and closed it he's the most blessed of all the meek. They let his footsteps echo down the close. Their rhythm getting faster and faster as he goes. You can tell that even with his steps getting faster and faster, the length of his stride is getting longer and longer. He wants to put a fair oul distance between him and that flat. And quick. If that's an example of the families in this parish then God help him. He's in for a right rough time.

Back up in Caroline's house Maw has rounded on Wendy, her being a teacher and the priest being the Chaplain of four primary schools.

He'll report you to the School Board, Wendy.

So? says Wendy. *It was worth it.*

For the first time in years Wendy's reunited with her sisters fully. In a real way. The only way to really unite a family is against a common enemy. That's why funerals are so intimate and homely. A family against the biggest enemy of all. Death. And talking about death, what about the head in the fridge, Caroline's thinking. But she's not wanting to bring it up. The rush of bad emotions are coming back now Boyle's gone. The entertainment. If you have to live your life at this rate to keep away the pain of a broken heart she'll be dead in a fortnight.

He's lovely, that priest, Geddy says.

Jesus! They're chasing after priests now, says Oul Mary.

He's away to Spain next month, Maw goes.

Wendy's surprised at that. He's just there at the school and now he's off to Spain. Gallivanting. But Maw lets her know it's not gallivanting. It's a special walk between France and Spain and your feet are bleeding at the end of it. Gushing. Geddy thinks of Boyle hiking over the mountains. The sweat on his shirt. A secluded olive grove where Boyle bumps into her. In seconds they're in the dust whacking it into each other with a passion only reserved for films about priests as lovers. As Wendy's wondering who the new stand-in Chaplain for the school will be, Geddy's wondering just how long this holy man can keep it up. All she can see is the blue sky and the sunlight dappling through the olive trees above. Great place for an orgasm. Then she has a thought. She interrupts the discussion about who's going to be the new Chaplain.

Can I ask something? Geddy goes.

They ignore her. Oul Mary's on about what a clever man Boyle is.

He's a clever man, that Father Boyle. A clever man alright he is. Aye.

Writes letters to the Vatican, Maw says.

Can I ask something? repeats Geddy.

Wendy's all up in arms about how writing letters to the

Vatican doesn't necessarily make somebody intelligent. Geddy's still trying to ask her question.

Right! Shut up about intelligent. Can I ask this question?

They all look at her. She's got five seconds.

See if I got pregnant in Spain, would the wane speak Spanish?

What? says Linda.

They're all about to burst out laughing. They take the big breath that you always take before you let out a blast of laughing. But they don't get it out as laughter. There's a loud bang outside. A thump thump like Neds on the roof of a car. They look at Wendy with a that's-your-car-getting-wrecked look. Wendy's out the door screaming the odds before the Girls even let that big intake of breath I was talking about out.

Get away from the car you wee bastards!

Ah shut up you oul cow, is the reply to that.

Whooo! say the Girls.

Wendy's more angry at getting called oul than a cow. *Ah'm not old. Ah'm not old,* she shouts. *I'm young!*

Run up my fuckin ribs missus, the Ned shouts. He walks on realising he's dealing with a maniac. Not the usual mad woman that you can wind up and get to run out the close and then challenge them.

Going up Garfield's the night, Wendy? Geddy asks.

But Wendy doesn't answer. She comes in through the titters and giggles of the Girls. Right up to Geddy's face.

And you shut up and all, she says.

I heard the two of yees got a lumber last night, says Angie.

Thought you never got a lumber, Donna? Geddy says.

She lumbered Charlie Garrett, Wendy tells her.

Donna told me it was only you that got a lumber, Wendy, Geddy says.

Wendy sits down and takes off her shoes. What the fuck is she doing, is what Geddy wants to know. Wendy points out to Geddy some cuts on her heels.

And? Geddy says.

Them's some bad cuts there, hen, Oul Mary says.

Oul Mary's listening to the polis reports on her tranny. Geddy's eyebrows are knitted together in puzzlement. Wendy had to walk home last night. Her feet are killing her. That's how she got the cuts. No bird ever walks home if she gets a lumber. You make sure he's getting you a fast cab home as part of the deal. You only walk when you never got a lumber but all your pals did. And Wendy was out with Donna last night. Wendy walked it home so Geddy lets rip at Donna.

What are you playing at, Donna?

Would yees shut the fuck up about lumbers, Angie shouts.

When Angie asks you to shut the fuck up, you shut the fuck up.

Language, says Maw.

No fuckin wonder – men, men, men; that's all they ever go on about.

She started it, says Wendy.

That's it. Angie stands up. Her belly hits Maw and Maw decides if there's winding up to be done she's not getting left out.

Christ Angie, you're putting the beef on, she goes. *Your belly's hanging over your jeans.*

Are you calling me fat, Mother? Angie demands.

If the glove fits you can squeeze into it.

Linda's joining in and calling Donna, Geddy and Wendy a triple of slappers. Something you hardly hear. It's usually a pair of slappers. But a triple? You can always rely on Linda for something original. Geddy wants to know how Donna never told her she lumbered Charlie Garrett.

Angie tells them if they don't shut up she's going to kill them. They shut up instantly. Only now Donna starts growling like a dog.

Maw, Maw; there she's at them growling games again, says Geddy.

Donna – down! Maw shouts.

Donna bares her side teeth a few times. She can do that with either end of her mouth, Donna. Lift her top lip and stretch her bottom lip down so as her teeth are showing. All that and she keeps the front of her mouth closed letting this low long growl out. If you didn't know her you'd think she was crazy.

Stop growling! What've I told you about that? Maw says.

She lumbered my boyfriend and never told me, says Geddy.

One of the millions, goes Wendy.

Shut it, Posh Spice.

Make me.

I will.

Go on then.

Pishy drawers, Geddy fires out.

Wendy's tongue is tied that bad she can't even speak. She's looking for words inside her head but they're all running away from her. The only words that're not hiding are the ones a five-year-oul wane would use. That one phrase has shoved her back to her early days. It's not often Geddy gets to beat Wendy in an argument. It's not often Geddy gets to beat anybody in an argument, in fact. At last Wendy gets something out.

I had the flu, right?

If something works, why fix it is what Geddy's thinking as she calls Wendy pishy drawers again.

I was only five! And I was ill! Wendy says. She's trying to excuse herself. And, unexpectedly, Geddy comes back with some good patter.

Ill? You are *ill!*

Fuck up, power lips! Wendy goes.

Now they're on common ground. And in this culture most talk is fighting talk. Violence and the threat of violence is just another aspect of the culture. Something to be brought out the bag like any other social tool. Middle-class folks call it reverting to type but that's only fear on their part. Their inability to accept a whole culture for what it is. So, for instance, when a middle-class person like Wendy steps up into Uni talk and high-flying concepts to batter lumps out of us that's okay. That's fine. But they've used a weapon from their cultural bag that we don't have; knowing fine we don't have it. That is a form of bullying. So why then when we pull out the fists and the boots are they surprised? We're only responding exactly the same as them. Idiots.

Wendy and Geddy are confronting each other; hands on hips, heads stretched forwards and teeth bared. A classic Nedess pose. Wendy knows the rules of this game well. She shouts, waving her fingers in the air with her palms facing her own chest.

Come onnnnnnnnnnn! she roars. And she looks like nothing could stop her. Nothing could stand in her way. She should try that with the wee fuckers at school. Maybe then they'd stop running wild over the top of teachers. There's nobody'd tackle Wendy in this state.

Except Angie.

For fuck sake that's it, Angie says.

She gets the vodka bottle in her hand, holding it by the neck. It's not the first time Angie's crashed, usually empty, bottles over people's heads. Geddy and Wendy sit down. The power squeaks out them as they fold into the cushions.

Right, c'mon, we're family in the name of Jesus, Oul Mary says.

I'll tell you how Donna never said nothing, Angie goes.

Donna interrupts with a couple of Rottweiler growls but Angie tells her to shut up and she does. Instantly. If she had a tail she'd wag it for biscuits.

Donna never said nothing cos she dragged Charlie Garrett out the taxi and battered him up and down the main street.

They all stare at the growling Donna.

I don't know how yees never knew, says Angie. *It's all over the town.*

Did you, Donna? grins Linda.

Donna growls some more.

She flung him out the taxi cos he tried to slip the hand, Angie says.

So what's wrong with that? Geddy goes.

Donna stops her growling and blurts out, *There was four other people in the taxi when he tried it on. The freak.*

Don't call my man a freak! Geddy goes.

Donna leaps onto Geddy's back scrabbing and biting like a demon. They're all in there grabbing fingers and jumpers and hands. Angie pulls Donna's long locks back so she can't sink her gnashing teeth into Geddy's back. By this time Geddy's on her knees pushing herself up and down with her hands, trying to bounce the much lighter Donna off her back. They eventually untangle them. Angie stuffs Donna back on the couch. Maw lights a fag and Geddy fixes her hair. Maw blows a long line of smoke out and gives it her war cry.

Jees, yees must think yees're the cat's pyjamas. Listen, yees're my daughters and I can honestly say, hand on my heart, that yees're all a bunch of dogs. So sit down and stop talking about men.

Next thing Wendy comes out with her usual. All about if Maw had loved them better they wouldn't all be picking men that are no good for them. All that damaged-by-your-parents shite that people use as an excuse not to live their lives. Angie hates that so she tells Wendy to stop blaming everything on the fuckin past.

Aye, yesterday's history, and the morra's a mystery, says Oul Mary. All that wisdom pressed into one wee phrase.

There! Well said, Granny; yesterday's history, the morra's a mystery. Well said, goes Angie. She keeps clapping her hands and staring at Wendy till Wendy finds something interesting on the carpet to look at. Oul Mary reminds them all why they're there.

Is it not about time we got on with it?

It is about time, they all agree.

I know! Let's get on with the spell, says Donna.

We're forgetting what we're here for, goes Angie.

That's right – we're here for one lassie the night, says Oul Mary. *One lassie.*

Caroline! chants Linda.

Angie suggests they have a toast to the one lassie. A mark of respect and solidarity to Caroline. They all think it's a good idea. Caroline is warmly embarrassed by it. Geddy fills the glasses, half glad to get the bottle as far away from Angie as she can. Cos in this family you never know what might flare up next. The glasses are placed in a circle on the table and they all lift them once on the nod of Oul Mary.

Here's to Caroline! Oul Mary says.

To Caroline – Six Black Candles! they chant.

They knock the neat vodka back in one tug. Soon as the glasses chink off the table Donna defaults to her glassy-eyed routine again. They get to work.

The spell. The spell. The SPELL, Donna goes.

There's a flurry of silent concentration. Oul Mary pulls out a see-through polythene bag, the kind the butchers fling the sausages in. The Girls set about getting the stuff out. Linda and Angie lay the rug out and fix the tape to the pentangle. Geddy rustles about in the bag and gets the dod of turf out. Smiling at its width. Its succulence. Wendy rolls the bottle of graveyard water about meditating on the particles floating inside. Who knows, some of the molecules might be part of their ancestors. Come up here for a night out to watch the action. You never know. You never know at all what's going on. Oul Mary rolls the polythene bag together in her palms. It looks like that catchy moon stuff that Wendy does when she's stressed. You might be in the middle of ASDA at the bean tins and a wee woman with furry boots bumps into the trolley. Wendy starts hyperventilating. Next thing she assumes the wide-horse stance and starts doing catchy moon. It's a fuckin embarrassment. One time she was doing it, Angie went and phoned a doctor saying there was a madwoman loose at the milk and cheese. It was a laugh watching Wendy explain she was a schoolteacher and how dare they treat her that way. She'd be reporting them to their superiors. By the time they got out of ASDA the quarter-pounders were thawing out. Angie had to eat the four of them when she got home.

What's in the bag, Granny? says Donna. She's always eager to learn more about the Craft. Always eager to listen.

It's a buckin bag of air – what d'you think it is? says Oul Mary. Being as straightforward as usual. But explaining nothing. They all stare at her.

Och, yees're all amateurs, Oul Mary goes.

What's it for, Granny? Angie says.

Oul Mary makes them none the wiser by telling them it's air out the Chapel. They're like six moons in the universe of ignorance as they try to pull the meaning of this bag out of the deep blue sea that is Oul Mary.

The sanctuary! Oul Mary says. She says it like that finally explains it. Hammers the nail home. But it doesn't. She flings the bag. Up it goes. Taking a crazy trajectory through the room. It floats down and down and lands smack in the middle of the pentangle on the rug. The Girls are amazed. But still there's no answer.

I hope it's not Father Boyle's hot air that's in it, Angie goes.

The absurdity of it all gets to Linda. Since her aneurysm she's been a bit like that.

Ha, ha we're the Six Sick Sisters! Linda goes and laughs.

Angie points at Geddy and Donna and calls them Sick and Sicker. Oul Mary informs them of a drugs bust in Cadzow

Crescent. Linda thinks they don't get her joke about Six Sick Sisters.

No, you don't get it: six, six, six, she goes. She does it with that *boom boom!* look on her face. They'll get it now. She's sure.

We do get it; it's shite, Angie says.

Six, six, six! Repeats Linda.

She's still thinking they don't really get it. Angie tells her to wrap it or she's phoning the patter polis.

Just like you phoned the doctors on Wendy when she was tying herself in knots at the milk and cheese in ASDA, says Linda.

Linda and Angie laugh. Wendy wants to say something but she chooses not to. She chooses wisely. Geddy's still away back on the six, six, six joke.

What d'you mean, Linda – six, six, six?

It's in the Bible, Linda tells her.

Right! says Geddy, none the wiser.

Caroline, get Stacie Gracie's head, Oul Mary says.

Suddenly everything takes on a different tone. Serious. Darker. More sombre. Downright sinister. Caroline is stunned to a silence. She's half stepped and stopped. The Girls are looking at her; looking at Oul Mary; looking at her. Caroline's lips are quivering.

Now? is all she can say.

Oul Mary grins. She knows the dread running through Caroline's soul like electric currents.

Did you freeze it like I told you?

Caroline nods and takes another step.

Exactly?

Caroline nods again. Oul Mary turns to the Girls. The turn is signifying to Caroline to go and get the head. Oul Mary figures the more she talks to her the more chance her bottle will crash. So she strikes a pose that assumes Caroline is on her way to get the head. She reminisces about fifty or more years ago in Donegal how she used to do the same spell. Out the side of her ear she's listening to Caroline padding and shuffling into the scullery. Padding and shuffling.

When we had no fridges . . .

How did yees do it, Granny? How did yees do it? Donna says.

If you buckin shut up I'll tell you.

Donna shuts up. Oul Mary continues. *We had a hard time. We used to have to do these ones in the winter . . .*

As Oul Mary goes on about how they had to take the head up the Donegal Mountains in a pail of water to freeze it Geddy's still thinking about the meaning of six, six, six in Linda's joke. It was Errigle, the mountain. Two thousand four hundred and sixty-six feet high. Some climb. That reminds Geddy of the sixes.

We've got technology now, Granny, Wendy says. *Fridges.*

I know yees've got buckin technology. I even had to get somebody else to do the head for me. I wasn't very good at that bit . . .

Will I take it out, Granny? Caroline asks. She's standing alone in the scullery.

Oul Mary nods aye and starts lighting the candles. Pushing the spell forwards so that Caroline feels a beat behind. She has to open the door. She's got no choice. Geddy is starting to feel the force of it all too. She thinks maybe they shouldn't be fuckin about with this. With the forces of darkness and all that.

It's OK if you know what you're doing, says Donna. As usual giving herself the part of somebody that knows what they're doing.

Oul Mary can see in her peripheral vision that Caroline is at the fridge and she's reaching out to open the door. She's doing it that slow you'd think she was a statue. A doll. An effigy of herself.

How can you know what you're doing if you don't know what it is? Geddy asks Donna.

But Donna sees how crucial this moment is too. She tells

Geddy to shoosht. The room falls into solemn silence as Caroline opens the freezer door. The fog of frost oozes out and in the grey white you can see the outline of features. Female features beside the sweetcorn and boil-in-the-bag curries. Each side is one of the cheap lemon meringue pies.

Caroline leans into the fog. Stacie Gracie's blue eyes appear in a clearing. Slam! Caroline bangs the door shut.

I can't do this. It's crazy.

Come on, Caroline, don't bottle out now, Donna says.

They all start remonstrating with her. About how they've came here the night and she's an ungrateful bitch. They could have been at Memory Lane and on their way to Garfield's or anything. But no! They came round here to show solidarity with their sister. To help her through the bad times. They're crumbling her. She's like a bag of flour that the bag's just been pulled off. It stands, but one grain falls, and it all starts to go, cracking and crumbling. Tumbling down and down till it's a peak that's left there. Oul Mary sees what's happening and butts in.

Leave her, Oul Mary says.

Caroline! It's Stacie Gracie, Linda shouts.

Leave her be. I'll have a quiet word. Caroline! Oul Mary says.

She shuffles into the scullery. Right up to Caroline and whispers stuff in her ear. It could be Witchcraft stuff. It could be Oul Mary stuff. It could be plain woman to woman stuff. But nobody knows. None of them can hear. They can't even see her eyes. Oul Mary's turned her so that she's looking out the window.

Meanwhile back in the living room the Girls discuss what to do next. Geddy says she knew Caroline would bottle out at the last minute.

Shoosht, Geddy, cos that's the very thing that'll make sure she does bottle out if she hears it, Donna goes.

Wendy's sure Oul Mary will turn Caroline round.

Sure she's better than any horse whisperer you ever heard, she says.

As they look in it seems to be working. They can't see her face but Caroline's becoming more and more animated as Oul Mary whispers. Like she's a big mechanical doll and Oul Mary's pulling the strings. Loading the Duracells. But Linda thinks it's not looking good. By this time Angie's saying it's a lot of shite this Witchcraft business anyhow. Why the fuck she's there when she could had went to the bingo is beyond her. For the moment it looks like they've all forgot about the head in the fridge. This house would be quite an ordinary one if it wasn't for that. Oul Mary starts shuffling back into the living room leaving Caroline leaning on the sink and looking out the window. A position that marks despair in houses and closes all over schemes in Scotland. A woman with her fists clenched on the side of the worktop. Her chest leaning out over the abyss of the sink. And her eyes unfocused somewhere out there in the grey daylight streets or the night with its orange globes of sodium lamps and baseball caps bobbing along in the darkness. Oul Mary slumps on the couch as Caroline leans towards the window hypnotised by the distant lights of Easterhouse. The promise of another world to escape to. Easterhouse. Worse, but somehow better.

Give her a couple of minutes. She'll do it, Oul Mary tells the Girls.

They knew she'd do it, Oul Mary. Yip! If there's ever any talking round to be done she's the woman for that. She could talk the hind legs off a donkey, that one. The knickers off a nun. Caroline turns and strides in.

Right, get all the stuff packed up, says Caroline.

There's a wee bubble of silence before they all let rip with much the same stuff they said to her ten minutes ago. Angie lights up a furious fag. That's another bit of General Miscellaneous language. The angry fag. There's a whole language in there of looks and shifts and movements so that middle-class people don't know they're in a foreign country. They could be one step away from getting their head kicked in and they don't know. They're as well being in Uzbekistan. And you know what the sad thing is? They think they do understand. Socially, morally and academically. They'll be a long time waiting for a short walk off a cliff. Exactly. But anyway Caroline waits till they're all eyes staring at her. Like a bunch of owls in a night-time hedge.

Somebody get the head and stick it in the bin-shed, she goes.

You can't just stick the head in the bin-shed! Donna says.

You have to admit she's got a point there. Oul Mary shoves the arm round Caroline and reminds her, *It's not right darling to leave it half-finished. Not something as important as this. You never know what luck that might bring.*

I don't give two fucks, you wrinkly oul bag, is Caroline's unexpected reply.

If she's like that with Oul Mary she's as serious as she'll ever be about anything in her life. Linda has a go trying to win her round. Trying to get her to listen but that doesn't work either.

I'm listening to myself from now on, not a bunch of loonies like yous, says Caroline. She's levelling her eyes to each of them, pausing on each one long enough so that they know she means business. Donna goes to put her arm round her. *Get it all to fuck!* Caroline screams.

And she sinks down to the floor crying. The Girls look at each other for the affirmation of defeat that none of them are willing to say out loud. They start gathering the Witchcraft paraphernalia and stuffing it in bags and coats and pockets. Donna leans in and whispers to Oul Mary will she get the head. Oul Mary nods aye and whispers back. *Shove it in one of them ASDA bags. You don't want people talking if they see it on the way out the close.*

Donna goes to the fridge. She pauses before opening it. Not that she's scared. She's got a reverence for these things, Donna. No matter what you think of people that go about doing Witchcraft and trying to kill people with spells, you've got to admire those who have reverence for their work. Tradition. People that do their work right instead of half doing it and leaving you with the consequences. Donna says the wee prayer you say in Witchcraft for spells aborted. For spells gone wrong. For spells backfired. It deflects the power built up in the room to another cause. She opens the door. And even though the Girls are mostly not looking at the fridge they can feel that the door has opened. The chill in the fridge is much bigger than it should be. The Girls pause and there's a transcendental silence to the power of eight women. Donna puts her hands in towards the head and:

BANG

The front door crashes, bouncing on its hinges and the lock splintering the wood. There's Bobby in the middle of the room like a bad apparition of the very thing you never wanted the spell to conjure up. Like the Devil, Oul Nick himself. There's screaming and panic as the Girls rush to the fireplace end of the room gathering their thoughts. Donna slams the fridge door shut and stands with her sisters. Bobby's hand is in an almighty plaster cast with these wee elastic bands attached to his fingernails and stretching to another contraption on his wrist. It seems they've made some mess of his hand. A right fuckin shambles it is.

Bobby Again

Bobby shares his sneer out equally as his head pans the Girls stuffed up against the fireplace with the shock. But they're recovering. They see it's that prick Bobby and they're telling their bodies to relax, to move forwards. Get ready to attack.

Look what yees done to my fuckin hand, he says.

He's holding it up like it was an actual grotesque hand he found lying on the street. They burst out laughing. I mean, imagine it. This seething maniac standing in the middle of the room. The door still swinging on its hinges like a horror movie. Eight women crushed into the fireplace, their arses burning. And this loony with a stookie screaming at them. You just have to laugh. Oul Mary's the first in there with a missile.

You've got some balls coming back here, son, she says.

Who phoned you? Bobby goes.

That stumps her. *I haven't got a phone.*

Well, hang up, you oul cunt! he says.

He's leaning into her face like he's about to bite off her nose. He might have been a bit meeker than usual earlier on but his trip to Casualty's made a new man out of him. The Girls retaliate with some *Shut its*. A couple of *don't you talk to my Granny like thats*. One *who do you think you are?* And a *you're lucky we only broke your fuckin hand*. But he keeps his cool, Bobby.

It's Caroline I'm here to talk to, he says.

The Girls look at Caroline then Oul Mary. Oul Mary quickly adds up the situation. All the variables. And it's over in half a second later when she nods aye to the Girls. They take up position on the couch and the seats. Watching the show. Caroline steps out onto the stage. Folded arms, one leg forwards. Shoe up on its heel and waving the toe side to side.

Well, what is it then? she asks.

The Girls are taking in every movement. Every stretch and bump of the skin. Every in breath. Every out breath.

I want to talk to you, Bobby says.

And why should I want to talk to a hoormaster?

The Girls like that. They nudge with elbows and shuffle their arses further into the seats. It looks like being a good show. Bobby's starting to feel uneasy. His apoplexy has worn off and the draught coming in through the open door is chilling him.

I want you to call McGoogan off!

Give me the money then, Caroline says.

Call him off first.

Don't listen to him, Caroline, says Angie.

Geddy lets the cunt know he deserves all he gets from McGoogan but Oul Mary bumps her to shut up. She's got higher plans resting on this one.

D'you want me and the wane to be homeless? Caroline says.

And that's a good one. All the Girls agree on that.

You could have went about it in a more civilised fashion!

Aye, and you would have just gave me it. 'Here Caroline, no bother, if you want any more just ask!'

Bobby's bravado is fading and he's starting to see what a situation he's in. He decides to go for a softer approach.

I'm begging you to call him off, he goes.

But Caroline still wants to know if he'll see her and the wane out on the street. Turns out he's been to the bank this very day and he's going to give her the money in the morning. Angie half confirms it, she seen Bobby coming out the bank – she thought it was him. Could have sworn it.

You've got to wait a day – it's in an ISA, Bobby says.

It's a landslide.

Oh aye, right! they're all going. Bobby promises again that he'll bring it round but Caroline's not convinced.

Oh, honest Joe here. I'd be waiting on hell freezing over, she says.

Bobby's lost his bravado completely now. And that's when something funny happens. Oul Mary hands the vodka bottle to Angie. On the fly, like. Behind everybody's back. They're all too concentrated on Bobby and Caroline. The entertainment. Oul Mary's working six yards ahead of them all and three puddles deeper. She leans forwards to Bobby.

You look a bit pale, son, she goes.

The room's surprised. They look at her. What's she doing being nice to him?

Being stalked by a hit man does that.

D'you not want a wee drink? Oul Mary says.

That hits the spot. The Girls are turning their heads to each other and questioning. Bobby's not sure what's going on. Not sure at all.

I could be doing with something, he goes.

Get a vodka for yourself then, Oul Mary says.

Bobby looks about for the glint of a bottle. He sees it. Angie's got it but she's hugging it tight and glaring at him. It would take a brave man to go in there and fetch it. A right brave man.

There's another bottle in the freezer, Oul Mary says.

She's manipulating the situation so that Caroline will get back on track with the programme. The spell. She's good at that, turning even what looks like a lost cause to her advantage. Bobby walks slow towards the freezer. He's walking slow cos he's thinking they might bop him over the head when his back's turned. Every step's a step into the unknown. The Girls are too interested in what he'll think when he opens the freezer door and there's Stacie Gracie's big blue eyes staring out at him. He puts his hand on the handle. The Girls are watching. But Oul Mary's watching Caroline. When Bobby's hand rises, Caroline's lips fall open. When his hand touches the handle her mouth falls open. When his hand tenses up that microsecond before it tugs the door, Caroline shouts out.

Right!! Right! I'll phone him, she says.

Oul Mary nods to herself. She's back in the driving seat.

Angie, pour him a vodka, Oul Mary grunts.

Bobby by this time is looking at Caroline. If he ever felt like he knew what was going on in this room he's lost now. He's trying to make it only between him and Caroline again. he pulls a comment out of her with his questioning eyes.

I'll call him off, Caroline says.

Thank fuck! Bobby almost cries with relief but catches himself on.

On one condition, Caroline goes.

Bobby sighs at that. Gives her an okay-what-is-the-one-condition look.

You come back home!

The Girls are shocked. A big intake of breath and they chatter on about *what the fuck are you doing Caroline,* and *you, sir, get to fuck out of here,* and all sorts of abuse till Oul Mary settles them down. Bobby's got the panic. But he's holding it in. His mind remembers he was going for a drink. Now where was it. Ah! That's right. In the fridge. His hand reaches out and opens the door but Angie's onto what Oul Mary's up to. She steps in and hands Bobby a glass.

Here's your drink, Angie goes.

Bobby dunts the fridge door shut and takes the glass off Angie. Caroline's following him like a limpet mine. Stuck to his shoulder. Nagging.

Me or Stacie Gracie, she says.

Bobby's eyes are bulging at her as he swallows the big drink in a oner. When the glass comes back down he's smiling.

Oh! Don't make me choose.

Caroline lifts the phone and shows him the handle like it's an exhibit in a court case. Item A, m'Lud. The phone that was used to stove the estranged husband's napper right in.

I'll phone McGoogan. Call him off right now.

Even though that's quite an inviting prospect for Bobby he can't come back. His face lights up and without thinking he nearly answers *Aye,* but his sense comes back to him and he answers. No emotion. No sneering, just plain forward words.

I can't come back.

In the silence the phone going down is like a car crash. The wee *ting!* of the bell like a bell tolling for whom. And for whom the bell tolls is Bobby. But it could be Caroline with the awful ache of loss in her chest. And the big empty in her belly. The tears held back so that they seem to be stored in a tragedy pouch that starts at the back of her throat and ends just under the surface of her skin at the back of her neck. The hairs rising. Sticking up. The bell tolls for thee. But if no man is an island then no bunch of women are an archipelago. Caroline's at least got them. Her sisters. Her Maw. Oul Mary. That gives her the strength to hide the reverberations of the bell in the place we hide our pain. There's so much of it by the time we're in our late thirties we might explode if somebody lights the right fuse.

Fine! Fine! says Caroline.

Her words sound as flat as Bobby's but they're loaded with sisterhood. And the sisterhood's the stopper on her emotions.

Oul Mary sees the way things are going. She's happy. She cast her spell and it worked. There are all kinds of spells. All kinds of curses. In all walks and levels of life people are cursing others. Using their powers to manipulate the world. And in this big game everybody loses. Even the most powerful are manipulated. This is the secret that Oul Mary knew young. One of her most developed talents. The art of fighting without fighting. So Bobby hears the *Fine, fine,* from Caroline and now he's staring her out. Trying to weigh up the situation so that his words have enough venom to hurt Caroline but not too much so that the assembled Girls'll attack him. He loses his struggle and blurts his words from a screwed-up face.

Och, fuck it! You're getting fuck all money, you maniac!

Tell that to McGoogan, Caroline goes.

The threat of pain is written in the iris of her eyes. Bobby leans into her face.

Fuck . . . McGoogan, he says.

He pronounces each syllable like it's a separate sentence. The Girls let rip with *Aye, right, and wait till McGoogan gets a hold of you* and stuff. Bobby says he'll take his chances with McGoogan and Linda tells him to send her a postcard then, from Casualty. The Girls laugh.

I'm off! He says.

He steps towards the door but Caroline steps in front of him. Bars his way. This is getting interesting. Very interesting. Oul Mary is delighted. Bobby tries to get by but when he goes left, Caroline goes left. When he goes right, she goes right. Bobby stops exasperated and looks at her.

Right – the wane? Caroline says.

Fuckin leave the wane out of this.

Stacie Gracie or the wane! Caroline goes.

Pulling that one out the hat meets with the approval of the Girls. They cheer.

Yes, Caroline, on you go! shouts Geddy.

Don't be so fuckin daft, Bobby says.

He's trying to treat it like a side issue that they really shouldn't be talking about. But Caroline's not letting it go. She's got a club and she's going to use it.

It's your choice, Bobby. Stacie Gracie or the wane? she goes.

The Girls are tense with anticipation. How will this one turn out? But Oul Mary knows exactly how it's going to turn out. Exactly.

Fuck this, I'm out of here, says Bobby.

He squeezes round her. Caroline steps back into the room and delivers him an ultimatum.

You walk out that door, you're choosing her, a no good slutbag, over your own son.

Bobby hovers in the doorway. The fulcrum between married life and a life of drink and drugs and retaliatory infidelity. He does consider it for a second. Coming back. But how can he make a decision yes and lean back into that room. The fuckin House of Horrors. Only the Devil himself would go in there. Oh, and doesn't Oul Mary know that. Fine well show knows it. Fine fuckin well.

Bobby walks away. There's the receding shuffle of his footsteps getting faster and faster as he puts distance between him and them. Caroline screams down the close. She's bent over when she screams so that her arse is in the house but her upper body's in the close. Her head is a good couple of feet into the greyness of the busted lights.

Right, that's it, you right rotten bastard. You'll never see the wane again, never! D'you hear me!!?

When she's vomited all her words out she straightens up. Adjusts her clothes, and turns to the Girls. Oul Mary knows exactly what's coming. Exactly. Her plan has come together nicely, thank you very much. Caroline slams the door.

Right, she says, *get that head out the freezer.*

Yes! Stacie Gracie's head, says Donna. In she goes to get it.

Get this over with. I want her out my house for good, says Caroline.

Oul Mary puts her arm round her and orders everybody about their jobs with flashing eyes. Caroline is back on the team. The team's all over the place setting up the spell. Oul Mary shoves a chair up to the door cos no matter what happens this time, there's no way this spell's getting interrupted.

Six Black Candles

Minutes later the lights are down and the Girls move about frantically setting up the spell. Six Black Candles. All is well. The chair is snug against the broken door. The light in the scullery's been covered with a bit of that red plastic stuff you get off stage lights. Wendy stole it out the school. The six sisters are moving round the pentangle taped onto the rug. Their hands are joined and they're chanting. If the Provvy man came he'd get a right shock. They're circling the rug clockwise. Maw is circling anti-clockwise. The Girls raise their hands in the air and circle with palms touching. Angie and Donna are dragging/shoving Linda round in her chair. The red light from the scullery's coming through in shafts and filtering through the yellow light of the candles. It all seems like hell. Now and then the red light is disturbed by a shadow. That's Oul Mary moving about in the scullery.

And what's she doing in the scullery? She's over at the deep-fat fryer and she spits in it to make sure the fat is as hot as it can be. It sizzles up like snakes and settles back in a calm anger. She chants from the scullery into the living room.

Dead dead dead.

The Girls join in and continue as Oul Mary falls about her business.

Dead dead dead dead dead dead, they chant.

She gets the head out the fridge and bumps it down on the scullery table. She leans into the crazy living room and changes the chant.

Fry the head!

Fry the head Fry the head Fry the head Fry the head Fry the head Fry the head, they chant.

They circle through the bars of red and yellow light. Oul Mary drops the head in the deep-fat fryer. Up it froths and sparks like Andrews Liver Salts. The fat is running along the table and onto the floor but still the Girls chant and still Oul Mary mumbles her mad spells. Oul Mary watches the fat for a bit then changes the chant again.

Burn burn burn!

Burn burn Burn burn Burn burn Burn burn Burn burn Burn burn, they chant.

They're just into that when Oul Mary changes it again.

Out!

Out out Out out Out out Out out Out out Out out Out out Out out Out out, they go.

That's the signal for Caroline to come into the scullery and fish Stacie Gracie's head out of the big chip pan. Caroline leaves the circle. Even though her altercation with Bobby's gave her some added strength she still pauses as she leaves. The Girls notice this but Maw steps into her place and they circle all the more animated. Chant all the louder to spur her through to the scullery. As the Girls circle, each one turns their head to keep an eye on what's happening. The deep-fat fryer. Oul Mary's got a pair of them big wooden tongs women used to use to get their washing out of the tub and into the spin dryer before automatic washing machines were invented.

Oul Mary's waving the wooden tongs in the air like the crazy claws of some prehistoric bird. A Grannydactyl. She's clacking them together in the same rhythm as the Girls are chanting.

She hands Caroline the tongs. Caroline fishes the head out of the fryer and stands with it hanging out over the tiled floor like guilt. Fat dripping off like blood onto her shoes and the linoleum. Fear. She looks at Oul Mary for what to do next. With a wee imperceptible shove Oul Mary nods toward the pentangle and the circling Witches. Caroline's got no option. She pads in holding it way out in front of her. The Girls twist and turn trying to get a view of the burnt and singed head. A quick look at Caroline's face. How's she holding up? Will she make it through to the end? Once she's right in the living room the Girls break off and go behind her like a conga. She's the head. Or rather Stacie Gracie's the head. Out there in front is the head that Donna made out of straw days before. The photo of Stacie Gracie they cut out from photos of her and Bobby. They got Sam up the Quadrant market to blow it up to lifesize and stuck it on the straw head. Now it's all shrivelled and burned and you'd swear it was a real head. You can still see the blue eyes of Stacie Gracie peering through. Caroline lays the head in the middle of the pentangle beside the turf, the candles, and the graveyard water.

Blood! chants Oul Mary. Her voice punctuates the silence and they all start chanting again as the conga makes its way back into a circle.

Blood blood blood blood blood blood, they're going.

Caroline puts her hand out over the head. Oul Mary draws a needle from her shawl and pricks it into Caroline's thumb.

Ah, you fucker, says Caroline.

The blood drips out helped by Oul Mary squeezing the thumb from its base to its tip. Donna, second-in-command Witch, steers Caroline's hand so that the blood drips *drip drip plip* onto Stacie Gracie's head. Right on the eyes. With that done, Oul Mary rips the photo off the straw head and lays it flat in the centre of the pentangle. She places five of the six lit candles round about; one on each point of the pentangle. She sits the other one in the centre along with the photo. The Girls are in absolute awe. Then she does her spell. It's in Irish Gaelic but I've translated it.

The light that is in darkness is Caroline and she's in the centre of the star, and all power shall flow and the centre is the place of convergence of the streams.

Oul Mary turns to Caroline. But Caroline spouts out that she feels sick and runs to the toilet. They wait mid-spell, and that's like getting disturbed well on your way to an orgasm. They only noise is the fluttering of the candles, the breathing of the Girls, and then the retching of Caroline as she boaks her load down the lavvy pan. That breaks the trance. Angie leans into Wendy.

This is fuckin crazy! she says.

Just do it. It'll make her feel better, Wendy says.

Exactly, goes Linda.

Angie nods okay to Wendy and that's the first positive moment they've had for years. Even if the spell doesn't work at least it's gave them that wee moment of true sisterhood. A light that tells them there's a tunnel, and a tunnel they might start walking in order to absolve their differences.

The purpose of the spell is to kill Stacie Gracie the same way the guy that called Wendy a lezzy, the guy that called Donna a ghoul, and the plumber with the burgh that never plumbed Maw's washing machine in right, bit the dust. Caroline comes back in from the toilet looking a bit pale round the gills. Donna takes charge of the situation.

Right, Caroline. You've got to blow out and light the Six Black Candles. Just answer Oul Mary back every time you light one.

Caroline nods. Oul Mary hands Caroline six matches. She pushes Caroline down on her knees. Caroline starts blowing the candles out. The smell of the smoke from them reminds everybody of Chapel. And funerals. And weddings. And Lent. The whole Catholic experience is exploded into the molecules of smoke from snuffed candles. Caroline blows and lights. Blows and lights.

Get a bit of paper, Donna goes.

But they don't understand.

She's got to write Stacie Gracie's name on it and burn it, Donna tells them.

Wendy looks about and snaffles a bit of paper that's next to the phone. She gives it to Donna. Donna folds it funny and gives it to Caroline.

Right, Caroline, here.

Caroline holds the folded paper like she's been handed a tenner to go to the shops but nobody's told her what to get. When she speaks it's in the feeble voice of a child.

Pen?

Pen! Donna snaps.

Wendy hands Donna a pen. Donna does some funny stuff with the pen that looks like blessing but it's not. Now they're ready again. Oul Mary does the first part of the spell again like before, in Irish Gaelic (translated) (rough) (as fuck) and the Girls answer back in English.

Do we wish Stacie Gracie to burn in the fires of hell? Oul Mary chants.

Yes, we want Stacie Gracie to burn in the fires of hell, say the Girls.

Caroline sets fire to the paper.

Do you wish Stacie Gracie to die the unnameable death? Oul Mary wants to know.

And they do. The paper is shrivelling up.

As the paper shrivels so shall the life-force of Stacie Gracie, Oul Mary goes.

So shall the heart and soul of Stacie Gracie.

Will we shriek her into the fires of hell?

We will shriek her into the fires of hell.

The Girls shriek and shriek. God help the Provvy man if he turned up now. Through all the high-pitched yelling and bending down and waving hands and arms Oul Mary shouts at Caroline to blow out the candles.

Caroline! The candles!

Caroline gets down on all fours and moves about like a crazed dog huffing and puffing and blowing out the candles. When she's finished she turns to the Girls. They all relax and slump down exhausted. Oul Mary picks up her wee tranny and switches it on. Adjusts it till she finds the polis and shoves it against her ear.

Who wants to make a wee cup of tea? says Maw.

The Aftermath

Maw's asked them all to make a wee cup of tea but they've ignored her. She decides to put the pressure on Wendy.

Wendy?

There's a car chase, Oul Mary tells them.

Newsflash from Mary Duffy, armchair reporter, Donna says.

Maw's still trying to stare an answer out of Wendy.

It's always me, Wendy says.

Angie butts in and tells her she should make the tea cos it'd be a handy skill for when Father Boyle gets back from licking the Pope's arse and she gets the sack from school. She can get a job in Bite U Like up the street.

I'll maybe ask your Dessie to teach me the hammer! Wendy says. She moves off to make the tea.

Or I might teach you the slap on the fuckin jaw! Angie says.

She's threatening to get up out her seat but Donna dampens that down. She's too excited about the prospect of what might have happened to Stacie Gracie.

Phone her. Phone her. Phone that cow Stacie Gracie, Donna goes.

Caroline flinches at the thought of phoning the lassie that stole her man. It's weakening her like kryptonite. She's got her number. Had it for ages. And photographs. Little bits of paper and bus tickets that she fished out of Bobby's pockets when she was building up a picture of what she didn't want to believe. Watching the tide of jealousy and insecurity wash in round about her while proclaiming her feet are dry. Queen Canute. Geddy joins in now.

Aye, see if she answers, she goes.

The Girls stare at the phone, willing Caroline to go to it. To pick it up. To affirm their abilities as Witches. Now Angie's even forgot her tangle with Wendy. She's caught up in it. She wants Caroline to phone. Just to see if anything happened. Not that she thinks it did but it would be interesting if it did. Oul Mary butts in with a polis report.

They're moving at some rate of knots along the main street, the polis.

Wendy slides up to Caroline. Tells her in her ear that Stacie Gracie might be dead. That's an excuse for phoning up. Maybe they killed her. Maybe they actually killed her.

Phone her, Caroline, says Donna. She's pushing the telephone table closer to Caroline with her black nail varnished toes.

No.

How not?

I don't want to, says Caroline.

She moves more towards the scullery. Angie tries to persuade her. Linda accuses her of being feart. That does the trick a bit; she retaliates to that one.

I'm not scared.

Do it then, says Donna.

Angie lifts the phone and gives it to Caroline. Caroline hands it back to Angie and tells her to do it. It's one of them hand receivers with all the buttons on it. They kind you charge up. Angie looks at the numbers and they're staring at her like little expectant eyes. But she flips the phone to Geddy. Geddy dials the first part of the number then hangs up.

No. Somebody else do it. What if she's dead?

She won't be dead, Angie says.

There's a wee laugh in her voice. But her wee laugh is betrayed by the doubt. Linda comes to the rescue saying it's all just a laugh. But all the same, something might have happened.

She might have burned her fingers on the cooker, fell in the fire, fell down the stairs or just got this incredibly bad neuralgia.

Caroline's still not for doing it. The answer's still no. Linda wants to know if she's feart to phone cos it's Stacie Gracie. Talking to the woman that stole your man and all that; more nerve-racking than being up the court. Or is it that she thinks the spell's actually worked. The Six Black Candles. Is that what she's feart of?

I don't know, I don't know, I don't know, is Caroline's reply. She covers her face with her hands trying to hide from the rest of the Girls.

Christ, I think there's going to be an accident here, Oul Mary says.

None of them are listening; they're too interested in what Caroline's going to do.

That's it – you think this has worked, don't you? Linda says.

Caroline still doesn't know, doesn't know, doesn't know. Geddy calls it a daft spell and Angie agrees with a smiling nod. Oul Mary announces that the car the polis were chasing has just crashed into the Whifflet Bridge.

Don't mock it. What if it has worked? Donna says.

The room falls silent. It's only the electric whispers of Oul Mary's tranny. It hisses and it crackles. It crackles and it hisses. The Girls look from one to the other. From the other to the one facing up to the fact that aye, maybe the fuckin thing did work. Maybe like Bannan, McGowan and Cassidy's deaths, this is all true.

Oh fuck! I'm clearing this stuff up, Caroline goes.

She drops to her knees pulling in the candles and photos and bits of straw to the centre of the rug where's she kneeling pretty as a picture of frantic despair. She's just pulling one of the corners towards herself as if she's going to wrap the whole thing up like a giant Dick Whittington parcel when the couch starts playing 'Amazing Grace'.

The fuckin couch is playing 'Amazing Grace', Geddy says.

They all jump back. Oul Mary jumps up off the couch like there's a bomb under her arse. There's Caroline kneeling in the middle of all the Witchcraft stuff and the rest of them looking at the couch like it's a big telly. Donna's first to realise what's going on. She dives into the couch. Now it's a swimming pool and she parts the waves of the two big cushions. Down and down she goes, holding her breath. Swimming for oysters. Her hand feels something on the sandy bottom of the couch. She surfaces gasping for air, holding the object in the air. 'Amazing Grace' rings loud and clear through the room.

It's Father Boyle's phone, she shouts. *Daft cunts.*

She lets it play another verse – 'I once was lost but now I'm found', probably – then asks if she should answer it. Oul Mary's got definite views on that.

You can't answer a priest's phone, it's a sacrilege.

Angie wants to know how come answering a bit of plastic can be a sacrilege.

You never know who it could be on the other end, says Oul Mary.

It's the property of the Church, Maw goes.

Angie sniggers at Maw then answers Oul Mary. *Who could it be? God for fucksakes? 'Ah, God here . . . just phoning to say the earth's round . . . forgot to give that information. Hope I never caused too many problems. See yees all on Judgement Day. Bye!'*

Nobody answers her. The phone is on the last verse.

Och, give me the fuckin thing, Angie says. She grabs the phone off Donna. She presses the button. *Hello, Purgatory here.*

Maw and Oul Mary look away mortified. It's the Chapel

House on the phone and they want to know where Father Boyle is. The Girls can pick up the gist of it from Angie's answers.

No, he's not here, he's away to a wake. He left his phone here by mistake but he's just across the road. I could run ov . . . Aye, I can see it from here . . . OK. I'll get somebody to tell him . . . No, I know the exact house. Bye.

Angie clicks the phone off. *It's the Chapel House.*

And? says Donna.

Father Boyle's to go to the hospital. Last rites. A car accident.

That'll be the crash at the Whifflet Bridge, mark my words! says Oul Mary. *Mark my words.*

Angie wants to know who'll run over to the wake house and tell him. Nobody answers. They all make excuses. Feeble excuses and mumbles and avoiding eye-contact. The Girls are getting ready to leave. Maw and Oul Mary are more obvious. They stand up and get their jackets out the bundle that's flung in the corner.

Oh, I'm bucked, I think I'll go home to my tic, says Oul Mary.

Caroline panics. The last thing she wants is for them to go. To be left on her own. The last thing she wants is that big black empty feeling to come rushing back into her. To fill that place beneath her ribcage with dread and awe. With fear.

I'm pretty tired myself, Maw says.

That's making it all the worse for Caroline.

Don't go home the now, there's more vodka left! Caroline says.

They're just about to make their various excuses when Caroline's phone rings. Angie picks it up. Soon as Angie's got the phone up there's this manic laughter coming from it. The Girls are slipping about sliding their jackets on. Caroline knows that laugh is Bobby's.

That's Bobby! I'd know his laugh anywhere!

Bobby, on the other end, has heard the most amazing joke ever and he can't stop going into fits of manic laughter.

Angie's face is telling a story. Her face changes from anger to horror as the laughing maniac rambles on pouring out his crazy tale. Angie turns to the Girls and tries to relate the tale to them.

That cunt Bobby, laughing. McGoogan's crashed his car. He's in Casualty!

There's a beat while the Girls realise the implications. McGoogan's in Casualty. That means he won't get the money off Bobby. That means Caroline won't be keeping her house. That means the Six Black Candles was all in vain. All for nothing. They're a picture of disappointment. Their nails are out for Bobby and he'll be getting it sometime but for now their hearts are sore for Caroline. Except Donna. She's got other thoughts on her mind. Other implications. Angie has a go at Bobby down the line.

Shut your mouth hoormaster or I'll come round there and rip your balls off and you'll be in Casualty beside him.

As Angie rolls and rasps her words to their best effect Donna's down on the rug rummaging through the stuff. She eventually finds what she's looking for. It's the bit of paper with Stacie Gracie's name wrote on it. Most of it's burned but on the back of it she can see another name: McGoogan with his phone number. Caroline must have wrote it down when she was hiring him to slash the cash out of Bobby. Donna tried to get a word in but Angie's on a mission.

Oh, is that right? You can read me like a book? Well, listen here, Sonny Jim; I can read you like a fuckin pamphlet!

Donna checks the paper again to see she's not seeing things. Close. She flips it over and over. Stacie Gracie. McGoogan. Stacie Gracie. McGoogan. Stacie Gracie. McGoogan. Angie's still ranting. She's good. She's ripping Bobby to bits.

No. In fact, I take that back. I can read you like a fuckin stamp, she tells Bobby.

Then he says something. Her face twists. She turns to

Caroline and tells her Bobby says she's getting fuck all money now. He says some more and hangs up. Caroline's like a cowed dog. They're all round her comforting her and wondering how they're going to get out and catch the pub and the dancing now that she's in this state. That's when Donna shoves the bit of paper into the fray.

This has got McGoogan's name on it! she says.

The Girls gather round for a look at it. Passing it from hand to hand, flipping it over and showing it to each other.

That means nothing, Angie says eventually. *Nothing it means.*

It's got his fuckin name on it!! screams Donna.

There's a line of delight in her voice. The Girls are not too sure where they are now. Donna's eyes are wide in awe of their power and it's all too much for Caroline as she presses her hysterics back.

It worked! It fuckin well worked! Donna says.

But it was Stacie Gracie we were doing. Not McGoogan. It was Stacie Gracie, Caroline blurts out. She's not really talking to anybody but herself. She looks down into the circle. Stacie Gracie is grinning up at her through the debris of the Six Black Candles.

What about my money, my house! Caroline says.

The car burst into flames, says Angie.

Whifflet Bridge? Oul Mary wants to know.

Angie confirms that it was the Whifflet Bridge right enough.

Oh shit, he might die, Caroline goes.

The full implications are coming through to her now. Everything. The Girls bow their heads. Half in reverence for Caroline, half in reverence for the spell.

If McGoogan dies that means we've killed an innocent man, Caroline says.

Caroline, he won't die, says Linda.

Och, it's just a coincidence. There's accidents every night on my wee tranny, Oul Mary says. She's trying to convince them.

How do you know that? How do you know it's an accident? Caroline wants to know.

But Oul Mary doesn't choose to answer. She just ignores her and buttons up her coat. Maw's buttoning up her coat and all.

It's getting late, Mother! Maw says.

Her and Oul Mary drag the chair away from the door. The door blows open in a gust of chill wind. Oul Mary stands in the doorway the exact same way Bobby had stood in it earlier when Caroline made him choose between Stacie Gracie and the wane.

Aye, I'll have to away up the road. Are you coming? Oul Mary asks Maw.

Caroline's desperate. She knows soon as one or two of them go the whole circle'll break up and drop away into the darkness. Leaving her along high there over the wooden shutters and metal doors and harsh echoes of the scheme. She pleads.

Granny, don't go the now . . .

But Oul Mary ignores her.

Aye, it's getting late so it is. Very late, says Maw.

Maw!! is all Caroline can say.

Oul Mary and Maw move into the shadows of the close.

See yees all after, Oul Mary says.

The Girls answer and their goodnights go flowing down the stairs becoming emptier and weaker as they fall. When their voices have vanished there's nothing till Oul Mary shouts back up.

Never you bother your arse about McGoogan crashing his car, hen. See yees at Mass on Sunday?

They tell her they'll be there or *like fuck we will* or whatever. Caroline's on the couch biting her thumbnail.

I'm for the dancing – who's coming? Geddy says.

She's slapping her hands together and stretching a smile

across her big pink face. And Donna's up for it. Garfield's, that's where they want to go.

Yees can't go up the dancing after this, Angie says. She nods at Caroline. What she means is, *Yees can't go to the dancing and leave her depressed. What if she does something daft?*

Caroline, you come with us! Says Donna. She's hoping Caroline'll say no. Who wants a doomer hanging onto them all night when there's all that talent going about like shoals of nice fish.

I can't, says Caroline.

Thank fuck, say Donna and Geddy in their heads. But you've got to make a show of it so Geddy tries.

Come on, get another man. They're all the same from the waist down, Geddy says.

And from the waist up, goes Donna.

Wendy sees an opportunity to get away and all. She lifts Boyle's phone while Donna and Geddy are trying, not too hard, to convince Caroline to come to Garfield's.

Come on, Caroline, says Donna.

We'll have a great time – men! goes Geddy.

But Angie sees right through them.

Fuckin leave her alone, she's crippled, Angie says.

Donna argues that's just what she needs; a good night out.

Och just yous two get to fuck, goes Angie.

There's a tense beat, then Donna and Geddy head off. Linda sees her opportunity to leave and all.

Donna, going to bump me down the stairs? Linda says.

Donna and Geddy run away.

Cunts! Linda shouts.

Donna and Geddy don't want stuck with an emotional cripple for the night. And they definitely don't want stuck with a real cripple. Fuck that. Linda hears them leaving the close.

Wendy moves right in there. *I'll bump you down the stairs, Linda.*

D'you not want to stay here with Caroline? Linda asks.

I need to take this phone over to Father Boyle anyway.

Aye, you take the phone over, Wendy. Who else! Says Angie.

Wendy wheels Linda to the door and then goes and kisses Caroline on the cheek.

Love you. Don't worry, everything will be alright.

I've got to go, says Linda. She's thinking she can maybe catch Donna and Geddy down at Mitchell Street trying to flag a fast cab. They can't knock her back then.

Great! Everybody's suddenly in a hurry, Angie says. Her fists are on her hips like a cartoon. A specific cartoon in fact: that black cook on the *Tom and Jerry* cartoons.

See you the morra, Caroline, says Linda.

Caroline can only nod. Her support is going bit by bit. Linda and Wendy leave. Caroline and Angie listen to the *bump bump bump* of the wheelchair going down the flight of stairs. When it's only silence Caroline bursts out greeting. Angie leans over and rubs her back in wee circles.

Don't worry – I'll stay here the night.

Thanks, Caroline says.

She speaks through tears and snotters. Angie hands Caroline the phone.

Phone my house and tell them I'm staying here the night. They'll listen to you.

Caroline wipes the bottom of her jumper over her eyes. Wipes the snotters away. Takes a deep breath and looks at the numbers on the phone.

I'll make us tea and toast. I love that before I go to bed. Mind we used to make it at night when we were wee? Angie says.

Aye, and we used to eat it as we made it!

One for them, one for us!

Aye.

Caroline's eyes glaze over and Angie takes that as a signal to go in the scullery and make the tea and toast.

Right – enough toast to choke a horse! Each! she says.

Caroline dials up on the phone. Angie can hear the faint ring of the phone in the quiet that's here now that everybody's gone.

Let it ring. They'll be playing that Dreamcast thing, she shouts.

She flings six slices of pan into the grill. It's one of them grills where the three slices closest to you lip over the edge but once they're toasted on one side they all fit. You'd think they'd measure the bread before they made cookers, Angie's thinking when she hears Bobby's name.

Hello? Bobby? Is that you? Caroline says.

Angie comes in from the kitchen. Not with a stride. Or a walk even. She unobtrusively comes in and watches Caroline with a look of loving concern.

Bobby? It's me, going to not hang up. Please, Bobby! Caroline says.

Angie looks at Caroline. Caroline looks at her. That is sisterhood. That moment is worth all the moments from the whole crazy night. That is the love Caroline had been searching for. Needed. The Girls looked for it for her too. But Angie knew where it was all the time. It was in a look. A non-critical look of unconditional love.

Okay. Okay, can we just talk? Says Caroline to Bobby.

Bobby asks if the Girls are still there. Caroline looks at Angie.

No. They're all away. Aye, I'm sure.

Angie ruffles Caroline's hair and goes back into the scullery. Turns the toast and hey presto, it fits. In the living room Caroline pleads with Bobby.

Can we meet up the morra?

Bobby talks, probably saying *like fuck – after what youse Witches done to me?*

I only want to talk.

And this time he's been persuaded a bit. He's probably thought about the consequences of not seeing the wane. Give him his due, he loves that boy.

Just me. I promise, Caroline says.

Bobby's saying yes – that's got to be a good thing, Angie's thinking.

Outside ASDA. One o'clock. Thanks, Bobby. Lo— He's hung up! Caroline says to Angie.

Everything okay?

Angie has no judgement in her tone. Nothing at all. Just a simple human question. There's a glimmer of hope in Caroline's eyes. A glimmer that's not been there for a wee while now.

I've to meet him the morra.

That's good, hen, you go and meet him, Angie says.

She holds Caroline tight in the middle of the pentangle. In the middle of the rug. In the middle of the room. In the middle of the house. In the middle of the street. In the middle of the scheme. In the middle of the town. In the middle of the country. In the middle of the planet. In the middle of the solar system. In the middle of the galaxy. In the middle of the universe. In the middle of the night. At the tail end of their history. The universe is a tear. And in that tear is hope and expectation. And the only thing that drives that hope and expectation is love. Love drives the universe.